BLUES
IN THE
DARK

ALSO BY THE AUTHOR

Novels

Evil Hours
Face Blind
Tom Clancy's Splinter Cell (as "David Michaels")
Tom Clancy's Splinter Cell—Operation Barracuda (as "David Michaels")
Sweetie's Diamonds
A Hard Day's Death
Metal Gear Solid (based on the video game)
Dark Side of the Morgue
Metal Gear Solid 2—Sons of Liberty (based on the video game)
Hunt Through Napoleon's Web (as "Gabriel Hunt")
Homefront—the Voice of Freedom (cowritten with John Milius)
Artifact of Evil
Torment—A Love Story
Hitman: Damnation (based on the video game series)
Dying Light—Nightmare Row (based on the vide ogame series)
The Secrets on Chicory Lane
In the Hush of the Night

The Black Stiletto Saga

The Black Stiletto
The Black Stiletto: Black & White
The Black Stiletto: Stars & Stripes
The Black Stiletto: Secrets & Lies
The Black Stiletto: Endings & Beginnings
The Black Stiletto: The Complete Saga (anthology)

James Bond Novels

Zero Minus Ten
Tomorrow Never Dies (based on the screenplay)
The Facts of Death
High Time to Kill
The World is Not Enough (based on the screenplay)
DoubleShot
Never Dream of Dying
The Man with the Red Tattoo
Die Another Day (based on the screenplay)
The Union Trilogy (anthology)
Choice of Weapons (anthology)

Nonfiction and Miscellany

The James Bond Bedside Companion
Jethro Tull—Pocket Essential
Thrillers—100 Must-Reads (contributor)
Tied-In: The Business, History, and Craft of Media Tie-In Writing (contributor)
Mystery Writers of America presents Ice Cold—Tales of Intrigue from the Cold War (coeditor, contributor)
12+1: Twelve Thrillers and a Play (anthology)

BLUES IN THE DARK

A NOVEL

RAYMOND BENSON

ARCADE
CRIMEWISE

An Arcade / CrimeWise Book
A Herman Graf book

Arcade Publishing books may be purchased in bulk at special discounts for sales promotion, corporate gifts, fund-raising, or educational purposes. Special editions can also be created to specifications. For details, contact the Special Sales Department, Arcade Publishing, 307 West 36th Street, 11th Floor, New York, NY 10018 or arcade@skyhorsepublishing.com.

Arcade Publishing® and CrimeWise® are registered trademarks of Skyhorse Publishing, Inc.®, a Delaware corporation.

Visit our website at www.arcadepub.com.

10 9 8 7 6 5 4 3 2 1

Library of Congress Cataloging-in-Publication Data is available on file. Library of Congress Control Number: 2019944897

Cover design by Erin Seaward-Hiatt
Jacket photography: © Johan63/Getty Images (piano player); © Vladimir Gappov/Getty Images (woman with pistol); © LPETTET/Getty Images (cityscape); © Kesu01/Getty Images (light)

Print ISBN: 978-1-948924-91-7
Ebook ISBN: 978-1-948924-92-4

Printed in the United States of America

FOR MY FAMILY

ACKNOWLEDGMENTS

The author wishes to thank the following individuals: (alphabetically) Rebecca Arends; Gil Bartal; J. H. Bográn; Elizabeth Fuller and Julie Grist of *Larchmont Buzz*; Will Graham; Nancy Johnson; Shannon Luders-Manuel; Josh MacNeal; Edgar Mariscal and the Dunbar Hotel; Laura Meyers and the West Adams Heritage Association; Jacki Morie of the West Adams Heights Sugar Hill Neighborhood Association; the Vernon Healthcare Center; Cy Weisman; and Jeffrey G. Weiss & David Bailey.

Special continuing thanks goes to Cynthia Manson, and to my team at Skyhorse Publishing—Herman Graf, Kim Lim, and Johanna Dickson. Finally, my love and appreciation go to my wife Randi and son Max for their help and support.

AUTHOR'S NOTE

Of course, this is a work of fiction. The character of Blair Kendrick didn't exist. The studio, Ultimate Pictures, is totally imaginary, as are its personages. The organized crime activities of Meyer Lansky are well documented, especially in Las Vegas, but his function as a movie studio investor is purely my invention. Likewise, my use of James Cagney as a costar for Blair Kendrick is also fictional, although he did make the film noir "comeback" gangster picture, *White Heat*, as mentioned in this novel. The "Wasco (California) Bass Player Farm" is another invented locale, as is "Our Lady of Hope Children's Home."

My descriptions of the neighborhoods of Los Angeles's West Adams Heights—"Sugar Hill"—are correct, although I have played fast and loose with placement of houses that are locations in the story. Karissa's home on S. Harvard Boulevard and Hank's dwelling on S. Hobart Boulevard are mish-moshes of mansions I explored there and are not real places. My depiction of the Dunbar Hotel and S. Central Avenue in the 1940s is as precise as could be achieved through in-person research and what could be gleaned from old photographs.

The bulk of this book was written primarily over the summer of 2017. The inspiration was a newspaper clipping that my now-ninety-eight-year-old mother had sent to me about new occupants of an old house doing renovations and uncovering a human skeleton in the walls. That got me thinking about secret histories of old dwellings. As a film historian and instructor, I am also rabidly interested in Hollywood and its evolution. The late 1940s period especially attracted me, for I'm a huge fan of films noir and am fascinated by the movement's traits of characters' motivations dictated by fate and destiny, the femmes fatales, and the often convoluted crime plots. Setting the tale in classic and contemporary Hollywood was a path that naturally worked for me.

Contributing to my formulation of the narrative were current events of that year. Racism and sexual harassment were significant parts of the national conversation, as they've always been in our history, and I was compelled to tell a story that addressed both as humbly and honestly as I could.

—R. B.
March 2019

1

THE MOVIE

The Present, 2020

The house lights dim to darkness and the advance press screening of the movie begins with the obligatory studio and production company logos.

Typical of most industry viewings, members in the audience who work at the organizations applaud when theirs is displayed.

It is immediately striking that, unlike most pictures made today, this one is not presented in a widescreen format. All movies made prior to 1953 were framed in the old aspect ratio that was more of a boxlike 4:3 rectangle, and the advent of anamorphic widescreen technology in the fifties changed all that, mainly because the studios wanted to combat the proliferation of television sets in the homes of potential ticket-buying audience members.

Another shock is that the new picture is in black and white.

The filmmakers are taking a huge risk in presenting such a throwback, retro picture for today's public.

Orchestral music on the soundtrack blares with a sassy, seductive theme that cries out: film noir.

If you didn't know better, you'd think you are really watching something that had been made in 1948. The crime pictures Hollywood churned out between roughly 1941 and 1958 fell under a stylistic umbrella that French critics later dubbed film noir because they were unusually "dark" in subject matter and tone. They were made cheaply, often by a director of Eastern European extraction, in startling black and white. Night scenes. Rain. Lots of smoking and drinking. Hard-boiled detectives. Bad girls whom the French critics later labeled femmes fatales. Seedy bars and motel rooms. Double crosses. Violence. Witty dialogue full of innuendo. The Postman Always Rings Twice. The Big Sleep. Out of the Past. Double Indemnity.

This new film projected at the press screening is a modern film noir.

The screen fades to black, and the orchestral music continues to swell as the title appears:

FEMME FATALE—THE BLAIR KENDRICK STORY

The audience applauds again.
And then a title card proclaims:

THIS IS A TRUE STORY.

2

KARISSA

Several Months Earlier, 2019

She hadn't expected to be thinking about murder that day, but within the hour that would be the case.

The anxiety of the previous night's restless sleep was just beginning to wane as Karissa Glover parked her blue 2015 Nissan Murano at the curb on South Harvard Boulevard. She placed the coffee cup from Executive Suites in the holder and sighed. She had once read that if you were anxious and worried about things in the waking world, then that was fodder for the subconscious to act out. Worries about her divorce, her housing situation, and, most of all, a new project for her film production company were taking a toll.

Snap out of it! She could hear Marcello, her best friend and business partner at the office, order her to do so with humor and reassurance. It was just after eight in the morning on a sunny, fresh Los Angeles day, and she knew that if she simply focused on the tasks at hand, she'd feel just fine. She took a breath and summoned a more upbeat, professional attitude.

Karissa looked through the passenger window at the house—a mansion, really—across the street. It was much too large for her, but it didn't appear as decrepit and in need of repairs as she had expected. Nevertheless, she needed a new home. She was sick and tired of renting a room at the Executive Suites. The divorce wouldn't be final until that damned Willy signed the papers. Selling their house in Van Nuys had happened too quickly for her to make other arrangements. Starting over at the age of forty-six wasn't pleasant.

How she'd come to be aware of the house on South Harvard Boulevard had been a lucky fluke. Two mornings ago, she'd gone into the Executive Suites lobby for the complimentary cup of coffee. Usually the place was sparsely populated at 8:30 a.m., but that day a few business types were there with the same idea. A striking woman in her thirties dressed in a sharp pantsuit stepped up behind her at the machine and said, "*Please*, Lord, caffeine!"

Karissa laughed and added, "It's one of His small miracles."

They stood at the amenities counter, doctoring their respective coffee cups with cream, and the woman asked, "Are you from out of town?"

"No, I live in LA," Karissa answered. "I'm house-hunting right now. This is just temporary."

"Ah. I hear you. It was only one night for me. Realtors' convention. I'll be out of here this morning. What are you looking for? Maybe I can help. I need to leave soon, but do you have time to sit for a minute?"

"Sure." They went to one of the few vacant tables.

"I'm Serena, by the way," the woman said.

"Karissa." They shook hands. "I work in Hollywood, so I'm looking for something that doesn't have an outrageous commute."

"You in the movie business?"

4

"I'm a film producer."

Serena raised her eyebrows. "Ah. Do I have a tip for you! Do you know West Adams Heights?"

"I know where it is."

"I just heard about an old house there—a gorgeous mansion—that's about to go on the market. I think you could get it for a song and beat the rush if you act quickly. It's just down the street from where Hattie McDaniel lived back in the forties. You know who I mean?"

Karissa smiled. "Sure. A lot of the black celebrities lived in that area in those days."

"Uh huh. Well, it's pretty much a melting pot now. You'll find all the options on the census form under 'Race.'" She winked at Karissa and whispered with a smile, "You'd fit right in."

Karissa was a little taken back by that remark, but she didn't say anything. Had Serena, who was African American, made the comment from an intuitive observation? Karissa always felt that her biracial ethnicity wasn't *that* obvious.

Serena dug into her purse and pulled out some listings on pieces of paper. She thumbed through them and found what she was looking for. "Here it is." She took out a pen, grabbed one of the Executive Suites notepads that was on the counter within arm's reach, and wrote down an address, phone number, and a name. She tore off the page and slid it across the table.

"Call the landlord, Mr. Trundy. I'm not representing the property, but you can tell him Serena told you about the house." She looked at her watch. "Oh, my, sorry, but I have to run. It was great meeting you, Karissa, and good luck!" Serena stood and they shook hands a final time.

Then the woman had rushed out of the lobby. Karissa had felt regretful that she hadn't asked Serena No-Last-Name for a card, but she was also bewildered and assuredly intrigued.

Now, after dutifully making an appointment with Trundy,

Karissa sat in her car across the road from the house in question. It was a two-story Mediterranean Revival mansion, an architectural style popular in the 1920s and thirties that evoked the look of a seaside villa. Very formal and symmetrical, with a low-pitched hipped roof and broad, overhanging eaves. This one was once a sparkling white stucco, but now the exterior walls had browned and the paint was chipped and flaking in several places. The roof's dark green shingles appeared to be sound enough, and the grounds were clean and manicured. Four big oak trees provided cover and shade over the lawn. While most of the mansions on the block had old but traditional wrought iron fences with gates surrounding the properties, this one didn't. The front yard was wide open to the street. A paved walk led from the sidewalk to a flight of six stone steps that rose to a stucco porch and the front door. A short wall surrounded the porch. A driveway on the left curved around to a garage on the side of the building. There were, however, wrought iron bars on the windows, which she supposed provided some security.

Karissa thought the street was a little too close to the Santa Monica Freeway, which was just a little over a block to the north. However, it was indeed a beautiful neighborhood, stocked with fashionable large homes of the same ilk. She was aware that West Adams Heights, once popularly known as "Sugar Hill"—and still called that by locals—was, as she had acknowledged to Serena, an enclave populated by black celebrities in the 1940s and fifties until the area's decline in the sixties when the construction of I-10 cut through the Heights and everything changed. Nevertheless, while it had been predominantly a neighborhood of African Americans, today the West Adams district was a hot, trendy locale of lively diversification.

Even Marcello had mentioned that Hattie McDaniel had lived on Harvard Boulevard when Karissa told him what she was going to do. McDaniel, the first African American to win an

Oscar—as "Mammy" in *Gone with the Wind*—had owned a home just up the street from where Karissa was parked.

"And Louise Beavers, too," Karissa had said to Marcello. Beavers, another popular black actress of the period, also owned a home around the block on South Hobart Boulevard. "So did Butterfly McQueen, Bill 'Bojangles' Robinson, Marvin Gaye, the Mills Brothers . . ."

In fact, *lots* of African American celebrities once lived in the different neighborhoods of the larger area known as West Adams. It had been one of the focal points of what was dubbed "Black Hollywood" in its day. Not anymore.

Ha! Maybe it is *perfect for me!* Karissa thought as she opened the car door and got out. She strode across the street, walking twenty feet to the stone steps. She climbed them and stood on the covered porch. To the left was an old wooden swing hanging from the stucco overhead. A tall potted plant with broad leaves stood to the right. A mail slot was built into the door.

Karissa raised a fist to knock, but the door opened before she could. A short black man who appeared to be in his sixties or seventies gave her a slight smile. He was dressed sharply, much like a Realtor hoping to make a sale.

"You must be Ms. Glover."

"Yes. How do you do?"

They shook hands. "My name is James Trundy. Please come in."

She stepped inside an expansive foyer that could have been frozen in time from the 1940s. Karissa wasn't an expert on design styles, but she was certain that nothing she saw was more recent than the fifties. An empty, old-fashioned metal hat rack that towered near the door was right out of the art deco period. The worn hardwood floor was probably due for a refurbish. A small, vintage lounge sofa with red upholstery stood against the wall on the right.

"Are you with the realty company, Mr. Trundy?"

"No, ma'am, I'm the landlord. I look after the house. I've been doing this for almost fifty years."

"My, my. Well, I'm captivated."

"Would you like to see the place?"

"By all means."

Despite the antiquity on display, everything appeared clean. The house *smelled* old, but it wasn't unpleasant. Trundy led her past the wooden stairs on the left that obviously led to the second floor and into a large dining room containing a long table set for fourteen. Visually, the space had an eclectic style of verdure artwork, heavy dark furniture, bright ceramics, and wrought iron accents. Oak floor. The wood-beamed ceiling sported carved rams' heads.

On one wall was a large painted portrait of a very pretty blond woman dressed in a formal gown.

"It's beautiful," Karissa said. She nodded at the painting. "Who is that?"

"She is the former owner of the house. She lived here in the late forties."

"Really? I'm surprised."

"Why?"

"Wasn't this a black neighborhood then?"

Trundy shook his head. "West Adams Heights started as an all-white neighborhood. When black celebrities started buying and moving in to houses in the early forties, there were residents who tried to get them evicted. There were covenants that prohibited black people from residing here. A number of those black celebrities fought back and won the right to live here in the state courts. That paved the way for the Supreme Court decision in 1948 that struck down legal housing discrimination." He nodded at Karissa. "But, in a way, you are correct. Sugar Hill became more of a black neighborhood in the late forties, fifties, and sixties. There were still white folks living here, though. Blair Kendrick was one of them, that is, until 1949."

Karissa wrinkled her brow. "Blair Kendrick . . . why does that name sound familiar?"

"She was an actress. Movie star. For a while."

"Oh, *right*. Isn't she that film star who was killed by the mob or something?"

Trundy pursed his lips and gave a slight nod.

"Wait. She made a few film noir pictures in the forties, right? Always played what they call a femme fatale—the bad girl. Then she got in trouble and . . . what? She was murdered?"

"Yes, I'm afraid so."

"Am I correct to say that she was killed because she witnessed a high-profile murder? Some Hollywood bigwig?"

"Eldon Hirsch. He was the head of Ultimate Pictures."

"Oh, right. I remember that now. She was under contract with Ultimate Pictures, wasn't she?"

"I believe so."

"And she *lived* here?"

"That's right. Many of her things are still in the house, too. Upstairs and in the basement, you'll find a lot of what they call 'ephemera.'"

"Oh, Lord. Let's keep looking."

He showed her the kitchen, which was big enough to accommodate three or four chefs at work. "Everything is functional, although a few appliances are in disrepair. I can show you which ones to avoid using. Not to worry—you have a stove and refrigerator. They were replaced within the last ten years. There's even a dumbwaiter." He pointed to a door at the side. "That leads to the servant's bath, and the door beyond that goes into the garage, where you can park your car. I'm afraid there is no automatic garage door. The garage is just open to the driveway."

"There's also not a fence around the property," Karissa said. "I noticed all the other houses on the block have these wrought iron fences."

"Those weren't built until the sixties and seventies. None of the houses had fences back in the day. No one was residing in this house during the sixties and seventies, so a fence was never erected."

"Is there much crime in the neighborhood? Would I be safe?"

He shrugged. "The neighborhood declined in the sixties, and there was a lot of crime then and the next couple of decades. Not so much now. The area has become quite diversified." Just like Serena had said. "Do you know the largest church catering to the African American community in Los Angeles is right here at the end of the block?"

"No, I guess I didn't."

"The First African Methodist Episcopal. Decades ago they met in a house in the neighborhood; now they have that big building on the corner." He looked at her as if he were trying to determine how much African American blood she had in her. Karissa, being light-skinned but certainly not pale enough to pass as white, often endured this kind of scrutiny from both races. It was not a pleasant experience, but she had grown up with it. "Are you from Los Angeles, Ms. Glover?"

"I'm from Sacramento originally, but I went to UCLA and stayed here."

Trundy nodded and then indicated a smaller, adjacent room off the kitchen. "The laundry machines here in the utility room are also functional." Another door led to a bright room with a dining set. A large window looked out into the backyard, which was not in as good a shape as the front. "This is the breakfast room, or 'morning room,' as they called it in those days."

"How quaint!"

He led her back through the dining room and under an arch to

10

the expansive "parlor," as he called it. It contained more antiques, as well as framed movie posters. Pictures that starred Blair Kendrick. A grand piano that had seen better days sat at one end of the room, adorned by several framed photographs. Blair Kendrick was in all of them, posing alone or with other stars of the day—Robert Mitchum, Ray Milland, James Cagney, Dana Andrews . . .

"Oh my gosh!" Karissa gasped. "Are those original posters?"

"I believe so, yes."

The Jazz Club. A Dame Without Fear. A Kiss in the Night.

"I love old movies, but I don't think I've seen any of these. I'm a film producer. I *work* in Hollywood."

"Do you now?"

"Yes, sir. I coproduced *Second Chance*, the one about the fellow who dies and goes to argue his case with Saint Peter so he can have another chance back on earth?"

Trundy shook his head. "I didn't see it. Sorry."

She raised her eyebrows and gave a little laugh. "Well, you weren't the only one. The critics liked it, though." She shook her head. "Those posters are probably worth something. I don't know why I haven't seen these movies. Do they crop up on Turner Classic Movies at all?"

"No," he answered with a curious finality.

Karissa stood in the middle of the room and surveyed it. She couldn't help making a full turnaround, taking it all in. "This is more like a ballroom! You could throw a nice party in here."

"I'm sure that's what it was used for, ma'am. You'll find that the piano has not been tuned in decades, though."

She went over to it and picked up one of the framed pictures, a typical studio publicity portrait. In it, Blair wore a striking string of pearls around her neck.

"She was gorgeous."

"Blair Kendrick was a flame that burned very brightly for a short time. Hardly anyone remembers her these days."

"She doesn't look like a femme fatale here."

Trundy made a disapproving grunt. "Shall we see the rest of the house?"

Karissa picked up on his tone and said, "Do you . . . I'm sorry, do you have a connection with Blair Kendrick?"

"I just look after her house, ma'am." He turned his head and gazed lovingly at the surroundings. "She'd be in her nineties if she were still alive. But she's buried in Westwood Village Memorial Park."

Karissa knew of it; many stars and Hollywood executives were interred there. Marilyn Monroe. Jack Lemmon. Natalie Wood.

"Who owns the house now?"

"An investment firm, or trust fund, or law firm, or something. I don't understand these things. I just collect my paycheck in the mail and take instructions from a group of attorneys."

"I see."

He next took her through double folding doors at the back of the parlor to the "conservatory," which was an enclosed porch that spread behind the parlor and kitchen. Large windows here also looked out into the backyard. A door opened to steps that led outside. The space contained two card tables and a pool table. *She must have liked to play games*, Karissa thought.

They went back into the parlor, out into the foyer, and to a room on the opposite side of the house, which he called the study. Inside was a desk, and more old furniture.

"Good for a home office," she said. "Is there, uh, cable? Internet?"

"I am arranging for that to be installed. You won't find a television in the house, though. If you want one, you'll have to supply it yourself."

Karissa wondered why the house wasn't already wired. "Mr. Trundy, how long has it been since someone lived here?"

"Decades. You will be the first renter since Blair Kendrick . . . moved out."

"Why hasn't the place been rented until now?"

Trundy held out his hands. "The owners didn't want to rent it. Now they do."

No wonder the house looks like it has just sat here since the forties . . .

"And the owners had you keep it clean all these years, but they never renovated it?"

"Me and my mother before me. Yes. Shall we go upstairs?"

"Please."

They ascended the curving staircase to the second floor, where entrances to six bedrooms jutted off a main hall. One of the bedrooms was full of boxes and a trunk. "Those are Ms. Kendrick's things. We've never known what to do with them. Maybe since you work in Hollywood, you might have a suggestion."

"You mean I can look through them?"

He just nodded and continued the tour. The master bedroom was again adorned with Blair Kendrick movie posters and photographs. A four-poster king-sized bed dominated the space. Floor-to-ceiling windows opened and looked out at the Santa Monica Freeway.

"It once had a much better view, I'm afraid," Trundy said.

"Oh, that's a shame, isn't it? Does it get very noisy at night?"

"It's about like what you hear now."

The sound of the speeding cars wasn't too obtrusive. Perhaps if she pretended the roar was the ocean and not that of traffic . . .

"You could always sleep in one of the other bedrooms," he suggested. "They are each equipped with beds and dressers."

"But this one's so exquisite. I'll think about it. So, tell me, Mr. Trundy. What's the rent? I'm not sure I can afford such an opulent place."

"One thousand a month."

Karissa's jaw almost dropped, but she retained her composure. *What a steal! Too good to be true!*

She made a face and pretended to peer at the furniture and walls more closely. The wallpaper was peeling in places. The dresser, bed, and nightstands were definitely . . . old. The initial impression of antique opulence had quickly given way to the truth that the house was badly in need of an update. Still—it was livable. She'd have everything she would need. As a rental, it could be temporary. Or not. Maybe she'd fall in love with the place and want to renovate it herself—if and when her next production made millions of dollars in profit. She almost laughed aloud at that thought.

She looked at Trundy, who raised an eyebrow, as if to say, *Come on. You know it's a good deal.*

"All right, I'll take it. When can I move in?"

"As soon as you'd like."

As they walked down the stairs to see the back porch and yard, Karissa said, "This place might be inspirational. My partner and I are developing a new movie. We'd like to do a crime story, a thriller. This business of Blair Kendrick being killed, and with her being a white woman living in this neighborhood when more black celebrities were populating it—I think there could be some social relevance. I'm going to have to dig into more of the history of West Adams Heights. What do you think?"

He paused and looked at her when they reached the floor. "Do you know anything about racism, Ms. Glover?"

She was a little shocked by his question. "Mr. Trundy, I'm mixed race."

"I can tell that by looking at you. How much? Half? A quarter?"

That made her prickle. "I don't know. I was adopted. I've never had DNA testing or anything like that. So, what do you mean? Because I'm mixed race, you don't think I've experienced racism in my lifetime?"

He shook his head. "My apologies, Ms. Glover. My question was way too personal. I'm an old man. I have old-fashioned ideas. And I don't know anything about the movies. I don't go to the movies."

She narrowed her eyes at him. "What's Serena's connection to you? I never found out her last name." He wrinkled his brow, and she pressed on. "On the phone I said that a woman named Serena told me about the place."

"Oh, yes. The owners must deal with her. I don't know her. Would you like to see the lease?"

A house with a history. A former owner involved in a juicy Hollywood crime. Karissa hadn't expected to be thinking about murder that day, but perhaps she *had* stumbled upon the genesis of her next film project.

After a moment's hesitation, she answered, "Please."

3

THE MOVIE

The advance press screening continues. After the main title credits, the theme music reaches a climax and then diminishes to underscore, as the film opens on an aerial view of Hollywood. Black and white. Day.

A female voice-over commences. "They say that Hollywood is a land of dreams. That's what I thought at first, too. I suppose for some, it is. For others, like me, it was the stuff of nightmares. Tinseltown, for all its glamour and glitz, for all its money and class, and for all its dedication to providing an escape for human beings via the flickering images on a movie screen, it's really just a big lie. I know. Hollywood seduced me, chewed me up, and spit me out. I was the celebrated 'bad girl' of crime pictures, and then Hollywood murdered me.

"My name is Blair Kendrick. It's time to set the record straight. This is my story."

Cut to the interior of a Hollywood soundstage, flooded with bright lights.

"I arrived in Hollywood in late 1946, innocent and bright-eyed, fresh off the bus from Chicago, Illinois. As soon as I had turned eighteen, I left home. My mother and father were glad to see me go. The less said about that, the better. I felt as if I had some talent—and I was blessed

16

with the kind of looks that seemed to me to be what Hollywood wanted. Sure enough, it wasn't long until I landed an audition at one of the middle-level studios, Ultimate Pictures. It wasn't a major like MGM or Paramount or Warner Brothers, but it was big enough for me.

Eldon Hirsch, the fifty-two-year-old mogul who ran Ultimate Pictures, paced behind three director's chairs that were set up near a camera. One chair was empty; the other two held the fidgeting director, Emil Winder, and the line producer, Buster Denkins. George Thiebault, a consummate studio cinematographer, stood behind the Arriflex 35-II camera. The auditions had been moving along for hours.

"Jesus, Emil," Hirsch said. "How many more starlets are we going to see today? Why can't you make up your mind?"

The director spoke with a thick Eastern European accent. "Eldon, we want to find the *right* girl, don't we?" His real name was Emil Weingold, but the studio had made him change his last name to Winder so that he wouldn't sound *too* Jewish. "We talked about this. We want someone unknown, someone *new*. We want the next Jean Harlow. The next Barbara Stanwyck."

"Why don't we just offer the role to Stanwyck? She was terrific as the bad girl in *Double Indemnity*," suggested Denkins.

Hirsch snapped, "Stanwyck's too big a star for a supporting part. You don't have the budget for someone like her." He grumbled under his breath for a few seconds. "You're right, Emil, we need someone fresh. Someone with chutzpah." He sat down in the empty chair and called to the stage manager, who was off to the side near a door, "Send in the next girl, Carl."

In the designated green room, Blair Kendrick—blond, brown-eyed, tall and long-legged, with the body of a ballerina—sat nervously as she watched the other starlet wannabes get called to the soundstage in the order in which they were signed in. Blair had arrived at eight o'clock that morning and found she was number seventy-two in line. It was now nearly two o'clock, and she was starving. The meager scrambled egg she'd had at the dingy diner on Hollywood Boulevard near her hotel wasn't enough. She, along with most of the girls, had already smoked a half-pack of cigarettes.

"Number sixty-nine!" the stage manager shouted when the door opened.

It wouldn't be long now. From the looks on the returning girls' faces, it didn't appear that the audition was going well. She had nothing prepared.

Suzie had told her about the audition, but how Suzie had learned of it, Blair didn't know. Suzie was a resident of the Hollywood Hotel, too. She'd said it would be a cold reading from "sides," which were select pages from a screenplay. "The audition is top secret, so don't tell anyone else!" Suzie admonished.

So much for confidentiality! There were over a hundred girls here.

It was Blair's second audition. The first had occurred on her third day in the city, also a referral from the only person she knew in Hollywood, a lecherous friend of her high school speech teacher who worked as a "grip," whatever that was. He had gotten fresh with her on the evening she'd met him for supper. She quickly realized he had no influence whatsoever in getting her an "in" to the business. At any rate, that first audition was a cattle call looking for dancers. Although she could dance, Blair wanted to act. She knew from the start that if she didn't approach her goal uncompromisingly, she'd be relegated to walk-ons or the chorus. Hit the ground running, that was her philosophy.

Blair Kendrick knew she had more smarts about the business

than most newcomers. How? Because she had had an education, she was well-read, and she watched a lot of movies. She studied the trades and followed the careers of her favorite stars. She understood that making it in Hollywood was not for the squeamish or naive. She may have been new to the city, but she wasn't stupid.

Her hotel was once a landmark destination. It had been built prior to the arrival of "the movies" in Southern California and was a place to be seen during the silent era and the thirties. However, by the mid-forties, the Hollywood Hotel had declined in both reputation and upkeep. That was why she could afford a room there by the week. It wouldn't be long, though, before she would be forced to either find a waitress job or move out.

For the audition, she had chosen to wear a pinstriped two-piece dress with a fitted blouse that had a double bow motif at the waist and a high neckline. Blair had seen a picture of Betty Grable wearing something similar, and it suited her.

"Number seventy-two!"

Oh my God, here I go!

She got up and approached the man with the clipboard.

"What's your name, honey?" he asked. She told him. "Follow me."

They walked out onto the large soundstage. The spotlights were blinding, but she could see the silhouettes of three men in chairs. A camera on a tripod stood next to them, and there appeared to be an outline of another person behind it.

"Blair Kendrick," the stage manager announced, and then he left her alone, vulnerable and exposed to the studio gods some twenty-five feet away who would decide her fate.

"Uhm, hi," she said, giving a little wave. She put her flat hand over her eyes, attempting to see who was in front of her.

"Hi, sweetheart, do you have the sides with you?"

"Sides? Oh, you mean the script? Uh, no, no one gave me anything."

She heard the men grumbling, and then one of them shouted, "Carl!"

The stage manager came running out. "Yes, sir?"

"She doesn't have sides."

"Oh, sorry." He looked at her and growled, "What did you do with them?"

"I never got anything!" she whispered.

"Did you pick them up when you checked in?"

"There was nothing to pick up; there was just this woman with a list at a desk . . ."

"Never mind, stay right there." He disappeared toward the green room.

Well, hell, she thought. Feeling self-conscious and embarrassed, she gave the men a shrug and a little laugh. "Wasn't my fault, fellas," she said.

She heard more mumbling. "Turn around, sweetheart," the man sitting in the middle ordered. He sounded German, or something.

"What? You mean . . . ?" She did a complete revolution on her feet, as if she were modeling a new dress—which she was.

"How tall are you?"

"Five-ten."

"Where are you from?"

"Chicago."

More mumbling. The same guy asked, "Can you say that without the accent?"

"What accent?"

The man laughed. "Honey, you have a Chicago accent. You say 'Chicago.' Like the 'a' in *snack*. We say, 'Chicawgo.' Like the 'o' in *dog*."

"Yeah? Well, you probably say *tomawto*, and I say *tomayto*."

The guy on the end laughed.

"What's your name again, honey?" the heavier man on the other end asked. He seemed to exude more authority over the others.

"Blair Kendrick."

Carl returned with pages in hand. He gave them to her and said with a low voice, "Don't lose *these*."

"I never *lost* the first ones because I never had them," she said aloud.

After Carl left the space, the man in the middle—she presumed he was the director since he was giving her most of the direction—said, "Okay, doll, you're Abigail. She's not a nice lady; in fact, she's out to squeeze our hero out of his money, and she uses her *feminine charms* to do it. You get my meaning?"

"Sure."

"Read that monologue up at the top of the first page. You see that?"

"Yes, sir."

She took a few seconds to compose herself, cleared her throat, and jumped in.

"Look, baby, I know you're married, but I can't help it if you do things to me. You make my heart just go all a-flutter and then my temperature starts to rise. It's the way you look at me, the way you touch me, the way your mouth moves . . . . You do these *things* to me, Freddie, and I have to do something about it. If you'll just sit down a minute, have a cigarette, maybe have a drink with me, I bet you I can do some of those same things to *you*."

Blair stopped, looked up, and waited.

Mumbling.

"You have a nice delivery, honey," the man in the middle said. "It's kind of like Lauren Bacall, only your voice isn't husky like hers. Do it again, please."

"You want me to lower my voice?"

"No, no, it's fine like it is. Try it again."

She did, not varying the inflection much. They seemed to like it.

For the next ten minutes, she read more lines and then did a scene with an actor named Johnny who stood in for whoever the real star was going to be. Then they had her walk up and down some stairs that were on part of a set stored at the back of the soundstage. After that, they asked her to kiss the actor. He really got into it, so she did, too. Then she read some more.

None of the other girls had auditioned so long. She took this as a good sign.

Finally, all three men stood and walked over to her. The middle guy introduced himself as Emil Winder, and he was indeed the director. The fellow on his left was Buster Denkins, a producer. The other man, the one who seemed to be the boss, was none other than Eldon Hirsch, the president of Ultimate Pictures.

"I'm honored to meet you all," Blair said. Her heart was pounding with excitement.

"Blair, we want you to do a screen test. George over there will shoot a little film of you. We'll do those lines you just read and do some of those scenes with Johnny. We just want to see how you look on the *big screen*. Is that all right?"

"Well, sure!" Then she held up a hand. "But can I ask a question?"

"What's that, dear?"

"Do you think I could get something to eat? I'm *starving*."

The men laughed.

Carl sent the remaining girls home and made a call for sandwiches to be brought in. The men huddled, spoke for a few seconds, and then nodded their heads as if in agreement.

Ultimate Pictures had found its next star.

4

KARISSA

The move-in went smoothly. The furniture from the house Karissa had shared with Willy Puma—soon to be her ex-husband—was in storage. She wondered if she needed any of it. While the pieces in the house on Harvard Boulevard were decades old, they were still functional and went with the antiquity of the mansion. A new mattress was in order, for sure, but other items? Best to keep them stored until she'd lived in the place for a while. Was her residency in Sugar Hill only temporary? She didn't know. She supposed that if she did decide to stay, then she would have to make the decision to modernize the entire place—or not.

There was a certain charm about the old house that was appealing. During her first day there, all Karissa could do was wander through and explore the many rooms. There were treasures to be opened and examined. Boxes, trunks, cabinets, and chests-of-drawers—all full of clothing and trinkets. The walk-in closet in the master bedroom contained vintage dresses, hats, and shoes. She had the frivolous idea of throwing a 1940s costume party for all her Hollywood friends.

Marcello Storm was also very impressed. Her colleague had come to help her move her things from the Executive Suites and the storage facility. A bulky weight lifter, he carried heavy boxes as if they were paper cups. When Karissa and Marcello were in college together, there were many who told him that he resembled a young Muhammad Ali.

"Girl, you're going to get lost in this place," he said, juggling some items while he ascended the stairs. "I hope you have a map."

Karissa laughed and said, "Oh, I know my way around already. It isn't *that* big."

"It's humongous. It's a regular Taj Mahal! There are probably secret passages that lead to other dimensions."

They reached the master bedroom. "Just put down the boxes anywhere."

He did and then went over to look at some of the photographs on the dresser.

"Blair Kendrick. She was something else."

"Do you know much about her? I was going to start googling her tonight once I settled in. She sounds fascinating."

"I guess she was."

"Did she really get killed by the mob?"

Marcello picked up another picture. "That's what they say."

"Who's they?"

He pulled out his cell phone. "I guess you don't have your Wi-Fi set up yet?"

"Not yet. I need to do all that. You're going to help me, right? The landlord just got cable installed today." She started opening the boxes and putting her clothing away. There was still plenty of room in the closet, despite the presence of the antique items.

He fiddled with his phone as he spoke. "Is that all I'm good for? A glorified IT guy? The hired help?"

"Yep, and he can also negotiate amazing movie deals—that's what you are."

"Ha! Yeah, well, I suppose it's getting easier these days, but Hollywood still belongs to middle-aged white guys."

Karissa laughed.

"It wasn't that long ago that Hollywood didn't make movies with or for black folks," he continued. "In the early days, we had to create our own underground system to make what were actually called 'race' movies that played in churches and rented halls and such."

"I remember my Film History class, Marcello. Thank God for Oscar Micheaux."

Marcello raised his eyebrows and nodded at her comment. "Okay, look here at Wikipedia." He indicated his phone. "Blair Kendrick. It says she was a movie star who perished in a suspicious automobile mishap after possibly witnessing the July 1949 murder of Eldon Hirsch, the president of Ultimate Pictures. Speculation is that the mob chased her from the studio after the hit, caught her, and did away with her, but the case was never closed." He started reading silently.

"Tell me more," Karissa said as she put her shoes away.

"It talks about her rise to fame in just two years, that she was under contract with Ultimate, and she made six movies. She was being groomed to be the next Barbara Stanwyck or Bette Davis, as she showed not only beauty but a talent for acting. Says that she started out playing femmes fatales in film noir pictures but that she might have elevated herself to A-level pictures in time."

"Keep going."

"Uh, she was born in 1928 in Chicago, Illinois, came to Hollywood when she was eighteen, and made her first picture in 1947. It was a supporting role in *A Kiss in the Night*. She was the bad girl." Marcello paused and said, "Mmm-mmpf."

"What?"

"I was just looking at her pictures here. She was one good-looking white lady, I got to say. You think she looks like Jean Harlow?"

"I don't know," Karissa said, emerging from the closet. "Blond and ivory skin." She shrugged and joined him to look at his phone. "Nah, she doesn't look like Jean Harlow. She's pretty, though."

"I don't think I've seen any of her films. It says *The Jazz Club* is the one that made her an overnight star."

"What year was that?"

"That was '47, too. It had some black actors in it—jazz musicians and such."

"I love film noir, but I don't think I've seen that one, either."

He scrolled down on his phone. "Okay, it says here that all her films were withdrawn from circulation after the murder. Huh. No wonder we haven't seen 'em."

"The studio did that?"

"I guess. Here's the stuff about the murder. Says on July 1, 1949, Blair Kendrick was seen entering the Ultimate Pictures studio lot in the evening around eight o'clock. The guard on duty at the gate, Barney Johnson, claimed she drove through in her Oldsmobile and waved hello. Since she was under contract, he didn't stop her, although he told the police that he hadn't seen her for months. A few minutes later, Johnson claimed that another car, occupied by a man at the wheel and a woman passenger, approached the gate. The driver shot him. He survived and lived to give a statement to the police, but he really didn't know anything. He couldn't identify the shooter. Eldon Hirsch, the head of the studio, was found in his office, shot to death. He'd also been robbed of a prized coin collection that he kept in a safe."

"Huh."

"Blair Kendrick's car and a car registered in Nevada were dis-covered the next morning all the way up on Mulholland Drive, where they had been involved in a bad accident. Both cars were burned up, charred to a crisp, and the Nevada one had an unidentified body at the wheel. Suspected arson on both cars. Blair was found on the road next to the Nevada car. Badly burned and unrecognizable. She was eventually identified and buried in Westwood Village Cemetery. God, she must have crawled away from the burning wreck and died right there on the highway."

"Jesus."

"Right? Look here. Says a studio executive, Buddy Franco, may have been involved. He went missing after the incident." Marcello clicked on the Buddy Franco hyperlink and reached a shorter entry on Wikipedia. "Buddy Franco was an executive vice president and studio fixer for Ultimate Pictures between 1942 and 1949. Well, look at this. Says he was a suspect in the murder of his boss, Eldon Hirsch! He had connections to the Las Vegas mafia and mysteriously disappeared the night of Hirsch's murder. No one heard from him for years until *1975*, when he was discovered in a diner in Las Vegas—shot to death by an unknown assailant. Police chalked it up to a mob hit. Again, nothing was ever proven, but it's suspected that Franco may have been responsible for what happened on Mulholland Drive."

"Oh, wow. It's ironic that she played femmes fatales in her pictures. Why the hell did she live in this house, though?"

He kept reading. "Says here that she was a controversial figure even before her death because she chose to live in West Adams Heights—called 'Sugar Hill'—among mostly African American movie stars and celebrities. Hmm. Doesn't say why. Did Stepin Fetchit live here?"

"I don't know. I think his star stopped shining by the late

forties. Besides, he represented a characterization of a black man that I find offensive."

"That's true. By then we had actors playing real roles and not just butlers and maids and Tarzan natives. Remember James Edwards?"

"Of course. The man who could have been Sidney Poitier if he hadn't pissed off the studios."

"Yeah, I guess he was deemed too 'uppity.' I think he also slapped a white woman in public. I'm sure that went over well in the early fifties, or whenever it was. What about Dorothy Dandridge?" Marcello suggested.

"I absolutely love her. I'm not sure if she lived in West Adams Heights. She was married to one of the Nicholas Brothers for a while."

"Now *they* could throw a mean tap dance. Who were some of the others during that period? Lena Horne and Pearl Bailey?"

"Uh huh. Ray Charles—his studio is a few blocks away on Washington, isn't it? The point is . . . why did Blair Kendrick live here?"

"I don't know, Karissa."

"Well, I'm going to find out, but not now. Come on, let's set up the Wi-Fi. We need to get to work on our new project."

It hadn't taken long to unpack all her things. All she'd really needed was everything she'd had at Executive Suites—her clothes, some files, a few books and CDs, and some personal keepsakes.

She set Julia—a very old rag doll she'd owned since she was a child—on Blair's dresser next to one of the glamour photos of the actress. The doll was a kind of good-luck charm for Karissa. It wore a simple dress with the name *Julia* sewn into the hem.

Julia had come along with Karissa on every move she'd ever made in her life.

"We're starting a new life, Julia," she announced to the doll. She didn't feel foolish at all, although she thought the occasion called for a couple of glasses of wine.

That night, Karissa stayed up way too late exploring the rooms upstairs, especially the one full of boxes and a trunk. According to Mr. Trundy, they contained personal items belonging to Blair Kendrick, packed away for safekeeping. Karissa wondered for whom they had been kept. From what she'd read so far on the Internet, Blair had left no family behind.

Her thoughts trailed to Trundy. A strange bird. Karissa figured him to be one of those old-fashioned black people who looked down on mixed-race men and women. She had found throughout her life that prejudice could come from unexpected places and ran both ways. It seemed that when it was convenient for someone to think of her as white, she was simply lumped in with the rest of the white population, but when that became inconvenient, then she became most definitely black, a token representation of the entire race. She'd felt the same thing in her conversation with Trundy.

Karissa thought about whether she should be snooping in the boxes. Mr. Trundy hadn't told her the things were off-limits. In fact, he had encouraged her to have a look. Perhaps because she worked in Hollywood?

She went to the trunk first and wiped it off with a kitchen rag. She was going to have to do a lot of dusting around the house. The trunk was unlocked, so she sat on the Persian rug and opened it. Inside were some items of clothing, a few stationery boxes, a stack of copies of the studio publicity portrait of Blair wearing the pearl necklace, and a couple of photo albums. She flipped one of the albums open and began to peruse.

It was fascinating. The book was filled with black-and-white pictures from yesteryear. Some appeared to be professionally taken—studio shots, glamour and publicity stills, and the like—others were candid, probably shot with Blair's own or someone else's personal camera. Karissa recognized parts of the house in some of the pictures—Blair had thrown a party at some point and documented it in photographs.

But Karissa was most struck by the faces in the photos—nearly everyone was black, except for Blair and a few others.

As she flipped through the album, she began to see more pictures that featured Blair and a distinctive black man. She was a tall woman, but he was taller, broad-shouldered, and extremely handsome. There were a few shots of him sitting at a piano, with Blair draped over the edge as if she were about to sing. Other pictures were taken in public, possibly at a nightclub, where the clientele was all black. Blair Kendrick was the only white woman there.

One 8x10 showed the two of them cheek to cheek, looking at the camera, with huge smiles and stars in their eyes.

They were in love, Karissa thought immediately. *Blair Kendrick was involved in an interracial romance.*

She searched through the book for identifications of the subjects. Nothing. She carefully removed pictures from the leaves to look at the backs. Blair hadn't written on them.

Who is this man?

These were taken in the late forties. An interracial romance would have been taboo. Karissa couldn't remember when California's "miscegenation" laws were changed. She pulled out her phone and looked up the date.

It was October 1948. California's Supreme Court determined that anti-miscegenation laws violated the Fourteenth Amendment of the Constitution. Of course, it wasn't until 1967 that the U.S. Supreme Court made interracial marriage legal nationally with the *Loving* case. But in California, it had been legal for nineteen years.

All the same, that didn't mean it would have been readily accepted.

Karissa looked at the 8x10 again and stared at the beautiful black man with sparkling, kind eyes.

Who are *you, mister?*

5

THE MOVIE

The flickering motion picture transitions to a montage of Blair Kendrick undergoing wardrobe fittings, hairdressing and makeup sessions, studio photography shoots, and more screen tests. Her voice-over continues.

"I was put through a battery of more screen tests and publicity photo shoots as part of a makeover to turn me into a Hollywood movie star. I didn't mind at all—it was all very exciting! I couldn't believe my good fortune. My dreams were coming true. Then, three days after I landed the part, I was invited back to Eldon Hirsch's office on the studio lot. At 8:30 p.m., I was told that it was to finalize my contract and celebrate with dinner and drinks. This was curious, for I had already signed my contract. But I supposed having dinner with the boss was just a formality, something I had to do as part of the game."

The screen tests had made the rounds at the studio. The various executives were impressed. The girl had *charisma*. Emil Winder absolutely wanted her for the role of Abigail in the picture, which was called *A Kiss in the Night*. It was a supporting part—the "bad girl"—who of course would pay for her sins at the end of the picture by dying. It was a juicy, meaty role, perhaps one that could steal the movie. Shooting was to begin the first week of December, and the release date would be as early as February or March of 1947. B movies were often made quickly, shot in two to four weeks. They utilized the services of contract players with one or two minor name stars, were usually made on existing sets, and were turned around in the editing room within a month. Add another month for publicity and promotional materials to be created, and it was ready for public consumption, often as the second feature of a double bill.

Blair's deal was a standard seven-year contract exclusive to Ultimate Pictures. She could be "loaned" to other studios if she was wanted by them, but Eldon Hirsch had to approve the moonlighting and Ultimate would receive 25 percent of her earnings. It was the way of the studio system. Some of the big stars were balking at the unfair, one-sided contracts. Olivia de Havilland had already won a Supreme Court decision in 1944 that stated a seven-year contract meant exactly that—seven calendar years. Prior to the ruling, studios didn't count actual days an actor wasn't working, thus sneakily extending the contract beyond the designated term.

It didn't matter to Blair. She was *thrilled* to be under contract with a Hollywood studio. She was about to make a major motion picture, and she would soon be hobnobbing with Tinseltown's elite.

When she arrived at the studio that evening, she stopped at the gate per procedure. She had already been introduced to Barney Johnson, an old-timer security man who had worked the gate for nearly twenty years. Chubby and all smiles, he was obviously taken with Blair's charm.

"Good evening, Miss Kendrick! How are you?"

"Fine, Barney. I have an appointment with Mr. Hirsch."

"Drive right on in. You can park in Lot C by the administrative building. Nice car you got there!" He patted the top of the brown 1941 Oldsmobile Series 60 sedan.

"Thank you, Barney. I bought it *yesterday*. It's used, made before we went to war. But I think it runs all right. I've never owned a car in my life. I learned how to drive in Chicago, though, and got my license there. I guess I'll have to get it changed for California, won't I?"

"Yes, ma'am, eventually I think you do. I'm sure there's no rush. It's a beauty."

"Thank you, Barney. See you later!"

She parked in the designated lot and got out. Blair eyed her wristwatch—she was a bit early, but the sun had already set. She wore a black V-neck dinner dress, a pearl necklace that was a sixteenth-birthday gift from her grandmother, stockings, and heels. She had no idea what Hirsch had in mind, but she wanted to look the part of a Hollywood star.

The building was practically deserted. Another security guard would normally be stationed inside the front door, but it was after hours. She knew the way to Hirsch's inner sanctum. His secretary, Camille Something-or-Other, was not at her desk. The lights were out. The only illumination came from the bottom slit of the closed door at the end of a long hall.

This can't be normal, she thought. Nevertheless, she took a deep breath, thrust her shoulders back, and marched with purpose down the corridor. Before she reached the door, it opened. Eldon Hirsch stood there, dramatically backlit.

He was wearing a satin bathrobe.

"Blair, my dear! Come in, come in. You look absolutely stunning. My, my."

"Uhm, thank you, Eldon." She didn't move.

"Please. Come in."

"Are we . . . are we having dinner?"

"Indeed, we are. The meal will be served in a while. We shall have drinks first and toast your future with Ultimate Pictures!"

She moved past him into the spacious room. Gold was the operative word in describing its color. The drapes, the carpet, and the lighting all glowed with a golden sheen. The studio mogul's office was as big as a basketball court in floor space. On one side was an elegant dinner table that sat ten people. It was covered with a white tablecloth and was set for two, one setting at the head of the table and the other directly at a right angle on the end. Lit candles provided "atmosphere." The middle of the room sported a sitting/conference area with comfy chairs and a couch, a coffee table, and plenty of ashtrays. The far end of the space was dominated by Hirsch's massive desk, which was big enough for six executives. His private bathroom was off to the side of the sitting area. There were no windows—just plenty of golden drapes and paintings by impressionists. Blair had no idea if these were originals or not, though she suspected they were.

"May I suggest a glass of champagne to start off our glorious evening?"

"Sure. Eldon, you're wearing a bathrobe."

He grinned broadly. "I like to be comfortable in the evenings. I often work late. I shower after everyone's gone home for the day, and I put on silk. Do you like it?"

Seeing that he was more than fifty pounds overweight and thirty or forty years older than she, Blair almost told the truth. Instead, she said, "You look very . . . relaxed." As for herself, she was beginning to feel a great deal of anxiety.

Hirsch went to the bar on one side of the room, pulled a bottle out of an ice bucket, expertly popped the cork, and poured two glasses that were already sitting on top of the bar. He handed one to her and said, "To the new star of Ultimate Pictures. Cheers." He clinked her glass.

"Thank you, sir." She sipped the bubbly liquid and felt a tingle run down her spine.

"You know how I knew you were the perfect girl to play Abigail?"

"How?"

"When you spoke with that sexy Chicago accent."

She rolled her eyes. "Oh, hmpf, that." She dived into it and said, "Dere's no way you're goin' to get me to talk dat way tonight."

"Oh!" He opened his arms. "That makes me just want to squeeze you!"

She ducked and smoothly maneuvered out of reach. Opening her purse, she pulled out a pack of cigarettes.

"Pardon me, Blair, I should have offered you a cigarette. Here, have one of mine." He produced a gunmetal case out of the pocket of his robe and flipped it open.

"Thank you." She took one and looked around for a lighter.

"Here you go." From his desk, he grabbed a heavy metal lighter shaped like a small elephant. The flame shot out of the upraised trunk with a flick of the thumb. Tentatively, she leaned in with the cigarette in her mouth. He got one for himself, fired it up, and replaced the elephant. Then, he moved toward the couch.

"Let's have a seat over here, shall we?"

Oh dear. Is this the famous Hollywood "casting couch" I've heard so much about?

Blair didn't know how to react. She didn't want to embarrass or anger him—he was the *boss!*—but she also felt trapped, with no alternative plan of action. Her nervousness escalated to genuine anxiety. Nevertheless, she sat on one end of the couch and crossed her legs. He plopped down way too close for comfort—as she had expected—and stretched an arm behind her on the back of the furniture.

"So, tell me about yourself," he said. "I know you're from

Chicago. When did you come to Southern California? Did you study acting? And do legs like yours grow naturally on every girl in the Midwest?"

She laughed uneasily. "No, I'm a freak of nature. No boys in my high school wanted to date me because I was taller than them. Mr. Hirsch, I arrived in Hollywood just two weeks ago. Yours was my second audition. And I've never taken acting classes. There were no such things where I went to school."

"Your *second* audition? My, you handled it like a pro. My dear, you're a *natural*. I can tell you're going to be a major star, Blair." He leaned in, too near her face. "If you trust me to help you, I *will* make you a big star. You'll, of course, need to follow my advice and instruction. I've helped many girls in their careers."

Blair pretended to focus on one of the paintings across the room. She stood and moved toward it. "Oh, is that a Monet?"

His voice betrayed his annoyance. "Uh, no, that's actually a . . . I don't know who did it; my interior designer chose it for the office. Very different from Monet." He followed after her, cigarette in hand.

She shrugged. "Well, art is not something I know much about. You've got a lot of nice art. Your interior designer has taste." She thought perhaps if she made out to be *dumb* then maybe he wouldn't be so much of a wolf. On the other hand, maybe he *liked* his women dumb.

Ah, she would try a different tack.

"So, Mr. Hirsch, are you married?"

He blinked and turned away. "Married? Oh, uhm, yes, I have . . . yes, I'm married."

"Oh, yeah? What's her name?"

"Beatrice."

"How long have you been married?"

"Twelve years. But let's not talk about—"

"You have kids?"

"Uhm, yes, a son."

"What's his name?"

"Justin."

"How old is he?"

"He's, uhm, he's seven. Or eight." He scratched his head and frowned.

"You don't know hold old your son is?"

"*Eight*. He's eight. Justin is eight."

Blair sensed she had him in an uncomfortable spot. "I gather Beatrice is younger than you."

"Uhm, yes."

"Is this your first marriage?"

"Beatrice is my third wife. But let's not talk about—"

"No, I find this terribly interesting!" She moved over to his desk. "What a beautiful specimen of furniture! You must feel very important working here."

He followed her, not exactly aware that he had lost control of the conversation. "Why, yes, I do. Isn't it magnificent?"

"And what are these?"

Lying on top of the desk were three open leather-bound port-folios. Inside, nestled into velvet-covered pieces of cardboard, were rows of coins.

"Ah, that . . . that is my coin collection."

"Coin collection?"

"Yes. It's . . . it's worth a lot of money."

"Really? How much?" she asked.

"I'd rather not say. Look here." He pointed to one that was a dull silver color and that featured a woman in profile wearing a headband with the word "Liberty" written on it. "This is a silver dollar from 1817, called a Capped Bust Silver Dollar. Very rare."

"Really?"

"And this one . . ." He turned a page in the portfolio and pointed to a silver coin showing a woman with long wavy hair.

"This is the Flowing Hair Dollar, minted in the year 1794! It's worth about . . ." He leaned in and whispered, "Sixty-five thousand dollars!"

"No! You're joking!"

"I am not."

"Oh my God! Show me another!"

He turned the page. "Well, there are quite a few in here that are very valuable. But here is the absolute most valuable, rarest coin in my collection." He pointed to a smaller, dull gray coin with stars circling a woman's head profile. She wore a crown. "This is a 1913 Liberty Head Five Nickel."

"That's a *nickel*?"

"Yes. Only five of them still exist that collectors know about."

"And how much is *it* worth?"

"Depends on who you talk to. Could be up to a half-million dollars."

"I don't believe it!"

"It's true, my dear." Suddenly, he leaned in, as if to kiss her, but she slipped away once again.

"So, you keep these here at your office?"

"Yes, in my safe there. I thought I would show them to you this evening. That's why I had them out."

She went back to the bar and grabbed the champagne bottle. "Mind if I refill my glass, Eldon?"

"Go right ahead. I like a girl who takes matters into her own hands." He strode across the room to be near her again. He started to put his arm around her back, but she skirted away.

Blair decided it was now-or-never time. She took a deep breath.

"Listen, Eldon, I like you, and I'm *very* grateful for the contract. I want to do my very best for you and Ultimate Pictures. But I am not the kind of girl who is going to, uhm, indulge in any whoopee with you or any other studio executive."

His mouth dropped and, for a moment, there was a fire in his eyes.

She held up a hand. "Don't get mad." Then she slinked up to him and slid her palm on his cheek. "I'm just going to have to get to know you better. I'm from the Midwest. Girls from the Midwest don't do anything *naughty* on a first date. This *is* our first date, right? So, maybe, if you're *patient*, Eldon, things might work out in the future. What do you say?"

The man tensed and turned as red as a tom*ah*to. She didn't know if he was going to strike her or melt.

To close the deal, she leaned in, shut her eyes, swallowed her pride, and kissed him lightly on the lips. Then she swore to herself that it would never, ever happen again.

The man's body relaxed slightly, and he resigned himself to the fact that he wasn't going to get lucky that evening.

"That's what I like about you, Blair," he said. "You have chutzpah!"

6

KARISSA

Karissa had always loved movies. Her first experience in a theater was seeing a rerelease of Disney's *Pinocchio*. It had thrilled and frightened her, and yet she had sung what she could remember of "Hi-Diddle-Dee-Dee" all the way home in the car. Kids' movies quickly became her weekend activity until she was old enough to see more adult fare. Her adoptive parents were indulgent and liberal when it came to Karissa seeing R-rated material, especially if they deemed the pictures to have socially important messages. By the time she had experienced the Coen Brothers' and Spike Lee's first films in the late eighties, Karissa knew she wanted to work in the business. She attended UCLA film school, acted some, made student pictures, and gradually gravitated toward the production side of the industry. Her twenties and thirties were spent on film shoots in any number of capacities from "runner" to "assistant to the producer." Her marriage to the actor Willy Puma when she was in her late thirties put a bit of a damper on her career—he had made their union all about *him*. That was finally over, and Karissa was determined to focus on taking her company to the top.

Stormglove Productions kept an office on South La Brea Avenue in a storefront near 2nd Street. The name was a combination of Marcello's last name—Storm—and Karissa's—Glover. The pair had known each other since UCLA, worked separately and together on various crew assignments once they'd gone pro, and eventually discovered a mutual desire to move into production development. They formed a partnership in 2010 and Stormglove was one of the producers of a well-received independent film that put them on the map. *Second Chance* had taken a top prize at Sundance and was on the short list at Cannes. Although not a blockbuster at the box office by any means, the picture had turned a profit. For the time being, Karissa and Marcello each had a safety net in savings.

Since then, Karissa and Marcello had considered, developed, and dropped a handful of other projects. When the ACLU, the NAACP, and the National Endowment for the Arts got together to create an original film festival that would highlight up-and-coming production companies, Karissa and Marcello applied to be a part of it. To their delight, they were accepted to submit a proposal. Now they had to come up with a script, production plan, and budget for a feature film over the next three months. A total of four pictures would be funded, produced, and distributed with the cooperation of several major and minor studios. It was a big deal, and the partners knew it could be the next step of their survival in Hollywood.

Stormglove's headquarters was a no-frills establishment. There was no front office receptionist. It was just a big room where Karissa and Marcello usually sat at separate desks. The only other spaces were a smaller conference room, which contained a coffee machine and a miniature fridge, and the unisex bathroom.

First thing that morning, Karissa brought in preliminary research materials and laid them out on the conference room table, where the couple had decided to brainstorm.

"What's all this?" Marcello asked.

"Biographical material on Blair Kendrick. I think I've already outlined the opening scene. She comes to Hollywood all bright-eyed, lucks out in an audition for Ultimate Pictures, strikes the fancy of studio head Eldon Hirsch, and is on her way to be a big star."

"The bloodshed obviously comes later, I guess. Karissa, I don't know. Why would we want to make a movie about a white actress who was a flash in the pan and was murdered?"

"I don't know yet, Marcello. That's why we need to keep digging and find out what really happened. I've barely scratched the surface just searching for stuff on Google. Don't you find it strange that there's not much out there about the murder? Or murders, if you believe some of the stories. They claim studio fixer Buddy Franco was maybe Hirsch's killer and possibly hers, too."

"There's not much out there probably because the police never solved the case. It went cold."

"I think I might have found something else about Blair Kendrick's story. Look here." She opened a folder and took out the photograph of Blair and the elegant, handsome black man. "Do you know who this is, by any chance?"

Marcello took the picture and stared at it. His brow wrinkled, and he said, "I think he looks familiar . . . shit, who is that?"

"Well, there are *dozens* of photographs of that man among Blair's belongings. In most of the shots, they look like they're awfully fond of each other. Look at their body language in the photo. Here are some more." She laid out four more pictures on the table. "What's the first thing you would say about the two people in those photographs?"

"That they look like costars. Actors in a movie. Or a stage show."

"But these two"—she pointed—"are not professional photos.

They're candids. Taken with a home camera. Look at the way he's holding her hand. Marcello, I think Blair was dating a black man. I want to know who he is."

Marcello rubbed his chin. "Well, if she was messing around with a brotha back then, I don't think she would've taken him home—they would've *lynched* him."

"But what if they were a couple? An interracial relationship in the forties. There could be something of a story for us here."

"She wouldn't have been allowed to date a black man, Karissa. The Production Code was still in effect. It was taboo. Actors had clauses in their contracts that forbade anything that was considered immoral. They must have been colleagues in something, not lovers."

"Marcello, there are too many pictures at my house for them to just be colleagues. We need to find out who he is. Come on, you know I have good instincts for a story. All I'm saying is we should find out more. You going to help me or not?"

He studied the picture again. "You know, he's probably a musician. I mean, he's sitting at a piano in that one." His eyes abruptly widened. "Wait a second. I remember!" He grabbed his phone and opened a browser.

"Who is it?"

"Hold on . . ." He thumbed the keypad and brought up a page with photos. "Yep, I was right. That's Hank Marley."

"Who?"

"Hank Marley." He paraphrased the description online. "A jazz musician from St. Louis who had his own band in Los Angeles in the late forties. He was going places, too, but, let's see . . . . Yep. He *disappeared*. Mysteriously vanished. Suspected of being murdered. He wasn't active very long. Says, 'What promised to be a stellar career was tragically cut short by Marley's sudden disappearance in 1949.'"

"Forty-nine again. That year keeps coming up in this story.

Marcello, we need to find out more! There's something here, I know it. We're uncovering something dramatic. Who can we ask about him?"

Marcello rubbed his chin and gave her back the photos. "Why don't I talk to some of my boys who play down at the World Stage on Friday? There's one guy who's pretty old. Maybe he knows something."

"The World Stage? The jazz club?"

"Yeah, it's not too far from where you're living."

"Angelina will let you go out late at night?" she teased.

"My wife won't have a problem with me going out and socializing if it's business, you know that. She might even want to come."

She paused, then raised her eyebrows at him. He cocked his head. "What, you want to go, too?"

7

THE MOVIE

A montage of scenes from a Hollywood premiere—limousines, stars in tuxedos and evening gowns, bright lights, photographers . . . and Blair Kendrick smiling and gushing for the press as she enters the theater. The voice-over begins . . .

"A Kiss in the Night *opened to the public in late January of 1947 and was a box office hit. Most of the reviews singled me out as the best thing in the picture. Columnist Hedda Hopper came out from one of those huge hats she wears to write, 'Newcomer Blair Kendrick is a spitfire. I wouldn't want to get on her bad side.' Her rival in the gossip trade in Hollywood, Louella Parsons, also mentioned me by saying, 'I hope Ultimate Pictures is treating Blair Kendrick well—she is destined to be one of the studio's shining stars.'*

"It was a whirlwind that barely allowed me to catch my breath. One thing I can say about Ultimate Pictures is that they had a good publicity department. Between the New Year and the premiere, I was photographed dozens of times for promotional stills that the ad boys would 'plant,' that is, deliver to newspaper and magazine offices. I did a few interviews for radio, and I was a guest on Jimmie Fidler's Hollywood on the Air.

"As for Eldon Hirsch, he continued his pursuit of me. I kept having to remind him he was married. I could tell he held it against me, but he couldn't argue with what I meant to the studio. If the picture had flopped, he probably would have canceled my contract and I'd have been out the door.

"Instead, I got the lead role in a new picture called The Jazz Club, *which started shooting in March."*

When Blair saw the set on the soundstage, her jaw dropped. Her experience in Hollywood was limited, but the extravagance of the production design for *The Jazz Club* flaunted the picture's A-list budget. "Tubby" Wheeler, the designer, pulled out all the stops to create a full-fledged nightclub interior with a bandstand, dance floor, and a couple dozen cloth-covered tables. New York's Cotton Club had been an inspiration, and it was as if that famed institution had been reinvented for the West Coast.

It was to be a singing and dancing crime movie. Hirsch ordered Blair to go to a vocal coach twice a week in between her promotional duties for *A Kiss in the Night*, even though she was already a decent singer. Rehearsals began in February so that the cast could learn the dance routines and musical numbers. Picking up the steps was no problem for Blair. As choreographer Lance Tooley told her, "You've got legs like a gazelle, and I mean that as a compliment."

Her character was that of Goldie, a gun moll who takes over her boyfriend/gangster's mob after he is gunned down. Originally a performer at "the Jazz Club," she turns the nightspot into a haven for music, crime, and sex. All this would be homogenized, of course, to satisfy the Production Code watchdogs at the Hays Office.

George Thiebault, the director of photography, and his team worked all morning on the lights for the day's shooting as the all-black band rehearsed their lively numbers. They reminded Blair of Cab Calloway's outfit, of which she was a fan. She had taken to jazz when she was a young girl watching *Betty Boop* cartoons. Calloway and his band, along with Louis Armstrong and Duke Ellington, had often made appearances in live-action bits in the shorts. Blair loved "Minnie the Moocher," the song that Calloway made famous, and Armstrong's "I'll Be Glad When You're Dead, You Rascal, You." She also owned records by Fats Waller. There was something about jazz and its musicians that spoke to her. Blair felt it in her bones.

The band slowed down the tempo with a blues number that she recognized as something sung by Jimmy Rushing on an old Count Basie recording. The pianist sang it mournfully, but with a smile on his face, the way many of the Negro singers did.

It was this enthusiasm for the music that drew her to step up to the handsome man at the piano. His hands gracefully flew over the keys. He cocked his head slightly and intently listened to the melody he was playing, his eyes closed. The man obviously felt the music deeply in a treasured place inside his heart. The fellow certainly had charisma; it oozed out of him. She guessed he was in his late twenties or early thirties, probably a decade older than she. She listened to the dreamy song until he lifted his fingers from the final chord, and then she said to the pianist, "Hi, there."

He opened his eyes and replied, "Well, hello, Miss Kendrick. How do you do today?"

"Oh, you know my name?"

"I sure do. You're the *star*. How could we not know your name?"

"Well, I don't know *your* name."

"My apologies. My name is Hank Marley."

She held out her hand. Surprised by this gesture, Hank blinked and hesitated before nearly touching her with his own hand.

"Go on, I won't bite," she said. He laughed and then followed through with the handshake. "Glad to meet you."

"Glad to meet you, too." He quickly let go and went back to the piano keys, turned his head to the drummer, and counted off. The band smoothly launched into a new number that jumped and jived.

She addressed all of them. "I simply *love* what you fellas are playing."

"Thank you," the drummer said.

It was a seven-piece band—piano, drums, bass, clarinet, saxophone, trumpet, and trombone. The tune swung, making Blair sway naturally back and forth. When that piece finished, she asked them for their names. There was a Jim and a Ray, a Charlie and a Francis, and a Billy and a Bobop.

"Bobop?" she asked.

The trombone player grinned, revealing pearly white teeth. "It's a nickname, but all my friends call me that."

"Not bebop?" She had heard of the jazz style, played by the likes of Charlie Parker.

"Nope. Bobop."

She laughed. "Okay, then!"

The assistant director called out through a megaphone. "All right, people, we're going to try a first take! Places, everyone. Extras, assume your positions."

"Patrons" of the nightclub entered the set. Some sat at tables, some stood on the dance floor in pairs, and others lounged around the bar.

"I'll talk to you later, fellows," Blair said, and she waved a little goodbye at Hank. She then ran over to where Emil Winder was standing with Thiebault.

"You ready, doll?" Winder asked in his trademark Eastern European accent.

"You bet."

49

"This is going to be fun. Okay, you know what to do. As soon as I call 'action,' you come in from the left side there, and the camera will pick you up."

"Okay."

She had started to move toward her mark when the line producer, Buster Denkins, stepped out of the shadows and stopped her.

"Blair . . ."

"Oh, hi, Buster."

"Listen, uhm, just . . . it's probably not a good idea to get too friendly with the colored help."

She furrowed her brow. "What do you mean?"

"Just what I said. You're the star. You keep to yourself and your costars. Let the band be the band. No need to fraternize."

"I was just being nice. I like the music. What's wrong with that?"

"Places!" the A.D. called.

"We'll talk later. You go," he said.

Blair rushed to her spot just off the set. Zelda, the wardrobe and makeup girl, quickly approached, touched up her forehead with some powder, and adjusted the shoulder pads on her blouse. Denkins's words, however, had ruffled Blair.

Who does he think he is? I can talk to whoever I want!

"Quiet on the set!" the A.D. shouted.

The camera started rolling.

"And . . . action!" Winder called.

As Hank Marley and his band started to play, he caught Blair's eye and winked at her.

Damn, he's simply divine! she thought. She blew him a kiss . . . and then strutted out into the lights.

When shooting wrapped for the day, Blair got out of her costume and makeup, put on her street clothes—which consisted of a simple red frock with a belt at the waist and a small hat—and left the dressing room. She spotted Eldon Hirsch down the hall talking to the director and halted in her tracks. Not wanting to go near him, she turned around and went the other way, back to the soundstage. One of the grips she had seen working on the set was there, busy loading lighting equipment on a dolly.

"Is there a way out at the back of the set?" she asked.

"Sure." He pointed. "Just go around the flats and you'll see a door back there. Goes to the rear of the building."

She followed his directions and ended up outside between soundstages on the lot. There, the band members were smoking cigarettes and passing a pint among them.

"Oh! Hello."

They greeted her warmly.

"You on your way to another stage?" Hank asked.

"No, I'm going home. Aren't you?"

"We have a gig tonight at the Downbeat Club."

"Oh? Where's that?"

"Central Avenue, down in Little Harlem." Blair had heard the term before. It referred to an area south of downtown Los Angeles—a nightlife center for colored people.

Bobop, the trombone player, said, "You should come."

Blair laughed. "Oh, I don't know . . . do, uhm, ladies like . . . me go to the Downbeat Club?"

Hank flashed a killer smile at her. "It's mostly a Negro clientele, but white people show up, too. You wouldn't feel out of place."

Ray, the bass player, spoke up. "That's right. We'd make you feel at home."

Blair blushed. "Oh, thank you kindly. I'd love to, but maybe another time. I'm pretty tired. That was a long day, wasn't it? I can't imagine how you can go on and work some more."

"Oh, we're used to it," Hank said. "Got to make a living!"

"I guess so. Well, I'll see you tomorrow."

They bid her good evening and she strode around the building to the front where she had parked her Oldsmobile. Her thoughts raced as she walked.

Was it her imagination, or did Hank Marley look at her differently than the other men? And—did it bother her? He was a Negro and she was white. It was supposed to bother her. But, somehow, it didn't. To her, so-called "racial differences" had always been a *so what?* issue.

As she drove to the Hollywood Hotel, where she was still living, she couldn't help but think how much she would have really liked to hear the band play jazz at a nightclub.

Three days later, after a particularly trying shoot on the club set, Blair left the soundstage by the back way again to avoid running into Hirsch. He had sent flowers to her dressing room, once more attempting to woo her into having dinner with him. One of the other actresses in the picture, Gloria Maddox, could see what was going on. Gloria had a supporting role as a waitress at the club who ends up helping "Goldie," her "boss."

"Honey, sooner or later, you'll end up on that couch," Gloria told her. "It happens to all the girls under contract."

"It's not going to happen to me. What, you had to sleep with Eldon Hirsch?"

Gloria shrugged. "I wouldn't be here if I hadn't. Once it happens, he forgets about you and goes on to the next girl. It's a small price to pay to get in the pictures, honey."

Blair was so taken aback that she didn't know what to say. It was as if she were somehow "uninitiated," like the rest of the sorority.

To hell with that, Blair thought. She was never one to follow the crowd. She had noticed, though, that the other girls in the cast weren't as friendly as they could have been.

She left the building through the back door. The musicians weren't congregated there this time. As she approached her car in the parking lot, her heart sank when she saw a flat tire on the Oldsmobile. Not one to curse—much—Blair said under her breath, "Well, hell." One thing she couldn't do was change a tire. She looked around to see if someone could help. Failing that, she marched to the gate to ask if Barney could lend some assistance. He wasn't there. A younger man with red hair and prominent freckles stood in the guard box.

"May I help you?" he asked.

"Where's Barney?"

"He's off today."

"What's your name?"

"Red."

She nodded. "I see. I'm Blair Kendrick."

"Uh huh?"

"The star of—oh, never mind. I have a flat. Can someone help me get it changed?"

"Uh, I don't know. You might need to call a mechanic."

"Do you have a number to call?"

"I don't know. It's after hours."

Well, hell, she thought again. Blair scanned the parking lot once more for a man—*any* man—who had more get-up-and-go than Red.

"Well, can I leave the car overnight? Get the flat fixed tomorrow?"

"Yes, ma'am, you can."

"Thank you."

She turned to make her move, and then she saw Hank Marley.

He was standing on the sidewalk outside the gate as if waiting for a ride. She went through the pedestrian entrance and approached him.

"Hi, Hank!"

He looked at her and gave her the same killer smile. "Why, Miss Kendrick, good evening to you."

"You can cut the 'Miss Kendrick' stuff, Hank. Please call me Blair."

"All right, Blair."

"What are you doing out here? Do you have a gig tonight with the other fellas?"

"Not tonight," he said. "I'm on my way home."

"Where is that?"

"Sugar Hill." When she cocked her head, he continued. "West Adams Heights. It's southwest of downtown. I rent a room in a house there."

"Ah. How are you getting home?"

"I'm trying to get a taxi, but they don't seem to want to stop for me."

"Why not—oh, I see . . ." She looked up the street. "If I can get you a taxi, can we ride together? My car has a flat and I probably can't get it fixed until tomorrow."

Hank blinked and pursed his lips. "Why, I . . ."

"It's okay. I don't give a damn what anyone thinks or says. We're friends, and we work together."

He shrugged. "All right."

"Come on." They walked to the corner of Melrose and Crescent Heights. Cars zipped past them. Blair immediately thought of the scene in *It Happened One Night*, when Claudette Colbert and Clark Gable were hitchhiking and Claudette caught a ride by hiking up her skirt and revealing a leg. Blair wouldn't have to do that, though. She spotted a yellow Plymouth taxi headed their way and waved it down. When it stopped, she leaned in the window.

"We have two stops. One in Sugar Hill, and the other at the Hollywood Hotel."

The driver frowned when he saw them together. "I don't think so," he said.

Before he could drive off, Blair said, "Wait! There's an extra five dollars for you if you take us."

Hank said, "Blair, you don't have to do—"

"Hush." She waved him off. The driver finally nodded, and they got in through the back door.

"You're at the hotel, miss?" the driver asked.

"Yes."

"I'll go there first."

"No, we're taking Hank home *first*," Blair replied firmly.

The driver grumbled under his breath and took off, making a turn and heading east.

Hank looked at Blair. She smiled at him.

"Thank you, Blair."

"You're welcome, Hank."

8

KARISSA

Karissa pulled into the Ultimate Pictures lot on Melrose after checking in at the front gate, where the guard verified her appointment. As she drove her Murano further onto the lot, she scanned the old buildings and smiled. Some of them had been standing since the late 1930s, when Ultimate Pictures was formed. Although it wasn't one of the early majors like MGM, Universal, Paramount, Columbia, or 20th Century Fox, Ultimate had carved a niche in Hollywood history throughout the forties and fifties as purveyors of moneymaking B movies and the occasional A-list picture. Karissa knew a little about its past. Eldon Hirsch had been a Jewish entrepreneur wannabe when other studio moguls like Louis B. Mayer, the brothers Warner, Jesse Lasky, and Darryl F. Zanuck had carved out their corners of Tinseltown. Hirsch got a slower start in the business, but he ultimately succeeded when— allegedly—he made some deals with shadowy figures of organized crime. It was true that Hirsch had his hands in the initial ventures of casinos and gambling in Las Vegas in the late forties, around the time that Blair Kendrick was beginning to make movies. No formal accusations were ever made, and Hirsch never faced any legal problems.

Instead, he was supposedly murdered by his "friends" in Nevada.

Her phone rang as she was getting out of the Nissan. Marcello's ID appeared on the screen.

"Hi, Marcello?"

"Hey, just checking in. You at the studio?"

"I just arrived, about to walk inside to see Derek. Ten minutes early. That's good for me, huh?" Karissa used to have a bad habit of tardiness, even for vital production appointments. But after the semi-success of *Second Chance*, she resolved to be punctual forevermore. And she was.

"Fantastic. You can finally drop your membership to Sorry-I'm-Late Anonymous."

"Well, I hope your meeting with the banker goes well. Get us some money. Lots of money."

"I'll try, hon. You just get what you can from Derek. He's a good guy, I think he'll cooperate."

Inside, the receptionist checked her in and pointed to the comfortable waiting room, where copies of *Variety*, *Hollywood Reporter*, and the *Los Angeles Times* were plentiful. A large TV screen displayed the latest Ultimate production, which was a comedy starring two actors—one white and one black—who had made the leap from a career in television sitcoms to the big screen.

Karissa sat on a couch and ran through e-mails on her phone until Derek Morton appeared from behind a door marked NO ADMITTANCE. They shook hands warmly.

"Come on back," Morton said.

His title at Ultimate Pictures was Assistant to the Head of Production. He was in his thirties, surfer-blond, and ambitious. Karissa and Marcello had met him at a Hollywood party some time back and kept in touch. "If you ever have something to pitch to Ultimate Pictures . . ." he had said.

He led her through the inner sanctum of the administrative building and into a conference room. He offered her coffee, which she declined. Then he shut the door and they began.

"So! I understand you and Marcello have a mysterious but fabulous idea for that indie film festival. We're one of the sponsors, you know."

"That's right, Derek, and I'm hoping you can maybe help us out—with some archives that perhaps exist somewhere in the dungeons of Ultimate Pictures."

He laughed. "I'll see what I can do."

"You know, I've never met Justin Hirsch. Is that possible?"

Morton shrugged. "He doesn't spend too much time in his office anymore. Leaves the running of the studio to others."

"How old is he now?"

"He turned eighty a couple of months ago."

"Wow. He's in good health, I take it?"

"He's as ornery as a tiger in a circus."

Karissa leaned forward across the table and spoke in a conspiratorial tone. "Well, our idea has to do with his *father*, in a way."

Morton cocked his head. "Oh?"

"Do you remember Blair Kendrick?"

Later when she reflected on their conversation, Karissa would swear that a shadow passed over Derek Morton's face as soon as she said the name.

"Uh, yeah?"

"Well, we want to do a movie about her. We see it as not really a biopic, maybe not even a 'true story,' but more of a modern film noir with her as the femme fatale in the movies as she really was—and, I don't know what yet, but including something else in her personal life. You know, 'young and popular actress becomes a mob target.' Of course, we'd have to deal with the murder of Eldon Hirsch."

Morton sat back in his chair. "What exactly do you want from us?"

"Access to your files on Blair. Screen tests. Film footage. Anything, really. Of course, our attorneys could work out some kind of deal for compensation. Hell, maybe Justin would want to get involved. Tell his father's story, you know?"

Morton drummed his fingers on the table and didn't say anything.

"What? Is there a problem?" she asked.

"It would be a controversial subject around here, Karissa. I know for a *fact* that Justin isn't a fan of Blair Kendrick. He hates her with a passion. I'll let you in on a little secret. Please don't share this with anyone, all right?"

"Sure."

"He keeps a poster of Blair Kendrick in his office. When he's stressed out, he throws darts at it. After her face is obliterated with holes, he takes the poster down and puts up a new one. This has been going on since he was made head of the studio *decades* ago."

"No way."

He nodded. "It's true. I don't think he's going to take kindly to a picture about Kendrick."

"But why? What does he have against her? *She* didn't kill his father."

"I have no idea." He shrugged and made a "don't ask me" face.

Karissa tried another strategy. "Well, what do you know about Buddy Franco? He was an executive at the studio during that time. A fixer."

Morton shook his head. "We don't use that 'fixer' term. That's a title for Eddie Mannix or Howard Strickling . . . or Ray Donovan, if you watch Showtime."

"Hm, from what I've read, Franco was there that night."

"He's something of a controversial figure here, too. *He* might have been the guy who pulled the trigger on Eldon Hirsch, and they were best friends! Franco was definitely playing footsies with the mob."

"Okay. So, are you saying we can't get into your archives?"

He shook his head. "No, I'm not saying that. Yet. Let me make some inquiries. There really shouldn't be a problem if you just want to do some research. I can tell you that if the movie goes into production, though, Justin's not going to be happy about it." Morton smiled. "I can always blame some dumb secretary for giving you access without realizing it was a sensitive issue."

She bristled at his description of an office worker. "Well, I wouldn't want anyone to lose a job."

"That won't happen. Is there anything else?"

"Nope. That's it."

"Right. Like I said, let me look into this. I'll call you in a day or two—is that okay?"

"That would be great."

Karissa drove home to West Adams Heights after the meeting. She had texted Marcello to say that she wasn't sure how it had gone. Derek Morton's reaction had not been what she'd expected. Whatever.

Marcello responded with a quick, "TTYL. See you at 7:30."

That night she had planned to meet Marcello for dinner and then go together to the World Stage and hear some jazz. Hopefully, they would be able to talk to some of the musicians who might know something about Hank Marley and Blair Kendrick.

As she approached the house on Harvard Boulevard, she saw

a familiar green Jeep Cherokee parked at the curb in front. "Oh, no," Karissa muttered, pulling into the driveway.

There he was, standing on the porch by the front door.

Instead of driving into the garage, she stopped the car and got out.

"Willy, what are you doing here?" She strode around her vehicle and stood on the grass, looking up at him.

Willy Puma was an actor who had spent several years straddling the line between A- and B-list action roles. He was mostly known for playing henchmen and had made a splash in a long-running thriller franchise called *Meat Grinder*. Big, beautiful, and also biracial, Willy had darker skin than Karissa. Most people—especially Hollywood casting agents—took liberties with his appearance. He was always placed in stereotypical black roles.

They had been married for seven years.

"How come you don't return my calls?" he snapped.

"Our attorneys talk to each other. You're not supposed to be here, Willy. Leave now."

"Come on, Karissa, *talk* to me. I just want to talk to you!"

"Well, I don't want to talk to you."

He stepped off the porch and came down the steps toward her. Instinctively, she moved a few paces back. He held up his hands. "I'm not going to touch you."

"That's right, you're not. Go away. And sign the divorce papers. Let's get it done with."

"That's what I want to talk to you about. Karissa, I don't want a goddamned divorce! I've changed my mind. I'm not going to agree to it."

She shook her head. "Uh-uh. Too late. That ship sailed when you cheated on me a third time, got drunk, and wrecked your car with your *woman* inside. They say, 'no publicity is bad publicity,' but in my case it was *bad publicity*."

"How many times do I have to say I'm sorry? I went and did the therapy thing! I did everything you wanted me to do. How can I make it up to you?"

Karissa felt her blood boiling. She didn't want to have this conversation—this *argument*—again. "You can't. Now leave. *Please.*"

He stood there, his jaw clinching and his hands trembling. Then, he slammed his right fist into the palm of his left hand. "This ain't over!" he growled, and he marched down the yard to his car.

Once he had driven away, Karissa weakly went back to her Murano and got in. Her hands were shaking as she started the engine and drove the vehicle into the garage.

I'm not going to cry.

She had already shed too many tears, although Karissa knew that the well would never dry up.

9

THE MOVIE

The film continues with a montage of newspapers spinning toward the camera—copies of Variety *and other Hollywood trade and gossip publications. Headlines read:* KENDRICK TO STAR IN "DAME" *and* BLAIR IS TOAST OF TINSELTOWN!

The female voice-over narration resumes. "The Jazz Club *wrapped in April of '47, and I was immediately signed to star in a picture called* A Dame Without Fear. *My 'bad girl' persona was really taking off. It would be a few months before* The Jazz Club *opened to the public."*

Shots of the actress playing Blair Kendrick flash on screen—she is modeling new clothes, being seen at fashionable restaurants, and caught in candid photographs with such stars as Cary Grant, Frank Sinatra, Robert Mitchum, and Ray Milland.

"*I was enjoying my newfound fame. As a single woman in the public eye, the studio fixed me up on dates with some big Hollywood names, but I went on them just to stay out of the clutches of Eldon Hirsch.*"

*Blair receives flowers in her dressing room. She opens the card to see a note—*May I see you tonight?—Eldon.

Cut to Blair parking her Oldsmobile against the curb of a dark street lined with nice mansions. She gets out, carefully looks around to make sure she's not being watched, and locks the door. She then moves down a sidewalk to a more modest one-story house.

"What Eldon didn't know—what Louella Parsons and Hedda Hopper and those awful gossip queens didn't know—was that I had embarked on something very dangerous. I couldn't help myself. When the heart desires something as strongly as mine did, you follow it, no matter what."

Blair hurries up a paved walkway to the front door. Before she can knock, it opens—revealing Hank Marley.

Blair rolled over and looked at the clock on the nightstand. 6:20.

The dawn seeped through the blinds in Hank's bedroom. It was time for her to get up and leave. She hadn't meant to spend the entire night, but they had fallen asleep sometime after one in the morning.

He lay on his side, his broad black back to her. His breathing was slow and heavy. Not snoring. With her gaze, she traced the shapes of the muscles in his shoulders and on his one visible flank. His short coal-colored hair beckoned for her touch, to slide her fingers gently over his scalp. His scent was that of long-dried sweat and a cologne he always wore. She didn't know what it was called, but it gave him a musky aroma that somehow reminded her of firewood.

It had been weeks since that first cab ride together, the result being a whirlwind of an intensely vivid dream that ignited every nerve in her body. It had been a wave of emotions and sensuality, a tsunami she couldn't and had no desire to stop. And yet Blair still wondered why she was attracted to him. She honestly had no idea. She recalled the stories about the Negro boxer Jack Johnson, and how he had been with a few white women, especially Lucille Cameron, one of his wives. Johnson had served a prison sentence for some ridiculous crime that was used to punish him for stepping out with ladies who "weren't his kind." Well, the attraction had to go both ways, didn't it? Those white women hadn't minded sharing their beds with a Negro man, either. Perhaps Hank was her own version of a Jack Johnson. Maybe it was just a sex thing, but in Blair's case, it was more than that. All she knew was what the lovely ache in her chest told her when she wasn't with him.

She quietly slipped out of the bed and put on the bathrobe he had given her. She left the bedroom, went into the hall, and entered the bathroom. When she was done, she primped for a moment in front of the mirror. The night had done a little damage to her face, for she hadn't bothered to remove her makeup. Now it was a bit smeared around the eyes and mouth. She couldn't believe she had slept that way, but one went with the flow. She used soap and water to wash most of it away.

Blair tread softly back to the bedroom. Hank had turned to face her side of the bed, but he was still asleep. She removed the bathrobe and slid under the sheets next to him. She cuddled against his body and he instinctively draped a strong arm around her.

"Good morning," he said.

"You're awake?"

"No. I am definitely dreaming."

She chuckled. "Then dream on." She kissed his forehead, but he moved his mouth up to hers and met it.

After the long kiss, he said, "Be right back." He got out of bed and padded, naked, to the door to use the bathroom, too.

Blair sighed.

God, what am I doing? Am I crazy? What's gotten into me?

She knew what she was doing was wrong. By society's standards, anyway.

But is it really so wrong?

For the past month, Hank had shown her what physical love could be. She'd had no idea. And she knew they had to be careful. Becoming pregnant would be a disaster—for them both.

Hank returned to the room and got back in bed with her. "Mmm, good morning, again," he said.

"Good morning."

"I'm still dreaming."

"We both are."

He started to sing a line from a song, the one about a lucky lady dreaming . . .

"What *is* that song? I heard you and your band play it that first time I met you on the set."

"Oh, that's called 'Blues in the Dark.'"

She raised her forehead. "Ah, right. Jimmy Rushing and Count Basie?"

He smiled. "1938."

"I like it. It's sad, but it's romantic. We're that, aren't we?"

"What you mean?"

"We're 'blues in the dark.' You and me. That's what we are."

He grinned. "That we are, baby."

A short silence. Then she asked, "You've never told me whose house this is."

"Some white guy who lives in Florida. He rents rooms to colored folks. It's kind of a dump, wouldn't you say? Not like the other houses on South Hobart Boulevard. Louise Beavers lives just a few houses down."

"Who else lives here?"

"My bass player, Ray, and his wife and son. Another Negro couple who are both dancers. That's it right now. Our landlord doesn't go in for all that covenant bullshit that prevents Negroes from living in Sugar Hill."

"I thought I heard those cases were over. Hattie McDaniel and the others—they won, didn't they?"

"In the state of California, yes they did. But I understand another case is going to the Supreme Court. I don't know when; soon. In the meantime, we get to stay."

"Good."

They lay in each other's arms for a while, and then she shook herself out of her reverie. "I have to go."

"I know."

"I meant to go last night."

"I know."

"Do you think anyone will see me?" The notion made her nervous.

"I don't know. I hope not." After a pause, he suggested, "You could do what you've done before—go out the back, around the side of the house, and then come up to your car. Won't be as noticeable."

"I think I'll do that."

"Or I could cover you with a blanket and carry you to your car."

She laughed and punched him lightly on the shoulder. He laughed, too, and kissed her again.

"Oh, Hank, what are we going to do?"

"Darlin', if you need to . . . if you *need* to end this . . . I will understand. I will totally understand, baby. You know that. I'd hate for it to end, but . . . well, I *know*."

"Hank, I don't want it to end. But what if someone finds out? It's a miracle no one has caught us yet."

"No one's coming in my room without me inviting them in. Mr. Smith and Mr. Wesson will make sure of that."

"Who?"

"Smith & Wesson. My revolver sitting in the nightstand on my side of the bed."

"You have a gun?"

"I do. A thirty-eight caliber. It's a real honey."

"Jesus." She shivered a bit at the thought. "The thing is . . . Hank, I *want* to be seen with you. I want us to be able to go out to restaurants. I want to go to the club and hear you play. I want to go dancing with you. I want you to be my date at the premiere of *The Jazz Club*."

"I don't think your studio bosses would like that very much."

"I know."

"Isn't there something in your contract about that?"

"There's a morality clause in everyone's studio contract. Relationships with someone of a different race are forbidden. It's so stupid. Why is this country the way it is?"

"It would take a philosopher much smarter than me to answer that. Darlin', I've lived with racism every day of my life."

His frankness shocked her. After a moment, she replied, "And *that* is so unbelievable." She looked at him. "Do you think maybe in ten, twenty, or thirty more years that things will have changed?"

His soft laugh was short and abrupt. "Baby, you are smart, talented, and good-hearted. But I got to say, you're naive. Sometimes I think you've been blind to what's going on between whites and Negroes in this country. What was it like in Chicago?"

She bristled a little, but then answered, "You're right, Hank. I grew up in a sheltered existence on the north side of the city. I never had much dealings with Negroes. I guess maybe I wasn't paying attention. I'm sorry."

"Don't apologize. I understand. Most people in this country are like that. *We* notice the discrimination. White folks, for the most part, take it for granted, I'm sorry to say. Please don't take offense, but Blair, you're going to leave here and go back to your white world and not face any of the danger *I* would if we're caught. I have a feeling it's going to take a long time for those kinds of things to change."

"Oh, Hank. We have to be careful. And, you know, I can

dream about things changing," she said. "Maybe it's naive, but think of a future when we could get married. Can you imagine that?"

"You and me? Married?"

"Can you see it? In your mind's eye?"

He gave a soft laugh. "I'd like to be able to imagine it, darlin'. But I'm afraid I can't. Don't get me wrong; I would love more than anything to be married to you. I just don't see it happening . . . except in a dream." He separated himself from her and grabbed a pack of cigarettes from the nightstand. He popped two into his mouth, lit them with a lighter, and handed one to her.

"You did that better than Paul Henreid did in *Now, Voyager*," she said with a smile.

"And you're a hell of a lot more beautiful than Bette Davis."

A moment of silence passed as they smoked.

"Hank?"

"Yes, ma'am?"

"What was your family in St. Louis like? You've never said much about them."

"Not much to tell. I didn't know my daddy. He upped and left when I was four. I barely remember anything about him." He held up his right hand, revealing a gold ring on his finger. "This is all that's left of my daddy. It was his wedding ring. Apparently, he left it behind when he walked out. My mother gave it to me, said I could sell it if I wanted to. I decided to keep it and wear in on my right hand just to—I don't know—have some sort of connection to the man who helped conceive me. My mother still loved him. She never hated him for leaving us, although I never understood why not. I guess love is a powerful thing when it's real. As for my mom, well, she died when I was fifteen."

"Oh, I'm sorry."

"Don't be. She had the cancer. It was a blessing. She worked her heart out as a maid. I loved her more than anything, but she was never a very happy person. After she was gone, it was just me and my little sister, Regina. She's two years younger than me."

"Is she still in St. Louis?"

"Nuh-uh. She's right here in LA. Plays the piano, too."

"Really? How come I haven't met her?"

Hank gestured with his hands. "I suppose it just hasn't worked out."

"You're not . . . it's not because I'm white that I haven't met her, right?"

"No."

"Hank, I think you're lying to me. You don't want your sister to know you're seeing a white woman."

"That's not true, baby."

"Well then, I want to meet her."

"All right, all right! You'll meet her. Lordy, woman . . ."

"Why isn't she living here with you?"

"She didn't want to! She wanted to make her own way. Regina lives in an ugly old apartment in South Central. I've been trying to get her to move. But what about you, Blair? Why did you leave Chicago?"

Blair sighed heavily. "My father owns a chain of liquor shops. He's done very well. We were never wanting for money. The problem was that both he and my mother liked to sample the goods a little too much—every day. My older brother, Tommy, was killed during the war. Battle of the Bulge. That really sent them over the edge. Mom would beat me. Dad would beat me. They tried to get me to marry some businessman my dad was friends with. He was twenty years older than me and fat. There was no love in our family. I got out of there as soon as I could."

They were silent for a while after that confession. Then she turned to him. "Hank?"

"Yes?"

"I . . . I never asked you this before."

"What?"

"Have you ever . . . you know . . . with a white woman . . . ?"

He shook his head. "Hell, no. You, my dear, are the first." He gave her a look. "And I *ain't* going to ask you the same question."

She laughed. "Oh, you don't have to, I'll tell you everything. Hank, you're really the first man I ever . . . well, there was this boy back in Chicago. Happened once. Didn't mean a thing. I'll always consider *you* the first."

Indeed, there had been Joey in Chicago, the boy who had taken her virginity at a high school graduation party gone out of control. The act had been awkward and passionless. Afterward, she felt ashamed, but he wanted her to stay in the city and marry him. She held no interest in that, but Joey kept pursuing her, thinking she would "put out" for him again, Instead, she left town. She told her parents her plans and didn't say a word to Joey. Her mother and father didn't care. To them, she had been just another mouth to feed, which took away from what they were able to spend on booze.

"The fact I'm a Negro doesn't make any difference to you?" Hank asked, drawing her out of the unpleasant memory.

"No."

"It's supposed to."

"Well, it doesn't. I mean, I know what the outside world thinks about it. I know we could get in a lot of trouble. But in my heart and soul, I don't care about that. None of that ever mattered to me. In my eye, you're just a man. And a damned handsome one, too."

She draped a leg over him and pushed her body on top of his. They kissed for a full minute.

When their mouths parted, Hank said, "Well, then, we're just going to have to be careful, won't we?"

She nodded, but then couldn't help but continue. "But I have to say, I might throw caution to the wind and challenge that studio contract morality clause. Olivia de Havilland took Warner Brothers to court and got some changes made. Maybe it's time someone stood up to them about *this*."

"Darlin', it's about a lot more than the studio contract. It's not legal for different races to get married. I'm pretty sure what we're doing right *now* isn't legal. We could go to jail, I think."

"Then we'll have to run away and find someplace where we can live the way we want to." The kissing continued for a while until she finally said, "Damn it. I really need to go."

She slid off him and put her feet on the floor. "But before I do . . . would you show me your gun?"

"My gun? What for?"

"Well, you know I had to shoot a prop pistol in *The Jazz Club*. I have to do it again in *A Dame Without Fear*. I think maybe I should practice shooting a real gun so I'll know what it's really like."

He put his hands behind his head on the pillow and grinned at her. "We could go out of town and find a place in the desert to take a crack at some bottles and tin cans. I'll show you how."

"Oh, that sounds like fun! When can we go?"

"Soon, baby, soon. You had best go before there are too many people on the street who'll see you."

She nodded, blew him a kiss, and put on the clothes she'd dropped on the floor the night before.

10

KARISSA

The World Stage was a performance and educational art space in Leimert Park Village, located in the heart of LA's African American community. Degnan Boulevard bisected the diamond-shaped triangle that made up the area with 43rd Street running east-west at the top, Crenshaw Boulevard jogging down from the northeast corner, and Leimert Boulevard going from the north-west corner to a point at West Vernon Avenue. At the bottom tip of the "diamond" was small Leimert Park itself. Degnan sported an art gallery, a Jamaican restaurant, a bookstore, a foster youth support center that provided arts education and other activities, a parking lot, and the World Stage.

Karissa hadn't been to the spot, even though it was about three miles away from her house in Sugar Hill. Over the past few years, much of her time in Hollywood had been spent in other areas. During her marriage to Willy, she had lived in Van Nuys and never had much opportunity to visit this side of Los Angeles with a majority black population. It wasn't that she wouldn't have felt at home, but that she knew from experience that color-ism factored into how she was viewed.

Willy, who was darker, once told her that she could "pass as white." It wasn't true at all. He'd said it to hurt her. It was an insulting comment, especially from her husband at the time. She fully acknowledged that she had grown up with a significant amount of privilege, considering that her adoptive parents had been white and had lived in a predominantly white upper-middle-class neighborhood. But that didn't mean she couldn't still identify with the black community. Especially regarding civil rights, the Black Lives Matter movement, and other issues involving race relations, Karissa knew where she stood.

Even so, throughout her life she lived daily with questions from strangers like, "What are you, exactly?" They always wanted to touch her hair. She was asked which "side" she preferred. She'd become upset with the limited options of races from which to choose on forms. She was told countless times that she was "exotic." She'd been asked if she was Middle Eastern. She perceived that some black people thought she was "stuck up," believing that she "behaved" as if she were fully white, while white people presumed the opposite—that she viewed them from the point of view of a black person. This was nonsense, of course. These daily microaggressions were indicators of *their* prejudices, not hers.

Sometimes, Karissa felt caught in the middle, blocked from both communities and never fully accepted.

But there were positive aspects to her identity, too, such as being able to comfortably chat up members of either race. She was instinctively aware of interracial families or couples when she saw them on the street or in the media. She received—and presented—the "black nod," that subtle acknowledgment African Americans gave to their peers, usually strangers on the street, to illustrate their shared solidarity. Karissa also typically felt comfortable in certain foreign countries where being biracial was a more accepted norm than in the United States.

Karissa and Marcello had dinner at Ackee Bamboo, just a few doors north of World Stage, prior to the nine-o'clock Friday night show. The jerk chicken was excellent, and Marcello devoured his ackee and salt-fish entrée. No alcohol was served, so they drank ginger beer.

"There's no bar at World Stage, either," Marcello said.

Karissa said, "I suppose we could go somewhere for a drink afterward if we want."

He shrugged. "No party animal activity tonight, I'm afraid. Angelina gave me the stink eye when I said I was going with you to hear jazz."

"I thought you were going to bring her."

"Nah, she wasn't interested. She thought it'd be more fun to take the twins to see the new Marvel superhero flick. Too bad we can't produce one of *those*."

"Tell Angelina I'll have you both over for dinner as soon as my kitchen is up to snuff at the new house."

"She'd like that."

Karissa cocked her head. "Wait . . . she doesn't know about . . . when we . . . ?"

Marcello vehemently shook his head. "She does not."

"That's good."

He looked at his watch. "Let's get going."

Karissa paid with the Stormglove credit card, and they walked over to World Stage, which looked more like a storefront for a dentist's office than a nightclub. Inside, the space was long and narrow with fewer than a hundred folding chairs on the floor. The tiny stage held a baby grand piano, drums, a double bass, and gear for guitar, woodwinds, and vocalists. Charlie Parker tunes from a bygone age piped over the PA as the nearly all-black audience waited for the performance to begin. Karissa and Marcello found three empty seats near the front and took two. The last open chair was grabbed at the last minute by a bald white man in a suit and tie. He smiled at Karissa and said, "I know, I'm overdressed." He loosened his tie and settled into his chair.

Karissa turned to Marcello. "How do you know these guys?"

"Butch is my man from San Diego. He's the sax player. Through him I know Zach, the drummer, and Carl, the keyboard guy."

"Think they'll know anything about Hank Marley and Blair Kendrick?"

"We'll see, won't we?"

The lights dimmed and the music faded out as a man wearing a kufi cap and caftan stepped onto the stage. He welcomed the audience to the show, made a plea for donations, and then introduced the band. "It is my pleasure to welcome to the World Stage once again—the Butch Johnson Hive."

The seven musicians took the stage—all black men who appeared to be various ages from twenties to sixties—and picked up their instruments. Butch, perhaps the oldest member of the group, stood in front, eyed the drummer and bass player, and gave them a quiet count-off. The rhythm section burst into a swinging fast tempo that recalled the bebop style of the forties.

Karissa spent the entire evening with a smile on her face, swaying and bouncing in her chair. This was the real thing. For the next ninety minutes, old-school jazz was alive and well in Los Angeles, California.

When the show was over, the band greeted the audience members and signed CDs at the back of the house. Marcello embraced Butch and slapped hands with the other musicians, giving them dap. He then introduced Karissa and explained that they had questions about some musicians of yesteryear. Three of the guys left for home, while Butch, Carl, Zach, and the bass player, known as "Hero," joined Karissa and Marcello as they walked out of the building. Mutually deciding there wasn't enough time to find a place nearby to sit and have a drink, they strolled down Degnan to the park and found some benches. The four musicians lit cigarettes. One had a pint of bourbon in a paper bag, which was passed around. There were plenty of people in the surrounding areas, including a couple of LA's finest sitting on police motorcycles on 43rd.

Karissa produced the photo of Blair Kendrick and Hank Marley, and the musicians took a look.

"I don't know who the white woman is, but I know that's Hank Marley," Butch said. Hero murmured an acknowledgment. "He was a piano man, had his own band for a while. Fine player. Ray played with him."

"Ray?" Karissa asked.

"Ray Webster," Butch said. "Bass player. He played with us when we were first starting out. We were friends, I guess."

Karissa and Marcello shared a look. "Is he . . . still around?" she asked.

"Yeah, but barely."

Hero, who was probably around the same age as Butch, addressed him. "How old is Ray? Gotta be ninety, at least."

Butch answered, "He turned ninety-four in February. He's not in good shape. Ray's in a nursing home. He's had all kinds of health problems. Heart attack, stroke, a little of this and that . . ."

"Is he cognizant? Would he speak to me?"

"I don't know. I suppose if he can *speak* then he might. Some days he speaks. Other days he doesn't. I visit him when I can."

"Did he ever mention Blair Kendrick?" Karissa tapped the photo as Butch handed it back to her. "That's who the woman is."

They all shook their heads. "Not that I recall," Butch answered.

As they spoke, Karissa noticed a man watching them from a bench not too far away, also smoking a cigarette. It was the same guy wearing the suit who had sat next to her during the show.

He appeared to be in his forties, was moderately heavyset, and his white skin stood out from those around him under the streetlamps. He was prematurely bald on top, with brown hair on the sides. He seemed to be glancing their way.

"When did Ray play with Hank Marley?" Marcello asked.

"In the forties. I think he was the youngest dude in Marley's band. Didn't something strange happen to Hank Marley?"

"He disappeared in 1949," Karissa replied. "No one knows where he went."

"I'm sure *someone* does," Hero said. "I heard Hank was killed."

"Murdered?"

Hero shrugged. "I guess. I don't know much about it."

"You think Ray would know?"

"Maybe."

Karissa saw the man in the suit stand and walk back up Degnan toward the club. She indicated toward him and quietly asked, "Does anyone know that guy?"

The musicians squinted; the light wasn't too good, but no one recognized him. "Never seen him before," Hero said. "Why?"

"Nothing. He was at the show, and he's been looking at us for a long time. So, where can we find Ray Webster?"

Butch replied, "The Vernon Healthcare place, not that far from here, over by the One-Ten."

"Thanks."

"One more thing . . ."

"Yes?"

Butch made a face and rubbed his chin. "Ray left some stuff with me. A couple of boxes of papers and things. I can see if there's anything in 'em that might be of interest."

"I'd appreciate that."

Marcello looked at his watch. "I better get going. Angelina will crack my head wide open if I don't make it home before midnight."

The others murmured other excuses. Karissa was feeling weary, too, especially after the stress she'd felt earlier that day when Willy had shown up at her door. She thanked the men, good nights were said all around, and everyone parted ways. Karissa walked up Degnan toward the parking lot across from the World Stage.

The bald man in the suit was standing in front of the World Stage, smoking another cigarette. "Hello again," he said to her with a smile.

She nodded at him. "Do you work at the World Stage?"

"No, ma'am, I just like to come here for the music."

She started to walk on. "Well, have a good evening."

Karissa got about ten feet past him when he spoke up again. "Oh, pardon me?"

She stopped and turned. Karissa's instincts kicked in. He liked to come for the music? *The band had never seen him before.*

Now on full red alert, she stepped back. "I have to go, I—"

"I have a message for you."

"What?"

"About Blair Kendrick and Hank Marley."

She felt a sudden, frightening adrenaline rush. "A message? From who?"

"Someone more important than you."

"What the hell is this?"

The man said, "Forget about making the Blair Kendrick picture. Her story can't be told because there is no story. Drop it and think of something else to do for your film project."

"What do you know about it? Who do you work for?"

He held up a hand. "Friendly warning. Stop asking questions about Blair Kendrick and Hank Marley."

"That's not very friendly. Go to hell." She swung around and continued walking toward her car in the lot, deftly pulling her car keys from her purse. She dared not look back. Shaken, she remotely unlocked her Murano, opened the door, and then turned to gaze back at the World Stage.

The man was gone.

She scanned the street and lot.

He was nowhere to be seen.

Karissa got in, locked the door, and started the car. She then tried to call Marcello to tell him what had happened, but she got his voice mail. Cursing softly, she pulled out of the lot and drove home toward Sugar Hill.

11

THE MOVIE

The motion picture on the screen transitions to a new montage accompanied by a reprise of the theme music as the Blair Kendrick character is seen at another Hollywood premiere. The Jazz Club *brings out major stars and press. Blair emerges from a limousine, and the camera bulbs flash in her direction. She smiles and waves, and her escort—her costar in the film—leads her arm in arm into the theater. A quick shot of studio boss Eldon Hirsch, standing in the greeting line, reveals a man frowning with frustration.*

The voice-over continues. "The Jazz Club *was the biggest hit in the history of Ultimate Pictures. I was the toast of—if not the town, then certainly the studio. The number of suitors who pursued me increased. Eldon Hirsch never gave up his harassment of me, and I steadfastly avoided his advances. It didn't make him happy, but there was nothing he could do about it. I was his* star."

Cut to Blair on a soundstage, holding a gun, speaking lines to another actor, and shooting.

"A Dame Without Fear *shot later in the year and was released in time for the Christmas holidays. Once again, my star shone brightly. By that time I had made* Killer Blonde, *and I was to start*

81

production on The Dark Lonely Night *in early 1948. It was around this time that I decided to take the plunge and buy my own house. I had left the Hollywood Hotel months earlier and was renting a place in Santa Monica, but that was too far from Sugar Hill and Hank Marley. I deserved better, so after the New Year in '48, I used my earnings to purchase a house on the street right behind Hank's."*

The Realtor phoned Blair as soon as the house became available. She went to Sugar Hill and met the man—who was white—at the beautiful Mediterranean Revival two-story home on South Harvard Boulevard. When Blair stepped out of her Oldsmobile and looked at the front of the mansion, her heart soared. She rushed up the walk to the front porch to greet him.

"Isn't this the same street where Hattie McDaniel lives?" Blair asked, after the initial introductions.

He pointed to the north. "Just down the block. At the corner."

"Oh, my."

"Want to look around the outside of the house first, or would you like to go on inside?"

"Let's go inside."

After the move-in was complete, Blair held a housewarming party and invited her colleagues and friends from the studio who were, of course, white. More than one of them expressed surprise that she had bought a house in Sugar Hill. Nevertheless, they came. Director Emil Winder and producer Buster Denkins were there, along with several of Blair's costars. Other Hollywood royalty attended, such as Robert Mitchum, Dana Andrews, Teresa Wright, and even Shirley Temple, who was not quite twenty years old. Director Jacques Tourneur was wooing Blair to star in a picture he was doing at another studio, and a hot new actor on the scene, Kirk Douglas, tried to convince her to talk to his agent about switching representation.

Eldon Hirsch, although invited as a courtesy, didn't show his face.

Several of the guests commented how "unusual" the party was, for the number of black attendees was striking. The "Negroes," as nearly every white person referred to them, were almost the majority. Blair had gotten to know quite a few members of "Black Hollywood" over the past several months, and her door was open to them. She had also employed two servants—a husband-and-wife team of maid and butler—both black—whom she paid very well. Georgeann and Sheridan were happy to have the jobs, and they were also complicit in the clandestine affair going on between Blair and Hank, sometimes acting as spies whenever Hank attempted to visit Blair at her house and making sure the coast was clear. Blair and Hank always used the back entrances of each other's homes, both of which were within walking distance. As there were no alleys in the neighborhood, the lovers used the narrow walkstreets, or paseos, that often existed between houses to slip from one block to the one behind. There were still small spots in which they could be seen, but if they only went at night and hurried . . .

Blair had invited Hank and the members of his band to perform in the room she had dubbed the "parlor," although it was large enough to be a ballroom. The grand piano she had purchased—but didn't play—was really for Hank. Inviting the band to perform was her trick to get away with having other Negroes at the party.

Through her relationship with Hank, Blair had gotten to know Hattie McDaniel, who was currently between husbands after divorcing her third a few years earlier. Louise Beavers was there with her new beau, Leroy Moore, as well as Eddie "Rochester" Anderson and his wife, Mamie. Superstar tap dancers the Nicholas Brothers were on the guest list, but only Fayad appeared with his wife, Geri. Howard, who was married to an up-and-coming actress by the name of Dorothy Dandridge, was a no-show. Bill "Bojangles" Robinson was another personage who was unable to attend, but Butterfly McQueen was there with actress Frances Williams, who had been instrumental in organizing black residents of Sugar Hill to fight the restrictive, segregationist covenants in the neighborhood a few years earlier in the decade. It was turning out to be a lively evening.

On the invitations, Blair had insisted that the party was informal. In keeping with the theme, she wore a black satin cocktail "wiggle" dress with a beaded bullet-shaped bodice and soft black tulle over the shoulders. It gathered at the hip on one side and fell in a skirt that had a small slit. The other women wore similarly occasion-appropriate gowns, while the men were dressed in suits. This wasn't an awards show after-party. Georgeann had brought in two other women to help with the food and drinks, and the party *swung* for hours. Hank's band played mostly music the white folks would appreciate—Glenn Miller and Benny Goodman hits—but they also covered popular numbers by Cab Calloway, Duke Ellington, and Billy Eckstine.

Blair spent most of her time entertaining in the parlor, dancing with various men from the studio, and raising eyebrows when she dragged Fayad Nicholas to the floor. The band picked up the tempo with Goodman's "Sing, Sing, Sing," and the couple "cut a rug," a recently popular slang term for dancing.

Afterward, to catch her breath, Blair went to the bar, where Sheridan served champagne to the guests. She asked for some water first, then took a flute of bubbly and downed it. As she stood and watched the festivities, she couldn't help but notice how the white people tended to stay on one side of the room, while the Negroes kept to the other half, near the band.

"Hello, Blair."

She turned to see Buster Denkins with his wife, whose name she had forgotten.

"Hi, Buster, are you having a good time?"

"Marvelous party, thank you."

She looked at the wife. "How about you, er, Carol?"

"Cathy. It's a beautiful home, Blair."

"I'm sorry, Cathy—my head is spinning. And thank you. It's something, isn't it?"

"When was it built?" Denkins asked.

"In 1918. There hasn't been much renovation to it, either." She nodded at the band. "The piano's new." She laughed.

"Nice to see Hank Marley here. The band did a great job in *The Jazz Club*."

"Yes. That's—that's how I thought of them to come play at the party. They were so good in the picture."

"There sure are a lot of Negroes here," Cathy Denkins said.

"Sure," Blair answered. "It won't be long before Sugar Hill is primarily a black neighborhood. I've gotten to know so many of them. Everyone is lovely."

"It wasn't always like that, was it?" Denkins asked. Blair shot him a look. "Sugar Hill, I mean," he added.

"No. When these houses were built, it was a white community. It was right before or during the war that movie stars like Hattie and Louise moved in. There were residents who objected and tried to get them evicted with restrictive housing covenants. Did you know there was a real estate firm called 'White and Christian'? And those weren't the proprietors' names." Blair rolled her eyes. "Disgusting way to treat human beings."

"The courts changed that, didn't they?"

"That's right, Buster. Hattie and Louise and Ethel Waters and others who simply wanted to live here were sued, but the state court threw out the case in 1945. Now a similar case has just been heard in Washington, DC. We're waiting on the result, but we're hoping the Supreme Court will decide that members of the Negro race will be 'accorded, without reservations and evasions, the full rights guaranteed them under the Fourteenth Amendment of the Federal Constitution.'"

"Sounds like you have that memorized."

"I've read the brief."

Cathy asked, "Why did *you* choose to live here, though?"

Blair took a sip of champagne. "I beg your pardon?"

"Why did you choose to live here with all the colored people?"

Blair looked from her to Denkins, who didn't seem fazed by his wife's question.

"Uhm, because I like the house? And because it doesn't matter to me. What difference does it make?"

Cathy blinked. "Oh, I didn't mean, well, you know . . ."

"No, I don't know. What did you not mean?"

Denkins interrupted. "Never mind, honey, let's have some champagne. Terrific party, Blair." He turned his wife to the bar, only to be greeted by another black face. Sheridan smiled and asked, "Champagne, sir?"

Stifling a laugh, Blair moved away and headed over to greet Hattie McDaniel.

The party wound down around three in the morning. Sheridan and Georgeann cleared away the remnants of discarded glasses, food trays, and the inevitable debris that accumulates during a party. The guests had all left, save for Hank, who, along with Blair, helped the two servants put things away.

"You don't have to do this, Hank," Blair said as she helped

Georgeann bring champagne flutes into the kitchen for washing. He was already at the sink, carefully wiping the dishes used for hors d'oeuvres.

"You *both* don't have to do this," Georgeann said. "Sheridan and I will take care of it. It's our job. You two go on and relax."

What she meant was, *you two go on and disappear upstairs.*

That was one reason why Blair liked the couple so much. They weren't prejudiced against the idea that one of their own was seeing a white woman. Blair had found this wasn't always the case. There were those in the Negro community who disapproved— and they had let her and Hank know it. She knew many more residents of West Adams Heights than those who had showed up at the party, residents she couldn't have invited.

When they were alone in Blair's bedroom, she removed her dress and began preparing for the night. As he undid his tie and threw his jacket over the back of a chair, Hank said, "You realize it's going to get out."

"What's that?"

"You and me. Us."

"Not if we're careful. We've been cautious." She took off the pearl necklace and placed it in a dresser drawer. It was her favorite, the one given to her by her grandmother. She'd worn it in studio publicity photographs, and several journalists had commented that Blair rarely posed for pictures without it. It had become a signature piece.

"Too many people know about us now. Not so many white folks, but plenty of mine. We can't guarantee everyone is going to keep quiet about it, Blair. There was a reporter here from the *California Eagle*." That was one of the newspapers that catered to an all-black readership.

She turned to him. Tired and not wanting to get into that kind of conversation, she held out her hands. "So, what do you want me to do? Stop seeing you?"

"I didn't say that."

"Well?" She shook her head. "If it gets out, then it gets out. If anyone gives us a hard time, then maybe we'll hire Loren Miller and he can take the case all the way to the Supreme Court the way he did with the covenant thing."

Hank chuckled. "I don't think it works that way, but I do admire your positive attitude." He took her in her arms. "You threw a wonderful party, my dear."

"And you played your little heart out. You fellas sounded fantastic. Everybody loved you. I couldn't stop dancing."

"And I can't stop loving you."

She pulled his head down and kissed him. "Come on, piano man, let's go to bed."

12

KARISSA

Karissa parked the Murano in the tiny parking lot in front of Vernon Healthcare Center, easily spotting Marcello's red Corvette in another space. She looked at her watch. On time. Marcello was generally always early. She got out and was surprised by how small the establishment appeared. Karissa had looked it up online and read that it held ninety-nine beds, as well as an in-house rehab unit, all fully Medicare- and Medicaid-certified. She imagined it mostly served the black community, given its proximity to downtown Los Angeles.

Marcello was waiting inside the small, but bright, waiting room. A couple of the other chairs were occupied. A security guard was stationed by the front door and a receptionist sat behind a window. There were no white faces in sight.

"Hey," she said. "Where's Butch?"

"He couldn't make it," Marcello answered. "He said he left word with the staff that we wanted to see Ray." They walked toward the receptionist's window to register their visit.

The door next to the receptionist was wide open. A man, probably in his seventies, emerged with a nurse. The name badge affixed to her scrubs identified her as "Sylvia." The man was a visitor, for he was dressed in street clothes. Smartly designed wording on his T-shirt read, "Nuts Are Sexy"—and to defray any confusion about what that meant, there was a drawing of an almond beneath the words. He and the nurse were engaged in quiet, serious conversation, momentarily blocking the receptionist's window.

"If I have to drive three hours to get here, then the person I need to see better keep the appointment," he was saying.

"I understand. I'm so sorry the doctor wasn't available. She had to attend to an emergency at the hospital, like I said. Do you plan to stick around? She could be back by three o'clock this afternoon."

"I can't wait that long; I have to get back to the farm. Please call me if my father takes a turn for the worse."

"Of course, and we'll call you if he takes a turn for the *better*, too!"

"Thank you." The man turned to see Karissa and Marcello standing behind him. "Oh, I'm sorry."

"That's all right," Karissa said.

He started to move past them, but when he exchanged glances with Karissa, he did a slight double take, blinked, and quickly moved on. Meanwhile, the nurse Sylvia had disappeared back into the care center hallway.

Marcello approached the receptionist. "We're supposed to visit Ray Webster. I believe his friend Butch Johnson made arrangements?"

The woman checked her computer asked for their names, and wrote out two visitor passes. Karissa and Marcello stuck them on their clothing.

"Room 111," she said, indicating the door. "Wait for Sylvia to escort you."

Karissa and Marcello found themselves in a hallway that

looked like any other nursing home or hospital wing. It was lined with doors to rooms, a nurses' station, and gurneys—some carrying people. It smelled like a nursing home, too, but the place appeared clean and orderly. It seemed like a decent establishment. Sylvia was nowhere in sight; she must have slipped into one of the resident's rooms.

"You okay?" Marcello asked her.

"What do you mean?"

"After last night. What you called me about."

"Oh. Yeah. His threat sure was creepy, though. Scared me at the time."

"I bet he wouldn't have said that to *me*. I'd knock his goddamned head off."

"Who *was* he, Marcello? Was he at the World Stage just to find me and deliver his so-called message? Butch and the other band members said they'd never seen him before."

"I don't know, Karissa. You know Hollywood. It's got a dark underbelly and there are no secrets. A lot of folks know what we want to do for the festival."

The nurse appeared from a room. "Hello, I'm Sylvia," she said, approaching them. "You're here to see Ray Webster?"

"That's right," Marcello said.

"Well, you're in luck. He's fairly alert today. I have to ask that you keep your visit short. He tires easily and we don't want to upset him. His blood pressure is high and he's at the age when too much excitement could bring on another stroke . . ."

The woman suddenly frowned. "Oh . . . I'm sorry, are you family?"

"Friends," Marcello answered.

She put a hand to her mouth. "Oh dear, I've said too much. I'm not supposed to talk about a resident's condition to anyone but family. I thought you were with his son."

"His son?" Karissa asked.

Marcello interrupted again. "We're close with the family, Sylvia, it's all right. We know all about Ray's condition. Don't you worry. We'll be careful with him. Thank you for your help." He took Karissa's arm and walked on to Room 111 with Sylvia behind.

Ray Webster shared a room with another bed that was currently empty. The ninety-four-year-old man lay with his eyes closed and mouth slightly open. There were various tubes connected to his arms and running under the covers, and a machine beeped softly next to his bed. Karissa thought he looked extremely frail and on death's door.

"Ray?" Sylvia said in that overly loud nurse's voice. "Ray, you have friends here to see you." She addressed them: "He must be asleep."

Marcello spoke. "Mr. Webster? Hello, Mr. Webster?"

Karissa tried. "Ray? Good morning, Ray."

It was the unfamiliar feminine voice that jogged him out of his dozing. His eyes darted to the visitors.

"There he is," Sylvia said, moving to the door. "I'll leave you to visit."

"Gregory?" he whispered.

"No," Marcello said. "We're friends of Butch Johnson. You know Butch? The saxophone player?"

"Butch?"

"That's right, Butch. Your friend?"

Webster's eyes jerked around the room.

"Butch isn't here, Mr. Webster, but we're friends of his and we wanted to talk to you. Is that all right?"

The initial confusion on the man's face seemed to subside, but his voice was weak. "Who are you?"

"My name is Marcello Storm."

"And I'm Karissa Glover. How are you feeling this morning?"

"Fine." He coughed a little.

She gave Marcello a glance and he nodded at her to go ahead. "Mr. Webster," she said, "we wanted to talk to you about your old friend Hank Marley. Remember him?"

"Hank Marley?"

"Yes. Didn't you play in his band a long time ago? Back in the 1940s?"

"Hank Marley . . . I remember Hank." A visible change rolled over his face that displayed a warmth of recall, but also a touch of sadness.

"You played bass for him?" Marcello asked.

"I played bass. Hank. Piano player."

"That's right," Karissa said. "Can I show you a photograph? I'd like you to look at it." She dug the picture of Hank and Blair out of her purse and held it close to his eyes.

"I need my glasses," Webster whispered.

They were on the nightstand by the bed. Marcello picked them up. "Here they are."

The man positioned the glasses on his face. He then took the photograph, held it at arm's length, and stared at it. He smiled.

"Oh. Hank. And . . . and . . ."

"Do you remember the woman?" Karissa asked.

He drew a slow intake of air and then spoke slowly and with effort. "Blair. That's Blair Kendrick. Oh my. I haven't thought of them in . . . . Where did you get this picture?"

"Well, sir," Karissa said, "I'm living in Blair Kendrick's old house in Sugar Hill. I found it there."

"Sugar Hill? You live in Sugar Hill?"

"That's right."

"I lived in Sugar Hill."

"We know. So did Hank Marley. You two were friends, right?"

"One of my best friends. He lived in the same house as me and my wife and son. He gave me my first job as a musician. I was twenty-one. I had to be twenty-one to play in the clubs."

"What can you tell us about Hank and Blair?" Karissa asked.

"They . . ." he sighed. "They were in love. They were so much in love. They were not two people; they were *one*."

The way he said it took Karissa's breath away. It was as if he were describing a romance that great poets might write about.

Then he shook his head. "But they couldn't do nothing about it. Not nothing, no way. He was a black man. She was a white woman. It was forbidden."

"How did they manage?" Karissa asked.

"They met in secret. Their houses were close; they walked to each other's homes, snuck in the back way. I sometimes saw her in our hallway. She was a movie star, did you know that?"

"Yes, sir."

"The studio would ruin her career. There were laws. Misce— missa—missagen—"

"Miscegenation laws."

"Yes." His eyes twinkled a bit at Karissa. "But it changed in . . . what year was it? When a black could marry a white?"

"In California, it was 1948."

He nodded. "California, not other states. Some states, maybe, but not everywhere. That was later?"

"Yes, sir. In 1967, that's when the Supreme Court made it a federal law that there couldn't be any discrimination of interracial marriage."

At that point, Webster looked at Karissa and smiled broadly, revealing very few teeth. "You're the product of that!"

"Sir?"

"You mixed. I can see that."

"Oh. Yes, sir. I'm biracial. That's correct."

"You half and half?"

"Uh, I don't know."

"One of your parents? Black?"

"I don't know. I was adopted."

He gave her that smile again. "Well, I can see it. You're part-sister. Maybe half. Maybe quarter. Maybe eighth. You're light-skinned. But I see it. You're a beautiful woman."

Karissa blushed and looked down. "Thank you."

"I bet white men say you're 'exotic.'"

She laughed. "I've heard that a few times in my life, yes."

He laughed hoarsely. "Bet you don't like that, huh?"

"Not really."

"I don't blame you."

"Mr. Webster—"

"Call me Ray, child."

"Okay, uh, Ray. What happened to Blair and Hank? I understand Hank just disappeared sometime in 1949. Do you know anything about that?"

Something passed over Webster's eyes and he coughed. Then he coughed again. Wheezing, he said, "They wanted to get married. Studio said . . ." He coughed again. ". . . they would blacklist Blair . . . threatened Hank . . ." The coughing became more pronounced.

"It's okay, Ray," Karissa said. "Take a breath. Do you need some water?"

". . . they were going to kill him . . ."

"Who's they?" Marcello asked.

Webster gasped for air and managed to say, "Fr—Franco."

"Franco?" Karissa asked.

The machine Webster was hooked up to started beeping. His eyes bulged and he appeared to have trouble breathing.

"Oh, dear, we need the nurse." Karissa placed a hand on Marcello's arm.

He said, "I'll find someone," and quickly left the room.

"Gregory . . ." Webster whispered.

"Gregory?"

"Talk . . . to . . . Gregory . . ." Then he gasped in pain.

Sylvia and another nurse rushed in with Marcello. "You two need to leave the room, please," Sylvia said.

They went out to the reception area. "Did he say anything else?" Marcello asked.

"He told me to talk to Gregory, whoever that is. He mentioned Franco—Buddy Franco—did you hear him?"

"Yes."

"The studio fixer. Did he do something to Hank? Was he the one threatening them?"

"Well, he figures in some of those stories you told me about the night Eldon Hirsch was shot."

They sat and waited. Marcello got on his phone, answered e-mails, and stepped outside to make a call, while Karissa thought about what she'd heard. It wasn't much. Webster had been surprisingly coherent for a little while. He probably knew more, if only she could get in and talk to him again. After fifteen minutes had passed and Marcello was back in the building, she approached the receptionist window and asked to speak to Sylvia. She was told to sit down and wait. After another ten minutes, Sylvia came through the door.

"How is Mr. Webster?" Karissa asked, standing.

"He's had a cardiac incident. You won't be able to see him now. I asked you not to excite him."

"We didn't mean to excite him; we were just talking to him," Marcello answered.

"I need to get back inside. What is it you wanted?"

"Sylvia, Ray asked us to talk to Gregory about something. Do you know who Gregory is?"

Sylvia frowned. "I thought you were friends of the family?"

"We are."

"Then you should know that Gregory is Mr. Webster's son. He was just here a little while ago."

Karissa felt her pulse quicken. "The man—he was maybe in his sixties or seventies—with the 'nut' shirt?"

"That was him, yes."

"Can you . . . can you tell us how to reach him?"

Sylvia shook her head. "Nuh-uh. You're not family. Next time he's here, I'll ask if it's all right if I give you his number. You leave me your name and number, all right?"

Karissa nodded. "All right," she said, handing the woman her business card.

Outside, as they walked to their cars, Marcello asked, "So, did that accomplish anything?"

"Sure it did. It was corroboration that something bad happened to Hank Marley—and it was because of his relationship with Blair Kendrick."

"He didn't exactly say that."

"Sounded like it to me. If only we could have kept him talking a while longer. He knows more. Maybe his son, Gregory, does, too. Let's put on our research hats and see if we can find him."

"There must be a few hundred Gregory Websters in Los Angeles."

"But do they all have sexy nuts?"

As Karissa drove away from the nursing home, something else about Gregory Webster other than his T-shirt struck her. She wasn't sure if it had been her imagination, but it seemed that, as he was leaving, the younger Webster had looked at Karissa in a way she couldn't quite put her finger on.

13

THE MOVIE

The motion picture shifts to a night scene, the exterior of the Ultimate Pictures lot. The camera pulls in slowly to the administration building and a single illuminated window amid the darkness. We penetrate the window and now are inside a spacious office that is lit only by a shaded lamp on a broad desk. The room is full of shadows, the setting reminiscent of something from a German silent film made by the likes of F. W. Murnau or Robert Wiene.

Eldon Hirsch sits with his coin collection, placing his newest acquisition in a slot in a binder. He has the means and the wealth that could give him great pleasure in life, but instead he is alone— an angry, unhappy man. A black-and-white publicity photo, framed and sitting on his desk, is a representation of the obsession that is eating his soul.

It is a recent still of Blair Kendrick, inscribed and signed, "To Eldon—Thank you very much for everything! X X O O—Blair."

"There he is, playing with his toys."

Hirsch looked up and squinted into the shadows. The tall,

shapely woman was a silhouette, but the white dress she wore took on a ghostly luminescence in the semidarkness. At first, he thought she was Blair, finally come to pay her respects, after hours, in the way he had been desiring . . . but then he realized he was mistaken. The woman's outline certainly resembled Blair's, but she was unfortunately someone else altogether.

"Malena?" Hirsch whispered.

"In the flesh and blood."

"How did you . . . ? I wasn't expecting you." His secretary, Camille, was gone for the night—but he thought he knew who might have let her in.

The woman strolled into the expansive office. She was in her early thirties, a lean, athletically built beauty who spoke with a faint Italian accent. She also had magnificent, flaming-red hair. Malena Mengarelli could have been a glamorous movie star if she had chosen that path. Instead, she had immigrated to join and sleep with her underboss in Las Vegas, who provided her with the means to enjoy an extravagant and indulgent lifestyle among a sinister family of colleagues. Malena wasn't exactly a *caporegime*, nor had she ever been "made," since women never received that honor. Nevertheless, soldiers in the organization did her bidding, and it was well known that anyone who refused her orders would soon, as they would say, sleep with the fishes.

Eldon Hirsch had no doubt that Malena Mengarelli was a very dangerous person.

"I was in town on business and I thought I'd drop in, pay a visit," she said. "You don't mind, do you, Eldon?"

"Not at all." He stood and started walking toward the bar. "Can I get you a drink?" Then he stopped and nervously moved back to his desk, reaching for the cigar box. "Or maybe you'd like a cigar? You like Cubans, don't you? Meyer told me so."

"Sure, I'll have a Cuban. *And* a drink."

Hirsch fumbled with the box and managed to produce a Havana original. He handed it to her and flicked a flame from his elephant lighter. Malena puffed it and sat in the chair in front of the desk. Hirsch returned to the bar. "What'll you have? Martini? Gin and tonic?"

"Bloody Mary."

Hirsch spent too much time preparing the drink, retrieving cold tomato juice from the little bar fridge and conscientiously adjusting the right ratios of juice to vodka to spices. When he finally brought it to her, she didn't thank him.

"You're not having one?" she asked.

"Uh, no . . . I'm not. You enjoy it. How have you been? You look well. You look beautiful, Malena. That red hair, God . . . you sure you don't want to be in a picture? Technicolor would do wonders for you. I could make you a star. You could be—"

"Hush, Eldon," she snapped. "Screw your shitty movies."

Even Eldon Hirsch was shocked when words like that were uttered by a woman.

Malena blew a few smoke rings. "This is good. I'm impressed."

"I'm glad you like it." He wanted to ask her why she had "dropped in" but knew to keep his mouth shut. She would bring up the agenda in due time.

She nodded at the coin collection, still spread out on the desk. "I see you're admiring your baubles."

Hirsch gave a little laugh. "Yes, yes. I can't stop handling them. They are something, aren't they? Their worth increases every day. In ten or twenty years' time—"

"I know, I know, they'll be very valuable. Screw your shitty coins."

The studio boss swallowed and sat back in his chair. He considered pressing the call button and having Buddy Franco step into the room. That, however, would be a huge mistake. Hirsch was fairly certain that Franco was behind her visit.

"Eldon, I've come to ask you about the loan. You know it's past due."

"Ah, of course. I thought that might be what you wanted to talk about." He sat forward with his elbows in the desk, his hands clasped below his chin. "The studio is making lots of money now. We're finally in the black. I'll be able to pay it back by Christmas."

"Christmas? Why not now?"

"All right. Sure. I can do that. Tell Tonino I'll send a check tomor—"

"You'll write one now, Eldon. Three hundred thousand. That's the down payment on the interest you owe. Tonino understands your liquidity problems, so he'll allow you to pay off the rest in installments. Just know that the interest increases as time marches on."

"Oh, I know. I'll do it right now." He opened a drawer and removed a studio check register. "Three hundred thousand? Made out to the same, uh, attorney?"

"Yes." She squinted at the register. "You don't want to use studio funds, do you? Won't that . . . look funny?"

Hirsch cursed to himself. He would have to write a check out of his personal account. "You're right, Malena. What was I thinking?" He laughed again and opened another drawer. He removed a different check register and wrote out the draft. Hirsch tore it off and handed it across the desk to her.

Malena glanced at it to confirm the check's accuracy and then opened the Prada purse in her lap. She dropped the slip of paper inside and snapped the bag shut.

"Have you had dinner?" Hirsch asked. "We could go to—"

"Don't have the time," she said. Malena abruptly stood, crushed the lit end of her cigar in the ashtray near his elbows, and left the drink virtually untouched. "See you later, Eldon. I have to run."

She turned and started to walk away from the desk, which was a relief to Hirsch. But then the woman stopped suddenly and turned around. "Eldon, you wouldn't be embezzling a portion of Tonino's profits from the studio, would you?"

Hirsch's stomach jumped into his throat. "Wha—what? What are you talking about?"

The woman's cold, dark eyes bore holes into his.

Christ. They know. Hirsch swallowed.

"Be careful, Eldon," she said. "I'll give you a few days to think about things. We'll have another talk soon, all right?"

He just stared at her, speechless.

"*All right?*"

"Sure, Malena. You're welcome to come back anytime. We'll do dinner."

The corner of her mouth turned up in a smirk. "I'm not one of your little starlets you screw on your couch here." She gave him a little wave and left the office.

Hirsch took a handkerchief from his pocket, dabbed his forehead, and pressed the call button attached to the desk. He heard the faint buzz elsewhere in the building. A few minutes later, another figure—this time a bulky, stocky silhouette—stood in the open doorway on the other side of the room.

"Did you want to see me?"

"Buddy. Come in. Close the door."

The man who entered was thirty-eight years old, had an army crew cut, and was still dressed sharply in a suit. Buddy Franco moved across the floor and took the chair that had previously been occupied by Malena Mengarelli.

"So, you're still here," Hirsch said. "Do you ever go home to your wife?"

"You know I don't leave the studio until you do, sir."

"And you should know you don't have to do that unless we talk beforehand and I need you for something."

Franco shrugged. "I'm like you, Eldon. I feel at home at the office."

Hirsch emitted a short laugh that sounded more like a snort. "Trouble with the old lady, Buddy?"

"Not really. I just have priorities."

Hirsch pulled out another cigar and offered the box to Franco. "Have a Cuban."

"Thank you, sir."

Both of them lit their cigars with the elephant lighter.

"Malena Mengarelli was just here."

Franco nodded. "I know. I let her in."

"I thought so."

"I couldn't very well refuse."

"No."

There was a pause as the men puffed. Hirsch considered the man who was the studio fixer at Ultimate. Could he trust Franco? The guy seemed to be very loyal. He had overseen the elimination of a number of problems that Hirsch hadn't wanted the press to find out about. He did as he was told and protected the boss. The two of them had become friends—perhaps. Or was it all an act? Hirsch knew very well how Franco had come to be employed at Ultimate. The question was—to whom was Franco *really* loyal? Hirsch? Or the boys in Vegas?

Franco nodded at the stogie in the ashtray. "She didn't finish hers."

"Waste of a good cigar."

"Everything all right?"

"She thinks I stole their money."

Franco's expression didn't change. After a beat, he asked, "Did you?"

"Of course not. I still owe them some cash on the loan, you know. I made a down payment."

"That should hold off Tonino for now."

"And Meyer will be happy." Hirsch drummed his fingers on the desk and looked away. "Beatrice wants to take Justin to the Grand Canyon this weekend. Wants him to see that big hole in the ground for his birthday."

"How old will he be?"

"Nine."

"I'm sure he'll enjoy it, sir."

"Are you kidding? Justin's a little brat." Hirsch inhaled on the cigar and blew several smoke rings into the air, just as he had seen Malena do. "What the hell . . . he'll probably grow up and take over the studio someday. I guess being a brat is a good qualification for the job."

Franco did not respond to that one.

Hirsch picked up a coin on his desk and held it between his thumb and index finger. It was silver-colored, with a man's head in profile wearing a wreath of leaves in his hair, like a Roman orator. "Do you see this, Buddy?"

"Yes, sir."

"It's a Barber quarter, S mint, from 1901. There are a lot of fakes out there, but this one's real. Just a little over seventy thousand were produced, and it's very rare."

Franco had indulged his boss many times regarding the coin collection. "Very impressive, Eldon."

"I'll say. Meyer found it for me. Someone he knew in New York acquired it—somehow. I didn't ask. I got it for a song. I guess it's worth about five hundred bucks. But who knows what it'll be worth when Justin's my age, huh?" He gave Franco a grin. "Part of it belongs to you, you know."

"I appreciate that," the fixer said. "But I'm not looking for you to cash in. You need to hold on to them. I don't care about my percentage until you decide it's time. Or until *Meyer Lansky* does."

"I know, I know. We all have a percentage, don't we? He

104

procures and gets thirty percent, and you get ten for, well, just being here."

"And the other sixty is yours, Eldon. He knows that, I know that. It's okay. It's part of your deal."

"Damn right, it's okay. Every man has a fetish." He laughed. "What's yours, Buddy?"

Franco didn't answer.

Hirsch slowly and lovingly rubbed a palm over one of the binder's pages. "I'm grateful he allows me to be the custodian. He knows I'll take better care of it than him."

"True, but Mr. Lansky can be very enterprising in other ways. How's the hotel doing?"

"They don't tell you? It's going gangbusters. He's really turned it around. That fucking Bugsy Siegel was going to lose everyone's money—I'm not surprised they bumped him off last summer. The hotel casino business in Vegas is taking off. In five years, there will be three or four more on the Strip, and I don't know how many downtown. In ten years, God, who knows what it'll be? It's going to become the Hollywood of the desert. The Pink Flamingo—well, now it's the *Fabulous* Flamingo—it started it all. Bugsy—may he rest in peace—was a visionary. But he sure was a fuckup. I'm going to the head. I'll be right back."

Hirsch got up and went to his private bathroom. Franco crossed his legs and continued to smoke. From his point of view, the studio mogul was certainly—and conveniently—in denial that the boys in Las Vegas had bankrolled Ultimate Pictures back when it was starting up. Hirsch wouldn't be where he was without them. They had also placed Franco at the studio to keep an eye on things. While he technically worked for Hirsch, the reality was a different story. Hirsch's "investments" in the casinos amounted to very little. The truth was that he owed the mob a great deal of money. Could the man also be *stealing* from them?

If they'd sent Malena Mengarelli to deliver a message, then perhaps, Franco thought, he should investigate the matter himself.

Hirsch returned, sat behind the desk, and resumed fiddling with his coins. "How's the musical doing?"

"It's on schedule."

"Is that Kraut director spending too much money?"

"We may need to go over the budget a little. The water fantasy sequence is going to cost more than anticipated. Can't be helped."

"I figured we'd lowballed it. All right, you can approve the extra dough, as long as it's not my arm and my leg. What about the war picture?"

"Doing fine. Wraps this week."

"Any trouble keeping Bill off the bottle?"

"I read him the riot act before we started production. He sobered up real quick."

Hirsch shook his head. "It's a shame when a star is a drunk. Or takes drugs. Have you heard anything about, uh, what's her name—Virginia?"

"Recuperating nicely, from what I'm told. You're not going to renew her contract, are you?"

"No. She was a mess. That piece Hedda Hopper did on her nearly took down the studio. What was she thinking, that girl? No wonder the Hays Office gets after us all the time. We ought to outlaw Hollywood parties for anyone under contract."

Hirsch took another drag from the cigar and then leaned forward. He spoke a little softer, as if he might be afraid someone else would hear.

"What have you heard about our girl?"

"She's still seeing him."

Hirsch slapped the palm of his hand hard on the top of the desk. The move was so sudden it made even Franco flinch.

"Goddammit." The man moved his head back and forth, as if he was searching for something. "Why the hell does she want to sleep with a colored boy? That goddamn nig—"

"They were seen at the Dunbar Hotel just the other night," Franco interjected. "Marley and his band were playing there. Blair was at one of the tables, alone, and then she was joined by some other coloreds from her neighborhood. After the set, she went off with Marley."

Hirsch closed his eyes and rubbed his brow. "If Parsons or Hopper or Fidler gets hold of this . . . Christ, what is she thinking? Doesn't she know she can't do this?"

"What would you like me to do, Eldon?"

"I want you to *stop* it, Buddy! Jesus, what do you think I want you to do?"

Franco nodded. "I assume you'd rather not approach this from Blair's side of things, but from Marley's side?"

"That's the place to start, certainly!"

Franco paused, inhaled on the cigar, and blew out the smoke. "Shall I hit 'soft' or 'hard?'"

Hirsch looked at him and answered, "Why don't you try 'medium' and see how that works?"

14
KARISSA

Karissa and Marcello sat in the Stormglove Productions office attending to various bookkeeping chores while discussing the elements of the Blair Kendrick story they had uncovered so far. The mystery of the man at the World Stage who had threatened Karissa had been pushed aside for the time being. As Marcello had said, "Chalk it up to another Hollywood bullshit scam."

Karissa wanted to return to the nursing home to see Ray Webster again. So far, attempts to contact his son Gregory had been fruitless. Googling "Gregory Webster" and "almond" or "nuts" indicated there was no man like him anywhere near Los Angeles.

"I overheard him saying that it took him three hours to drive to the nursing home," she said. "Where could that be?"

Marcello laughed. "Anywhere! In LA? Are you kidding?"

She had to agree with him. "Depending on the traffic, yeah, you're right. Hell, it could be San Diego, for all we know."

Karissa continued to work on spreadsheets on her computer, when her e-mail indicator dinged. She usually gave incoming mail a quick glance to see who they were from in case she could afford to open them later. This one, however, was from the festival people.

She started reading and immediately felt a rush of anxiety that only occurred when she knew she was facing something dreadful.

"What the *fuck?*" she gasped.

"What?"

"Marcello! The film festival has dropped us!"

"*What?*"

"Did you get this e-mail from Barbara? It was sent to you, too." Barbara was a producer in charge of the endeavor.

"Let me see . . ." He looked at his monitor and typed on the keypad. "Yeah." He read it and his eyes went wide. "What the hell is this?"

Karissa read it aloud. "'We are sorry to say that after further consideration, we have decided that Stormglove Productions' proposal does not meet the requirements set out in the production agreement.'"

"That's bullshit. Everything was approved."

"I'm calling her." Karissa pulled out her cell phone and dialed the woman's number. She waited a second and then groaned. "Voice mail." Another few seconds. "Barbara, this is Karissa Glover. Marcello and I just received your e-mail. What's going on? This can't be right, can it? Please call me back." She gave her cell number and hung up.

They looked at each other. Marcello pursed his lips, something he did whenever he was angry.

"What does this mean?" Karissa asked.

"I have no idea. It's got to be related to that guy the other night."

"I think so, too. Wait a minute."

"What?"

She picked up her phone again and dialed. "I'm calling Derek Morton."

"At Ultimate Pictures?"

She nodded. Her eyes brightened when he picked up. "Derek? Karissa Glover. Hey, listen, sorry to bother you, but I—what?" She listened. "Yeah, but listen, Marcello and I have been dropped from the festival and we want to know—no, I—Derek, wait." She winced. "Oh, come on, is it the subject matter? Because that's crazy. I don't see why—" Karissa made a circular motion with her index finger, indicating she was being given the runaround. "Derek. Stop, please, let me ask you a question. Is this Justin Hirsch's doing? You told me there might be a problem, so just tell me straight. Uh-huh. Well, what is it? What do you mean, you don't know? I think you do, Derek. Look, he can't just hand down an order to fire us. Yes, I *know* Ultimate Pictures is a major sponsor. So, he has that kind of power? Oh, for Christ's sake, just tell me the truth." She blinked, did a double take at her phone, and slammed it on the desk. "He hung up on me."

"Jesus. Was it Hirsch?"

"He wouldn't say, but what do *you* think? Eldon Hirsch's son doesn't want Blair Kendrick's story to come out. The big question is *why*. A lot of it is public knowledge!"

"Well . . . no, not really," Marcello said. "As we've discovered, there's also quite a bit of mystery we don't know."

She leaned forward and looked at him. "They're hiding something. What if *they* killed her?"

"They? Who?"

"Buddy Franco. The studio fixer. He was supposedly connected to the mob."

"Karissa . . ."

"You have to admit there's something fishy about all this. There's so much we don't know. Think about it. How come we haven't seen any of Blair's movies? The studio withdrew them decades ago. They don't want her to be remembered.

And what happened to Hank Marley? *He* disappeared, too, vanished around the same time that Hirsch was shot and killed in his office at the studio. And that guy Franco—he went missing, too, until, God, nearly thirty years later, when he was executed in a Las Vegas diner. What the fuck, Marcello? There's a hell of a story here!" She stood and started pacing around the room.

"So, what are we going to do?"

Karissa stopped and leaned over her desk toward him. "I'll tell you. We're going to develop the movie anyway. Screw the festival. We'll keep going. We'll find another studio that will work with us. If we have to fund the picture ourselves, go into production, and finish the damned thing—and *then* find a distributor—then we will. Plenty of people do it that way."

Marcello raised his eyebrows. "Are you that dedicated to this story to go through that kind of shit?"

"Aren't you?"

"Well . . ."

"Okay, fine, I realize you're not as committed to it as I am. Marcello, there's something *here*. I really believe that if the truth comes out, there will be fireworks."

"What if Hirsch tries to stop us? He has the money and the lawyers to do that."

"On what grounds? We're not stealing anything from him. Is *he* developing a movie about Blair Kendrick and Hank Marley? No, he just doesn't want one made. He can't stop us. We don't work for him. Fuck Justin Hirsch."

Marcello laughed.

"What?"

"It's the old Karissa Glover I used to see back at UCLA. Whenever you hit an obstacle, you'd get all mad and forge ahead despite everything just to prove you could surmount the problem."

"And what's wrong with that? It's why I'm a damned good producer! And so are *you*." Marcello held up his hands in surrender. "So, are you with me or not?"

"All the way, babe. All the way." He held up a palm and she high-fived it.

15

THE MOVIE

The film shifts to a nighttime exterior of the Dunbar Hotel, the center of African American nightlife on Central Avenue in 1940s Los Angeles. The block is jumping, as cars and taxis pull up to the front of the hotel and let out the likes of Duke Ellington, Louis Armstrong, and Joe Louis. Black couples and singles mill around on the sidewalk, dressed to the nines for a night on the town. The fashion for women is small waists, full skirts, and long hemlines. Waves, rather than curls, is the order of the day. The men are in single-breasted or double-breasted suits with center vests and peaked lapels. Wide, short ties in a Windsor knot come in patterns and are adorned with tiepins. No man is without a hat.

The camera moves around the building as the voice-over resumes.

"Central Avenue was where it was at for the Negro community. Everyone went to the Dunbar Hotel to see and be seen. It was where the black entertainers stayed, since they weren't allowed to use white hotels. Mind you, they could perform *in white hotels, but they couldn't sleep there! The strip in front of the hotel was for cruising, where the locals showed up to hold up the wall and show off their new threads.*

"*Next to the Dunbar was Club Alabam, a hugely popular night-spot for jazz, and just a few doors down from that was the Downbeat Club, a more intimate setting where the audience could see a show by the likes of Charlie Parker or Dizzy Gillespie—up close and personal.*"

We are now inside the Dunbar Hotel, moving through its grand art deco lobby with Spanish arcade–like windows and open balconies.

"*I would sometimes accompany Hank to the Dunbar on nights we thought not too many people would be there. After all, our relationship was controversial on both sides of the color line. Musicians and show-business people tended to accept us more than regular folk. The Negro movie stars like Eddie 'Rochester' Anderson and Louise Beavers didn't seem to have a problem with seeing one of their own with a white woman.*"

The camera moves into a small lounge, a cocktail bar, with room enough for a piano on one side. Hank Marley is sitting at the keyboard, a cigarette hanging out of his mouth. Ray Webster stands next to the piano with his upright bass, thumping away as the pair play lively acoustic jazz pieces. The place is packed.

"*The Turban Room was a little place downstairs inside the Dunbar where Hank occasionally played with Ray Webster, just as a duo. There wasn't enough room in there for his full band, although they often played in the larger Club Alabam out back, the Downbeat Club, or a place called the Last Word, across the street.*

"*There was one evening that I had to work late at the studio shooting* The Dark Lonely Night. *Hank was at the Dunbar with Ray, doing what he did best . . .*"

Ray Webster launched into an opening riff for Earle Hagen's "Harlem Nocturne," arranged for piano and bass, which was one of Hank Marley's signature pieces. When his fingers hit the keys, the patrons applauded and *ooh*ed and *aah*ed in appreciation. Hank grinned broadly and nodded at the listeners.

"Thank you, thank you kindly."

The music didn't stop the chatter, though. The Turban Room was a bar, not a concert hall. The musicians played as drinks were served, cash flowed, and people socialized. Cigarette smoke filled the crowded room, the lighting was low, and the ambiance was cool and smooth. Hank loved to play at the Dunbar, often more so than in the bigger joints that paid better. There was something about the intimacy of the place, the closeness of the customers, and the one-on-one sparring with the young bass player he had hired. Ray still had a lot to learn, but he was good—damned good. They made a swell team.

The next song in the set was "Woody 'n' You" by Dizzy Gillespie, which was an unusual piece to be heard on just piano and bass, but they made it work. Hank swayed and bounced his shoulders as his fingers flew over the keyboard. Ray emitted a moan of delight as he felt the spirit of the music. He plucked the strings of the double bass with verve and abandon. When the tune was done, the entire room burst into applause.

Hank spoke into the microphone on the stand beside the piano. "Thank you, ladies and gentlemen, thank you very much. I must say you're all looking mighty fine tonight all decked out in your going-out clothes. I see a whole lot of beautiful people. Yes, sir. Ray and I hope you're enjoying yourselves."

There were some affirmative shouts of joy.

"Good, good. Here's a little number that is something of a personal piece for us."

The duo launched into a dreamy version of "Blues in the Dark," and Hank sang in a passionate, woeful timbre. For a moment, the conversations in the bar ceased completely as the song cast a spell over the crowd. Women closed their eyes and smiled. Men moved in place with the melody. It was three minutes of pure magic. The applause that erupted when the music stopped indicated how potent the arrangement was.

"Thank you, thank you. You are all very kind. Well, Ray and I are going to take a short break. We're the Hank Marley Duo, and we'll be back in a little bit. Don't go away now, y'hear?"

Hank and Ray nodded at each other and left the band area, which was more of a corner than a stage, and slithered through the crowd. Ray stopped at the bar to get a drink and Hank went out of the lounge, upstairs, and into the hotel lobby. He greeted several acquaintances, including the acclaimed architect, Paul Williams. It was a sea of lovely black faces and a handful of whites, but the woman he'd hoped to spot wasn't there.

He went outside and greeted Delbert, the doorman, and offered him a smoke.

"No, thank you, Hank, not while I'm on duty, sir."

Hank tapped a cigarette out of the pack for himself. Delbert was ready with a light, and Hank allowed the man to fire it up. "Thank you very much." Then he walked north along Central to the Club Alabam's awning. The doorman there, Eugene, also greeted Hank. A poster proclaimed the appearance of Joe Turner, a blues singer who had appeared in Duke Ellington's musical revue *Jump for Joy.* Hank knew Curtis Mosby, the club owner, and probably could have ducked in for a few minutes to listen to a couple of numbers before heading back to the Dunbar, but he decided to continue his stroll outside and enjoy the cigarette.

He passed the Downbeat Club, crossed 42nd Street, and kept walking north at a leisurely pace, nodding at various pedestrians and couples who were strolling in the opposite direction. Music from the various clubs on the block drifted through the night air, creating a muffled, but pleasant, cacophony of clashing melodies and rhythms.

Blair . . .

Hank often wondered if he was doing the right thing with her. The relationship could hurt her career. Although opportunities for black people in Hollywood had improved during the past decade, it was still a segregated, closed world. The precious white stars had to be protected so their public images remained sanctified. All in the name of the box office dollar.

He had read in the *Sentinel* that a case could be going to the state courts that challenged miscegenation laws. If that passed, then he and Blair could get married. Even so, that didn't mean it would be accepted by her studio. Was it selfish of him to keep the relationship going? The problem was—he really loved her. He had been with several women in his thirty years on earth—all black, of course—and he had loved several of them. Blair, though, was different, and it wasn't because she was *white*. Joe Hardy, a fellow he played cards with sometimes, said something the other night about that. "You only like her 'cause you're getting some *white* meat." Hank would have punched the man in the face if others at the table hadn't held him back.

Later on, Bobop, his trombone player, asked him over drinks, "Could it be true, Hank? That this is all about her being white? Don't be mad, I'm asking as your friend. Do you know what you're doing?"

Sure, there was a taboo element to it. Something . . . foreign. But all that ceased to matter when he considered Blair herself. Blair could *talk* to him. She understood his moods and his tastes and his *music*. He loved her fire. The racial difference simply didn't enter the equation when they were alone. It only came into play when they were with other people, outside the privacy of the bedroom.

Lost in his thoughts, Hank didn't notice the black Cadillac that passed him slowly heading south. It pulled over to the curb behind him. Besides the driver, there were three passengers inside—all white men.

Buddy Franco got out with two cohorts—big, burly guys who might have been wrestlers. Without warning and with no concern that they could be seen by dozens of pedestrians, the men quickly moved behind Hank. One of the bruisers clasped his hands together to form a battering ram of knuckles and swung hard into the middle of Hank's back. The musician toppled to the sidewalk.

Women screamed. Men shouted, but no one dared to interfere. These were white men. *Undercover police? Probably. Don't get involved. Walk away. Watch from a distance.*

The two thugs started to viciously kick the fallen man. Hank cried out as the hard shoes pummeled his ribs, his belly, his back, his legs, and his face. After a full thirty seconds of punishment, Hank Marley lay helpless, limp and bloody.

Franco stooped to speak softly into the man's ear.

"Stop seeing Blair Kendrick. This was just a warning. The consequences will be far worse if you don't do what I say. Do you understand, *boy*?"

Hank could only groan.

"*Do you understand?*"

Hank nodded.

Franco stood and gestured for the men to follow him back to the car. They got in and it took off down Central, turned a corner, and disappeared.

The distant music from the jazz clubs faded away completely. Hank ceased to hear the traffic noise on the street next to him. There were muted cries nearby, and someone calling for help. He felt bodies near him, hands gently moving him, and words asking if he could hear what was being said.

An eternity passed, and then he was aware of a familiar voice. "Hank! Hank! Delbert called an ambulance. Hold on!"

It was Ray.

Hank reached up and grabbed his bass player's collar. "No . . ."

"What? Hank, you're hurt bad! We got to get you to the hospital—"

"Just take me . . . home . . . take me home . . . no hospital."

"Hank—!"

"I . . . mean it . . ."

Ray Webster did what Hank asked. He enlisted some friends from the hotel to help him carry Hank to his car, and then he drove his injured friend to their home in Sugar Hill. Ray roused his wife, Loretta, out of bed to help attend to Hank in his room. Ray called the studio and left a message for Blair, who was busy shooting night scenes. Then, together, Ray and Loretta cleaned and bandaged up their friend and sat with him during the night, while their five-year-old son, Gregory, slept in his own room.

16

KARISSA

On Sunday, Karissa decided to pick up where she had left off and continue exploring her house on Harvard Boulevard. Who knew what other treasures that belonged to Blair Kendrick she might find?

The bedroom where the trunk was also contained several cardboard boxes. She opened them, one by one, and was disappointed to find mostly paperwork pertaining to Blair Kendrick's activities at the studio, such as scripts and publicity stills. One box held a collection of the latter that were pre-signed, apparently to mail to fans. Karissa figured they might be of value. Autographed photos of a murder victim/actress present at the murdering of a Hollywood studio head? Someone could make a killing on eBay, but it wouldn't be Karissa. She left the pictures in the box, save one that she would take to the office for inspiration.

Inside another box were copies of the *California Eagle*, the oldest African American newspaper published in the western United States. Karissa knew that it had started in the late 1800s under a different name and was changed to the *California Eagle* not long after the turn of the century, staying in print until the 1960s. The box in the bedroom held various issues from the late 1940s.

Blair had marked the issues on the fronts with a pen, indicating page numbers within. Karissa examined one and found a piece on Hank Marley and his band, who were appearing at the Last Word nightclub. Another paper had a photo of Hank and the band performing at Club Alabam. Yet another featured a photograph of the audience at the Downbeat Club—and there was Blair Kendrick at a table with Hank. The caption read, "Jazz musician Hank Marley out on the town with actress Blair Kendrick."

The last *Eagle* in the box was dated January 1949. Karissa recalled that Eldon Hirsch had been killed in July 1949. *This might be significant*, she thought, and so she went downstairs to her laptop computer and began to search various subjects via Google.

First, she studied Blair Kendrick's filmography. She had made three pictures for Ultimate that were released in 1947—*A Kiss in the Night*, *The Jazz Club*, and *A Dame Without Fear*. Three more movies came out in 1948—*The Dark Lonely Night*, *The Love of a Killer*, and *The Outlaw Lovers*. The IMDb website indicated that Blair had begun production of a picture called *The Boss and the Blonde* that was to be a 1949 release, but production was never completed. It had been scrapped by the studio in January of that year.

Karissa searched online for *The Boss and the Blonde* but found very little to explain why the studio had canceled the film. Apparently, it was to be yet another film noir with Blair playing a gun moll to a powerful mobster who was none other than James Cagney. The actor had not portrayed a gangster since the 1930s. It was to be something of a return to that type of role for Cagney. When *The Boss and the Blonde* was stopped, Cagney instead made his mobster comeback for Warner Brothers in the classic *White Heat.*

Next, Karissa looked for any information about Blair Kendrick in January 1949 and found a couple of references to the cancellation of the title by Ultimate Pictures, but again with no reason why it had happened. A search for her name in February 1949 produced no results. The same was true for March and April. Then, when Karissa typed "Blair Kendrick May 1949," She was linked to a scholarly article on a political website that referenced a *Los Angeles Times* story on the House Un-American Activities Committee and its "Red Scare" witch hunt. Fortuitously, in the same column and in a sidebar unrelated to the main piece, Karissa discovered one of Hedda Hopper's gossip columns. "Where is Blair Kendrick?" Hopper asked. "The feisty blond actress has not been seen or heard from in Hollywood since her last starring vehicle was canceled by Ultimate Pictures. When I spoke to studio executive Buddy Franco about it, he replied that Blair had become gravely ill and production was halted. Franco wouldn't elaborate on Blair's condition or where she was convalescing."

Wow. What the hell had happened to her?

Karissa printed out the page and continued to look for further mentions of Blair in the following months. Nothing in June. Then, in July, the murder of Eldon Hirsch. Lots of hits there with speculation that Blair Kendrick had witnessed it and was killed by the perpetrators. The charred body by burned cars on Mulholland Drive, identification made by the jewelry—her signature pearl necklace—that the corpse was wearing, and the subsequent burial in Westwood cemetery.

What was the mysterious illness she had contracted? Had she experienced a "nervous breakdown," as they called it back then? Karissa had to admit that Blair Kendrick exhibited a recklessness by having a love affair with a black man in the late 1940s. It could have been detrimental to her career—and perhaps it was.

Karissa's initial instincts to create a film around the actress, portraying her as a femme fatale who, in real life, had been a victim, seemed to make more and more sense. But why was Ultimate Pictures so dead set against her making the picture? Something wasn't clicking.

She decided to research the history from another direction. She googled "Hank Marley 1949" and found a few hits about his disappearance: he was reported as a missing person in early February of that year. That meant he had most likely vanished in late January—the same month that Blair Kendrick had become "ill" and her movie was canceled.

A coincidence? Karissa thought not.

The *California Eagle* had been archived online, where it was accessible and free to the public. Karissa searched for mentions of Hank within the paper and found plenty dated throughout the late 1940s. However, there were no links to issues in 1950 or '51, though there were a handful for 1952. Karissa clicked on each one, and every time she was sent to a page that proclaimed, "Sorry! This issue is missing from the archives!"

That's odd, Karissa thought. She then remembered the other newspaper that catered mostly to African Americans—the *Los Angeles Sentinel*. She looked for archives online and learned that they were accessible at the UCLA Library.

Hm. Field trip.

The Charles E. Young Research Library was an impressive building on the north end of the UCLA campus. As Karissa walked the familiar grounds of her alma mater, she reminisced about the many hours she'd spent here preparing for exams, writing papers, or researching various topics that piqued her interest. While the UCLA library was comprised of several physical locations, the research library was perhaps Karissa's favorite. It contained documents, books, journals, newspapers, and digital files from all over the world in many languages.

Inside, Karissa located the microfiche for the *Sentinel*, which was first published in 1933 and still in circulation. She went through the index to locate dates and issues in which Blair Kendrick and/or Hank Marley were mentioned, but they were mostly duplications of news in the *California Eagle*. She then wrote down the entries from 1952 and went to collect the film. Once she had the microfiche threaded into a machine, she scrolled to the appropriate issue.

The microfiche abruptly ended. In fact, it had been cut. The rest of the film was still spooled onto the small reel. She threaded the remainder and saw that the page she'd been looking for was missing. It was as if someone had deliberately deleted it from the archive and hadn't bothered to splice the fiche back together.

Karissa spent the next hour checking the other 1952 reels. They, too, were missing the pages she wanted. She picked up the various reels and took them to the help desk.

"I want to report some vandalism on these microfiches," she said to the librarian, carefully displaying the damaged microfiche.

"That's horrible!" the librarian said. "Thank you for pointing it out."

"Is there any other way I can see these issues?"

"They're also online. Let's go look."

Together they got behind a terminal and searched for the desired issues.

The situation was the same. The online issues, too, were missing.

"This is freaky," the librarian said. She suggested that Karissa try some other libraries. Karissa thanked her and left. *A disturbing development*, she thought.

She decided to drive back to the east side via the 10 and

entered downtown to visit the Los Angeles Public Library on 5th Street. But after checking the catalog, she found that there was only online access with ProQuest, the same service used by UCLA. They would be the same files. Just to make sure she wasn't going mad, Karissa searched for the missing issues and, sure enough, they weren't there.

Somehow, someone had erased articles from 1952 about Hank Marley.

The library closed at five on Sunday, so Karissa stopped in Little Tokyo downtown for dinner at Kura Revolving Sushi, a restaurant where various plates of *nigiri* moved on a conveyor belt by one's seat and she could pick whatever she wanted and pay by the plate. Karissa sat at the bar, so as not to take up a full table, and found herself next to a Caucasian man around her age, dressed as if he had just come from the beach.

During the meal, she noticed that he kept glancing at her. Finally, after he had paid his bill and was ready to leave, he got up the nerve to say, "Excuse me, I was just curious, are you, what, Middle Eastern?"

Oh, no, here we go again, Karissa thought.

"No, I'm not."

"Oh, sorry. You're mixed, aren't you, what, part black and part white?"

"I'm biracial, yes."

"That's interesting. Well, I think you're gorgeous. Very exotic looking, if you don't mind my saying so."

"Actually, I do."

"It was a compliment."

"Not really."

"Oh. Well, *sorry*." He got up.

"You want to touch my hair, too?" she asked.

With that, he turned and started to leave, but then swirled around to face her again. "You know, I *was* going to offer to buy your dinner and see if you'd like to have coffee when you were done, but now I won't."

"My loss, then. Have a good evening."

"Bitch," he said, and left the restaurant.

Karissa sighed heavily, took a moment to breathe, and finished her meal.

It was dusk when she pulled into her driveway in West Adams Heights. Instead of entering through the garage entrance into the house, she walked around to the front yard to pick up the newspaper she had neglected to retrieve that morning. She looked up at the porch and saw pieces of mail sticking out of the slot in the door, stuck.

As she went up the steps to the porch, she suddenly had a sensation that she was being watched. Karissa turned to look out to the street and saw a black SUV sitting at the curb across the road. It was now too dark to discern clearly what the make and model was, but she didn't know brands of cars by sight anyway. What concerned her more was the silhouette of a man who was sitting in the passenger seat. The orange dot of an ember at the end of a cigarette glowed against the shadow. His hand moved the cigarette and flicked the ashes to the asphalt through the open window.

He was watching her.

She dug her cell phone out of her purse. Karissa was ready to dial 911, but she stopped and asked herself if she was overreacting. The man could be waiting for someone. He could be totally harmless, and perhaps he wasn't actively watching her. He'd probably only just spotted her crossing the yard. But after the incident at the restaurant and the creepy guy at the World Stage the other night, Karissa felt justified in her paranoia. She went ahead and dialed the numbers. She was put on hold, of course, and she unlocked the front door and entered the house from the porch. After locking the door behind her, she walked through the foyer to the kitchen and made sure the door to the garage was locked.

When the dispatcher finally came on the phone, she reported that a suspicious person was sitting in his car in front of her house. She was told a patrol car would swing by in a few minutes.

Karissa hung up, went to the front of the house, and looked out a window.

The SUV was gone. Now she would appear foolish to the cops who showed up.

Her phone rang, startling her. The caller ID indicated it was Marcello.

"Hey," she answered.

"Hello there. Did you have a productive day?"

"Just uncovered more mysteries. How about you?"

"Well, I just got some bad news. Ray Webster died today."

"Oh, *no*."

"Yeah. Butch told me. Apparently, that cardiac incident the other day was pretty serious."

"Oh, gee, I'm sorry to hear that. We need to redouble our efforts to find his son. Does Butch know how to reach him?"

"I asked," Marcello said. "He had a number for him, but it's no longer good."

"Sounds like Gregory Webster doesn't want to be found," Karissa said. "What's *that* about?"

"Who knows. Anyway, Ray's funeral is in a few days. Gregory will probably be there, don't you think?"

"Can we go?"

"I don't see why not if it's a public funeral. I'll find out from Butch."

*

Karissa tossed and turned and slept fitfully, but she awoke with a start at 3:05 a.m. She got out of bed, went to the bathroom, and splashed cold water on her sweating face. It had been a nightmare that, of course, she couldn't recall much of now. She remembered the emotions in it, though—an urgent need to hide from something or someone that was looking for her. Her parents were both present in the dream, but they couldn't help her. It was a recurring dream that Karissa always had whenever she felt stressed or worried.

Karissa had never known her real parents. Her adoptive parents, a white couple, were warm, God-fearing souls who had given her a wonderful upbringing. She was an only child in the household, although there was once a time when they had considered adopting another. It never happened. Karissa had a sudden desire to phone her parents in Sacramento—but that, too, was out of the question. Her father, Thomas Glover, had died of a freak heart condition when Karissa was in her thirties. Her mother, Belinda Glover, had succumbed to breast cancer only six years ago. Sometimes it saddened her that she had no real family left.

Although she had asked on several occasions what they knew about her birth parents, the answer was always a big zero. The adoption agency had told them Karissa was an orphan. She had been left at the doorstep one morning, a toddler secured by a belt in a basket, accompanied only by her Julia rag doll and a note that said she was eighteen months old and that her parents had been killed. An accident? No one knew.

Karissa had no memory of those earlier years. She had assumed a traumatic event at that age could be somewhat recalled, but according to a therapist she had seen during college, it was entirely possible that her brain had blocked it out. Karissa chose not to be hypnotized, which may or may not have induced some memories. The problem was a mind that young simply didn't have the maturity to understand the incident and put it into a cohesive narrative.

Julia was the only link Karissa had to those early times. The rag doll that now sat on Blair's dresser was the single memento from her short life with her real parents. She'd taken good care of it throughout the years, periodically repairing any tears in the fabric and cleaning the dress that bore the stitched name *Julia*.

Unable to sleep, Karissa picked up the doll and went downstairs, poured a small glass of red wine for herself, and sat in the parlor with Julia, the ghost of Blair Kendrick, and other phantoms of the past.

17
THE MOVIE

The next montage, scored by dramatic orchestral rearrangements of the main theme, reveals Blair receiving a phone call at the studio, becoming alarmed, and rushing out to her car. She drives recklessly through the dark Hollywood streets until she reaches Sugar Hill. Ray and Loretta Webster greet her at their house.

"I had just finished shooting some nights scenes, and we'd wrapped for the day when I got the call from Ray. Hank was hurt. He was hurt bad. I had to get to him. My love . . . my love . . . ! What did they do to you? Oh my God . . . !"

The Websters take her into Hank's bedroom and Blair stifles a scream. She then indicates that she will take over and thanks them.

Blair returned to Hank's bedroom, carrying the bowl of ice and more cloths. Earlier, she had tried to convince him to go to the hospital, but he stubbornly refused. He was convinced nothing was broken.

"You could have internal injuries," she said as she sat on the bed next to him. "They kicked you in the stomach. Hank, when you went to the bathroom, was there any blood?"

"No, I don't think so," he said weakly.

"Well, keep an eye out for that." She wrapped some ice in a rag and gently massaged the red bruises on his face. "This will help the swelling go down. Does it help the pain?"

"Yes. I feel fine now."

"Ha. That whiskey I gave you is what you're feeling. Hank, honey, you're going to be sore for days. How are your *hands*? They didn't hurt your piano-playing fingers, did they?"

"No, thank God. They spared me that horror."

She wanted to cry. Blair hated to see him so battered. "And you sure you don't know who they were?"

"Just white men. Probably from your *studio*." He said it with venom in his voice.

That made her feel terrible. "They're bastards, Hank. I bet Eldon Hirsch sent them. He must have gotten wind of us. Don't you think?" Hank nodded. "In fact, I bet I know who it was. There's this guy who works at the studio. His name is Buddy Franco. Did he have a crew cut, like he just got out of the army?" Hank nodded again. "Late thirties, maybe forty years old?" Again, the affirmative response. "That's him. They say he's a studio executive, but he's really a fixer. He makes studio problems go away. That's his job."

She leaned over and opened the nightstand drawer. The revolver was still there. "Maybe you should carry this around with you to your gigs," she said.

"Honey, if I did that and the police stopped me for any reason at all and found that, I'd go to prison for life. Hell, they might just go on and shoot me, no questions asked."

She picked up the gun and held it in her hand, pointing it at the far wall. "I'm getting pretty good at hitting the targets, aren't I?"

"Yes, you are. You're a regular Annie Oakley."

Blair laughed and put the gun back in the drawer. "Well, keep the thing handy here. You have a right to defend yourself."

Hank cleared his throat and spoke. "Baby, we have to . . . we have to stop this."

"What?"

He opened his eyes a little wider, despite the puffy, purpling flesh around them. "If we don't stop seeing each other, they'll be back. Honey, I . . . I don't care what they do to me; it's *you* I'm concerned about. They will ruin your career. I knew a fella once. This was back in Missouri. He and a white girl got together only one time. He was lynched by a mob, and *she* was killed by her own father."

"That was Missouri. This is California, Hank. That's not going to happen here. Not in 1948."

"They gonna hurt you other ways."

She laid her head on his chest. "Oh, Hank, I can't bear the thought of not seeing you anymore, but I don't think I could take seeing you hurt again, either. If it means keeping you out of harm's way, then . . . then we just have to be more *careful*. We can't be seen in public. We have to just see each other at our homes. The way we started out. We got too careless and too cocky, going out together where we could be spotted." She raised her head and looked him in the eye. "I believe these crazy laws keeping apart people who love each other are going to change soon. If we can just hold out. That case is going to the California courts this fall."

"They won't win. The racism in this country runs too deep."

"Hank, I'll say it again. This is *1948*. It's time that we get rid of racism once and for all!"

Hank started to laugh in a soft, hoarse whisper, which caused him to cough.

"Take it easy, Hank. Here, have some water." She handed him a glass that was on the nightstand.

"Baby," he managed to say after taking a sip, "I told you before and I'll tell you again. You're naive. Racism's not going away that easily. I think we're going to have racism in this country for a long, long time. Probably forever."

She held him by the upper arms, leaned in close to his face, and kissed him a few times around the sore spots. "So, what are you saying? Do you think we should stop seeing each other?" she asked softly.

"Yes, I do. For your protection."

"I don't care what the damned studio does to me. Fame is fleeting. If we do it, it's for *your* protection. I'm not going to let them hurt you again. Oh, but Hank, it will be horrible without you."

"I think we should try, baby."

"Maybe you're right." Her eyes welled. "This is all my fault."

"Don't be silly."

"Ray and Loretta probably blame me for what happened."

"They don't. Ray and Loretta like you a lot, and they respect how *I* feel about you. Get it out of your head that it's anybody's fault."

She stood and paced the floor. "Oh, how I hate that creep Eldon Hirsch! All he wants is to get into my pants. That's why he's doing this. He's jealous."

"It's in your contract, Blair. The morals clause."

"I know, I know. But lots of stars get away with stuff they're not supposed to do. This is all about his precious ego. I hate him. I hate him and his stupid office. I hope he loses that coin collection he loves so much. That would hit him where it hurts."

18

KARISSA

Ray Webster's funeral was held at Spalding Mortuary on S. La Brea Avenue, a little over three miles from West Adams Heights. Marcello picked Karissa up in his red Corvette, and they rode together to the service, which was to take place at 10:30 in the morning. Marcello had checked with Butch, and the occasion was open to the public.

They parked in the small lot on S. Mansfield Avenue, a smaller street that diagonally intersected with La Brea where the funeral parlor stood.

"I hate funerals," Marcello quietly said as they got out of the car. "Really hate them."

They walked around to the front of the lightly tan-and-white structure and joined a few others who were just arriving as well. Karissa and Marcello followed them inside and signed the guest book that was on a podium by the chapel doors.

It wasn't large, but it was a sufficiently comfortable sanctuary with two rows of pews, the ever-present gold cross on the wall at the front, and the open casket on display at the end of the aisle. The room had a bright, orange glow to it, due to the color of the wood paneling on the ceiling. Soft, recorded organ music consisting of hymns piped in through speakers.

Ray Webster lay peacefully inside the casket, dressed in a simple suit, his hands crossed over his chest.

Roughly twenty people were in attendance, all black. Marcello spotted Butch and the other members of his band—Hero, Carl, and Zach. They greeted each other and sat together in the same pew.

"I don't see Gregory Webster—do you?" Karissa whispered to Marcello.

"Nuh-uh."

Then, as if on cue, the family entered, which consisted of Gregory and a woman, presumably his wife, who appeared to be around the same age as her husband. She wore a black dress and he was in a dark suit. Another man, probably in his late forties or early fifties, walked on the opposite side of the woman with his arm around her. The trio solemnly made their way down the aisle to the front and sat in the first pew.

The service, led by a black minister in robes, moved relatively quickly. The minister led the mourners in a hymn, which was accompanied by an elderly woman at a piano behind the pulpit. She had silver-white hair and appeared to be as old as Ray Webster had been. Her playing was tentatively competent, and Karissa got the impression that she might have once been a decent pianist in her day.

The minister then delivered a short but respectful eulogy that highlighted how Webster had been a "good soul," was a pillar of the community, and at one time was an admired musician. The minister acknowledged Ray's son, Gregory, his wife Carol, and their son, William, who had flown in from New York. He also mentioned a great-niece—a Ms. Brantley—who was unable to attend the funeral but had sent some words of remembrance to be read aloud.

The whole thing was over in fifteen minutes. Instructions were given regarding interment at Angelus Rosedale Cemetery, which happened to be in West Adams Heights just north of I-10, not far from Karissa's home.

"We're not going to the cemetery, are we?" Marcello whispered to her.

She shook her head. "Not if I can get a word with Gregory."

The three Websters got up and walked up the aisle to the exit before the rest of the attendees were dismissed. They stood together at the outer doors of the funeral home, shaking hands and greeting the visitors as they left. Karissa and Marcello bid the musicians goodbye and took their positions in line. Karissa overheard a woman ask if there was a repast being held anywhere, but the couple shook their heads.

When Karissa and Marcello stepped up, Gregory's eyes widened. The same look he had given Karissa at the Vernon Healthcare Center came over his face.

"My condolences, Mr. Webster, Mrs. Webster," Karissa said. Marcello repeated the same words, shaking Gregory's and William's hands. Karissa continued, "You don't know us, but my name is Karissa Glover, and this is Marcello Storm. We're filmmakers, and we'd like to talk to you sometime about your father, and specifically the years in the 1940s when he played with a musician named Hank Marley."

Gregory and Carol shared a look that exhibited what could only be described in Karissa's mind as *fear*.

Then the man aggressively shook his head and whispered, "No, no, not here—go, go, I can't talk to you."

"But I—"

Carol Webster snapped, "Leave us with our grief. Go."

Marcello quickly chimed in. "We're very sorry. Come on, Karissa."

Karissa felt terrible. "Yes, we're sorry. Forgive me."

136

But Gregory and his wife and son had already turned away from them and were greeting the next people in line.

Karissa and Marcello went down the steps outside to the pavement.

"Was that strange to you, or am I imagining things?" she asked.

"I'm not sure. He chased us away, but he was also acting like he had something to say to you."

"I know, right?"

Then she stopped dead in her tracks.

"What?" Marcello asked.

"Over there. That black SUV."

Across Mansfield Avenue and on the far side of La Brea, near a Popeye's Chicken joint, sat a black BMW X5. A bald Caucasian man was in the passenger seat, watching them—with *binoculars*.

"That's the guy from the World Stage!" Karissa spat. "Oh my God, it's the car that was in front of my house the other night. That fucker is stalking us!"

Marcello immediately crossed Mansfield at a fast pace. He ran to the edge of La Brea, but traffic was too heavy for him to jay-walk into the street. When the BMW's driver saw that he had been spotted, he put down the binoculars, pulled away from the curb, and sped into the throng of cars traveling north on La Brea. Marcello shook a fist in that direction and returned to Karissa.

"Did you get a good look at him?" she asked.

"Not really. All I could tell was he was a white guy who looked like Bruce Willis with hair on the sides of his bald head. I'd like get my hands on him."

Karissa had no doubt that Marcello could probably take on the creep.

"What's going on, Marcello?" she asked.

"I don't know. Let's get out of here."

She turned back to the entrance of the funeral parlor. "I wish we could talk to—"

The Websters were still greeting visitors, but they had been joined by the old woman with the white hair who had played the piano. Her hands were clasped with the couple's in solidarity.

The four of them were looking straight in their direction.

19

THE MOVIE

The film cuts to a montage of pages slowly tearing away from a desktop calendar—February 1948, March, April, May . . . . In between are various clips of Blair Kendrick in the studio, attending premieres, and being photographed. Her voice-over continues.

"The months went by so fast I could barely stop for air. The Dark Lonely Night *was released in early 1948 and was a massive hit for* Ultimate Pictures. *I then began work on* The Love of a Killer, *even though MGM asked Eldon Hirsch if I could be loaned out for something they were doing. Eldon refused. Although I had found success playing 'bad girls' in these crime pictures for Ultimate, I longed to do something different. Hell, I could sing and dance—I wanted to do a* musical, *but that wasn't in the cards."*

Cut to an exterior daytime scene, somewhere in the desert outside of Los Angeles. Blair and Hank are together, and she is target shooting with bottles and cans. Holding Hank's revolver, she holds the gun with an outstretched arm, takes a bead on a target, and shoots three rounds in succession, hitting all the bottles. Hank then sets up more targets on a rock and she does it again.

"But while my career was blooming, things weren't so great in my *personal life. Hank and I stopped seeing each other after he was beat up by Buddy Franco and his goons. We resolved to be friends, but of course, it didn't work. Three months went by before both of us were going crazy without each other. By May, we were sneaking around to each other's houses again. The only thing we didn't do was go out in public together."*

Cut back to the desktop calendar—the pages for June, July, August, September, and October disappear. More movie posters and soundstage shots of Blair working . . .

*"*The Love of a Killer *came out in the summer of '48 and was again a big hit. The reviews of my performance were especially good. I was kind of surprised, for I felt the role didn't challenge me; it was pretty much the same thing I'd been doing in previous pictures. But it was nice to be liked.*

"And then toward the end of October, as I was beginning production on The Outlaw Lovers, *I started to notice I wasn't feeling too well."*

A little dizzy, Blair emerged from the women's restroom of the studio soundstage and made her way back to the lounge where she sat, lit a cigarette, and put her head back.

Oh God, I just want to die . . . What is wrong *with me?*

The nausea had reached a tipping point and she had been forced to rush to the toilet and vomit. It was the third time this week. She had been in the middle of a take for *The Outlaw Lovers* when she suddenly bolted off the set and ran into the corridor. The director, a man named Richard Tanner, shouted "Cut!" in a none-too-pleasant tone. When she returned, he chewed her out.

"Blair, if you need to go, you have to hold it until the take is done. Don't you *ever* ruin one of my takes again. I don't care if you *are* Eldon Hirsch's little princess. This is *my* set!"

It was as if he had slapped her. *Little princess?* What the hell did that mean?

She pointed a finger at him, squinted her eyes, and growled, "Don't you ever talk to me like that again, Dick. *I'm not feeling well.*"

"Well see the nurse, for God's sake. We have a picture to shoot."

"I'm fine now. Let's do the shot."

Now it was the lunch break, but Blair had no appetite. The mere thought of food made her queasy. She never got sick. Was it a stomach bug of some kind? Had she caught it from somebody? Zelda had been out with the flu, but that was a month ago. No one she knew had anything serious.

Perhaps she just needed rest. She and Hank had been rather lively in the bedroom as of late. After their "time off" from each other in the spring, they now coveted whatever precious hours they could spend together. They saw each other only at night— either in her bedroom or his . . .

Richard Tanner walked by with a tray of food from the commissary. He didn't even look at her or ask how she was feeling. *Where did the studio find him, anyway? Who does he think he is?* She had had enough experience in her two short years in Hollywood to recognize the difference between a good director and a talentless hack. Tanner had supposedly come up through the ranks, although she had never heard of him. *The Outlaw Lovers* was his first picture at the helm. Instead of working *with* his actors, he treated them like slaves.

Little princess, am I? I'll show him.

Blair forced herself to stub out the cigarette and stand. She marched to the administrative building, breezed past the security guard, and approached Camille, the main bastion of defense for the studio head. The woman was an old-timer, about sixty years old, and hard as nails. She protected her boss as if he were the president of the United States.

"Is Eldon in?" Blair asked.

"Hello, Blair," the woman said, looking her up and down. "Do you have an appointment?"

"Do I *need* an appointment?"

Camille shrugged. "I suppose not. You *are* Blair Kendrick, after all." She picked up a phone and pressed an intercom button. "Sir, Blair Kendrick is out here, wants to see you. Fine." She hung up and jerked her head at the door behind her. "Go on in."

Blair walked down the long corridor and entered the inner sanctum. Normally she was loath to even be within ten feet of the studio boss. He had never given up his lecherous advances, but he seemed to have taken her rejections in stride.

The man kept the spacious office dimly lit, creating an ominous atmosphere of intimidation for anyone who came to meet with him. The desk, on the other side of the room, was bathed in a pool of light from the lamps around it. It was almost as if it were nighttime. The golden glow of the room didn't help her equilibrium one bit.

"Eldon?" she called.

"Blair, my dear! Come forward! To what do I owe the pleasure?"

She strode across the carpet. He had one of his coin collection binders open in front of him. There were three loose coins on the desk, and she must have interrupted him in the act of securing them on a page. Was that all he did every day?

It was then that she realized she was wearing a bathrobe that covered only a nightie, and she had slippers on her feet. It was her costume for the picture, and she hadn't bothered to change out of it for lunch. No wonder Camille had given her the stink eye.

"It's that director, Dick Tanner," she said. "He acts like he's Cecil B. DeMille or William Wyler, and he treats me like I'm a chorus girl."

Hirsch made a face. "What happened?"

She told him the story. As she did so, she began to feel woozy again. She wavered on her feet, and Hirsch stood. "Blair, sit down. No, come over here and lie down. You're awfully pale."

She put her hands on his desk to hold herself up. "I'm sorry, Eldon. You're right, I don't feel so good."

"Come on, honey." He came around and led her to the couch.

She plopped down and stretched out. The room was spinning.

What the heck is wrong with me?

"I'll get you some water," he said. He poured a glass from a pitcher at the bar and returned, sitting by her and helping to prop her up so she could take a few sips. He then placed the glass on the coffee table and held her hand. "Maybe we're working you too hard."

She closed her eyes and shook her head. "I like working hard."

"Well, I must say it's paying off. *The Love of a Killer* has made the most money of all your pictures so far. The public loves you."

She kept her eyes shut, willing away the nausea. "That's nice to hear, but it's not my *best* movie. I must say I didn't like it much."

Hirsch shrugged. "Who cares? The audience did. There's even some buzz around town that you might be considered for an Oscar nomination."

"What? Really?"

"Just rumors, but that's how these things start, you know."

"I think *The Jazz Club* is the best thing I've done. I keep doing the same thing, Eldon. I'd like to branch out. Try something different. I play the same character in every picture."

"Maybe so. But you know what, Blair? I wasn't going to tell you until *Outlaw Lovers* wrapped, but we're giving you a raise."

"You are?"

"Yes, my dear. You'll be getting another ten thousand a picture, *plus* a little share of the profits . . . if you're a good girl!"

She had never heard of a star receiving a share of the profits. She opened her eyes and looked at him. "Are you pulling my leg, Eldon?"

"As much as I'd like to pull on your leg, sweetheart, I'm not. You know Jimmy Stewart just negotiated a profit-sharing deal for his next two pictures. *Harvey* and some western. The writing's on the wall. All the major stars are going to want points. It's a changing business." He leaned in closer to her. "And I've got the integrity and foresight to embrace it. I'm willing to go along with the trend. Perhaps." He put a hand on her forehead and then lightly ran it through her blond hair. "So . . . if you're *good*, maybe you can share a little in the profits, too."

She was suddenly aware of his breath, his weight, his oily hair, and his thick lips that so desperately wanted to kiss her. It repulsed her even more, practically turning her stomach. She rolled to the side and nearly gagged.

"Oh, poor dear," he said. "I'd better call the studio nurse."

Blair waved at him. "No . . . don't . . ." She managed to control the urge to throw up. Instead, she sat upright, reached for the glass of water, and took another swig.

"Well, I'm going to tell Tanner to call off shooting for the day," Hirsch said. "You need some rest."

"No, no, I'm feeling better." He moved in even closer. *Why in the devil would he want to get all mushy with me when he knows I'm about to retch?*

It had been a mistake to come. A moment of uncontrollable ego on her part. She should go back to the director, apologize, and get on with the work. She waved him away.

"Are you sure? We can't have our biggest star getting sick," he said.

"I'm fine." She took another sip, finishing the glass. "Thanks for the water. That helped a lot."

"Good. Now remember what I said about being a good girl, and maybe that raise will materialize."

She looked him square in the eyes. "I thought you said I already have the raise."

"Oh, you do, but you still have to, uh, earn it, you know."

How was she supposed to take that? The guy didn't give up.

"Oh, and, uh, Blair," he continued, "I hope you're not, uh, seeing a certain individual anymore."

This brought on a stab of anxiety. "What?"

"Just remember what your contract says. If it got out that you and . . . and . . . a *Negro* are having relations, I'd have to cancel that contract. You'd be out of a job, you'd never get an Oscar nomination, and you'd never be able to work in this town again."

She stood on wobbly legs. "Is that a threat, Eldon?"

He stared at her. "*Are* you seeing him, Blair?"

"I'm going back to the set, Eldon. I'm not even going to indulge you this conversation. Thank you for the water and for the raise and for everything you do, but you're being a silly little boy to think *that* about me!"

She turned and started to cross the carpet to the exit, but he got up, grabbed her by the hand, and pulled her back to him. His arms went around her and he pressed her body into his. His big belly took up most of their body contact. "Oh, Blair, my beautiful Blair," he moaned, "how can I convince you other than just tell you straight out? I love you. I think you're the most wonderful girl on the planet. I would leave Beatrice and get a divorce if you just gave me the word that you'd be mine. I would shower you with flowers and diamonds and money, lots of money. I am dying for you!"

"Eldon, stop!" She struggled against him, feeling terribly ill again. "Let me go, I'm going to be sick!"

"What can I do to convince you? Oh my God, that mouth of yours. I must have it!"

He leaned in to kiss her . . . and she heaved—all over him and the gold-colored carpet.

20

KARISSA

On the morning after the funeral, Karissa drove to the far west side of Hollywood and parked in the free lot by the Pierce Brothers Westwood Village Memorial Park and Mortuary. She was surprised by its deceptive size. Located on Glendon Avenue, the cemetery was tucked away between tall buildings and not visible to the street. Karissa had read up on the site before coming and learned that it originally opened in 1905, but it had been a burial ground since the late 1800s. Many of Hollywood's elite were buried there, but the graveyard also contained many people who were not famous at all. Besides traditional graves in the ground with markers and tombstones, crypts in walls surrounded the property.

It was a fresh, clear morning, and already tourists were wandering around the grounds searching for their favorite stars' resting places. Even Karissa was impressed by the roster. She'd known about some of them like Marilyn Monroe and Natalie Wood, but she also saw crypts and markers for Burt Lancaster, Don Knotts, Ray Bradbury, Hugh Hefner, Fanny Brice, Truman Capote, Dean Martin, and so many more that it was overwhelming. Karissa had to smile at the humor exhibited on some of the stones. Jack Lemmon's read simply, "Jack Lemmon in," as if it were a movie poster. Billy Wilder's epitaph was "I'm a Writer but then Nobody's Perfect."

Karissa finally found what she was looking for. It was a simple marker flat on the ground, not far from where Eva Gabor was interred.

BLAIR KENDRICK 1928–1949

That was it. Nothing to indicate who she was. No one had placed any flowers on the grave.

Karissa wished she had thought to bring a bouquet or an arrangement. She sighed, not particularly understanding why she had felt the need to visit the cemetery. Looking at her watch, she realized she had to get to the Stormglove office. It was going to be a busy day.

Late afternoon. Karissa shut down her computer and prepared to head home. Marcello had left earlier, as he had some personal errands and also wanted to check out something. It had been a long day of reaching out to contacts at various studios. Both she and Marcello had gone through their address books in attempts to find a producer or company executive who might be willing to listen to their pitch to make the Blair Kendrick movie. Karissa had also written a long, passionate letter to Barbara at the festival, hoping that she would listen to reason. Perhaps she would realize that whatever pressure Ultimate Pictures was putting on her to drop Stormglove from the endeavor was steeped in the personal history of the Hirsch family. That alone should not be criteria for canceling Stormglove's involvement.

Karissa was also intrigued about the older woman they had

seen at Ray Webster's funeral—the one with the white hair who had played the piano. It was entirely possible that she had been a contemporary of Ray—and, in turn, Hank Marley. How could they find her again? Gregory Webster and his wife Carol had also piqued Karissa's interest with their surprising reaction to her approach. More important, they had seemed genuinely unsettled by her presence.

And then there was the man in the car across the street, watching them with binoculars. Could it be possible that the Websters knew he was out there? Who *was* that guy?

Her cell phone rang before she stood to leave her desk. Marcello.

"Yes, sir?" she answered.

"Barry Doon."

"What?"

"I believe that's his name. The guy who was watching us at the funeral. In the BMW."

"Oh my God, Marcello, are you a goddamned mind reader? I was *just* thinking about him!"

"Well, I think I found out who he is; that's what I went to check out. He's an executive vice president at Ultimate Pictures, but he's really a modern studio fixer. He makes the studio's problems go away."

"His name is *Barry Doon*?"

"Yes, ma'am."

"How did you find out?"

"I reached out to my bro, Lewis, in LiUNA, the utility workers' union for our favorite industry—Hollywood motion pictures. He was recently on a couple of productions at Ultimate. I described the guy, and Lewis thought it might be Doon. Are you still at the office? Bring up Google."

"I was just about to leave. I'll look on my phone." She put him on speaker and switched apps. "Okay, I'm typing in his name."

There were a few hits for Barry Doon—IMDb and a few mentions from trade sites.

"Click on Images," Marcello prompted.

Sure enough, the bald man appeared in a handful of candid shots.

"Oh my God, that's him."

Doon was in a couple of pictures with Justin Hirsch, the eighty-year-old head of the studio, and with various stars in others. There weren't many.

"Now we know what we're dealing with," Marcello said.

On the way home, Karissa stopped at her Chase bank drive-through ATM to get some cash. She slipped her debit card into the slot, punched in her PIN, and requested a hundred dollars. A message appeared on the screen—INSUFFICIENT FUNDS.

"What the hell?" she said aloud. Reached through the driver's-side window once again, she punched in her request a second time. INSUFFICIENT FUNDS.

Now alarmed, she went back to the main menu and pressed the command to see her balance. Her heart pounded in her chest when she saw the result—$0.00.

"No, no, no, that's *impossible!*" she snapped. She retrieved her card and drove out of the lane. She was about to pull into the bank's parking lot when she saw that the bank had closed for the day.

"*No!*"

She found a customer service number at the back of her debit card and, using the Bluetooth capability in her car, gave the voice command for her phone to dial it. Nothing happened. Karissa pulled her cell phone out of her purse and manually dialed the number. Again, it was as if the phone was dead. It was turned on, but the app didn't work.

"Oh my God . . ." Now, panic overtook anger.

What to do? It was after hours. Should she go to a police station?

No, the Stormglove office had a landline. She'd head back there.

Shaking, Karissa drove out of the lot and merged onto the road back to La Brea. The entire way she cursed and hit her fist on the steering wheel, urging the traffic to move faster. It was maddening. The rush-hour chaos on the Hollywood streets bottlenecked and eventually the Murano came to a complete stop two blocks away from the office. Tears formed in her eyes as she prayed that she hadn't been hacked. Perhaps it was just a freak computer glitch going on with her bank account and phone.

Finally, traffic moved. She made it to the storefront and parked in her designated spot. Karissa got out, ran up the outer stairs to the door with the Stormglove logo on it, unlocked it, and went inside. She grabbed the handset off the phone on her desk and—there was no dial tone.

"No!"

She slammed the receiver down and collapsed in her chair.

And then Marcello rushed in, his eyes wide, sweat pouring down his face. He had his cell phone in hand.

"Karissa! My goddamned phone isn't working. I came back to use—"

"I know—mine, too, and our landline is dead."

"Wait, what? Yours, too?"

"It's worse than that, Marcello. My bank account has been emptied. I stopped by Chase on the way home, and there's no money." She slapped a hand on the desk. "Damn, I didn't think to check the Stormglove account, I just looked at my personal one. Oh, Jesus, what the fuck, Marcello?"

"What? Your bank account? What about *mine*?"

*

They drove together to another Chase and discovered that the Stormglove account had been emptied and frozen, as well as Marcello's personal checking account. Then they visited an AT&T outlet to inquire about their cell phones. They were told that both accounts had been closed a few hours earlier. They filed official reports of fraud. The representative worked on their accounts and, after nearly an hour, eventually got everything restored. Marcello immediately called his wife and asked her to check other personal financial accounts held in her name. Then he called Stormglove's attorney, a man named Tony Davenport. Karissa phoned Chase customer service and reported what had happened.

When all was said and done, the couple was reassured that everything would be fixed and that no funds would be permanently lost. However, it might take up to forty-eight hours for the "investigation" to be completed and the money returned.

Deciding that they both needed a drink, Karissa and Marcello went to the Parlor on Melrose Avenue and ordered some stiff ones.

As they collapsed in weariness from the adrenaline expenditure, Karissa asked, "So is this the work of Barry Doon and Justin Hirsch?"

Marcello just looked at her. "Who else?"

It was after sunset when Karissa reached her home in Sugar Hill. She pulled into the garage, got out of the car, and unlocked the garage door to the house. It still felt as if she was entering a palace much too large for a single person to occupy. It was too soon for Karissa to feel completely "at home" here, but she did love it. She couldn't wait to throw a party in the house, but that would have to wait until she had something to celebrate. The start of production on a new film would be nice, but even that was the least of her worries after the day's events.

Karissa walked through the kitchen to the hallway that led to the entry foyer. Mail was on the floor, having fallen through the slot. She opened the front door and stepped out on the porch to scan the street, making sure no suspicious BMWs were in surveillance mode. Then she noticed a small package wrapped in brown paper at her feet. It was slightly too large to have fit through the mail slot. The package was addressed to her, but there was no postage on it. It had been hand-delivered by someone. Karissa took a quick look at the street again and returned inside, locking the door behind her.

Yesterday she would have thought she was being paranoid. There hadn't been a real reason to fear Barry Doon or any other studio henchmen that Ultimate Pictures sent out to intimidate her. Hollywood could be a rough town, but there usually wasn't a need to be overly dramatic.

But after what had happened that day, the game had changed.

Justin Hirsch had accomplished what he had set out to do—kick Stormglove off the festival project and scare them with financial terrorism—but there wasn't a legal foot for him to stand on when it came to stopping an independent production of their film. She was reminded of how William Randolph Hearst had done everything in his power to halt the making of Orson Welles's *Citizen Kane*. RKO Pictures refused to buckle under Hearst's pressure, and the picture got made anyway. Unfortunately, none of Hearst's newspapers would advertise the movie, and *Kane* tanked at the box office during its initial run. It was nearly two decades later that the film was dusted off, reevaluated, and declared one of the greatest motion pictures ever made.

Not that she and Marcello could produce anything of that caliber. But still . . .

Karissa took the mail into the kitchen. She disposed of the

junk in the recycling bin and then opened the small package with a pair of scissors. The box contained a jewelry bag made of black velvet, tied with a golden drawstring.

What?

Karissa undid the easy knot and pulled the thing open.

The bag held three old coins. Karissa poured them out into her palm. She didn't recognize them as anything in circulation today, and she wasn't completely sure they were from the United States until she examined them. One was about the size of a quarter, a very dull and faded silver, with a man's head in profile wearing a wreath of leaves in his hair, like a Roman orator. The year on the coin was 1901 and the words "In God We Trust" arced above the head. Another was a discolored gold or bronze with an Indian head on it, dated 1911. The back featured an eagle, with the words "United States of America" above it and "Ten Dollars" beneath the bird.

A ten-dollar coin? What would it be worth now?

The third coin was also a dull silver color. It had a woman in profile wearing a headband with the word "Liberty" written on it. The year marked it to be from 1817.

"Oh, my Lord," Karissa muttered. "That's old."

What is this all about? Who put this box on my porch?

Then she recalled—when Eldon Hirsch was killed, his safe had been opened and robbed of a rare coin collection.

"Oh, shit."

21
THE MOVIE

The flickering image on the silver screen reveals iconic views of Hollywood streets and soundstages, and then it cross-fades to the desk calendar again, the pages of months ripping away—October and November 1948, leaving December in place.

"I finally went to the doctor," the actress's voice-over continues. "He confirmed my worst fears. At the same time, The Outlaw Lovers *was rushed through postproduction so that it could be released in time for the Christmas holidays.* The Love of a Killer *was starting to appear on some critics' Top Ten lists of '48. Right after the New Year, I was supposed to start shooting another picture,* The Boss and the Blonde, *with none other than James Cagney as my costar. But I was frightened. It could all come crashing down."*

The camera slowly pulls in to a nighttime exterior shot of Blair's house in Sugar Hill, focusing on the illuminated bedroom window . . . and we, ever the voyeurs, penetrate the glass and invade a couple's privacy in a way that can only happen in a motion picture.

"You're being awfully quiet tonight," Hank said as they lay on their backs, cigarettes in their hands. When she didn't answer, he spoke again. "Is anything wrong?"

Blair sighed. "Oh, Hank. I have something to tell you."

"What's that?"

She raised herself up on her side, supported by her elbow. The mattress's box springs creaked loudly. She had been meaning to buy a new one for some time.

"I'm going to have a baby."

Hank blinked in succession a couple of times, his eyes on her. Then he smiled. "Really?"

"Yes. You remember when I kept getting nauseous a month or a month and a half ago? Well, it wasn't the flu; it was morning sickness. Morning sickness that lasted until noon. When it went away, I forgot about it and ignored it. But then, well, I'm a woman, you know, and we know when things start happening to our bodies. I was afraid, Hank. Is it terrible that I didn't want it to be true?"

"Blair, honey—"

"No, don't answer that. Anyway, I waited until last week to go to the doctor. That's when I finally got it confirmed. I'm pregnant, Hank. Two and a half months, maybe three."

Hank took a drag off his cigarette and then said, "Sweetheart, I think I'm smart enough to know that it could be upsetting to you no matter how I respond. Inside, truthfully, I'm jumping for joy. My heart is jivin' and dancing and singing. I want to break out the champagne and celebrate. But then, I look at you now, and I see how *you* feel about it. I can tell that this doesn't make you very happy. And I understand. I know why. And I'm fully aware of what this means for *us*. So that's why I'm not acting like a fool and running around crying, 'Hallelujah' and 'Praise the Lord.' Because that would upset you even more, wouldn't it?"

She chuckled a little. "Yes, it would. Although it might also make me laugh."

His eyes twinkled at the easing of her tension. "I do hope I can say that you make me proud, and that I love you more than anything else God put on this earth."

"Yes, you can say that, and I love you, too." She sat up and stubbed the butt out in the ashtray on the nightstand. "But we have to face facts. This is not a good thing for us, Hank."

"No, I suppose not."

She looked off, away from him. "Should I . . . should I get rid of it?"

Hank reached over to his nightstand and put out the remains of his own cigarette. He then sat up behind her and took her in his arms. "Honey, I would never tell you what you should do about this. Just know that I will stand by you. I will give you my opinion, for whatever that's worth, and I will give you my advice, which ain't worth nothin', and I will give you my support, which I hope might be of some value to you."

"I wouldn't even know how to go about it. I mean, there are other actresses who have . . . I'd have to ask someone . . ."

Hank cleared his throat. "I know a doctor. He's . . . he's a Negro doctor. He's a good man; he knows what he's doing."

Tears formed in her eyes and slowly trickled down her cheeks. They were silent for a few moments, and then she slowly shook her head. "I don't think I can. I can't do it, Hank. I can't get rid of our baby." She turned to face him. "The law is changed in California. We can get married. We can have our child."

"But honey, what about your career? Legal or not, the studio won't stand for their star actress to marry a Negro."

"Well . . . I'll just have to give up acting, then."

"Give it up?"

"Hank, they're not letting me do the kinds of roles I really want. I'm sick of playing these bad girl parts. I've asked over and over if I could be in a *comedy*, or a *musical* . . . anything but a crime picture. Eldon Hirsch won't loan me out to other studios—they've asked and he's always refused. It's like he's punishing me for not going to bed with him."

"You don't really want to give up being in movies, Blair. I know you. This is your life."

She stood and started to pace. "But I would if it means keeping you and the baby. Other interracial couples are getting married since the law changed."

"We couldn't travel out of state as a man and wife. We'd have to always stay in California."

"So? Where else are we going to go? We could move out of Los Angeles and go somewhere else in the state. San Francisco's a nice place."

"How will we live? My work is here, honey. I have a pretty good thing going with my band and all. It's hard to start all over again as a musician in a new town."

"I know. I'd get a job."

"Doing what?"

"I don't know! Are you trying to talk me out of this?"

"I'm not trying to do anything, honey. I'm just showing you all the angles."

"Well, are you willing to do this with me? Do you *want* to get married?"

Hank got out of bed and came to her. Once again, he took her in his arms. "Sugar, I want to marry you. I just don't want to see you get hurt. I don't want to see you turn your back on a successful career."

"To hell with it, Hank. For all the fame and money and glamour and glitz, there's something rotten to the core about it all. I've been thinking about this for days. I *do* want out."

"Well, then, I guess that settles it." He got down on one knee with her hands in his. "Will you live with me so we can make our own blues in the dark? Will you marry me, Blair Kendrick?"

She laughed and got down on the carpet with him. "Of course, I will." They kissed and toppled over on their sides, laughing. After a moment, she said, "How about this? I make *The Boss and the Blonde*—I mean, how many times does a girl get to do a movie with Jimmy Cagney? That should be finished by February, and then we'll do it. I don't care if I'm showing. Then we'll see what happens. Maybe nobody will say a damned thing and we can continue as we were. They can't fight the law. On the other hand, if we get run out of town, so be it."

"Sounds like a plan to me," he said.

After the rather quiet New Year, Blair reported to the set for the first day of shooting of *The Boss and the Blonde*. She had been studying lines the previous evening and was having difficulty memorizing them. Her mind was elsewhere. Nevertheless, she was ready to get started. She knew the lines would come; they always did. Her meeting with costar James Cagney the day before had gone very well. He seemed to be enthusiastic about the picture and said that he looked forward to working with her.

She sat in front of the mirrors in the dressing room, the bulbs brightly lit around her. Zelda came in with her makeup box. "Here we are again!" she chirped. "How are you this morning, Blair?"

"Fine, Zelda, and you?"

"Oh, just peachy." She squealed a little. "I just met Jimmy Cagney! Oh, my heart's all a-flutter. That was sure exciting."

"He's very nice, isn't he?"

Blair sat in the high chair while Zelda applied the pancake

base. As she did, Blair held the script in her lap, going over the dialogue again.

There was a knock on the door.

"Come in," Blair said.

Buddy Franco, dressed in his trademark suit, appeared in the doorway. Blair thought that the temperature in the room might have dropped ten degrees. "Excuse me, ladies," he said. "Zelda, can I talk to Blair alone for a minute?"

"Sure." Zelda put down her brush, wiped her hands on a towel, and left the room. Franco shut the door and stood in front of Blair.

"What is it, Buddy?" she asked.

"You ready to start shooting?"

"Of course."

"Good, good. This is a big one. Eldon's very excited about it. Jimmy Cagney and all."

"I am, too. What do you want, Buddy? I need to concentrate on these lines."

"Well, I hate to bring this up again, but it seems that a certain Negro was seen coming out the back door of your house the other morning."

Blair stiffened.

"You've been warned about this before. This is the last time I'm going to say it." He placed his hands on the arms of the chair and leaned in so close that she couldn't have squirmed out if she'd wanted. "Blair, you have to stop seeing the—uh, I can't be responsible for what happens to him . . . or to you . . . if you don't. I've been instructed to take the matter into my hands again, and I will. So, tell me now. I want to hear it from you. Is it over?"

Blair's heart pounded in her chest.

"*Is it over?*"

"Buddy. I'm about to start shooting an important picture. You said so yourself. Why do you want to come in here and try to scare me? I don't know what you think you've seen or who told you what. Now, get out of here. I need to work on these lines. I don't want to have to talk to Eldon about this."

"Eldon's not going to take your side anymore, honey. He's the one who told me to come in here and . . . *talk* to you."

Blair swallowed. The only thing she could do was to lie. After all, she was an actress.

"It's over," she said. "Now go away."

He released his hands from the chair and stood straight. "All right then."

"And if I catch anyone spying on me at my house," she added, "I'm calling the police."

He smiled in his oily way. "You do that." He opened the door and called. "Zelda? She's all yours."

When the makeup girl returned, Blair was crying.

"Oh, honey!" Zelda gasped. "What happened?"

"Could you give me a minute or two, please, Zelda?"

"Uh, sure. I'll be outside if you need me. Can I get you anything?"

"No. Thanks."

Zelda tentatively moved back to the open door and waited.

"It's all right," Blair said. "Just give me a minute."

"Okay." The door shut, and then Blair threw the script across the room.

22

KARISSA

The next morning, Karissa took the coins with her on the way to the office. Before leaving home, she had spent some time on the phone with her bank and learned that there had been some progress in restoring both her account and that of Stormglove Productions. Apparently, the correct passwords had been used to empty and close the accounts online, which indicated that the computers she and Marcello used had been hacked. It was extremely disturbing. The recovery of the actual funds was going to take longer and would require the involvement of their attorney, but fortunately Tony Davenport was already on the case. Karissa was lucky that she had reported the crime the same day it had occurred. If more than twenty-four hours had elapsed, it would have been more difficult to prove that she and Marcello had not authorized the closing of the accounts.

In the meantime, she had no funds aside from the cash she carried in her purse.

Earlier, Karissa had Googled "coin collectors" and come up with a gold and rare coin dealer on Wilshire Boulevard and Kingsley Drive, which wasn't far out of the way from the office.

She parked on the street in front and went inside. No one else was in the shop except for the short, bald man behind the counter. He wore thick glasses and was probably in his sixties, though it was difficult to tell for certain. He greeted her with a cheery, almost singsong Eastern European accent, "Good morning, good morning, welcome, welcome. My name is Seymour, and here's my card. How may I help you, young lady?" He handed her a colorful business card with his name, a cartoon caricature of himself, and the store information on it.

That made her smile. "I have some coins here I'd like to get appraised, if you do that."

The man shrugged. "I can do a ballpark verbal appraisal for you at no charge. If you want a notarized document for insurance or tax purposes, we charge fifty dollars per piece."

"Ballpark estimate would be just fine, thank you."

"Okay, what do you got?"

She dug the jewelry bag out of her purse and poured the three coins into her palm. She then laid them one by one on the black velvet pad on the counter.

The man stared at the coins without moving. Then, after nearly a minute, he picked up the one marked 1817. He eyed it carefully and turned it over. His hands shook a little. After a bit, he placed the coin back on the pad and took the Indian head piece from 1911. Once again, he examined both sides closely. Finally, he picked up the 1901 coin, scrutinized it, and placed it back on the pad.

Seymour cleared his throat. "Where . . . where did you get these?"

She was prepared for that question. "Oh, they're part of a family heirloom. My mother left those to me along with some other odds and ends. I thought because of the age that they might be worth something."

Seymour nodded. "Yes. Yes, they are worth something." He

cleared his throat again and picked up the 1817 coin. "I have never seen one of these. Only pictures. If it's real."

"I'm pretty sure it's real," Karissa said.

He laughed a little. "There are only a handful of these in existence. Fewer than ten."

That made Karissa gasp a little. "Really?"

"Really."

"So . . . how much is it worth?"

Seymour held up a hand as if to say, *hold on*. He placed the coin down and picked up the 1901. "This one is a Barber Quarter S. Maybe. There are a lot of fakes out there. I would have to consult my coin guy, but this one—it's in pretty good shape—this one might be worth as much as thirty thousand dollars."

Karissa gulped. "Really?"

"If you were to sell it, you wouldn't get that much. I think the last time it was auctioned, the buyer paid around thirty-six thousand dollars. So that's what you'd insure it for."

"And if I were to sell it?"

"You're free to shop around, but I'd give you twenty thousand for it."

"Twenty thousand dollars."

"Yes, ma'am."

Holy shit.

"What about the other two?" she asked.

"Well." He picked up the 1911 coin. "This, I'm pretty certain, is a D Indian Head Gold Eagle. I've seen one of these before. The condition a coin is in is everything. This one is in spectacular condition. I know of one in this condition that sold at auction for sixty-five thousand dollars."

"Sixty-five—!"

He replaced the coin on the pad and picked up the 1817 item. "If I'm correct, this is a very rare coin. Just a handful are known to exist. It's called a Capped Bust Silver Dollar. I'd go out on a limb and say it's worth half a million dollars."

"You're not serious."

He replaced the coin. He cleared his throat. "Did your mother have any other coins?"

"Not that I know of."

Karissa stared at the objects as if they had magical powers. She considered scooping them up and returning them to the bag, but then she remembered she was flat broke. She picked up the Barber Quarter S. "You can give me twenty thousand dollars for this now?"

"I can write you a check."

She handed it to him. "Okay." She picked up the remaining coins and put them in the bag. His eyes followed them, as if he was sorry to see them disappear.

"If you decide to sell them," he said, clearing his throat again, "would you consider coming back and selling them here?"

He wants them. Should I try to bargain with him?

"Maybe. Like you said, I should shop around." She indicated the Barber Quarter. *What the hell. I need funds now. He seems honest.* "That's a cheap one. I'll let that go now." She reached out and grabbed his wrist. "Are you giving me a fair price, Seymour?"

"Yes, ma'am. Better than fair."

"How much will you sell it for?" He hesitated. "Please be straight with me."

"I will be asking thirty-five thousand for it."

"That's a fifteen-thousand-dollar profit!"

"Yes, ma'am." He shrugged. "We're a business. That's the way it works."

She reflected on his words. "Twenty-five."

Seymour hesitated.

"And I promise to return to you if I decide to sell the others."

The man pursed his lips. "Twenty-two-five?"

Blair smiled and nodded. "Okay. Twenty-two thousand, five hundred."

In the parking lot, she called Marcello to tell him about the coins.

"And you didn't tell me this last night?" he asked.

"I wanted to find out more about them first," she said. "They might have been fake."

"You probably shouldn't have sold that one."

"I need the money. The other two are worth a lot more. I'll hold on to those. The big question is—who sent them to me? Do you think they might be coins from Eldon Hirsch's collection?"

"At this point, I'll believe anything, but that's pretty far-fetched."

"Marcello. Think about it for a second. What if the coins are the ones that were stolen from Hirsch? It means the killer and thief knows about us—about *me*. Maybe I wasn't supposed to sell them. What if they are . . . ?"

"What?"

"A warning."

"What are you doing now? Are you coming in to work?"

"I'm going to deposit this check, and then I'm going home to stash the coins."

"I'm coming over. I want to see them."

Karissa's stomach lurched when she saw Willy Puma's green Jeep Cherokee parked in front of her house. "Oh, no," she muttered. Still, she pulled in to the drive and left the car outside, in front of the garage. Before she allowed herself to get angry, Karissa thought that perhaps Willy had brought the signed divorce papers.

Fine.

She went around to the front yard. Her ex was sitting on the porch swing.

"This is kind of nice," he said. "You could sit out here and sip mint juleps like they did in the Old South."

"Willy. I hope you're here to deliver the signed papers."

He didn't answer. Instead, he patted the seat of the swing. "Sit by me for a minute."

"No. Do you have the papers?"

"Not today."

Karissa took a deep breath. "I'm going inside. Please leave."

He held up a hand. "Wait a minute, Karissa. Just listen to me. Okay?"

"What?"

"Are you trying to make a movie that will ruin my boss's reputation?"

She furrowed her brow. "What are you talking about?"

"I understand you're trying to make a movie about that crazy actress back in the forties who killed Justin Hirsch's father."

"What do you care?"

He stopped the swing and stood. "Because I'm starring in a new movie that Ultimate Pictures is making."

"You are?"

"Yes, indeed." He put his hands on his hips, striking a pose like that of Yul Brynner in *The King and I*. "I'm going to play the bad guy in *Hellhole Six*."

Karissa almost made a face. The Hellhole franchise was, sadly, a cash cow for Ultimate Pictures and the brainchild of Justin Hirsch. Like Meat Grinder, the series that had given Willy his break, they were violent, nasty, and sexist films that appealed to a low common denominator audience.

"Congratulations. You needed the work."

"I did, and I got it. So, what about this movie you're making? I can't have my wife doing anything that's going to jeopardize my relationship with Justin."

She felt her face flush, first from his description of her as his wife, and then from the implication of his words. "Did . . . did he put you up to this? Are you on a mission from *Justin Hirsch*?"

Willy shook his head. "No, no . . . he just . . . you're just not going to do it, Karissa. Wouldn't be right."

"What the hell are you talking about? I'm making a *movie*; there's no right or wrong about it."

"He just doesn't want you making the movie. I can't let you do it."

She moved away, off the porch and into the yard. "*Let* me? What kind of sexist shit is this? Sorry, Willy, I'm going to do what I want. I'm not your wife anymore."

"We're not divorced yet."

"*Then sign the papers, Willy!*"

"I don't think I will."

"Damn you!" She whirled around and nearly screamed at him. "Why do you persist on this? Why do you want to *torture* me?"

"Torture you? How the fuck am I torturing you?"

"By showing your goddamn face! Get out of here!"

"Look, I know you're still upset about the accident—"

"The *accident*? Willy, I told you if you cheated on me again—after two other times—then that would be it. I told you if you continued to drink and do cocaine, that would be it. You were fucking high on coke and booze, and you wrecked your car with another woman in the passenger seat. She sued us, and I had to pay your *homewrecker* with money I made from Stormglove Productions!"

"It was an accident!"

"Your goddamned lying lawyer turned it into an accident when the city tried to press criminal charges. The jury believed you because you're a fucking movie star. We both know damned well it was no accident. But her *civil* suit was a different story, wasn't it?" Karissa felt as if she might explode. "Why you persisted on chasing other women when you had *me . . .*!"

"Karissa, you refused to have my babies!"

"What's that got to do with it? I'm not going to argue about this again! You know the doctors said it would be dangerous if I tried to have children after that ectopic pregnancy. I wanted to adopt. *I* was adopted. But you didn't want that. Your macho pride wouldn't let you."

"Oh, that's right, let's pull the I-can't-have-children card. You just didn't *want* to have children! Your career was more important!"

"You *bastard! Get out of here!*"

"Karissa?" It was Marcello. She swerved around to see her partner on the lawn. He had pulled up in his own car during the argument. "What's going on? You okay?"

"Well, well, if it isn't the slick snake who fucks my wife," Willy said.

Marcello's eyes narrowed. "What? I . . . do not!"

"Willy!" Karissa snapped.

"You don't?" Willy laughed. "Oh, then I must be mistaken."

"Get out of here, Willy." She held up her phone. "Do I have to call the police?"

"Come down off that porch, Puma," Marcello said. "We can settle this right here."

Both men were built like gladiators. Karissa didn't want to witness a bloodbath. "Shut up, both of you." She punched 911. "It's ringing, Willy."

Willy held up his hands. "Oh, great, you *know* what happens when you call the cops on black folk. Fine. I'm going. You just listen to what I said, though. Don't screw up my movie!"

He stormed off the porch, strode across the grass, and got in his Cherokee. Karissa ended the call before the dispatcher answered. Willy screeched his tires as loudly as possible as he drove away.

"Are you all right?" Marcello asked.

"Yeah. Thanks."

"He's such an asshole. He never did like me."

"Yeah."

"I'm sorry he brought up that . . . you know."

She shrugged. "We don't need to talk about something that happened one time in a moment of weakness and alcohol and stupidity after Willy and I separated."

He nodded. "You and I go back a long way. It's part of who we are."

"You're my best friend, Marcello. It's behind us. End of story. And who is he to bring up infidelity, right?" She sighed. "Come on inside. I'll show you the coins."

"That's fine, but I also came to tell you something else."

"What?"

"I know where Buddy Franco's *daughter* is. She's alive and living in LA."

23
THE MOVIE

The screening of Femme Fatale—the Blair Kendrick Story *continues as the scene shifts to shots of Blair on various sets on soundstages as her character a) robs a bank, b) drives an automobile with rear-screen projection of a cityscape in the back window, and c) is slapped by a man whose back is to us, falls to the floor, and shoots him with a gun that was hidden in a holster on her thigh under her dress. The voice-over narrates.*

"Production was delayed a couple of weeks due to unforeseen circumstances in Jimmy Cagney's schedule, so we didn't start until the end of January in 1949. By the time February rolled around, we had less than a half hour of footage in the can. I was a little worried about my health—and of course the baby's, too. The movie was very physical, and I had to do some stunts without a double. Meanwhile, Hank and I were counting the days when I could walk away and we could start a new life together."

Zelda powdered Blair's face, the final step in the morning's makeup session. The actress was due on the set in a half hour.

"There you go, honey," the woman said. "You need help with your costume?"

"No, thank you, Zelda."

"All right, you call me if you need me." Zelda packed up her makeup kit and left the room. Blair got out of the high chair and closed the door. She didn't want anyone to see the coming struggle.

She had noticed a week earlier that the costumes were becoming snug. Today's was a high-waisted pair of wide-leg pants and a simple blouse, buttoned at the collar—something that might have been worn by Katharine Hepburn or Marlene Dietrich. When Blair put on the pants, she had to suck in and strain to fasten the snap. The belt helped, but she was terribly uncomfortable. Getting through the day's shoot was going to be an ordeal.

When she was dressed, she took one more look in the mirror at her face and makeup, took a deep breath, and left the dressing room, ready to report to the set.

"That's a wrap!"

The assistant director called it, indicating they were done for the day. Blair was exhausted, hungry, and depressed. She wasn't happy with her performance so far. She hadn't bothered to watch the dailies, and she had overheard the cameraman telling the grip, "She's not at a hundred percent." Her costar, too, seemed not to have his heart in the picture. Blair had heard that although Cagney had agreed to do the movie, he had never really wanted to return to the tough-guy gangster roles that had made him famous in the early thirties.

The mood on the set was dark.

Blair headed for the dressing room, eager to get out of the tight clothes and off the lot. She and Hank had planned a quiet dinner together at his house, and she couldn't wait to relax in front of his fireplace. It was an unusually cold February in Southern California, and the blaze in the hearth was going to feel cozy.

"Miss Kendrick?"

She turned to see one of the PAs in the corridor, a young man in his early twenties.

"Yes?"

"Mr. Hirsch would like to see you."

"Can I get out of costume and makeup first?"

"I believe he wants to see you as soon as possible. I'm supposed to escort you."

Damn. "Oh, all right." She turned and followed the PA out of the soundstage and into the brisk breeze. She hadn't bothered to get a coat because it was a short walk to the administration building. They were there in five minutes, but still she shivered and rubbed her arms over the sleeves of the blouse.

She thanked the PA and approached Hirsch's first lieutenant. Camille didn't look up from whatever she was working on. "Go on in," she said.

Blair opened the door behind the desk and went down the dim hallway toward the light at the end. Hirsch's door was ajar. She suddenly had butterflies in her stomach; somehow, she knew this wasn't going to go well.

"You wanted to see me, Eldon?" she asked from the open doorway.

He was behind the broad desk, silhouetted by the standing lamp behind him. This time, his head was not looking down at his coin collection. He sat straight, focused ahead, right at her.

"Come in, Blair."

She strode across the gold-colored carpet and paused at the spot where she had made a mess a few months earlier. "Oh, I see you were able to clean the spot. Again, I'm so sorry about that, Eldon."

"Never mind. Come here."

He motioned to the chair in front of the desk, and she sat. He had a cigar going, but he offered an open metal cigarette case to her.

"No, thank you," she said.

He snapped it shut, placed his elbows on the desk, and clasped his fingers. "I've seen the dailies."

"You always see the dailies. Don't you?"

He shrugged. "Not when I'm confident things are going well. Apparently, *The Boss and the Blonde* is not. And I don't think it's the director's fault."

"Eldon, the script . . . well, I don't think it's very good."

"The script is fine. It's *you* that's the problem. Actually, it's you and Cagney both. There's no chemistry. What's wrong?"

She shook her head. "I don't know. I guess I'm just not feeling it this time. I can't speak for Jimmy."

Hirsch took a drag of the cigar and blew smoke in her direction. "I've noticed something else in the dailies."

"What's that?"

"You're gaining weight."

She laughed nervously. "I am? Yeah, well, lately I've had a hard time keeping my girlish figure. The holidays last month, you know . . ."

"That's not it. You're pregnant, aren't you?"

The knot in her stomach exploded.

"Eldon . . ."

"Well? You *are*, aren't you!"

She looked down and nodded.

"It's *him*, isn't it? The *Negro*. He's the father?"

She nodded again. Then she met his eyes and said, "We're going to get married as soon as the picture wraps."

"The hell you are."

"Eldon, you can't stop us. It's legal now in California. Hank and I can get married."

"It may be legal, but it sure isn't *right!* Are you nuts? You'll ruin your career. I can't have my star actress married to a goddamn *Negro!*"

"Eldon! Please don't say that."

He pointed a finger at her. "Get rid of it. That's an order. I'll have Buddy arrange it. He'll be in touch with you. I want it done this Friday so you'll have the weekend to recover and be back on the set on Monday."

"No, Eldon, I won't do it."

"The hell you won't! You want to keep your job, don't you?"

"No. I don't. You can fire me, Eldon. I was going to tell you when the picture was done. I'm through."

He stared at her as if he was looking at a freak of nature. Finally, he said, "Are you out of your pretty little mind? You think Ultimate Pictures is just going to let you walk away? You're our biggest star. I think you just need some rehabilitation. A vacation. We'll get you fixed up, take care of your little 'problem,' and then send you somewhere nice and quiet so you can *get your fucking marbles back.*"

"That's not going to happen, Eldon."

"Oh yes, it is!"

With that, she stood. "Are we done, Eldon? I'm awfully tired and I'm hungry and I've had a long day. I'll work on that chemistry with Jimmy." She turned and started to walk away.

"Blair, I decide when a meeting is over!" She kept going. His voice rose higher as the distance between them increased. "Blair, I will make sure you never work in this town again! I'll scrap the picture! Better to do that now than take a hit at the box office! Do you hear me?"

She was at the door. "Blair!"

She walked out and shut the door behind her. She and Camille shared a glance, but the women said nothing to each other. Blair continued out of the office and, with her head held high, marched back to her dressing room. Only when she was behind the closed door did she crumple into a chair, trembling and sobbing.

The setting in the film shifts to nighttime in Eldon Hirsch's office. The studio mogul sits alone at his desk. The coin collection is tucked away in the safe, out of sight. He sits and stares at the signed photograph of Blair Kendrick. Hirsch reaches out and, with two fingers, lightly caresses her face over the glass frame.

He had been expecting the knock on the door.

"Come in."

Malena Mengarelli sauntered in slowly across the long expanse of the carpet. This time she wore a tight-fitting black dress that accentuated her tall, hourglass figure. The muted lighting sparked highlights off her red hair.

"Hello, Eldon."

"How are you, Malena? How's Tonino?"

"Tonino is fine."

"Won't you sit down?"

"No. You know why I'm here?"

Hirsch inhaled deeply and exhaled. "Yeah. I still owe a couple of payments on the loan."

The woman with the cold, steel brown eyes shook her head. "No, that's not why I'm here. You've been diligent in keeping up with those. Sort of." She opened her Prada Galleria handbag and removed a Colt police revolver. No frills. A swing-out cylinder, double-action, .38-caliber. She didn't point the gun at him, but simply held it flat, horizontally, in the palm of her right hand, as if she were making an offering of it to him.

"What's that for?" he asked.

"Oh, I'm just allowing you to admire it. You see, it's going to be the death of you. This very weapon will be the cause of your demise, Eldon, and I will have the pleasure of pushing the button, you might say. Tonino—and your good pal, Meyer—recognize that I have a certain penchant—and *talent*. You know that, right? Don't answer, it was a rhetorical question." She replaced the gun in her handbag. "Twenty million."

"What?"

"That's the figure that seems to be missing, Eldon. Twenty million dollars. That's a lot of money, even for Tonino and Meyer."

Eldon swallowed. "I swear, Malena, I don't know anything about—"

"Shut up, Eldon. Nothing points to you. You're right. If you've done anything with our money, you've covered your tracks well. We're going to keep digging, though. Tonino has employed some excellent auditors. It might take a couple more months, maybe three, for them to get to the bottom of it. In the meantime, just keep up with your loan payments. But if there's anything else on your conscience, you have a little more time to clear it. However, be aware that the consequences will come with no warning. It will happen when you least expect it. That's all. Good night." Then she turned and moved across the floor to the exit, her hips swaying.

Damn it to hell. Now it was imperative for Ultimate Pictures to churn out a couple of big hits as quickly as possible. He couldn't lose Blair Kendrick now. The entire studio, his career, and his *life* depended on personally earning twenty million dollars to replace what he had deftly and secretly lifted over time since 1939, when Ultimate Pictures was founded. He was a very wealthy man, but he didn't have that kind of money to dole out in one lump sum. He had squandered so much of it—gambling, women, partying, cars, travel, rare coins . . .

He'd been a fool.

And the only man Hirsch would have thought he could trust—Buddy Franco—was assuredly reporting back to Vegas about everything the studio head did.

At least Franco would take care of the dirty work that needed to be done regarding Blair, and none of that could wait any longer.

24

KARISSA

The destination was a movie memorabilia shop on Hollywood Boulevard, located in the touristy area where the Walk of Fame adorned the sidewalk, the kitsch "museums" dotted the storefronts, and throngs of visitors amassed to take selfies with street actors dressed as Iron Man or Darth Vader or Wonder Woman.

Vivian's Movie Store was one of many of its ilk. There, fans could buy film posters, glossy stills, celebrity autographs, toys, magazines, books, and other ephemera associated with Tinseltown. Karissa generally avoided these kinds of places, but she understood their value for tourists who wanted a tangible keepsake of the Hollywood dream.

She rode with Marcello in his sporty red Corvette and they parked at a meter. Being mid-day, the boulevard was crowded and lively. A motley crew of black teenage hip-hop dancers occupied an area of the sidewalk in front of an empty storefront next to the shop, music blasting at a high volume. A small crowd had gathered to watch.

Marcello approached the kid with the speaker hooked up to his phone, leaned in, and told him, "I'm digging the act and the music, man, but just some friendly advice . . . you might want to turn down the volume, or else the cops will come and make you leave." The young man just glared at Marcello, who shrugged and went with Karissa into the shop.

The shop smelled musty, as if stuff had been stored there for decades. It was a small, one-room space that was jam-packed with material. If Karissa had wanted to browse, she wouldn't have known where to start.

An obese woman who reeked of tobacco smoke sat in a chair behind a counter. She appeared to be in her late eighties, but Karissa figured she was younger than that. A lifetime of unhealthy food choices and smoking had taken a toll. If she was indeed the daughter of Buddy Franco, then she had to be around seventy.

"Hello," Karissa said to her.

The woman narrowed her eyes at them. "Could you please tell those hoodlums outside to take their damned music somewhere else?"

Karissa and Marcello looked at each other and subtly gave each other the nod.

Marcello replied, "Ma'am, seems to me they're just having fun, trying to make a buck. The music *is* loud, and I actually told them that before we came in."

"Well, it's driving me nuts. How can I help you?"

Karissa said, "Are you Vivian?"

"I am. Vivian's Movie Store, that's my name on the marquee. What are you looking for?"

"Was your father Buddy Franco?"

The woman frowned. "What is this?"

Marcello took over. "Ma'am, we're film producers. We're doing some research into the period when your father was an executive at Ultimate Pictures. You *are* Vivian Franco, aren't you?"

"I was, before I got married to Pete Modesky. You're making a movie about my father?"

"Well, not exactly," Karissa said, "but he might play a part in the story we're telling. I was wondering if we could ask you a few questions about him and his work at Ultimate Pictures."

"You're paying me?"

Again, the producers eyed each other. Karissa said, "Sure, we could pay you fifty dollars for a few minutes of your time."

"No, I mean for the rights to use him in your movie. You're going to pay me for that, right?"

Karissa answered, "We're just doing research right now, Mrs. Modesky. We don't even have a script yet."

The music outside started up again. The woman looked away and cursed under her breath. Then she said, "All right. Fifty dollars." She held out her hand. It was obvious that the movie memorabilia business wasn't doing so well.

Karissa gave her money from the cash she'd withdrawn after depositing the check from the rare coin store. Once Modesky folded the bills and stuck them in a drawer, she asked, "So, what can I tell you?"

"How long did your father work for Ultimate Pictures?" Karissa pulled a small notebook and a pen out of her purse.

"He started there in 1942, I think. He was still married to his first wife then. My mother was his second wife, whom he married in 1944. I was born in '45. Yeah, I'm old."

"Did he have other children?"

"He had a son from the first marriage, Michael, but he died in an industrial accident when he was twenty-three. I was the only child from the second marriage."

"May I ask what your mother's name was?"

"Ruth Dayton." She shook her head. "My mom eventually got a divorce and remarried after he flew the coop."

Karissa made notes as they spoke. "So, he worked for Ultimate Pictures from 1942 up to . . . 1949?"

"Yeah, that's when he left my mom and me. Just vanished

without a word. Then he shows up dead in 1975. We didn't think he was even alive before that."

"We're sorry about that. It's a mystery, isn't it?"

"Ain't no mystery. He left us, hid for years, then gets himself popped by the mafia."

Karissa nodded. "We're aware of that story."

"Story? It's no 'story.' It's fact. Some hit woman bitch walked into that diner and shot my father in cold blood."

Karissa and Marcello shared a glance. "A woman shot him?"

"Yeah. Probably Malena Mengarelli."

This was all new material for the producers. "Who?"

"You don't know about Malena Mengarelli?"

"Afraid not," Marcello said.

"She was a mobster moll in Las Vegas, but she was a god-damned killer. She's the one who killed that studio boss in '49, the same night my dad disappeared. Everything about my father's death points to a mob execution. Witnesses in the diner said it was a middle-aged woman, and that had to be Malena. It was her M.O. to a tee. There was no trial 'cause they never caught her! She vanished, probably fled to Mexico or somewhere."

"How old was he when that happened?" Karissa asked.

"Sixty-five."

Karissa decided to go in a different direction. "Do you know very much about Blair Kendrick?"

"Not really. Who does? She was on the 'scene' for only three years. She was at the studio when what's-his-name . . . Hirsch . . . was shot. The killers chased her out of the studio lot all the way up to Mulholland Drive, can you believe that? They got her there. But she was nuts, you know. My mother told me that Blair Kendrick had had an affair with a—with a colored man, and she got knocked up with his baby."

Karissa's jaw dropped. *A baby?* "How do you know that?"

Modesky laughed. "You didn't know that? My father shared

that bit of studio gossip with my mother. Yeah, that actress was having one of them interracial relationships in the *1940s*! It was revolting! Only a crazy woman would do that."

Marcello started to speak up, but Karissa jumped in ahead of him. "What happened to the baby? Do you know?"

"She got rid of it, or it died, or something. Not sure she even had it. She probably had an illegal abortion. It wasn't legal back then." The woman said this as if the act was the most disgusting thing she could imagine. "Besides, you couldn't have a mixed-race baby in those days. Well, you could, but you'd get in trouble. Just wasn't right. Still isn't."

On cue, the loud music outside cut off in the middle of a number. The woman's words were a sucker punch to Karissa's stomach. "Excuse me?"

Vivian Modesky narrowed her eyes at her. "Oh, I'm sorry, I guess you're one of those. Which one was black, your momma or your daddy?"

The nerve of this woman!

Karissa looked at her partner. "Come on, Marcello, let's get out of here."

"What, was it something I said?" the woman asked.

"Thank you for your time."

They started to go out the door.

"You're going to pay me to use my dad in the movie, aren't you?"

They slammed the door behind them. A couple of beat policemen were talking to the teenagers, so they scooted past them and walked to the car. When the couple was inside the Corvette, Marcello said, "Well, I hope that was worth fifty bucks."

"A sad, unhappy, miserable woman—that's the vibe I got. Did she get that racist attitude from her father? Well, it was worth it to find out about Blair and Hank's baby. Do you think it's true?"

Marcello shrugged. "How should I know? That's an interesting angle, though."

She put a hand on Marcello's arm as he started the car. "What if the studio made her have an abortion? They did that in those days, you know. Several famous stars were forced to have abortions. Or they got sent to draconian asylums for drug rehabilitation, or they were sent away—period—to get them out of the public eye. That's what those studio fixers did; they took care of 'problems' like that."

"Could be. And what about that hit woman? Malena Mengarelli?"

"The plot thickens!"

"Come on, let's get out of here. I feel like I need to take a shower after talking to that lady."

As Marcello drove away, Karissa reflected on the day's events. Was the fifty dollars well spent?

There was a baby.

What had happened to him or her?

That evening, in the house on Harvard Boulevard, Karissa wandered through the upstairs rooms, looking at the various boxes of stored items that once belonged to Blair Kendrick. She was still flummoxed by the place—its untouched treasures, its strange history. She decided to try her landlord again.

She located his number in her cell phone's contacts and dialed it. She was surprised when he answered.

"James Trundy."

"Oh, Mr. Trundy, this is Karissa Glover."

"Yes?"

"I'm so sorry to bother you this late in the evening."

"It's all right. What can I do for you? Everything okay at the house?"

"The house is wonderful. Listen—please, I need to know a little more about it. It's research for my work. Who owns it? You once told me that the house is owned by an investment firm or a trust firm. Can you please give me the name of the company?"

"Just a minute, please." He put down the phone. Karissa waited a few moments and then he returned. "The name of the company is Azules Oscuros S.A."

"It's Spanish?"

"Yes. I think so."

She had him spell it out for her, as she didn't speak the language.

"Where are they based?"

"It doesn't say."

"What doesn't say?"

"I'm looking at my pay stub. There is no address for Azules Oscuros S.A."

"And you get your paychecks in the mail?"

"Yes."

"Have you ever met anyone from the company? How did you get the job?"

Trundy paused and said, "Miss Glover, I'd rather not talk about this anymore. Do you like living in the house?"

"Oh, yes, I do!"

"Then, please, let it alone."

She was never going to get anywhere with him, she could see that. "One more question, Mr. Trundy, and I'll let you go. Why are all of Blair Kendrick's things still here? How come they were never moved out?"

"It's by order of the company that owns the house. Everything stays."

"And you never rented it out before?"

"Miss Glover, like I told you before, you're the first person to rent the house since Miss Kendrick died in 1949."

"You mean no one wanted to?"

"No, the company only recently opened it up for rental. You were the first person who was interested."

"Thank you, Mr. Trundy."

"Goodbye." He disconnected the call. Karissa swallowed hard, struggling with the mystery before her as a chill slithered down her spine.

THE MOVIE

25

THE MOVIE

"I reported to the set the next two days," the voice-over resumes as we see Blair driving her Oldsmobile to the lot. "The filming became more of a disaster. Everyone knew the picture was going to be a turkey. My costar expressed grave doubts to the director. As far as I know, he didn't put any of the blame on me."

Cut to the interior of Eldon Hirsch's office. Buddy Franco leans over the desk, nodding at the boss's instructions.

"As for the directive that Buddy Franco had given me, I ignored it. I had made up my mind that I was having the baby and giving up being a Hollywood star. Unfortunately, the studio brass had other ideas."

Blair sat in the dressing room after the day's work, smoking her sixth cigarette. She had removed her makeup and costume and was ready to go home. However, she had been hit with a wave of depression and couldn't get herself to move. The rumors were flying that the production was going to be canceled. After the assistant director had called a wrap for the day, Cagney had leaned in to her and said, "I'm sorry about this; I think it might be all my fault." Blair shook her head and said, "No, Jimmy, it's mine." He shrugged as if to say, *It is what it is*, and then added, "Whatever happens, it's been a pleasure."

Now it was after dark. Most of the crew had left and Blair felt completely alone in the building. *What are you going to do?* she asked herself. *Sleep here overnight?* Concluding that this was not a good idea, she stubbed out the butt and stood. She opened the jewelry box where she kept her treasured pearl necklace when she was working. She held it in her hands and thought briefly about her time in Chicago as a younger person. Her sixteenth birthday. A kind grandmother she barely knew. It was ironic that the necklace had become part of the "Blair Kendrick" persona in movieland publicity. She fastened it around her neck, grabbed her coat out of the closet, and prepared to depart.

When she opened the dressing room door, Buddy Franco stood in the hallway, as if waiting for her to come out.

"Buddy!"

"Blair."

"What are you doing here? I was . . . I was just about to go home."

"Come on, I'll walk you to your car."

"Uh, okay."

She turned out the lights and shut the door, and then she walked with him through the corridor and out the talent entrance to the parking lot. Blair's Oldsmobile sat where she'd left it that morning. A recent model black Cadillac sat next to hers. She had spotted vehicles like it at the studio and figured they were owned by Ultimate Pictures. In fact, she'd seen Franco driving one, or rather, *riding* in one with a studio employee at the wheel. There was a man in the driver's seat now. A couple of other cars were in the lot, dark and empty.

Along the way Franco had not said a word.

Blair approached the Oldsmobile and said, "Well, thank you for escorting me out, Buddy, I'll probably see you tomorrow."

He let her open the door and get inside. Then he leaned in, placed his right hand behind her neck, and, with his left hand, covered her mouth and nose with a cloth that smelled of strong chemicals. He pressed it hard into her face. Blair struggled and kicked and beat him with her fists. Her screams were muffled. The man was strong; she couldn't break free, and his grip on her head was so tight that she was afraid she'd snap her neck if she fought too hard. Then, she began to feel light-headed. The smell of the chemicals was overpowering. The sweet odor permeated her sinuses and she felt it in the back of her throat. Within seconds, it was as if the smell itself had become a living thing and was enveloping her brain, her eyesight, and her hearing. The world was fading away, and she could no longer raise her arms. She felt her body going limp, and darkness flooded her consciousness like black oil pouring into and clouding up a tank of water. Blair gasped for breath but there was no air to cling to. She was aware of her falling to the side on the car seat and then . . .

She wasn't sure if it was a dream or something that had really happened.

Her eyes were open, attempting to focus on what appeared to be a stuffed teddy bear that sat at a right angle to the horizon, the top of its head pointing to her right. She quickly realized that the left side of her face was flush against a pillow. She was lying on a bed, facing a wall, and the bear was sitting next to her.

What the hell?

She immediately attempted to sit up but was hit with a wave of nausea. The room spun like a crazy carnival ride. She groaned loudly and then turned over to face the rest of the room. Blair started to retch, and she fell the few feet down off the bed and onto the hard surface.

When she opened her eyes again, the teddy bear was still staring at her. It had a goofy smile, almost as if it were saying, *Ha ha, look at you, you fell off the bed!*

Blair groaned again as her vision focused a little sharper than before. She moved and lay on her back. The ceiling had a water stain that spread across the area to a crack that ran half the length of the room. She turned her head and saw the rest of the space. It was a bedroom—a child's bedroom, for there were other signs that a little boy had once occupied it. There was a map of the United States on the far wall. Next to it was a black and red pennant with the words, "Los Angeles Angels," a minor league team that Blair vaguely knew about. A small bookshelf contained children's books and a few volumes of encyclopedias. Next to it was a door to a closet. The foot of the bed pointed to a wall with a window that was covered by drapes decorated in baseballs and bats.

She was in someone's home.

It all came crashing back to her. Buddy Franco. The parking lot outside the soundstage. The cloth at her mouth. Blair swore she could still taste the chemicals. Chloroform? Whatever it was, it had knocked her right out.

The head of the bed butted against a wall. A few feet beyond the bed to her right was the door to the room. Blair summoned the strength to sit up, place her feet on the floor, and take a few deep breaths. She was barefoot but still wearing the clothes she'd had on at the studio—a pair of slacks and a blouse. Her brassiere was still intact underneath.

A nightstand next to the bed held an empty glass, a plastic pitcher of water, an ashtray, a pack of cigarettes, and a lighter. A small alarm clock indicated that the time was 2:14. The afternoon, obviously, as sunlight filtered in from the window.

Oh God . . .

She grabbed the pitcher and poured the glass full. Her mouth and throat were as dry as the desert and scratchy as hell. She gulped the delicious liquid, finished it, and poured another. She then reached for the cigarettes—and hesitated. Her craving could wait. She was desperate to use the toilet.

Blair managed to stand. She saw her flats sitting neatly on the floor next to the bookcase. Ignoring them for the moment, she took a few steps to the door and tried the knob. To her surprise and relief, it opened.

A hallway stretched to the left. Her room was at the end of the corridor. She spied an open door a little farther down, and her instincts told her it was the lavatory. She bolted to it, went inside, and shut the door.

The place was clean and usable. A mirror reflected a woman who had seen better days. She had no makeup on her face, exactly as she'd left it at the studio, and her blond hair was tangled in a mess. Her eyes were bloodshot. Her blouse was stained with what was probably her own vomit.

Strangely, her pearl necklace was still around her neck. They hadn't bothered to remove it.

First things first. She used the toilet and washed her face and hands with the soap and washcloth that were sitting on the counter along with a larger bath towel. There was also a bathtub with a shower, covered by a flimsy curtain on a rod.

She opened the door and moved farther down the hall to an open space, a den of sorts that contained a sofa, chairs, a coffee table, a radio console, and racks of magazines and books. A large picture window on one side revealed a beachscape, the ocean stretching far into the distance. Some steps on the far side of the room appeared to lead to a kitchen area. An archway to the left went off to the front of the house and a hall to another bedroom.

A large woman sat on the sofa with a newspaper in her hands. She wore a simple housedress and an apron. She might have been a maid, but somehow Blair didn't think so. The woman's face resembled a squashed apple. It was square, and she had tiny eyes buried in folds of flesh that were positioned above chubby cheeks and a small, puckered mouth. She looked to be in her forties.

The woman turned to address her. "Oh. I see you are awake. How do you feel?"

She spoke with a thick accent—German or Polish or Hungarian—something like that.

"Where am I? Who are you?" Blair's malevolence was potent in her tone.

The woman stood. While she was shorter than Blair, she was built like a wrestler.

"You must sit and relax. You can call me Leni."

"Where am I?"

"You are safe. We are by the sea. You will be cared for."

Blair entered the room. "What the hell are you talking about? I want to go home."

Leni shook her head. "That is impossible. You are our guest for a while." She nodded at Blair's stomach. "I am midwife. You will have your baby here."

"The hell I will!" Blair stormed to the archway and saw the front door at the end of the foyer. She ran to it and tried the knob, but it was locked. Blair turned back to see Leni standing behind her. "Let me out of here. Now."

"I am sorry, but you cannot leave. Sit down and relax, or I will be forced to make you do so."

Blair approached the woman, prepared to strike her if necessary. "*Let me out of here!*" She grabbed the woman by the shoulders and—

WHAM!

Leni had slugged her in the nose. Blair fell backward onto the tiled flooring. The stars spun in her vision and the pain was intense. Blood poured from her nostrils. She cried and choked and spat, writing uncontrollably.

The woman left her there. Blair was too stunned to get up. After a moment, Leni returned with a wet cloth. She squatted next to her and placed the rag on Blair's face.

"Hold this and press."

Had the woman broken her nose? It felt as though she had.

"Now listen to me," Leni said as tears ran down Blair's face. "This is your home for the next few months. You cannot leave. Your car is parked in the garage and I have the keys. You are miles from Los Angeles. You will be cared for. You will be fed and you will have many books and magazines to read, and we have a radio to hear the programs to keep you entertained. In time, if you show me that you can be trusted, we can go outside and walk on the beach for a short distance. Do not try to escape. I have orders to kill you if you do. During the war I worked in Germany in a place where pain and suffering was the order of the day. If you think the police will be looking for you, you are mistaken. The studio has put out a statement that you suffered a nervous breakdown and you are recuperating at a health facility away from the public eye. No one will miss you. Make the best of it and I will not have to hurt you again."

Oh God, oh God . . .

The wheels in Blair's head turned. What had happened in the parking lot? After he'd knocked her out, Buddy Franco must have driven her in her car to this place. She guessed that the driver of that Cadillac had followed along to bring him back to the studio, leaving Blair's car here along with her—out of sight. No one would miss her except, of course, for Hank. And Georgeann and Sheridan. Would they contact the police? If the studio had truly issued that statement, then the police would ignore them. Hank wouldn't believe it, though. He would know something was wrong. *He* would look for her. *He* would find her.

Blair opened her eyes, holding the wet cloth to her face. Leni stood over her, rubbing her fist.

"Get up," the woman commanded.

When Blair didn't move, Leni bent down and roughly pulled her up by the arm. Blair managed to stand on wobbly legs.

"I will take you to the bathroom to clean up. You might want to take a bath. You smell. I've already cleaned up after your vomit twice. Now come on."

26

KARISSA

Karissa and Marcello sat with their attorney in the Stormglove office conference room. Tony Davenport, an African American man in his fifties, listened to the journey they had undertaken thus far in attempting to bring Blair Kendrick's story to the screen. They outlined the alleged efforts by Ultimate Pictures to stop them, including being dropped from the festival, the threats from studio fixer Barry Doon, and the hacking and financial crimes against them.

"But you don't know for *certain that* it's Justin Hirsch who's behind it all," he said.

"Well, no," Karissa answered, "but, come on. Barry Doon works for Hirsch. That's a fact."

Davenport gave her a nod. "I'm willing to accept that. Before I tell you my thoughts, please explain why you think making a movie about this white woman from the forties is so important to you."

Marcello looked at Karissa and tilted his head, as if to say, *The ball's in your court.*

"Tony, as you know, I'm renting a house in West Adams

194

Heights, the old area they called Sugar Hill." Davenport nodded again. "The home belonged to Blair Kendrick. I've provided you copies of the lease and other documents about the owners, a company called Azules Oscuros S.A. It would be helpful to know who they are and where they're located. My landlord, James Trundy, either doesn't know anything or he's not talking."

"Spanish?" Davenport asked. "Azules Oscuros S.A.?"

"Yes."

"I speak Spanish. It means 'dark blues,' and the S.A. part stands for *Sociedad Anonima*, or an 'anonymous partnership.'"

"Dark blue, as in the color?"

"Literally, yes, only plural. Like a bunch of dark blues."

Karissa looked at Marcello, and he shrugged. "Not sure that makes much sense," she said. "Anyway, the more Marcello and I have uncovered about this woman's story, the more I see parallels with the racism and sexism in Hollywood today."

"So?" Davenport asked. "That doesn't answer my question."

"I see Blair as an antihero. She's played femmes fatales, which are typically 'bad girl' characters, but look at the position she was in. She was in love with a black man, had a relationship with him that was public, and *maybe* they had a baby together. He disappears, is maybe murdered. Eldon Hirsch is killed, and allegedly Blair was there when it happened. She ends up burned to death up in the hills on Mulholland Drive. Throw in the mystery of the rare coins that supposedly belonged to Hirsch and the involvement of the mob, and it gets more complicated. If these are facts, then the movie could be a powerful statement. Even if what I just described isn't the truth, the story has drama and mystery. It's a modern film noir. It could be a fascinating crime drama."

"But who's the hero? If Blair dies, who saves the day in the end?"

Karissa held out her hands. "I don't *know* yet!"

Davenport looked at Marcello. "You agree this is a viable project?"

Marcello grudgingly nodded. "At first, I was skeptical, but I've come around. I'm more concerned about why we're being targeted, and whether you can do something about it. Can you, I don't know, send a 'cease and desist' letter to Justin Hirsch and his bulldog? We're not trampling on anyone's rights here. This pattern of intimidation needs to stop."

Karissa added, "I want to hire a screenwriter and get started on this. But if Ultimate Pictures continues to harass us, that's going to be difficult. I've already started a rough draft, just something that defines the structure of the thing. But I still think we need a top-notch screenwriter."

Davenport leaned back in his chair. "Well, I hate to break this to you, but I've learned that Ultimate Pictures is developing their own story about Blair Kendrick and Eldon Hirsch."

Karissa and Blair simultaneously reacted. *"What?"*

"They've registered a treatment with the Writers Guild. I have a copy of the registration here." He handed them each a sheet of paper from his briefcase.

The producers scanned the one-page document. "Oh, for crying out loud," Marcello said. "This is practically a recap of a Wikipedia article. It's just a synopsis of what we all already know about the murders."

"Exactly. They may not even be making a movie about it at all. It's possible they're just trying to prevent you from 'copying' their so-called treatment."

"This is bullshit," Karissa said.

They heard the jingling bell of the front door opening. Marcello stuck his head out of the conference room door. "Oh, hey, Butch. Come on in."

The leader of the Butch Johnson Hive entered the room with a cardboard box in his hands. "Hey, man. Hey, Karissa."

Karissa introduced him to Davenport, and the men shook hands. "You brought Ray's stuff?" she asked Butch as he set the box on the table.

"Yeah, this is what I told you Ray asked me to hold on to for him," Butch said. "I don't think there's much here of interest. Some old photos and some sheet music."

"Let me see!" Karissa pulled the box to her.

Davenport stood and started packing up his notepad and pen. "I think I better get back to my office. I'll draft a letter to Ultimate Pictures and let you see it. I wouldn't worry too much about the Writers Guild thing. We can get around that."

"There is one thing we could do, you know," Marcello said.

"What's that?"

"Go public. Put it on our Facebook page. Tweet it. Tell the world we're being harassed. Get this Barry Doon character on video the next time we see him."

Karissa looked up. "Really?"

"That could backfire," Davenport warned. "The Hollywood community could very well ostracize you for attacking a studio. We can't prove the attacks on *you* are from them since it's just speculation; whereas if you do it to Justin Hirsch in public then there's no question that you're attacking *him*."

Marcello frowned. "Yeah, you're right."

Davenport smiled and shook everyone's hands. "Try not to stress. We'll get through this. Let me know if anything else happens. In the meantime, I'll get to work and try to find out if there really is a 'contract' out on you. Nice to meet you, Butch."

When Davenport was gone, Karissa started going through the box. As Butch had said, there were newspaper clippings, old photographs, and some sheets of staff paper on which music notes were written. Some of the photos were duplicates of ones she had seen in Blair's collection.

The most recent clipping was dated February 1949. It was an

ad for the Downbeat Club from the *California Eagle*. Appearing on a Friday night—Hank Marley and His Band.

"This must have been right before he disappeared," Karissa said, showing the others. She looked at Butch. "I understand you know Ray's son, Gregory?"

"Only by sight. He was at the funeral, you know."

"Right, and we tried to talk to him. He acted very strange."

"He's a strange dude," Butch said. "As long as I knew Ray, Gregory never lived in LA."

"Where does he live?" Marcello asked.

"I don't know. Somewhere north of LA, I think. I told Marcello I used to have a phone number for him, but it's out of service."

"Does he have anything to do with nuts? Farming nuts, that is," Karissa prodded.

Butch frowned. "Something like that. He owns an orchard or farm or something." He held out his hands. "Sorry, I don't know much. Ray and I were friends, but he never talked much about his family. I don't think I *ever* had a conversation with Gregory. I shook his hand and gave him my condolences at the funeral. I'm not sure he knew who I was."

"Very strange," Karissa muttered. She continued to look through the photos in the box. "Seen that one. Got that one. Oh, that's a nice one. Seen that one." She stopped and stared at one picture in her hand. "Hey. Marcello, look at this."

It was a worn, black-and-white snapshot of a young black woman in front of a small ranch house. She wore a simple dress and her textured hair was straightened, as was the style for African Americans in the thirties and forties.

He studied the picture. "Yeah? Who is she?"

"Doesn't she look familiar?"

His eyes widened. "The pianist at the funeral! With the white hair! Only young!"

"That's her. I'm sure of it. She spoke to his son and daughter-in-law at the funeral. Ray Webster certainly knew her when he was alive. And you know something else?"

"What?"

"I swear I've seen that house before. It's in my *neighborhood*, Marcello."

"Your neighborhood has big houses. This isn't a big house."

"No, there are small houses, too." She slapped her hand on the table. "Damn, I know I've seen it before." She pointed to the visible edge of the structure next to it in the photo. "This here is a big mansion next door to it. On the other side is another big place. But *this* one, it's a teeny little old house stuck in-between the two big ones. It's cute, but it looks like it's out of place when you see it. I remember driving by and noticing it. I thought to myself, *Who lives in there? A hobbit?* It stood out because it's so small. Damn, where did I see it?"

Marcello said, "Knowing you, Karissa, you'll think of it in the middle of doing something else. But you can't believe that woman still lives in that same house now?"

"Why not? You saw her at the funeral. She has to live somewhere. It's *possible*."

Marcello handed the photo back to her. "I guess we better find it, then."

27

THE MOVIE

The film rolls on. We see a nighttime exterior shot of the Downbeat Club on Central Avenue, the sidewalk busy with pedestrians dressed in their best going-out clothes. The photography accentuates the contrast between the bright spots of light of the street and the cars moving up and down the congested road that is the center of black nightlife in Los Angeles 1949, and the dark of nearly everyone's skin.

The camera zooms in slowly on a placard that reads: TONIGHT! HANK MARLEY AND HIS BAND!

Lively bebop jazz music ramps up on the soundtrack and we move inside . . .

The club was packed. A blanket of cigarette smoke hovered over the tables as the patrons danced in their seats. Cocktail waitresses moved in between arms and legs, doing their best to keep up with the demands for drinks. Most of the clientele had saved their meager dollars earned during the week for the obligatory weekend night out at one of the swinging clubs that catered to them. While occasional white jazz enthusiasts supported these clubs, they were, for once, the minority here. Central Avenue was known as Little Harlem, only on the West Coast, where one was proud to be referred to as a "Negro," and the less savory epithet derived from that word was rarely heard.

The Downbeat Club was one of the hot spots of the scene, and to be able to perform there was a privilege. Hank Marley took the responsibility seriously, but he also knew that the audience was there for a good time. He led his band through many popular numbers made famous by Duke Ellington, Louis Armstrong, Dizzy Gillespie, Charlie Parker, Cab Calloway, Earl Hines, and Lester Young, and he made sure he added a joyful spin to the arrangements.

Hank's fingers danced on the piano keyboard while Ray Webster plucked the strings of the upright bass, deftly keeping time with Jim, the drummer. The brass and woodwind section—Bobop on trombone, Billy on trumpet, Charlie on clarinet, and Francis on tenor saxophone—filled out the sound as if they were a hundred-piece orchestra.

The set had started at ten o'clock, and now it was nearing midnight, about time to wind down. As was his custom, Hank launched into the opening chords for one of the band's signature pieces.

"Folks, we now come to the end of this glorious evening," he said into the microphone—to which the audience shouted protests—"aw, thank you kindly, ladies and gents, you know if we could stay here all night playing for you, we would. Anyway, as we always do at the end of our shows, we like to bring things down to a nice little piece of dreamland. Each of us in the band would like to dedicate this number to our respective ladies, those bewitching creatures who we love and who love us."

The band broke into "Blues in the Dark" as the audience applauded. After a moment, they quieted down and listened to the melancholic, soulful lyrics.

As he sang, Hank heard someone in the back of the room say, a little too loudly, "Aw, he's singing about that *white* woman . . ."

This was followed by several "shh's" and "hush nows," but Hank ignored it all. He didn't care what they thought. The emotion he put into the performance was effortless, as his heart was heavy.

For he had no idea what had happened to Blair. She was missing, and he knew that the excuse from her studio—that she was "convalescing" at a secret resort—was bullshit.

Hank walked to the bus stop after saying good night to the rest of the band members. They had gone across the street to the Dunbar, where there were women to meet and drinks to consume. They wanted to spend a few more hours enjoying the night that, by their design, belonged to them. The pay for the gig often didn't go far, but these simple pleasures had a priority over the daylight realities of living in what was predominantly a white world.

Hank hadn't felt like partying. Blair's absence deeply concerned him, and he wasn't sure what to do about it. As he didn't own a car—he depended on buses and taxis to get around—it was difficult for him to do any investigating into her disappearance. She'd been missing for a week. He knew Blair would have said something to him if she'd really gone to a health clinic. That story was nonsense.

Something bad had happened to her.

He had mentioned it to a patrolman he was friendly with—the Los Angeles Police Department had a history of employing Negroes on the force since the 1880s—but the lawman was unable to find out anything except the studio's standard line. In Hollywood, that was the final word unless there was real evidence of foul play.

Hank had been to Blair's house and spoken to Sheridan and Georgeann. The housekeepers were just as mystified and frightened as he. The fact was that one morning Blair had gone to the studio for work, and she hadn't come home since. Her car was unaccounted for, too.

Could the disappearance have something to do with her plans to leave show business? Had she spoken to Hirsch, that awful studio head, and told him what she planned to do? Blair hadn't said she was going to do so; she had simply informed Hank that she wanted to wait until her latest picture finished shooting.

Hank also feared for the life inside Blair's womb. His baby was in trouble. Mother and child—vanished. His overactive imagination created all sorts of horrendous scenarios that replayed in his mind. Had she been harmed? Had she been *killed*? After what Buddy Franco and his henchmen had done to *him* last year, Hank believed anything was possible.

The bus was late. Hank looked at his watch and thought about trying to flag down a taxi. He'd been paid for the gig, but after splitting the money seven ways, what he had in his pocket would last only a few days.

This music business is a racket, he thought. But it was all he knew. He had loved the piano ever since his grandfather taught him how to play "Chopsticks" on an old honkytonk when Hank was six years old. Then, a white woman in St. Louis had given a couple years' worth of lessons to him and his sister, Regina, as payment for their mother cleaning the teacher's house. Hank was forever grateful to his mother for doing that extra work just so her children could learn to play the piano.

From that point on, Hank had taught himself the rest. He listened to all the greats as he grew up—Scott Joplin, Fats Waller, Jelly Roll Morton—and slowly developed his own style of playing. By the time he had left home and settled in Southern

California, he could hold his own against the powerhouses who were staples of the black jazz scene.

That didn't mean it was easy to make a living.

He thought about Regina and her current gig at the First A.M.E. Church, playing piano for the choir. Perhaps he should have grabbed that steady engagement when it had been offered to him. Turning it down had been a mistake. He'd wanted to concentrate on jazz and blues, not church music. Regina, meanwhile, was doing fine. He resolved to make attempts to see her more often. It was a shame that she had met Blair only once.

A pair of headlights heading his way along Central interrupted his thoughts. They weren't the only ones on the road at that time of night by any means, but the car was moving slowly, as if it were about to pull over to the curb and stop. Ever since the incident outside the Dunbar a half-year earlier, Hank found that such sights made him nervous. He dug into his pocket and grabbed his pack of Chesterfields, tapped out a cigarette, and put it in his mouth. Before he could light it, the car that was approaching *did* stop.

It was a black Cadillac, just like the one he had encountered before.

Hank dropped the pack on the pavement when he saw Buddy Franco emerge from the back seat, followed by the same two white thugs who had beaten him up before.

He considered running, but it was too late.

The first henchman pointed a handgun at him.

"Get in the car," Franco said.

The cigarette fell out of his mouth. Hank raised his hands halfway. "What is this?" he asked.

"We're going for a ride." The other man moved behind Hank and prodded him in the lower back with another pistol.

"What if I don't?" Hank asked.

Franco gritted his teeth. "Then we'll shoot you, right here in the street. No one will care."

Hank Marley took a deep breath and then nodded. He got in the back seat of the Cadillac.

28

KARISSA

Karissa arrived at the house on Harvard Boulevard at dusk and pulled into the garage. It had been a productive day, but still a frustrating one. She and Marcello still didn't seem any closer to resolving what direction they should take. Part of her wanted to drop the idea of doing a film about Blair Kendrick because it seemed so fraught with problems, not to mention the threats to her career and personal life. On the other hand, she was determined to forge ahead and stand up to the bullies who thought they could dictate what her company could make or not. Some intangible force was pushing her toward uncovering Blair's story and the truth about what had happened to her and Hank Marley.

She entered her home, put her purse on the kitchen counter, and walked through to the foyer. The mail had already been dropped on the floor through the slot. Still, she had gotten into the habit of peering out the door to check the front of the house. Opening the front door, she stepped onto the porch, and her eyes caught a splash of color over by the swing.

A vase containing a bouquet of flowers sat on the seat.

"What in the world?" she said aloud.

She walked to the swing and saw a little white envelope addressed to "Blair" attached to the vase with tape. The flowers were peonies, carnations, and roses. Very pretty.

If this is from Willy, trying to get in good graces with me again . . .

Karissa took the envelope in hand and opened it. She removed the card and discovered that nothing was written on it. The front and inside were blank.

"What the—?"

The bullet struck the front of the house before she heard the retort of the gunshot in the street. It took a full second or two to realize what had just occurred. By then, another round thudded into the front door as she instinctively jumped backward and leaped to the floor of the stucco porch. The scream came next as she rolled.

Panicking, Karissa started to crawl to the door, but stopped when she saw that would break what cover she had. Instead, she slithered closer to the protection of the short wall that ran along the edge of the porch. Could a bullet go through the stucco? It wasn't very thick.

She reached for her phone—but gasped when she remembered that she'd left her purse in the house. She was helpless.

The sound of a car revving its engine broke through her thoughts. Wheels screeched on the road and the automobile took off. Karissa raised her head above the wall and saw a black sedan speeding away. It had happened too quickly for her to get a good look at it.

Breathing heavily, she got back on her feet, gazed into the yard and street, and figured she was safe. Her heart was pounding in her chest like a drum. Her legs shook as she struggled to keep from collapsing.

Was it Barry Doon's car? The BMW?

She couldn't swear to it.

Karissa bolted for the front door and went inside, leaving the flowers on the porch. She ran back to the kitchen, found the phone in her purse, and dialed 911.

The police had come and taken her statement. A forensics team arrived a little later and pulled the two rounds out of the front of the house, bagging them as evidence. Now there were two ugly holes, one in the exterior wall and another in the door. The cops had also taken the vase of flowers and the card. Karissa assumed they'd check for fingerprints.

Curious neighbors had come out of their houses to investigate why police cars were congregated in front of the mansion. *Nothing to see here, folks, move along . . . !* She was embarrassed and mortified that she would be the subject of gossip and mistrust in the neighborhood. Whatever goodwill she had hoped to establish with her neighbors after moving in was now dashed.

A plainclothes officer who introduced himself as Detective Madison interviewed her after he arrived on the scene a couple of hours after the incident. He seemed weary and disinterested, as if a drive-by shooting was nothing new. Karissa told him her suspicions.

"Let me get this straight," he said. "You think this was done by an executive at Ultimate Pictures in an attempt at stopping you from making a movie?"

"I know it sounds incredible, but, yeah, that's what I think."

He looked at his notes. "And you think the shooter's name is . . . Barry Doon?"

"That's right."

"You sure about that?"

"No, I'm not sure at all. I didn't see him. I just know that he's verbally threatened me and my business partner, and we've caught him stalking us."

"He said he was going to kill you?"

She shook her head. "No, he didn't say that exactly. He just—"

"How did he threaten you?"

Karissa was tired and annoyed with the man's line of questioning. "It was more like intimidation. He told me not to continue my research."

"Or else what?"

"Or else . . . he didn't say. It was an implied threat."

The man looked skeptical. "Uh huh." He wrote something down and reread his notes. "These flowers that were delivered, you don't know who sent them?"

"No."

"Ex-boyfriend? Ex-husband?"

"Like I told the other officers, I'm in the process of a divorce. My ex-husband is an actor, Willy Puma."

"Willy Puma? The guy from *Meat Grinder*?"

"That's him."

"Huh. I like those movies." He wrote it down. "You think he might have done this?"

"Honestly? No."

"Well, we'll see if he has an alibi. You have his contact information?"

She gave him Willy's address and phone number. "Look, Detective, those flowers were placed on the swing so I would be forced to walk over and stand in a spot that made me a target. Whoever had the gun was waiting for me to do that."

"Good thing he missed," the man said.

Duh. Karissa wanted to shake him.

The detective eyed the distance between the bullet holes and where she had been standing. "If you ask me, whoever it was is a lousy shot. Or he intentionally missed you."

It was nearly eleven o'clock when Detective Madison finally gave her his card, gathered his things, and departed, saying, "If you have any more trouble, don't hesitate to call."

Oh, thanks, that's very helpful.

When she was alone in the house, Karissa texted Marcello and asked him to call her if he was still up. It seemed he wasn't.

She was starving but was too exhausted and wired to do anything elaborate for a late dinner. Instead, she had a bowl of cereal and four glasses of wine.

It was pathetic.

When she was finished, Karissa sat in Blair Kendrick's easy chair near the grand piano in the parlor. Photos of the movie star were all around. The actress in them stared at her, all smiles and bright eyes.

Halfway drunk, she asked aloud, "Is it worth my life to make a movie about you? Why should I? What happened to you and Hank Marley? What happened in that studio office when Eldon Hirsch was killed? Did you really have a baby? Who the fuck *were* you?"

Karissa wondered if the now-familiar ghosts lingering in the expansive ballroom of the old house would answer her questions, but the room around her remained silent.

29

THE MOVIE

The music on the soundtrack shifts into a plaintive melody that evokes a darker mood. The scene is a daytime exterior shot of a shoreline, with the Pacific Ocean stretching far to the horizon. The camera moves in to a lone house set on a cliff above the beach. An unpaved drive leads to it from the main road above. A tall wooden staircase covers the rocky bluff and connects the house's sun deck to the sand below, a distance of approximately forty yards.

We slowly zoom in on the picture window that faces the sea. A very pregnant Blair stands behind it, looking out, her hands over her swollen belly.

"The days, the weeks, and the months passed slowly," *the voice-over tells us.* "I was a prisoner in the house. The horrid woman, Leni, acted as maid, cook, and jail guard. She was very cruel at times, punishing me for the slightest infractions by taking away privileges such as listening to the radio or not allowing a walk outside.

"When I was 'good,' I wasn't mistreated. The food was fine, but that really didn't matter. I wanted to go home. I craved getting out of that house."

211

Cut to a shot of Blair and Leni strolling along shoreline, the tide lazily lapping at their bare feet. The camera catches a glimpse of the pistol tucked in the waist of Leni's pants.

"*Every now and then, Leni escorted me down those rickety steps to the beach, where we would walk along the shore. Leni always warned me not to speak to anyone if we happened to come across another beachcomber, but we never saw a single soul. From what I could gather during the conversations we had, the house was located near Malibu, far from the metropolis of Hollywood. I learned over time that it belonged to Eldon Hirsch himself. A getaway beach property that he hadn't used in years. My jail cell was the room his own son had used when the Hirsch family went to the beach together—once upon a time.*

"*Even though my Oldsmobile was parked in the garage, hidden from sight, I couldn't get to the key, which Leni kept on a ring with all the other house keys. The thought of escape was futile.*"

Blair got up from the bed in her room, put on the house slippers that had been provided for her, dressed in the tattered bathrobe, and opened the door. Leni had given her free rein of most of the house now. As it was April and she was seven months pregnant, trips to the bathroom required easy access. For the first six weeks, Leni had kept her locked in the room at night, but after a couple of accidents, the woman relented. Nevertheless, Blair was prevented from exploring anywhere else but the bathroom, den, and kitchen. The doors to the deck, Leni's bedroom, and the garage were locked. The front door was locked and barred. So were all the windows. The only exception was the den's picture window, which could slide open to the deck. Blair would have to strike the pane with something hard, like a chair or a big rock, to break it.

At night, Leni fastened a built-in gate at the end of the hallway to keep Blair confined to her bedroom, the hall, and the bathroom. While Leni slept, there would be no trips to the den or kitchen. Furthermore, there were no utensils in the kitchen that could possibly be used as weapons. No knives, forks, or pans large enough to be bludgeoning instruments. Leni kept them under lock and key, producing them only at mealtimes. There was no telephone in sight.

Blair thought that she might as well have had a ball and chain attached to her ankle.

The pregnancy seemed to be going all right, though. She had seen no doctors since her abduction. Blair could only assume that the baby was healthy. The bigger question was—what was going to happen to the child after it was born?

She often wondered if it would be a boy or a girl. Would the baby's skin coloring favor Hank's or hers? Probably a mixture of both, a lighter shade of dark than its father's shade. Sometimes Blair lay awake at night fantasizing about a life with Hank and the baby, living somewhere free of prejudice and hate, a nonexistent paradise where Hank could make plenty of money playing music and she could continue to act in pictures.

Then her thoughts would always go to Hank. Was he all right? Was he working to find her? Blair had asked Leni about him at one point, but either she didn't know or she refused to say anything. Leni frankly didn't seem to know much at all about what was happening outside the house. She never left. Food and supplies were brought to the place by an unseen delivery person. Blair knew it was a man, for she'd heard his voice—probably one of Buddy Franco's goons or maybe even a studio runner, some poor kid who had simply been told to deliver groceries to the house, unaware that a prisoner was being kept inside.

Sometimes, when the stillness of the day got to both women, there were attempts at conversations. They often didn't go well.

"Do you work for Buddy Franco or for Eldon Hirsch?" Blair once asked.

"That is not your concern," Leni answered with her nose in the air. "Shall I make coffee for us?"

"You said you're from Germany. Were you a Nazi?"

Leni only gave her a chilling smile.

"How did you get to this country? If you worked in one of those camps, like you say, why aren't you in prison? Didn't they arrest all the Nazi guards?"

The woman simply shook her head and tsk-tsked. She then delivered a short speech in her heavy accent. "You may be a beautiful and popular Hollywood actress, but you understand very little about the world. Money and knowing the right people—that's what it takes, *ja*?" She shrugged and made a little wave with her hand. "I got to this country and found my way to my current employers through a relative. Now, I am grateful for a job I can do, here by the sea, where no one knows me or how to find me."

Blair found it all so incredibly bizarre and downright . . . nasty. The woman could have been a stereotypical antagonist in one of the films noir in which Blair starred, right out of central casting.

Franco had visited once. Two weeks after she'd been kidnapped, he showed up at the place to outline the situation. He explained that she was being kept out of the public eye "for her own good." The studio had put out a statement that she was suffering from mental and physical exhaustion—what people called a "nervous breakdown"—and that she was being cared for in a resort facility away from the attention of Hollywood press. Franco told her that if she "behaved," then the baby would be taken to a reputable adoption agency and would be given a loving home. However, if she did not cooperate—the child would not live to see its second day.

Blair begged him to give her news about Hank. Franco said, "The Negro is not my concern, nor should he be yours."

She formed a wad of saliva in her mouth and spit in his face.

Franco glared at her, wiped himself with a handkerchief, and got up to leave. He told Leni, "For that, make sure she gets no radio for a week."

The radio had been a lifesaver of sorts. Aside from the few magazines and books that didn't interest her much, the set provided entertainment that passed the time. The broadcasts of dramas, comedies, variety shows, and music were something Blair looked forward to every day. For that alone, she had acquiesced and resolved to "behave."

Blair could only hope for a miracle to liberate her from this hell.

In clichéd 1940s style, the motion picture once again focuses on a close-up of a paper calendar. The month of April 1949 is ripped away, followed quickly by May, and then we settle on June. Cross-fade to Blair in bed, writhing in pain. Leni is acting as midwife.

"My belly grew bigger and bigger, and I became more frustrated and angrier. All the while I kept my eyes and ears open for any kind of possible escape route. But then, in mid-June, right on time, my water broke one morning and the contractions began. By the middle of the afternoon I was in the throes of labor, and Leni had to fulfill one of her primary functions for me and my baby."

An old-fashioned, wordless montage, accompanied by dramatic, swirling orchestral music, depicts a succession of images. Blair is in bed, her face twisted in agony. Sweat pours off her skin. Leni carries a pot of hot water into the bedroom. A clock reads 3:05. Leni offers a glass of water to the patient, and Blair strikes it away—the glass smashes on the floor. Leni yells at Blair. Blair screams. The clock now reads 4:35. The sweat has soiled the white sheets on the bed. Blair's hands clutch towels. A close-up of Blair's wide eyes exhibits fear and pain. Leni mouths orders to push, but not kindly. The clock reads 5:20. Now Blair is bucking and writhing. Leni squats on the bed between Blair's legs and shouts commands. The clock reads 6:05.

Fade to black.

The ordeal was over. The child, a girl, was born at 7:36 p.m. She had skin that was a light olive-brown, dark eyes, and jet-black, fuzzy hair that barely covered her little head.

Blair was exhausted, weak, and sore. Leni removed the baby from the bedroom soon after she'd arrived, saying that the child would be cleaned and wrapped in warm blankets. Blair had to lie in the wet, bloody bed for another hour before Leni returned to help her out so that the sheets could be changed. She also brought something for the new mother to eat.

There was still no sight of the baby. Anguished, Blair begged Leni to allow her to see her daughter. The woman must have had some sort of remaining maternal empathy in her soul, for she acquiesced and brought the baby back into the room. Blair held the little thing in her arms and began to nurse. It was all new to Blair. Nothing in her experience had prepared her for becoming a mother, but some things in life happened naturally. This seemed to be one of them.

Suzanne.

That's what Blair had decided to name her. There was no reason for it. She just liked the sound of it.

She held the little miracle as tears of wonder filled her eyes. There were also tears of anger. Blair's daughter had been born in captivity, and for that she could never forgive Eldon Hirsch, Buddy Franco, and the woman called Leni.

Blair spent the first night together with her daughter. They slept soundly and peacefully, although the baby woke twice, wanting more nourishment. In the morning, Leni came back into the room and took the child away to change her. Luckily, it seemed the midwife had diapers on hand.

But when Blair asked Leni when she could have Suzanne back, the woman replied, "Best not to become attached or name her. She will be adopted. You will never see her again."

With a cry, Blair attempted to get out of bed, but she was too weak to fight with the woman. Leni forced her back, left the room, and locked the door. For an hour, Blair was inconsolable. She beat on the walls, screamed for Suzanne, shouted obscenities, and eventually crumpled into a quivering mess of sweat and tears.

She thought she heard a car leave the house. Forcing herself to stand, Blair went out into the hall—but Leni had put the gate up. The woman was gone. Where was her baby? Had Leni taken Suzanne someplace? Blair called out in despair, but there was no one to answer her. Unable to act, she went back to her bedroom, cried some more, and eventually fell asleep.

That afternoon, before even a day had passed, Blair heard a car outside. Had Leni returned? Would she see Suzanne again?

Voices. A man and a woman. Leni and . . .

No. Buddy Franco.

Blair shrunk back into the bed, cradling her legs and clutching the teddy bear that she had unwittingly been using as a surrogate child over the last several hours.

The door opened and Franco came into her room.

"How are you doing, Blair?"

"Go to hell."

He didn't react. Instead, he sat on the edge of the bed and attempted to adopt a physician's bedside manner.

"Blair, I'm sorry to have to tell you this. This morning, Leni noticed that your child was having trouble breathing. She got word to me. I was prepared to take the baby to a pediatrician, but . . . it happened too quickly. There was nothing that could have been done, even if an ambulance had been waiting here at the house."

Blair stared at him with watery eyes. "Wha—what are you saying?" she asked hoarsely, fearful but somehow already knowing what he was going to tell her.

"The baby is dead, Blair. She died. I'm sorry."

The rage rose slowly, developing first as a rumble in her chest. Then the heavy breathing picked up, and then Blair screamed. "No! I don't believe you! Where is she? Bring me my baby! Bring her to me!"

Leni rushed in to help Franco subdue her. They held her down on the bed as she battled them with what little strength she had. It took a full six minutes of thrashing and wailing before Blair's energy finally gave out. She was completely spent.

Franco stood. "I'll make the arrangements to see that the baby gets a proper burial. Look on the bright side, Blair. You'll be here another week or two. You'll recover from the childbirth and get strong again. And then . . . you can leave. You can go back to work. And we can put this unpleasant business behind us."

She barely opened her eyes to look at him. "Bright side?" she whispered through clenched teeth. "You're a goddamned monster."

Franco shook his head as if to say, *What's the use?* Then he turned and left the room with Leni, locking the door behind them.

30

KARISSA

The next morning, despite the lack of sleep, Karissa drove to Vernon Healthcare Center again. After parking and entering the building, she approached the receptionist and asked if she could speak to Sylvia, the nurse they had dealt with on their first visit to see Ray Webster. Karissa lingered in the waiting room until Sylvia appeared in the open doorway to the facility.

"Yes? You wanted to see me?"

"Oh, hi, Sylvia. Do you remember me? I came here with my business partner a little over a week ago to see Ray Webster."

She nodded. "Yes, I do."

"Could I speak with you privately? I'll just take a minute of your time."

"Come on back."

When they were at the nurse's station, Sylvia asked what she could do for her.

"I really need to contact Mr. Webster's son, Gregory. I'd left my name and number the last time, and you'd said you would try to get ahold of Gregory and ask him to call me. Were you successful?"

219

Sylvia shook her head. "No, ma'am, I wasn't. I did try and phone Mr. Webster—Gregory, that is—and the number was no longer in service. I meant to call you right then, but there was an emergency with a patient and then, well, I had to do something else and it slipped my mind. We're always very busy here. I'm sorry."

"That's all right. Do you know where Gregory lives? I understand he had to drive a good distance to visit his father."

"I seem to remember he lives up north somewhere. The only contact information we had for him was the phone number. He didn't have financial responsibility for his father's care. Medicaid handled all that."

"Any idea where 'up north?'"

She pursed her lips. "Hm. When I asked him where he lived, I'm pretty sure he mentioned the Bakersfield area."

Karissa thought about that. Not tremendously helpful, but it was something. "Okay. Thanks."

She arrived for her lunch date with Marcello at Musso & Frank Grill on Hollywood Boulevard, one of the oldest landmarks that was still in business. It had first opened in 1919 and was a favored eatery among Tinseltown's elite for decades until it became more of a tourist attraction. Still, one never knew when a celebrity would pop in for a meal, as they often did. Karissa and Marcello liked the atmosphere of the place, the brown-and-maroon color scheme, and the first-class white tablecloth and red-jacket service.

Besides, Marcello had learned that Justin Hirsch ate there at least once a week, often a Tuesday, and often alone.

Today was Tuesday. Would they get lucky?

They were shown to a booth, and Marcello immediately asked for a beer, while Karissa requested just water. Not one to waste any time, Marcello promptly ordered the daily special—corned beef and cabbage. Karissa went for the salmon fillet. When the waiter departed, she then told Marcello about the previous evening's events on her porch—and how it was a fluke that she was still alive and now sitting across from him and telling him the story. In the middle of it, the beer arrived and Marcello took a long swig. When she was done, he let out a loud breath and said, "My God, Karissa, I'm sorry. Jesus. Are you all right?"

"Yeah. Just didn't sleep much. I'll probably go home after lunch, if that's okay with you."

"Hey, I'm not the boss. You can do whatever you want, my dear."

"Gee, thanks. Can I ask for a three-week vacation, too?"

The waiter delivered the food and the couple began to eat, although Marcello slowly picked at his food.

"I thought you were hungry," Karissa said.

"I was until you told me what happened. Jesus, Karissa, this is serious. Are we playing with our lives here?"

Karissa snorted and said with sarcasm, "Hey, when we made the decision to come and work in Hollywood, our lives went out the window!"

"I'm not joking! They better not come to *my* house and start shooting. I've got a wife and kids. I'll go Jason Bourne on them if they try it."

"Yeah, well, they might go *American Sniper* on you before you even know they're there. Try not to worry. To tell you the truth, the more I thought about it during my sleepless night, the more I'm sure the shooter missed me on purpose. I think he was just trying to scare me. It's made me more determ—" She inhaled sharply, grabbed him by wrist, and whispered. "He's here. He just walked in the door."

"Hirsch?"

"Uh huh."

She knew the man who entered the restaurant was eighty years old, but he appeared to be younger. He was in excellent shape, obviously someone who remained physically active. His face was weathered and tan. He had white hair, was tall, and he carried himself with the distinguished air of someone important.

"Is he alone?" Marcello asked.

"Uh huh."

"Oh boy, here we go!"

"Let's wait until he's seated and ordered."

Hirsch sat at a table for two near the back, in the corner, away from most of the other guests. No one would have recognized him except for hardcore Hollywood history buffs. He was the type of studio executive who shied away from publicity and broadcast award shows—unless, of course, he was certain he'd be winning something.

He was now positioned behind Karissa, in Marcello's line of sight.

"Has he looked our way?" she asked.

"Nope. He acts like he's the only one in the joint."

They continued to eat in silence. When Karissa had had enough of her meal, she stood. "I'm going. Why don't you pay the bill? I have a feeling we won't be welcome in here after I'm finished with him." She already had her cellphone in her hand. "I'm going to record our conversation."

"No. It's illegal. Not without him consenting."

"Oh."

"I'm going with you. I can back you up *and* solve the recording problem. I can be a witness to the conversation."

"All right. Let's do it."

"Hey. I said earlier that I wasn't the boss. That title belongs to *you*. Now go get him."

Karissa took a breath and they strode across the floor past other diners. She reached his table and Hirsch looked up.

"Mr. Hirsch?"

"Yes?"

"I'm Karissa Glover. This is Marcello Storm. Stormglove Productions."

There was a slight pause. She thought she detected a little twitch in his right eye.

"I know who you are," he said.

There was only one extra chair. "May I sit down?"

"I'm having lunch."

"This will only take a second."

He glared at her but gestured to the opposite seat. She took it and studied him for a moment. Marcello remained standing.

"Well?"

"Why are you trying to stop me and my partner from making a film about Blair Kendrick and what happened in 1949?"

Hirsch put down his fork and folded his arms across his chest. "What makes you think I'm trying to stop you?"

"Aren't you?"

"Not that I'm aware of."

"Mr. Hirsch, in the past week, my partner and I have had our bank accounts hacked and money stolen. We have received verbal threats from your lapdog, Barry Doon. He *does* work for you, correct?"

"Mr. Doon works for me, yes. If he's done anything to—"

"Someone tried to kill me last night at my home, Mr. Hirsch. He shot at me from the street. Was it Doon?"

"I don't know what you're talking about."

Karissa's heart was pounding furiously, the adrenaline pumping hard. She paused and took a deep breath. The man was lying. She knew it. She felt it.

"Look, Mr. Hirsch, I don't know how Blair Kendrick figured into your father's death, but by all accounts, she had nothing to do with it. Whatever happened is history. You can't censor history."

The man's face was gradually turning red. "Miss Glover, my father was murdered. A valuable fortune was also stolen from him that was to have been passed down to me and then to my own children. Blair Kendrick had something to do with it."

"She was a victim, too! She was killed by whoever murdered your father."

Hirsch pointed a finger at Karissa. "We at Ultimate Pictures don't want her name to become known again. We've taken all her pictures out of circulation. A film about her will give her unwarranted attention, and that will put a spotlight on my father's murder. We don't want that. It's a promise I made to my late mother, and it's an oath I took when I became the head of my father's studio when I was eighteen. *Eighteen!* And if you and your partner continue to go down this road, you will be *playing with fire.* Do you understand me, miss?"

"Is that another threat? You'll have us killed? Is that what you're saying?"

The restaurant manager was suddenly at the side of the table. "Mr. Hirsch, is there a problem?"

Hirsch growled, "This woman and this man accosted me while I was having lunch. Please get them out of here."

"Better come with me, madam," the man said, gently touching her arm.

Karissa violently pulled herself away from the manager and stood. "Is this really about Hank Marley, Mr. Hirsch?"

"Madam, please," the manager continued, "I don't want to have to call the police."

"Let's go, Karissa," Marcello said softly.

"Huh, Mr. Hirsch?" she continued. "Did your father do something to *Hank Marley?*"

Hirsch exploded. "*Get her out!*"

Karissa held up her hands. "I'm going." She started to walk away, but then turned and delivered a parting shot. "This isn't over!" Then, ignoring the stares of the other patrons, she and Marcello marched across the length of the restaurant. She went out the front door while Marcello paused to pull out his wallet and count out several bills to the maître 'd.

Outside, she told him as they walked to their cars, "I'm not sure he revealed anything useful, but I recorded it anyway so we can transcribe exactly what he said in there. Then we can erase the recording."

He laughed. "Good plan. By the way, you were great in there. *Boss.*"

31
THE MOVIE

An exterior daytime shot of the house on the beach cross-fades to the interior, where we find Blair sitting at a table in the kitchen, having breakfast. Leni watches over her.

Voice-over: "Two weeks after the baby was born, I felt stronger, although my grief took a terrible toll on my emotional stability. I was moving around better, but I was harboring a darkness that was struggling to be released. There had been no word from Buddy Franco, though. I had no idea when they were going to let me leave, or if they even were. It was now July 1949."

Blair took a final bite of the scrambled eggs and washed it down with the rest of the coffee. She wiped her mouth with a napkin and sat back in her chair. One thing she could say about Leni was that she was a decent cook.

"All done?" the woman asked. Without waiting for an answer, she took the plate and utensils to the sink and began to wash them by hand.

Blair eyed the iron skillet that was still on the stove.

"When do I get to leave, Leni?" she asked. "I'm feeling well. I could go back to work."

Leni turned to look at her. "Your breasts are still sore, *ja?*"

Blair frowned. "A little. But that's normal, right?"

Leni had told her that by simply not stimulating the breasts after the birth of a child, the production of milk would cease after a few days. Some women experienced pain from engorgement, and that was true for Blair. From the third day to the tenth, she was very uncomfortable. Leni had provided ice bags and aspirin, which helped. The aches were now subsiding.

"Still producing milk?"

"Not much. A few drops."

Leni shook her head. "Better not go until breasts are better." She moved to the table and suddenly reached out to fondle the pearl necklace around Blair's neck, but Blair jerked her upper body away.

"Don't touch that."

Leni held up her hands. "Sorry. It is nice necklace." She took the coffee mug and went back to washing.

Blair gazed at the skillet.

"I think I'm fine, really. Can't you contact Buddy? Please. I've been here for months."

"Mr. Franco will decide when is best for you to leave."

Blair slowly rose from the table and feigned stretching. "Ohhhhh. I've been lazy and have gained weight."

"We will go walk on the beach this morning," the woman said, her back still to her.

She's gotten careless, Blair thought.

She took a few steps toward the stove, reached out, and took the skillet by the handle. It had cooled enough to grasp. As it was made of iron, it was heavier than she expected. She then approached Leni from behind and said, "Don't you want me to help you with the dishes, Leni?"

"No, no, you go and rest."

Blair raised the skillet and brought it down with force on the back of the woman's head. Leni jerked and wobbled on her feet for a couple of seconds, tried to turn, and then collapsed like a ton of blubber. The heavy woman was out cold on the floor. Blood began to pool on the linoleum from the back of her grayish hair.

Oh my God, is she dead?

Blair stooped to examine her. She wasn't sure how to check for a pulse, but then she remembered that once in a picture her character had to do just that to an actor. She took Leni's wrist and felt around.

There.

A slow beating in the vein.

Blair exhaled loudly, relieved that she hadn't murdered her, although the monster probably deserved it. It was possible the skull was fractured and she would die anyway.

In shock at what she had done, Blair crumpled into one of the kitchen chairs and sat there for several minutes as the rage slowly subsided and she came to her senses. She had just struck down another human being. What had become of the warm, sunny actress known as Blair Kendrick? She was not surprised that she felt no remorse. It was as if she was completely detached from the violence she had just enacted.

Finally, she rose, searched Leni's apron pockets, and found the ring of keys. She hurried to her room to dress in the clothes she'd been wearing when she was first brought to the house. Then, she returned to the kitchen. Once again, Blair stooped to feel Leni's pulse.

Stillness. Just like the cold, distant silence in Blair's heart.

She stood, now a real-life femme fatale, and walked away with only a single thought.

To hell with her.

*

Feeling as if she was operating in another reality, Blair drove the Oldsmobile away from the house on the beach. It had taken a few tries to get the car started after it was immobile for so long, but eventually the engine kicked over. She had no idea where she was, but she followed the unpaved road until it came to a real highway. Following her instincts, she turned to the south and followed the coastline to a gas station. There, she stopped, went inside and asked to use a phone. The young man working there said they didn't have one, which she knew was a lie. She then asked how to get back to Los Angeles, and he looked at her as if she were mad. He finally told her to keep following the road and that soon she would see signs pointing the way.

It took over an hour for her to get to Hollywood and then to the area of Los Angeles she recognized as West Adams Heights. Sugar Hill. Instead of driving to her house, she went straight to Hank's home on Hobart. She parked at the curb and, not caring if anyone saw her, hurried up the walk to the front door. Knocking repeatedly, she called out, "Hank! Hank, it's me! Open up!"

The door swung open, but it wasn't Hank who answered. It was a young boy, about six years old.

"Wha—is Hank here? Who are you?" she stammered.

"I'm Gregory."

Then she remembered. Gregory Webster. Ray and Loretta's son, the little boy she often caught sight of when she visited Hank's place.

"Oh! Gregory. Hello. Do you remember me? I'm Blair Kendrick."

He nodded but eyed her suspiciously as if he wasn't sure.

"Is Hank Marley here?" The boy shook his head. "What about your daddy? Is he here?" Again, the head shake. "Your momma? Is she home?" No. "You—you're by yourself?" Gregory nodded. "Well, where are they? Where's Hank? Where's your daddy or momma?"

"Momma's at work. I don't know where Daddy is. We haven't seen Mr. Marley in a long time."

"What?" Gregory just stood there. "How long has Hank been gone?" The boy shrugged.

The panic that consumed her was overwhelming. Maybe Sheridan and Georgeann would have some answers. If they were still at her house.

"Tell your daddy that Blair was here. Will you do that? Tell him I need to speak to him right away!"

Gregory nodded.

She turned and started to go back to the car, but then she stopped. Returning to the open door and the boy who was still standing there, she said, "Will you let me come inside for a minute?"

The boy seemed to trust her. Perhaps he had remembered who she was—a friend of the family. He stepped back so she could enter.

"I'm going upstairs to Hank's room. There's something I need to find in there. Is that all right with you?"

He didn't say anything, so she went ahead and climbed the stairs. Hank's old bedroom looked untouched. The same bed and furniture occupied the space, but there were also obvious signs of other people living there—mainly women's things that belonged to Loretta Webster. Ray and his family had expanded their territory in the house.

Blair went to the nightstand and opened the drawer.

It was as if she'd found buried treasure.

She picked up Hank's Smith & Wesson and examined it. It was unloaded. A box of cartridges was also in the drawer, so she took that as well.

Blair turned and hurried down the stairs, past little Gregory who had remained in place, watching the frenetic white woman run around his family's house.

"Bye, Gregory," she said. "Remember—tell your daddy I need to talk to him."

She ran back to her car, started it, and drove around the block to her own house on Harvard Boulevard. The grass had grown long in the yard. What plants that had bloomed in the flower beds and pots on the porch were now long dead. The tears began to flow freely as she pulled in to the drive and got out. She went into the garage and tried to go in through the door there, but it was locked. She didn't have her own house keys. They had somehow gone missing at the house on the beach.

Blair ran around to the porch. The front door was locked, too. No one was inside.

"No! Oh, God."

She looked out into the street. How long would it be before Buddy Franco and his hoodlums discovered she had escaped? This would be the first place they'd search for her. She had to get in and out quickly.

Blair went down the steps and into the yard again, back around to the garage, and to the door inside. Surely if she applied enough force?

She raised her leg and stomped on the door with the sole of her shoe. Again. A third time, harder. Then another kick.

The lock broke.

Blair pushed on the door and she was inside.

Except for the amount of dust that had accumulated, everything appeared the way she had left it. The furniture was still in place. After a quick look around downstairs, she went up to the second floor. Her bedroom was intact. Her belongings and clothes were still in the dresser and closet.

She took the only suitcase she owned and opened it on her

bed. She started stuffing it with clothes and other belongings until it was full.

"Blair?"

The voice was coming from downstairs.

"Blair, you up there? It's Ray!"

She ran out of the bedroom and called from the top of the stairs. "I'm here, Ray!" She flitted down to the first floor and ran into his arms.

"Oh, Ray, I'm so happy to see you!"

"Where you been, Blair? We been awfully worried!"

"Forget about that—*where's Hank?*"

He gently pushed her away and looked at her. "Blair, you don't look so good. Are you all right? What happened to you?"

She shook her head. "Ray, I was kidnapped and held prisoner. Oh, God, Ray, I had a *baby*. Hank's and my *baby!*"

His eyes went wide. "Wha—well, where is it?"

"Dead. She died. Ray, I killed someone, the woman who was guarding me. *Where is Hank?* Why won't you tell me where he is?"

"Blair, please. Slow down. Hank—he's been missing since February. No one's seen him. Everyone thinks something bad happened to him. We had a gig at the Downbeat Club one night. He was going to catch the bus. Me and the other fellas, we decided to go over to the Dunbar to have a drink. I almost went on home, but then I changed my mind and wanted that drink. Anyway, I ran to the bus stop to tell Hank I'd buy him one, too, 'cause he *needed* it. He was missing you so bad. I saw him with some white men getting into a black Cadillac."

"Oh, no."

"They drove away. And that's the last I saw him."

She crumpled to the floor and started to cry. Ray got down on his knees with her. "Most of his stuff is still in his room, but we've been using it a bit. There are a couple of other families in the house now. I won't let 'em touch Hank's room, so Loretta uses it."

She sobbed into his shoulder as he held her.

"Gregory—my boy—he said you was at the house. You were in the bedroom . . . ?"

She lifted her head and nodded. "I took Hank's gun. I have it."

"Blair . . . "

"I'm going to do something about this, Ray. Will you help me?"

"I don't know, Blair . . ."

"I can't stay *here*. They'll be coming after me. I've got to flee. Get out of town. But first I need to do something. Will you *help* me?"

Ray rubbed his chin. After a moment, he said, "Darlin', I made a promise to my best friend, Hank. He made me swear that if anything ever happened to him, Loretta and I should do everything we could to protect you. You know what? I made that promise. You're family, Blair. I'll help you."

32

KARISSA

Karissa and Marcello received welcome news the next day from Tony Davenport. The attorney had managed to completely reverse the fraudulent pilfering of their bank accounts and received an "all clear" from their financial institution. New security measures were put in place so that it would be very difficult for something like that to happen again. Davenport also said that his firm was carefully looking into Azules Oscuros S.A., but they were hitting a brick wall. It was definitely a shell company, which meant it was masking the true proprietors.

Now back to square one, the producers set out to continue approaching studios to finance what they were calling *Femme Fatale—The Blair Kendrick Story*. It was time to initiate the hiring of a screenwriter who could put something on paper. They met with Miranda Jenkins, the talented scribe who had penned *Second Chance* for Stormglove. Another candidate was Jules Franken, an older writer whose work with several independent production companies was well received. Both were black, which would highlight Stormglove's aim for diversification. After all-day interview sessions with both candidates, they went with

Jenkins, having enjoyed working with her before. She wanted thirty thousand dollars to develop a spec script.

"Do we have that kind of money in the Stormglove account?" Marcello asked Karissa after the writer had left the meeting at their office. "I mean, I know we do, but can we afford to do without it right now?"

"I know what you're saying," Karissa answered. "We need the capital for expenses, the rent, and paying our attorney, among other things. But this is important."

"Normally, we'd make a deal with a studio first, and *they* would pay the writer."

"I know, but in this case, we need to be going out with a script, don't you think? Hirsch and Ultimate are probably putting out the word against us to other studios, just like William Randolph Hearst did to Orson Welles. We need to show whoever we talk to that we've got something worthwhile."

"Funny how the name Hirsch sounds a lot like Hearst. So how do we get the extra thirty grand?"

"I think I have a solution. You may remember I was given some found funds that we can use for development."

Karissa revisited Seymour at the gold and rare coin collector shop on Wilshire. After the familiar playful haggling with the sweet old man, Karissa sold him the D Indian Head Gold Eagle ten-dollar coin from 1911 and walked out of the place with a check for fifty thousand dollars. After depositing the check at the bank, Karissa drove home. For the first time in several days, she felt confident and reasonably happy. The incident at Musso & Frank's with Justin Hirsch had reenergized her. While the situation between Stormglove and Ultimate Pictures was by no means resolved, she felt good enough about the confrontation that they were probably safe to proceed with the picture.

Did she feel any guilt about selling coins that were possibly stolen from Eldon Hirsch?

Not really. She couldn't say she did.

Karissa drove south in the left lane on Western Avenue toward the I-10, taking the most direct route to her house. Traffic was starting to build, as the rush hour usually began by 4:00 p.m. Cars were going slow, and both lanes were full.

Out of the corner of her eye, Karissa noticed a black sedan pull up beside her in the right lane as she waited for a light at Washington Boulevard. She casually turned to look—and froze.

Barry Doon was behind the wheel of his black BMW, and he was staring at her.

Oh, Christ, she thought. *Is he going to pull out a gun and shoot at me?*

The light turned green up ahead. As the cars began to move, she swerved over into the left turn lane. The oncoming traffic was heavy, but a guy driving a pickup truck was looking at his phone and didn't move up with the cars in front. A space opened, and Karissa sped through it onto Washington.

Her nerves shattered, she drove along, cursing to herself. Was Doon heading for her house? What should she do?

She came to a right turn onto Harvard Boulevard, so she took it. Karissa wasn't familiar with much of the street geography in the part of West Adams Heights north of the freeway; it would be easy to get lost. The section of Harvard she was on, however, curved back to the west and became W. 21st Street, before circling back up to Washington. She thought that perhaps Harvard may have been a through street before the interstate was built. I-10 cut across it directly to the south, and her home was on the other side of the freeway.

Karissa took a left onto Washington and made her way back to Western Avenue. She turned and went south again, crossing the interstate on the overpass. Normally, she would turn left onto

W. Adams Boulevard, make another left onto Hobart, make a quick right on W. 25th Street, go around the traffic circle to Harvard, and she'd be home. But the BMW was there on Adams, in the opposite lane, pulled over to the curb. Doon spotted her, shot out into traffic, and made a screeching U-turn to come back up behind her. Karissa kept going east on Adams, for once wishing she could move faster. She was not one to be a daredevil behind the wheel of a car, but she was prepared to attempt a *Fast and Furious* maneuver if she had to.

Traffic moved along for several blocks. She could see the BMW in her rearview mirror, three cars behind her. The only thing she could do was try to lose him. But then what? He knew where she lived.

She reached for her purse on the passenger seat, opened it with her right hand while keeping the left on the wheel, and dug for her cell phone. She attempted to pull it out, but it got caught on the edge of the purse and slipped out of her hand, falling on the floor of the passenger side of the car where she couldn't reach it without unbuckling her seat belt and leaning way over.

There was another opening in oncoming traffic, so she recklessly made a left turn onto S. Congress Avenue, heading north. The BMW tried to follow her, but Doon was stuck waiting for a break in the oncoming traffic before he could make the turn. In the meantime, Karissa pulled a fast right onto S. 24th Street, going east again. She sped along as fast as she dared, barely halting at the stop sign at Normandie, and zipping through another miraculous break in the heavy traffic on that avenue to reach the other side. Continuing to travel on 24th, she didn't see the BMW in the rearview mirror. Perhaps she had lost him. She could stop, pull over, and get her phone. But then what? Call the police again? *Hello, there's a car following me, and I think the driver wants to shoot me.* Would they think she was nuts? Maybe not—they already had a case on file that she was the victim of a drive-by shooting. The problem was that the cops didn't seem to believe that a Hollywood studio executive was the one who had done it.

Eventually Karissa made a right turn to go south on S. Catalina Street, heading back to W. Adams Boulevard. Just to be safe, she made another left on 25th to lose herself further in the grid-maze of side streets of Sugar Hill. She crossed Vermont Avenue, continued east on 25th, and finally headed south again on Ellendale Place. She meant to turn right and head back west on Adams, but she was confused and went east instead.

And then she saw it.

The little house. The tiny house that was in the old photograph, the one she knew she'd seen before. The one with the pianist from Ray Webster's funeral, taken when she was a young woman.

Karissa saw an empty space at the curb on the right and managed to swing over. She parallel parked the Nissan and sat there for a moment, catching her breath. She checked all her mirrors for the BMW—no sign of Doon. She unbuckled the belt, reached over, and grabbed her phone—but then stopped. At this point she felt silly about calling the police. What the hell would she say? Instead, she put the phone back in her purse and exited the car.

Karissa approached the house. It looked like a garden shed compared to the large structures on either side of it. She wondered if the owner had been solicited to sell the property numerous times over the years and refused; hence, its incongruous appearance on the boulevard. It hadn't changed much since the old photo had been taken, but recent paint jobs, more modern landscaping, and better window frames had given it a facelift. A wire fence surrounded the yard. She opened the gate and walked to the front door.

Was she crazy? It was entirely possible that the pianist never lived there. She may have been posing in front of a friend's house. Or she may have had moved away a long time ago.

Karissa rang the bell. The worst that could happen was an awkward exchange—"Oops, wrong house"—and she'd leave.

To her surprise, the door was opened by James Trundy. Her landlord.

For a second, she was speechless.

"Ms. Glover?"

"Mr. Trundy! What are you doing here?"

"My mother lives here. What are *you* doing here?"

"I—well, *maybe* I'm here to see your mother. Is she, by chance, a pianist?"

He looked up and down the street and then held the door open wider. "You had better come in before someone sees you."

As she stepped inside the small entryway, Karissa thought, *What did he mean by that?*

"Please come this way," he said.

They didn't have to go far. Trundy led her into a small living room that contained a couch, coffee table, another chair, and a television. Through an arch was a kitchen and eating area. Another arch must have led to one, maybe two bedrooms.

The white-haired African American woman sat on the couch.

"Momma, you have a visitor," Trundy said.

The woman's jaw dropped. She said, "Oh, Lord, she can't be here!"

"She is, so we might as well talk to her." He turned to Karissa and said, "Ms. Glover, please meet my mother, Regina Trundy. Her big brother was a man named Hank Marley."

33

THE MOVIE

Ominous music builds on the film's soundtrack as we see a long exterior shot of the Ultimate Pictures lot. It's just after dusk and the sun has gone down, but it's not completely dark yet. Very few cars are in the employee and visitor parking area.

"I must have gone mad while I was at that house on the beach," the voice-over tells us. "I was going into the lion's den, but all I could think of was getting revenge. I didn't care if I was sent to prison or if I was killed. I had played criminal bad girls in movies, so I guess life was about to imitate art."

We see Blair's Oldsmobile drive off the main street and pull into the lot.

Barney Johnson's jaw dropped when he saw who had driven up to the gate. In his twenty-four years of guarding the main entrance to Ultimate Pictures, he had never been so flustered.

"Miss Kendrick? Is that really you? I can't believe it!" He stood up from the stool inside the little guardhouse.

She smiled at him through the driver's window and rolled it down. "Hi, Barney! You miss me?"

"I sure did! We all did! I was just about to leave to go home. Are you—are you feeling better? We heard you . . . we heard you were under the weather for a while."

"I was, Barney, but I'm much better now. Got a doctor's release and everything!" She blew him a kiss.

The wrinkle of his brow didn't exhibit certainty. Blair realized she didn't look so great. She wasn't wearing makeup, her hair was a mess, and she hadn't had a bath since the day before she'd left her prison on the beach. No wonder he was looking at her funny.

"Oh, Barney, I know I don't look like my usual glamorous self. I don't have a bit of makeup on, as you can see. I'm going to the hairdresser first thing in the morning. Please understand. I, uh, I just got out of bed. I've been resting all day, and I decided on a whim to come to the studio and see Eldon. Your wife doesn't get out of bed looking like a movie star, does she?"

Barney laughed. "No, I guess she doesn't. She's as pretty as a movie star, though, in my opinion!"

Blair laughed, too. "I bet she is. Now could you please open the gate so I can go inside?"

"Sure, Miss Kendrick. It's very good to see you again!"

He ducked back into the booth and raised the long, slender barrier. Blair figured it really wasn't much of an obstacle. Someone could drive right through it if they wanted.

She gave him a wave, drove on in, and parked in an empty spot. She didn't recognize any of the cars there, but three of the studio's black Cadillacs were sitting in the lot.

Blair took her purse and got out of the car. She went across the pavement to the door where another security guard would typically be posted at his desk, but she knew he would already be gone for the day. Camille, the ever-watchful Cerebus guarding the entrance to the Underworld, had also left for home hours before. There was nothing and no one to get in her way.

Barney Johnson scratched his head. He had never seen Blair Kendrick look so . . . *distraught*, despite her cheerful greeting. Instinctively, he knew something was wrong. Several minutes went by before he decided to do something about his misgivings. He reached for the phone to call Buddy Franco's office. He knew that Camille had left for the day, but the boss was still there along with Franco.

Another car—a black Cadillac Sixty Special in all-new sheet metal—pulled up to the gate. Very fancy, like the one Buddy Franco drove. Two people in the car—a man driving and a woman in the passenger seat. Had he seen her before?

Barney leaned out the checkpoint window. "May I help y—?"

The gun blast hit him across the right collarbone. He fell to the floor as the car burst through the flimsy gate into the lot. The guard attempted to stand and sound the alarm, but blackness fell upon him with the weight of the world.

The thin strip of light under the door at the end of the hallway revealed that Eldon Hirsch was inside.

Blair suddenly had the sensation that she was no longer inside her body. It was true that she hadn't been thinking straight for months. The ordeal at the beach had seriously damaged her, both physically and emotionally. She was intellectually aware of that truth, but at the same time she didn't know how to deal with it. Only one thing propelled her forward, and that was to avenge what had happened to her. Someone had to pay for the pain and suffering she had endured. Someone had to be punished for what she feared had become Hank's and her baby's fates.

Slowly, she walked down the dark corridor toward that slit of light. As she did so, Blair opened her purse and retrieved the Smith & Wesson, now fully loaded with six rounds. She held it in her right hand behind her back and slipped the purse strap over her left arm. As she moved toward the door, it appeared as if it was retreating, away from her. The hallucination was disorienting. *Why am I not getting closer to that office?*

But then, suddenly, she was there. She had no sense or memory that she had traversed the corridor. The door was right in front of her, slightly ajar. She pushed it open with her left hand. There was no squeak or creak, so Eldon Hirsch didn't hear her. He sat at his desk on the other side of the dimly lit room, the golden glow of the lamps' illumination reflecting off the carpet and furniture.

The devil is bathed in the effervescence of the fires of hell.

That thought almost made her laugh, but she remained silent.

Hirsch was studying something on his desk. Binders. The coin collection, of course, that he loved so dearly.

She began to move toward her nemesis. Blair made it halfway across the room, to the point where the sofa and coffee table were located. It was the spot where she had become sick and thrown up on him.

I'm going to do a lot worse to you now, Eldon.

He sensed her presence and looked up.

"Who's there?" He squinted. "Who is that? Malena?"

She stepped forward. "It's me, Eldon."

His eyes bulged. "Blair?"

"That's right."

He reached for the phone on his desk. She brought the pistol out from behind her back and pointed it at him. "Hands off. Put your palms flat on the desk."

"Blair! What are you doing? Put that gun away."

She crept closer until she stood just on the other side of the desk, the gun barrel five feet from his face.

"I, uh, I heard you were recovering nicely," he said, his voice quavering. "That you were ready to come back to work! That's, uh, good! I have a number of projects I think you'd be really good in."

The sweat beaded on his forehead. His eyes darted nervously. His hands shook.

"Trying to sweet-talk me, Eldon?" she asked.

"Blair, I'm just happy you're back. Oh, and I'm so sorry to hear about your child. That's a tragedy. If he had . . . if he had survived, we could have found him a good home, and—"

"She."

"What's that?"

"The baby was a *she*, Eldon. And if she had lived, the home she deserved was with me and Hank. What happened to her father, Eldon? Where's Hank?"

His mouth trembled, and he said, "Blair, wait a minute. I don't know anything about—"

She pulled the trigger. The recoil thundered in the cavernous office. The bullet missed, sailing just over his left shoulder and striking the wall behind him. Had she missed on purpose? She didn't know. It had the desired effect, though—it had scared the bluster out of him. He yelped and started to cry. "Blair! Please, don't. You don't know . . . . Listen, I have a wife and a son and a—"

"Studio? You have a wife and a son and a studio? Tsk tsk, Eldon. You cheat on your wife all the time. You barely pay any attention to your son. All you love is that coin collection. How would you feel if you lost it?"

"Blair. Wait. You don't understand. The collection—it's not all mine. I share it. I just manage it, I do all the work and the collecting."

"What are you talking about?"

Eldon held up his hands. "Put the gun down, and I'll tell you."

"No."

"You know, the guards will come running. They probably heard that shot."

"What guards?" she asked. "They've all gone home. The only one here is Barney, and he's way outside and was about to leave. Nobody can hear what goes on in this office."

"Buddy's here."

The mention of his name produced a sharp intake of breath. Blair wanted to find *him*, too. "Where?"

"In his office. Upstairs. You know where it is."

She nodded at the binders. "What were you saying about the coins?"

"I have friends in Las Vegas. One of them, a guy named Meyer Lansky. Maybe you've heard of him. He's in the casino business there."

"Meyer Lansky's a gangster."

"Yes."

"You share a coin collection with a gangster."

"Yes."

"Are they stolen?"

Hirsch hesitated. "Maybe some of them are. I don't know. The ones I acquired were . . . supposed to be . . . legitimate. Where he gets his, I don't know."

"And they're all there in those binders?"

Hirsch nodded.

"So, you're telling me that these coins belong to the *mob*?"

"Well . . . and me, too . . . and Buddy . . ."

She fired the pistol again, this time hitting him squarely in the left shoulder. He screamed and jerked back in his chair, but it was such a strong, heavy piece of furniture that it didn't tip over with his weight. He continued to blubber and cry, clutching the wound with his right hand. "Blair! Please! Agh! Call an ambulance!" Blood began seeping over his shirt, between his fingers.

"Tell me the truth, Eldon. Those coins were acquired illegally, right?" She pointed the gun at his face.

His eyes were headlamps of fear. He nodded furiously. "Yes."

"You imprisoned me for months. Kidnapped me."

He continued to move his head up and down. "Blair! Please! I'm sorry . . . !"

Another shot. This one struck his right shoulder. Another scream.

"*What happened to Hank?*" she shouted.

Sobbing, practically dripping off the chair, Hirsch managed to say, "I really . . . don't know! You'd . . . have to . . . ask Buddy."

"But he's dead? Hank is dead?"

Hirsch squeezed his eyes tightly shut. He reluctantly nodded.

Blair shot him again. This time the round hit the middle of his chest, just over the sternum. The studio mogul slumped in the chair. No more cries. No more trembling. No more movies.

Time stood still. Blair could feel herself breathing. She could see and hear the things around her, but it was as if everything was now in slow motion. She knew what she'd done, but she was not inside her body. She was floating along the ceiling, looking down, watching the two figures on opposite sides of the desk.

The next thing she knew, she had gathered the coin binders and tucked them under her left arm, the purse still dangling there. She turned and rushed out of the room, only to meet Buddy Franco coming in.

He had a gun, and it was pointing at her.

Instinctively, the lessons Hank had taught her paid off. Without hesitation, she simply raised her right hand and squeezed the trigger. The bullet caught Franco in his side, causing him to fall and drop his weapon. He lay on the floor, unmoving. Blair stood over him for a moment. Was he dead? She thought so, but she didn't really want to stick around.

Then Franco's eyes opened. He tried to move but it appeared that he couldn't.

"Help me . . ." he whispered.

"Why should I? You killed Hank. And you know what? I don't believe my baby just *died*. You killed her. Didn't you!"

Franco attempted to shake his head. "Orph . . ."

"What? I can't hear you!" Blair shouted at Franco.

"Orph . . . nage."

Blair's heart leaped. "What? An orphanage? You took her to an orphanage?"

"Yes. Just . . . got back . . . from there . . ."

"Where? *Where?*"

"I'll tell . . . if . . . help me . . ."

Blair squeezed her eyes shut and opened them. The man wanted her help? He'd tell her where her daughter was if she *helped* him?

"*Where is she, Buddy?*" she shouted at his face.

He flinched, and then whispered, "Santa . . ."

She reached in and shook him by the shoulders. "Tell me! Santa what?"

". . . Barb . . . ara."

"Santa Barbara?"

Franco reached for something in his jacket. Blair was ready to strike him with the butt end of the pistol, but he pulled out an envelope. With a trembling hand, he gave it to her. In the stark illumination of Hirsch's office and through blurry eyes, she caught the words "Children's Home" embedded in the return address on the envelope. She quickly looked inside and noted that it contained a form of some kind.

"All right, Buddy, I'll—"

But Franco's head had dropped, his eyes closed. Was he dead or only passed out? She didn't know and didn't care.

Her child was alive!

But with the elation came the feeling of panic. She turned to head out the office door—and collided with an elegant, beautiful woman in a white dress. She had bold red hair that appeared to be a circle of flames around her head.

"Who are you?" the woman snapped, surveying the scene. "What have you done?"

At first, Blair was frozen. She couldn't move or speak.

The woman eyed the coin binders under Blair's arm. "Give me those!" She started to reach for them.

Blair snapped out of her immobility, pointed the gun at the redhead, and shouted, "Out of my way!" The woman snarled and raised her hands halfway. Blair pushed past her and ran down the dark hall to the front of the building.

A gunshot resounded behind Blair. A round missed her by a few inches and tore a chuck out of the wall beside her.

Blair burst outside to the parking lot. She reached her car, threw the binders, gun, and purse on the passenger seat, and got in. She tried to start the Oldsmobile, but the engine coughed and sputtered. Another seizure of anxiety coursed through her chest.

The woman in the white dress emerged from the building, aimed her Colt .38 at Blair, and fired. The passenger window shattered, and Blair screamed.

Malena Mengarelli strode determinedly toward the Oldsmobile. Blair turned the key again—and this time the engine kicked over. She backed out of the space with a screech and drove toward the gate.

Another round smashed the rear driver's-side window. Blair slammed the gear into first, stepped on the pedal, and released the clutch. The Oldsmobile shot forward. It didn't register to her that the gate was missing. She hurtled past the seemingly empty guardhouse and onto the road like a demon from hell.

34

KARISSA

Karissa's eyes darted from her landlord to the old woman on the couch.

"You're Hank Marley's sister?"

Regina Trundy nodded. "Sit down, child. You shouldn't stay here long. They'll be watching us. It's why we haven't made much of an overture to you before."

"I don't . . . I don't understand."

The woman patted the sofa next to her. "Sit, please, child."

Karissa did so. Trundy sat in the other chair.

"Men are after you, aren't they?" the woman asked.

"I suppose you could say that. Someone tried to kill me the other day. Mostly they've just tried to scare me into not making the movie I want to do."

"It's about Blair and my brother?"

"Yes."

She nodded. "Good. That story needs to be told."

Karissa looked at her landlord. "Mr. Trundy, why didn't you tell me about your mother? I've been asking you questions about the house and all."

He displayed his hands and said, "It was for your protection, and ours. These men mean business."

"Why? It's history, isn't it?"

"Is it that man Barry Doon who has been harassing you?" the woman asked. Karissa could see that, despite her age, Regina Trundy had her wits about her. There was intelligence in her eyes and a feistiness in her spirit.

"Yes, that's him."

"He may be associated with that movie studio, but he's really a gangster. He works for bad men in Las Vegas who have been in bed with the Hirsch family for years and years. They own a large piece of the studio."

"Ultimate Pictures?"

"That's right."

Trundy continued. "From what we understand, Eldon Hirsch made a deal with the devil a long time ago. The mob bankrolled the studio when it started up. They get a piece of the profits every time the studio makes a movie that is successful."

"That's extraordinary," Karissa said. "How can that be allowed to happen?"

Trundy answered, "We can't answer that. It's too complex for us to understand, and frankly that's a whole other world. The son—the guy who runs the studio now . . ."

"Justin Hirsch."

"Yes, him. He's still beholden to the gangsters. If you ask me, he's a madman. He's harassed us for years. My mother and I, and my own family—we just want to live our lives peacefully and forget all that stuff that happened in the past."

"What *did* happen?"

Regina placed a hand on Karissa's. "Honey, my brother was murdered by those men."

Though Karissa was unsurprised, she still gave a start. "I

know that he disappeared in 1949, but no one ever reported what had happened to him. Do you know more about it?"

Regina looked at her son and cocked her head at him. He replied, "We know that a friend of Hank's—Ray Webster—saw him get into a car with a man named Buddy Franco. I guess you could say he was the Barry Doon of that time, the fixer for Eldon Hirsch, who was the head of the studio. Franco was also a mobster who answered to his bosses in Las Vegas, although he was on the payroll of Ultimate Pictures. You're right, no one knew what happened to Hank, but in 1952, a skeleton was found out in the desert between here and Vegas. There was a hole in the skull, indicating the man had been shot. Because it was a skeleton, the medical examiner was unsure what other tortures the poor man had to endure before he was killed."

"And that was Hank?"

Regina nodded. "The skeleton's bony finger still wore a ring—a gold wedding ring—that once belonged to our father. I had engaged a lawyer back then to try and find out what happened to Hank. He learned of the discovery in the desert and did some investigating. The police never officially identified the remains, but my lawyer attempted to get it in the papers."

"The African American newspapers," Trundy said. "The *California Eagle* and the *Los Angeles Sentinel*. They ran a story about it that year, but no one paid any attention."

Karissa winced. "When I tried to find those articles, I discovered someone had censored them. They were completely missing from the archives at the library and online."

"I'm not surprised," Trundy said. "The studio didn't want anyone to know they were responsible for the murder of a black man. I'm sure there were bribes and payoffs to law enforcement in the region where the skeleton was found. You see, if it had come out, the studio's stock would have fallen, and the mob in

Vegas wouldn't have been very happy. They wanted to protect their investment."

"They also didn't want it known that Blair Kendrick, a white woman, was seeing Hank, a black man," Karissa said.

Regina laughed a little. "Yes, that would have been bad PR, too. An interracial relationship of that type at that time was forbidden. California may have made it legal for white and black people to get married, but that didn't mean everyone was all for it. Not on your life! I understand that Blair became pregnant with Hank's child and they wanted to get married. Buddy Franco kidnapped her and took her someplace. She was held against her will for months until she had the baby."

"*Kidnapped* her? Oh, my God! What happened to the baby?"

"We believe Franco murdered her. We really don't know for sure. Considering the evil that was inside those men, I wouldn't put it past them."

"Oh, my God. That's awful. Do you think it's *possible* that the baby lived and is still alive?"

Trundy shrugged. "I suppose anything is possible, but I highly doubt it."

"What about the house, Mr. Trundy? Now can you tell me who owns it?"

Trundy answered, "We honestly don't know. Someone set up a shell company with some lawyers that would handle Blair's house and belongings. That company at first paid my mother to be the landlord to the house, and now I do it. We're not supposed to sell it, and we were recently told to rent it to the first person who came to ask about it. That was you."

"That's all you know?"

"The company was set up to run itself by a lawyer or lawyers in some foreign location," Trundy added.

"I don't mind saying that the company has kept my son and me comfortable. Tried to get *me* to move into the house," Regina said, "but I love this little place too much. I've been here forever it seems. I never wanted to move."

Trundy nodded. "Anyway, those studio people have hounded us forever, asking questions about Blair and a bad woman named Malena Mengarelli. Not only them, but the police. The mobsters from Vegas. I can't tell you how many times they've interrogated us. They want to make sure we say nothing about Hank. If we started talking about what happened to him, they'd come after *us*. We shouldn't be talking to *you*, but my mother and I just happened to discuss it yesterday. I knew you were looking into all this. We felt that if you came to us, we should speak. Those people also seem to think we know something about a missing coin collection that's worth a fortune. Apparently, it was jointly owned by Eldon Hirsch and the Vegas mob."

Karissa thought about that. She wasn't sure if she should mention that someone had sent her three of what she assumed to be the missing coins. "So, what role did Ray Webster have in all this?"

Regina said, "Ray would never talk about it. He helped Blair in some capacity after she escaped her kidnappers. He was hounded the rest of *his* life, too."

"Is that why his son is so hard to find? I'd love to talk to him."

"Gregory?" Again, Regina shared a glance with her son and then said, "Gregory knows some things, but he keeps his whereabouts secret even from *us*. He doesn't want those studio and gangster thugs to bother him. He had to sneak in and out of the city to see his father."

"Do you know where he lives? I've heard it was in the Bakersfield area."

"That's all we know, too," Trundy answered.

Karissa sighed heavily. It was all clear now. The reason Justin Hirsch was going to great lengths to stop her film and even *kill* her if he had to was not just to protect his father's "legacy," such as it was, but to protect the studio from legal culpability in past murders. Maybe there were even more bodies in the desert that Justin didn't want uncovered.

Hollywood's dark underbelly.

The sound of a car door slamming outside alerted them. Trundy went to the window and peered through curtains. "Oh, Lord, it's Barry Doon. He's coming to the door." He turned to Karissa. "Quick, go out the back. Hurry!"

Karissa jumped up and followed the man, pausing long enough to turn to Regina and say, "Thank you for talking to me!"

"Run, child! Do *not* call the police! We'll handle him."

Trundy held the back door open and she hurried into a small yard. The wire fence continued around the tiny house to the back. Where was she supposed to go now? She moved around to the side of the building and paused there as she heard Doon banging on the front door. "Open up, Mrs. Trundy!"

Karissa waited. Then, her landlord's voice mixed with Doon's. She couldn't understand what they were saying, until Doon said, "You better let me in. I'm going to have a look!"

After a moment, Karissa bolted out to the front of the house. The gate had been left open, so she ran through it and out into the street. Her car was parked just a few doors down on the other side. She figured Doon must have seen it and assumed she was inside the Trundy home. Karissa quickly got inside the Murano, buckled up, and started the engine. As she pulled out of the space, she glanced at the little house to make sure Doon hadn't seen her, and then she drove away.

She prayed that the Trundys would be all right. Karissa considered calling the police anyway, but Regina was probably right—bringing in the cops would cause more trouble than they'd want. She had to trust that Doon would not harm them, especially now that he knew Karissa was on to him. Now she had to take the risk of going home, if she should at all. Maybe she could go to Marcello's? Maybe—

Her phone rang. The caller ID indicated it was her ex, Willy. Great. That was all she needed. But on second thought—perhaps this could be helpful.

"Willy?" she answered.

"Hey, Karissa. I'm at your house."

"What? Why?"

"I brought you a present. You're going to like what I have to say. Are you at the office? I thought you might be home. I could come back in—"

"No! Stay there, Willy! Please! I'm on my way. I'll be there in five."

35

THE MOVIE

The sun is setting. As the camera follows the Oldsmobile along Crescent Heights Boulevard, the urban landscape thins out. We're heading into the Hollywood Hills. Soon there are no buildings at all as the car repeatedly climbs and dips. Cut back and forth to a close shot of Blair behind the wheel, tears streaming down her face as she tries to concentrate on her driving.

"I didn't know what I was doing," the voice-over says. "I was supposed to meet Ray after my 'visit' to the studio. Depending on how it turned out, he was going to help me get away, but I completely forgot and absent-mindedly found myself heading out of the city. Before I knew it, I was in the Hollywood Hills. I didn't want to turn around. I wanted to get lost. I was afraid. I knew that I'd done something terrible. Did I regret it? No, I didn't. But that didn't mean I thought I wouldn't have to pay for it when my soul was eventually judged at the gates of heaven. I had sinned, but that's what 'Blair Kendrick—the Bad Girl' would have done, right? A tagline on one of my movie posters was 'Her Sins Will Shock You!' I guess they really would now."

*

The two-lane road turned into Laurel Canyon Boulevard and ascended higher, winding around sharp curves and treacherous drop-offs. Blair didn't know where the road would lead. Sometimes the road narrowed and there was a cluster of houses, but then it opened up again to wild country. Blair had been acquainted with some stars who lived in the Hollywood Hills, and she'd been to some parties there, but she had no clue as to the exact geographical locations. In those instances, she had ridden in a limousine or studio car and had rarely driven her own automobile to such functions.

She was forced to change gears often on the tricky road. Her speed had lessened considerably, and she didn't feel safe. The image of that strange woman bolting out of the studio door with gun in hand—firing at her—was imprinted on her retinas. Was she following her now? And what about Buddy Franco? Was he dead or merely wounded? One thing was certain: she had to flee the city—and do it quickly. She dared not go back to her house. Her half-baked plan of quitting the movie business was now a reality. Blair Kendrick was no longer a star and would never make another picture again.

The erratic movement of lights in her rearview mirror jerked her out of the delirious reverie. It was a car, hot on her tail some fifty to a hundred yards back. Every time she went around a curve, Blair lost sight of it, but whenever the road managed to straighten for a short stint, the car was there.

Franco. Pursuing her in his Cadillac.

Or was it? He would have been in no condition to drive.

That woman with the gun?

She instinctively stepped harder on the gas pedal, attempting to go faster, but the climbing and snaking was too hard on the car. She was afraid she'd drive off into a precipice. She was in canyon country now.

A road sign indicated that she was approaching Mulholland Drive. She made a right turn and found herself on an even more meandering path. She had been on the scenic boulevard in the past—she and Hank had driven up to a lovers' lookout somewhere along the way to sit and contemplate the city lights. The lonely road was a symbol of Hollywood dreams.

Why was it so dark?

"Oh, Jesus," she muttered, as she realized she didn't have her headlamps on. The sun had set, and it was as if she were following a barely visible ribbon illuminated only by the moon and stars. She flicked the lights on, which made the road clearer.

But that only made her car more visible to her pursuer.

Who was crazy enough to build such a hazardous road? she wondered, reminding herself to pay attention. The headlamps shot straight beams of whiteness that cut through the black to reveal a highway that moved as if it were alive. A writhing, untamable beast upon which her car had to traverse. The sides were nothing but tall, thick trees, rocks, and cliffs. Every now and then a bend revealed a darkness off the side that might as well have been a bottomless pit. It probably went all the way to hell.

The pinpoints of headlights behind her were still there and getting closer. Whoever it was would soon catch her and kill her. She would never make it to the end of this insane road. Either that or she would end up at the bottom of a canyon, burning in a fiery wreck.

Perhaps that's what she deserved.

Unless . . .

She set a trap.

Maybe she could cause *it* to have an accident.

Mulholland Drive was silent and empty. It seemed they were the only ones up in the hills. Only once did another car pass her, and it was going down to the city. Could she get away with it?

258

At one point along the road at which she had a good vantage of the serpent road behind her, she saw not only the pursuer's headlights, but those of another vehicle behind his. Did they belong to a car driven by one of Franco's henchmen? Was that driver going to help the other car's occupants murder her and then bury her body somewhere out here in the canyons?

She had to do something.

A long arc ahead provided the opportunity. Blair cut her own headlamps and slowed down to a stop. In a flurry, she grabbed her purse, the gun, and the coin binders, and got out of the car, leaving it in the middle of the lane. To the left of the drive was a steep drop into nothingness. To the right was a tall, rocky cliff. She moved forward toward the cliff and along the stone wall, running ahead perhaps fifty feet. She heard the approaching Cadillac and saw its beams from around the bend of the rocks. They grew brighter as the car rumbled closer.

Then it was there, barreling ahead. Although she was some distance away, she could swear she saw the driver's eyes bulge when he saw the Oldsmobile in the middle of the road. It was too late to stop. He pulled the wheel to the right, but the Cadillac hit the back of Blair's car anyway and then plowed into the rocky face of the cliff.

Blair held the pistol and strode forward, pointing it at the wrecked Cadillac. She stopped ten feet from the wreckage. The Cadillac's lights cast an eerie glow over the scene that reflected on the stone and trees around them.

The woman from Hirsch's office sat in the passenger seat, her head resting against a spiderweb crack in the windshield, blood streaming down her face. The driver looked like a hired thug. He, too, had blood on his head and face, but he was conscious.

The other pair of headlights that had been behind the Cadillac now appeared from around the bend. The car stopped before it could collide with the chaos of metal on the road. But Blair was too intent on finishing this business to notice the second driver.

The injured driver's door had opened. Grimacing, the man moved and raised a pistol, pointing it at her.

Blair squeezed the trigger of her own gun and was startled by the jerk of the recoil and the loud reverberation of its retort across the canyons.

The man slumped in the seat and no longer moved.

"Blair!"

The voice startled her out of her one-track state. She turned to see the other car sitting in the road, idling, its headlamps illuminating the scene brighter than before. A black man stood in front of the car, his hand outstretched to her.

"Blair, it's me, Ray!"

"Ray?"

"When you didn't show up where we were supposed to meet, I drove to the lot and saw you leave. Then I saw them take off after you. I followed you both. Come on. We've got to get out of here!"

In a daze, Blair nodded and went to him. He opened the passenger door of a green 1939 Ford Coupe. "Wait," she said. She moved past him to the side of the road and threw the Smith & Wesson out into the precipice, where it disappeared into the darkness below. She then returned to the car and got inside with the binders and purse in hand.

Ray sat behind the wheel.

She said nothing. Her face was blank, eyes staring ahead as if she were in a trance.

"You don't own a car, Ray," she said with remarkable clarity after a while.

"No, Blair, I don't. This here belongs to Bobop. He lent me the car tonight for our plans, remember?"

"Oh. I forgot."

He was about to drive away, when Blair whispered to him.
"Wait."

"What?"

"We can't leave the scene like this."

"What are you talking about, Blair? We got to get out of here!"

She swallowed and uttered a coarse laugh. "I've made enough crime movies to know. There's something I have to do."

Blair explained to him what she had in mind. Ray's eyes grew wide, frightened by what she had just suggested. "I'll do it all myself if you won't help me, Ray."

"No, I'll help you," he finally said. "Those people deserve to burn in hell. There's a can of gasoline in the trunk of the car. I used it earlier to fill her up."

They both got out and went to the other wrecked car. The woman hadn't moved. Blair thought she might be dead. Was her name Malena? Hirsch had called out that name, as if he'd been expecting her.

Blair hesitated for a few seconds, and then she unfastened the pearl necklace that was her signature accessory. She hung it around Malena Mengarelli's neck, locked it in place, and walked away.

"Do it, Ray," she said.

He began to douse both cars with gasoline.

As they drove away from the two infernos on the lonely mountain road, Ray asked, "Are you all right, Blair?"

She didn't answer. Instead, her eyes were on the HOLLYWOOD sign that brightly shone on the hill up ahead. It had recently been refurbished by the Chamber of Commerce. For years it had said HOLLYWOODLAND, but the sign had

261

declined into disrepair and even lost a letter or two. Earlier in 1949, the sign had been rebuilt without the LAND part.

HOLLYWOOD. Built on dreams.

Sure, she thought. *Just dreams. Like blues in the dark. Nothing more.*

36

KARISSA

As Karissa approached her house on Harvard Boulevard, she saw that a green Jeep Cherokee was parked in front at the curb. She drove onto the driveway without entering the garage, parked, and strode around the house to the front yard to address her ex-husband, who sat on the porch swing with a big grin on his face.

"Willy! You—"

He shook his head. "Now don't go shooting off your mouth, Karissa, not until you hear what I have to say."

She started up the steps to the porch. "Willy, I need your help. Someone is—"

The screeching of brakes in front of the house interrupted her. Barry Doon's BMW made a reckless stop at the curb behind the Jeep. The man got out and aggressively approached Karissa.

"Oh my God," she gasped, running up the steps to the porch. By then, Willy had gotten to his feet.

"I want to talk to you!" Doon shouted from the yard.

"Who the hell is he?" Willy asked.

"A very bad guy. And he works for *your* studio, Willy. He

263

wants to kill me," she said, moving closer to her ex. Despite their history, she felt safer next to him.

Willy looked at her. "He wants to *what*?"

Doon reached the bottom of the steps and addressed Willy. "Step aside, Mr. Puma. This doesn't concern you. I need to speak to *her*."

"Who the hell are you?"

"I work for the studio that makes the *Hellhole* movies, so back away."

"I'm staying right here. You say what you need to say to both of us."

Doon's face turned red with anger. "Fine!" To Karissa—"What were you doing talking to the Trundys?"

"Get out of here before I call the cops," Karissa said.

The man pointed to her. "You're making this much worse for yourself, lady!"

"*Hey!*" Willy snapped. He moved down the steps. He out-weighed Doon by thirty pounds and sported a set of pecs that could intimidate a wild beast. "What's the problem here?"

Doon backed away. "Easy, Puma. I told you I work for Ultimate Pictures."

"So? Are you threatening my ex-wife?"

The man held up his hands. "I just want to talk to her. There's a, uhm, a *legal* issue that we're trying to work out."

"Then have your lawyer contact her lawyer. *You* best get the hell off this property."

Doon blustered, "Watch it, Puma, don't forget you've been cast in *Hellhole Six*."

"Yeah, and I have a contract of *steel*, too. Get the fuck out of my face before you don't have one anymore."

Doon glared at him and then at Karissa. He pointed at her again. "Keep your nose out of Justin Hirsch's business if you know what's good for you!" Puma lunged at him and Doon

264

jerked back. "I'm going! Your boss is going to hear about this, Puma." The man went back into his car, burning rubber as he went.

Willy climbed the stairs back to the porch.

"Thank you, Willy," Karissa said. "I hope you don't get in trouble for that."

He waved a hand at her. "I don't give a shit. My manager, my agent, my attorney—they'll give the studio fire and brimstone if they try to can me. Are you all right? Is this about that movie you and Marcello want to make?"

"Yeah. There's some real stinky history at Ultimate Pictures, Willy, and this movie would bring it all out. I'm real close to solving a puzzle." She exhaled heavily and sat on the top step of the porch.

"Well, I hope you do." He went back to the porch swing and picked up a large envelope he'd left there. "Look." He sat beside her and handed it to her. "The papers. All signed."

She took them and felt her eyes well up. "Oh, Willy. Really?"

"Really."

She opened the envelope, pulled out the papers, and saw that they were indeed signed. "Willy. Thank you."

"No problem. Hey, I'm sorry. For everything. I know I've been a jerk."

Karissa was flustered. "What . . . changed?"

Willy shook his head and grinned. "Well, you know my mama . . ."

Karissa blinked. "Celia? What about her? Is she okay?"

"Oh, yeah, she's definitely okay. As ornery as ever. You know how opinionated she can be."

Karissa thought she knew where this was going. "Oh, yeah. Your mama's the only person I know who could tell you what to do."

"Don't you know it? Well. She's taken your side in all this, and she gave me hell about all the shit I caused in our marriage. She really let me have it. When she found out I hadn't signed the papers and was putting you through . . . well, let's just say she laid down the law."

Karissa laughed. Her former mother-in-law was indeed a force to reckon with. "Tough-guy Willy Puma. Bested by Dear Old Mom."

Willy guffawed. "Please don't tell my fans. At any rate, I know she's right. And you've been right, too, all along. I'm sorry. I hope you can forgive me, and let's try to be friends from here on out."

"Sure, Willy. Thank you. And thank Celia for me."

"Oh, no. I ain't telling her that you know she whooped my ass." He stood and took a few steps away from the house. Then he turned back and approached her. "Let me know if you have any more trouble with that guy."

He held out a hand. She clasped it in hers and squeezed.

"Don't be a stranger," he said, and then Willy Puma crossed the lawn, went out the gate, got in his Jeep, and drove away.

Karissa wanted to collapse on the steps. The flow of adrenaline had been nearly nonstop for the last couple of hours—the car chase around West Adams Heights, the revelation of James Trundy and Regina, and the small satisfaction she felt with Willy and Doon's confrontation. She had no energy left.

She let herself into the house through the garage and picked up the mail off the floor that had fallen in through the front door. More of the usual junk, plus a letter-sized envelope addressed to her. The return address was a P.O. Box in Wasco, California. Where the hell was that?

Karissa tore open the envelope—inside was an informational pamphlet folded to fit the Number 10 envelope, all about Our Lady of Hope Children's Home.

An orphanage in Santa Barbara, California.

"What the . . . ?" Karissa opened it to see photos of nuns with babies, older children, and Catholic iconography. A heading indicated that the facility had been in operation since 1921 and had worked for decades to place abandoned or orphaned children in loving foster homes.

Folded inside the pamphlet was a letter-sized piece of paper that was a photocopy of an "intake form." On it was information about a child who had been brought to the orphanage in 1949.

"Oh, Lord."

Karissa examined the envelope again. No clue as to who had sent it.

After putting her car in the garage and locking all the doors for the day, Karissa sat at her computer and pulled up Google Maps. Wasco was located roughly thirty miles from Bakersfield. Interestingly, a state prison was also in Wasco. A tiny place with a population of around 25,000, the town didn't appear to have much else going for it.

Could that be where Gregory Webster lived? Had he sent the envelope? Karissa trusted her instincts, and this time they were telling her the answers to these questions.

The intake form was dated June 17, 1949. The child was described as a Negro female newborn with the name "Jane Doe." Karissa knew that the Census forms in those days allowed only one race to be selected. Someone's handwriting in the margin noted: "Parents—one white, one black? Unknown." The baby had apparently been left at the front door one night, wrapped in a blanket and lying in a pasteboard box. By the time a nun opened the door, whoever had brought the child had vanished.

The baby was pronounced "healthy."

Could this be Blair Kendrick's baby? It had to be. Karissa got up from the computer and paced the floor. *Someone is watching me. There's a guardian angel at work here. I'm being manipulated. Why else would I be sent this material? Blair Kendrick is dead, so who else could it be? Gregory Webster? Blair's baby, now grown, in her early seventies? Did the rare coins come from the same person? What is going on here?*

She looked at the time and saw that it wasn't quite five o'clock. A lot had happened since that insane lunch with Marcello at Musso & Frank's!

Back at her computer, she found the orphanage online and verified that it was still in Santa Barbara. She then looked up the Wasco post office, dialed the number, and asked to speak to a supervisor. When a man got on the phone, he sounded annoyed.

"This is Stevens, can I help you?"

"Hello, I'm calling from Los Angeles. Is it possible to find out who owns a specific P.O. Box there in Wasco?"

"What do you mean?"

"Oh, I received some mail, and the return address is just a post office box in Wasco. I'd like to know, uhm, who I'm doing business with."

"Lady, we can't give out that information."

Of course they can't.

"Even if it's a matter of money? What if they're owed a good deal of money?"

"Ma'am, I still can't do it except under special circumstances, like harassment or child pornography or something else criminal. Or if the person is deceased, or any number of things, but I can't just give it out. You might need a court order. Why don't you come in to the post office in person?"

"I might do that. Thank you."

It figured that they'd honor the privacy of a P.O. box owner. Now the question was, after a night's sleep—should she drive first to Santa Barbara or go straight to Wasco?

37

THE MOVIE

The motion picture shifts to a daytime exterior shot of Westwood Village Memorial Cemetery. A casket is lowered into the ground.

The voice-over relates, "The plan worked. The police thought Malena Mengarelli's body was mine. We were roughly the same build, and she was wearing my signature necklace. She had apparently regained consciousness as the flames overtook her and crawled out of the car and died on the highway where they found her. The studio paid for a quick and unpublicized burial. Her tombstone bears my name. I later learned that the woman was a killer who worked for the Las Vegas mob. They certainly weren't going to tell the police the identity of the corpse in the grave."

Cut to a daytime exterior shot of Our Lady of Hope Children's Home in Santa Barbara. A montage depicts nuns with children playing in the schoolyard, nuns watching over babies in a nursery, and the Mother Superior in an office checking records.

The voice-over continues, "After that horrific incident in the Hollywood Hills, my friend Ray Webster helped me hide. I heard through the grapevine that Buddy Franco had survived the nightmare at the studio. He essentially left Los Angeles and disappeared, leaving a wife and daughter. No one knew where he was, but I was afraid he'd be looking for me. I was shuffled between several of Ray's musician friends, but eventually I went to Santa Barbara to search for my daughter."

The camera pulls back from the outdoor playground and pans across streets and up to an overlooking hill. A dark 1947 Chrysler Windsor sits at a curb. Blair, now with dark hair and wearing a scarf and sunglasses, sits in the driver's seat. She holds binoculars and is watching the orphanage.

"I dyed my hair brown and did my best to change my appearance. I used Eldon Hirsch's coin collection to provide myself with a means to live. I'd sell one coin at a time, and that would last me quite a while. Finding dealers who were trustworthy was difficult, but I did it. I couldn't have word get back to the mob that those coins were turning up. I lived in a run-down boardinghouse, and every day I'd wait until Sister Agnes—I found out her name—brought baby Jane outside for some fresh air. Jane, for Jane Doe. That's what the orphanage called her. Not as good as Suzanne, but I liked it."

Cross-fade to a shot of a black couple leaving the orphanage. The woman is holding a baby. The man shakes hands with the Mother Superior as they say goodbye.

"And then . . . about three months after Jane's arrival at the orphanage, she was adopted by a nice Negro family that lived in Phoenix, Arizona. So that was my next destination. As much as I wanted to make contact with them, I was afraid my background— my existence—would be discovered."

A POV shot of what Blair sees through the binoculars pans over to the street. Parked across from the orphanage is a black Cadillac. Buddy Franco—now bald and sporting a mustache—and another man sit in the car, watching.

"You see, I soon learned that Buddy Franco had survived my gunshot and had changed his appearance. He, too, was watching the movements of my daughter, probably hoping I would show up.

He was correct. I showed up, all right, though at a distance. I had to be very careful as the months—and years—crept by . . . until it was 1952."

The Good Word Baptist Church catered to Negroes, but the congregation held a few specks of white among the many black faces in attendance one Sunday morning. The folks were dressed in their best suits and dresses, despite the lack of an air conditioner and the temperature outside of ninety-four degrees Fahrenheit. And it wasn't summer yet.

Blair sat in a pew toward the back of the sanctuary, near the aisle in case she needed to make a fast escape. She didn't want to get overconfident. Although she had not seen any signs of Buddy Franco or his minions in months, Blair was smart enough to know that they could appear at any time.

She enjoyed the gospel choir in the church. It made her feel good. The music, with its similar roots to jazz, reminded her of her time with Hank. Blair didn't take much stock in the other parts of churchgoing. She had long relegated her soul to a destiny of misfortune. There were times when she was compelled to walk up the center aisle to the front of the church and confess her sins. "I am a murderer," she imagined herself saying in front of the families in attendance. But she also thought, fitfully and hopefully, that if they knew the circumstances behind the killing, somehow they wouldn't hold it against her.

It's no use telling yourself that it was justified, Blair thought. *You've made your bed and now you must lie in it. But enough with the self-pity! Focus on why you came this morning!*

Blair gazed toward the row of pews in the front. A family of three sat in the fourth row closest to the pulpit. The man, a car mechanic by trade, had his arm on the back of the pew, indicating that the pretty housewife and the nearly three-year-old girl

271

sitting beside him were under his protection. They seemed to be happy. Blair had moved to Phoenix to be near her daughter and to watch her grow. Jane was a bubbly child. Every time Blair saw her, she was laughing at something. She couldn't remember ever seeing Jane cry.

Blair began attending their church after a year of watching and waiting. It had taken her that long to make sure Franco wasn't on to her. She had seen him several times walking with a cane, but that didn't make him any less dangerous. Blair knew that Buddy Franco had a contract out on her, and he would stop at nothing to find her. Luckily, he hadn't spotted her so far.

One day, she watched him from afar as he rang the bell and entered Jane's home. Blair didn't know what he'd told the adoptive parents. Surely, they must have wondered why this strange man was visiting them and asking questions. Nevertheless, he had left them alone and driven away. That was when Blair knew that she could never speak to Jane or her family. She had been hoping that there might come a time when she could casually approach them as a fellow church member, introduce herself by her new name—Penny Miller—and perhaps be friends.

Too risky.

Blair had to be content with just being in proximity to her beautiful little girl, but not interacting with her. After all, it wasn't only Blair's life that was at stake. Her presence could place little Jane and her loving parents in jeopardy.

The Tumbleweed Truck Stop was located just outside of city limits on Highway 60. It consisted of gas pumps, a convenience store, and a small café, in three separate buildings. The black family who ran the establishment lived in a house—a shack, really—that was part of the café. The business barely survived, as most travelers stopped closer in to the city. It was also apparent that the Tumbleweed catered mostly to Negroes; somehow, drivers on the road could tell the establishment was not often frequented by whites.

Blair didn't need to work. The money from selling the coins was supporting her just fine. But she toiled in the truck stop convenience store for something to do so that she wouldn't go mad from boredom. The family who owned the truck stop had befriended her at church, so she'd thought, *why not?* As the place was situated out of town and not too far from Jane's home, it suited her. The apartment building where she lived was only a mile away, too. It seemed to be out of the way and safe.

She had just finished restocking the Hershey candy bars in the rack near the cash register, so she took a moment to wipe the sweat off her face with a cloth and drink some water. It was terribly hot in Phoenix. She didn't think she'd ever get used to it.

It was always something of a novelty when the bell rang, triggered by a car running over the black rubber hose that stretched across the pavement by the gas pumps. Blair didn't need to do anything; Leroy would take care of the customer and fill up the car. Nevertheless, she always looked out the glass door to see who might be pulling into the remote rest stop. The sight of an old green Ford coupe that was on its last legs made her smile. The two Negro men heading her way were like angels from heaven.

She stepped outside to greet them, holding out her arms. "Ray! Bobop! How lovely to see you!"

They both gave her warm hugs, even though a black man embracing a white woman in 1952 was something for which they could get in trouble in Arizona. Luckily, there were no white locals around.

"What a surprise," she said. "Come on inside, I'll buy you a Coke." She looked back at the car. "I can't believe that old thing is still running, Bobop."

"I can't either, Miss Blair."

Ray jerked his head at him. "Shh!" he whispered. "Her name is Penny now."

"Oh, right, sorry, uh, Miss Penny."

Blair laughed. "It's all right, no one can hear you out here where Jesus lost his sandals."

She led them into the store and purchased three bottles of soda from the vending machine. They stood in the path of the standing electric fan that blew hot air through the small store, enjoying their drinks. At least it was a breeze that moved.

"How are things in LA?" she asked.

"Well, uh, Penny," Ray began. "I have some news for you, and it's not very nice news at that."

"Oh?"

Bobop looked down. He seemed to be glad it wasn't him who had to tell her.

"Well? What is it?"

Ray took a breath and spoke. "Some people found a body in the Mojave Desert between LA and Las Vegas. A skeleton. The police won't do nothing about it. They won't investigate it or try to find out what happened. To them it's just some sorry skeleton in the desert."

"What are you telling me?" she asked, starting to tremble.

"It's Hank."

She put a hand to her mouth. "Oh my God."

"He was shot in the head. Who knows what else was done to him? He was left out there to rot."

Blair turned away to face the desert landscape outside the door. She couldn't hold back the tears. "How do you know it's him?"

"Regina had a lawyer working for her who was trying to find out what happened to Hank. He was able to get word about the discovery of the body from a policeman contact he knew. Anyway, this was on the finger of the dead man's right hand."

Blair looked back at Ray. A gold ring lay in his palm. She took the ring and examined it.

She nodded. "This was Hank's daddy's wedding ring. Hank always wore it."

"Regina said you should have it."

Her hand clutched it tightly. Tears continued to roll down her cheeks. She was not surprised to hear the news, but the confirmation was enough for her to finally mourn him properly. Still, the wound would never be healed.

"Aw, child," Ray said. He took her in his arms again and let her cry against his shirt.

Later, when they finished a meal of bacon and eggs at the truck stop café, the trio sat back in the booth and lit cigarettes. They were the only ones in the joint.

"How's Loretta and little Gregory?" Blair asked Ray.

"Oh, they're fine. Gregory's getting bigger. Turned nine years old!"

"Oh, my. Well, give Loretta my love."

"I will."

"What do you hear about 'Blair Kendrick?'" she asked.

Ray shook his head. "That's something else I wanted to talk to you about."

"What is it?" she asked.

"Franco is alive and living in Las Vegas."

She nodded. "I've seen him."

"He knows *you're* alive, Blair. He's looking for you. Some of his flunkies came around asking me about you. They harassed Regina Marley. Darlin', I think you're in danger. Those gangsters in Las Vegas have the money and means to find you sooner or later."

She had been in denial of that truth for some time. "What do you think I should do?"

"I think you have to leave the country."

She put her head in her hands. Then she abruptly hit her fist on the table. "Goddamn it. You know, I've been thinking that this was getting too dangerous for Jane. That I can't do it anymore. That staying here is too selfish. That I have to go away, for her sake." She got up from the table and paced. "But where can I go? I don't know anyone anywhere."

"Well, now," Ray said. "I have a friend in Costa Rica."

38

KARISSA

Karissa hit the road in her Nissan Murano after she'd had breakfast, and, on a whim, stopped by the bank to withdraw a sizable amount of cash from the money she'd received from the coin dealer. She then dialed Marcello.

"What time are you meeting me in Wasco?" she asked him.

"Later today," he replied. "I've got this parent-teacher thing at my kids' school this morning. You're on your way to the children's home in Santa Barbara first?"

"Heading out now."

"Okay, call me when you leave Santa Barbara. It'll probably take the same amount of time for you to get to Wasco from Santa Barbara as it will for me to get there from here."

They hung up and Karissa drove on. Feeling like a woman possessed, she was determined to get to the bottom of the remaining mysteries. The key to finding the answers was in one of the two towns.

Like all Los Angelinos, she thought of her route in terms of highway names. It was a straight shot to Santa Barbara on the 101. That took her through Hollywood, into the Hills near

Universal City, and into the San Fernando Valley where the 101 became the Ventura Freeway. Then through Sherman Oaks, Woodland Hills, Thousand Oaks, and finally all the way to the coast and the scenic drive north. It wouldn't take too long, a couple of hours, if traffic wasn't bad.

It was around the area of Mussel Shoals that she noticed a black car in the rearview mirror that was shadily familiar. It was too far back to know for certain, but Karissa couldn't help but land on the obvious possibility—that Barry Doon was on her tail. Cursing softly to herself, she stayed the course, maintained her speed, and gripped the wheel. The car behind her kept its distance on the highway as well, not inching forward or back. Karissa decided to take the next exit to see what would happen. She pulled off the road at La Conchita and drove across a set of railroad tracks. She wanted to stop at a gas station, but the one on the corner was closed and abandoned, so Karissa drove farther into town. It was a typical beach community with weather-beaten houses built among the rocky shoreline. Keeping one eye on the rearview mirror, where she could still see the 101, she pulled over to the curb of a residential street. The black car sped past the exit, continuing its way north.

She waited a minute, then turned around and got back on the highway. The road continued through Carpinteria and Toro Canyon. However, as she approached the Santa Barbara city limits and a denser landscape of urban development, she saw the black car behind her again. Was she being paranoid, or was it the same vehicle? It seemed so. How had he gotten behind her again without her seeing him? It continued to travel at the same pace at the back as it had before. Karissa knew she was no expert at surveillance techniques or—what did they call it in action thrillers?—*E and E.* Escape and evasion.

Should she call the police? What would she say, exactly? *Hello, there's a car following me on the highway.* Well, duh, cars do follow you on the highway. Without real evidence of a threat, the cops would do nothing.

She really didn't want to slow down enough for him to get closer so that she could identify the license plate.

Her anxiety crept up again.

The only thing Karissa could do was to keep going. Eventually, her GPS directed her to take one of the Santa Barbara exits, and she drove into downtown. Perpetually glancing at the rearview mirror, she found that the black car was no longer there. The relief she felt was only a little comforting, for she sensed that Doon—or whoever he was—was still in the vicinity.

Karissa drove up to Our Lady of Hope Children's Home and parked in the visitor lot. As she got out of the car, she took a good look at her surroundings. A tall cliff with a road atop adjoined the property. There was no indication that she was being watched.

It was a pretty place, very tranquil. She imagined that back in 1921, when the orphanage was founded, it had been in a more rural setting. Over the decades, the city must have grown around it. The building was white and resembled a church. The property was surrounded by a fence and appeared to be very secure. A playground was next to the structure, but there were no children present at that time.

Karissa went inside and approached a nun at the front desk. She pulled the old intake form out of her purse.

"Hello, is there someone I could talk to about this?"

The nun wrinkled her brow and looked at the form. "Oh my, that's old. What did you want to know about it?"

"Anything I can find out."

"Well, you know our records are confidential."

"I understand that. Please, it's important. Is there a supervisor or director I can speak with?"

"Why don't you have a seat? I'll see if I can get someone."

The reception area was empty. Karissa sat in a chair and focused on the Catholic iconography on the walls. The literature available for reading consisted of brochures about adoption and right-to-life information, magazines published by the Catholic Church, and Bibles. None of this bothered Karissa. She had been raised to respect religious beliefs, and she had attended a Protestant church for most of her childhood with her own adoptive parents.

Being in the orphanage brought back memories of her childhood. As she had been adopted herself, Karissa admired what any organization did for children who needed homes. She often thanked the Lord for her loving adoptive parents, who'd welcomed a strange two-year-old mixed-race child into their own home without hesitation. She often wished she could remember something—anything—about her real mother and father during those first two years of her life. It was why she had held on to the old rag doll, the one with the name "Julia" stitched into her clothing. The doll was her only link to her birth parents. But recalling any relevant memories was impossible. It didn't matter much anyway, for she considered the couple who had raised her to be her true father and mother.

"Ms. Glover?"

The voice jolted Karissa out of her thoughts. She looked up to see an older nun, perhaps in her sixties, standing in an open doorway. She stood up.

"Hello, I'm Mother Superior Phyllis Anne. Would you like to come back to my office?"

"Yes, thank you, Reverend Mother."

Karissa followed the woman through the door and into a hallway. She had expected to hear crying infants and laughing children, but it was unusually quiet. They went into a small office near the front. The nun offered Karissa a seat and took her place behind a desk.

"I don't hear any children," Karissa said.

"They're in another wing," the Reverend Mother said. "This is just the administrative area. We *do* like our silence over here." She laughed a little. "Now, what can I do for you?"

Karissa showed her the form. "I'd like to know if there is anything—anything at all—that you can tell me about this child."

The woman adjusted her glasses and scanned the page. "Oh, dear. This is before *my* time. How extraordinary. Is this—is this somehow a part of your family?"

"No, no, it's . . . well, it's a long story. I'm a filmmaker, and I'm doing research and . . ." Karissa realized that the tale was so complicated that she couldn't easily describe why she wanted to know these things. "Let's just say I'm interested in finding out anything I can about what happened to that child. Was she adopted? And by whom?"

The nun shook her head. "That kind of information is strictly confidential, Ms. Glover. Besides, for a case this old, those records would be locked up in storage." She handed the paper back to Karissa. "I'm sorry I can't help you."

Karissa nodded. She opened her purse, took out an envelope that contained the cash she had withdrawn from the bank, and counted out several bills. The Mother Superior's eyes went wide as she watched the money being counted and placed on the desk.

"What if I were to make a little donation to your orphanage?" Karissa asked. "Here's five thousand dollars. Do you think maybe you could find that information and tell me? After all, it was a long time ago."

The nun swallowed and said, "We've been needing to repair some of our playground equipment and upgrade a couple of computers. What kind of time frame do you have?"

"I need the information as soon as possible."

"Give me your phone number. It might take me a few hours. I'll call you when I have something. Is that all right?"

39

THE MOVIE

The motion picture's momentum builds as the audience sits in antic-ipation. The people in attendance know that they're in the final act—and that revelations will be forthcoming.

There are shots of different calendars for subsequent years, tearing away quickly—1955, 1958, 1962, 1965 . . .

We see a tropical beach, the ocean's waves gently lapping onto the shoreline. Costa Rican children run about and play. A lone woman sits in a recliner underneath an umbrella. She wears a modest swim-suit and sunglasses. Her hair is dark. She is the Blair Kendrick character, her appearance modified, older.

"With Ray's help, I fled to Costa Rica and led a quiet, anonymous life in Puntarenas. I won't bore you with the details, but I snuck out of the country with a fake passport under the name Penny Miller. Ray's friend, a Honduran named José Bográn, was a lawyer there. Apparently, José had once lived in Los Angeles and knew Ray from before. José helped me incorporate a private company with funds I continually received by selling off the rare coins, a few at a time over the years. There were fake partners and stocks that made it look like they were the investors, which hid my identity. I named it Azules

Oscuros S.A., which meant "Dark Blues"—an in-joke that would mean nothing to anyone but me and Hank. The company managed my house on Harvard Boulevard back in Los Angeles because, only God knows why, I wanted to keep it. Maybe I really was crazy. I thought perhaps someday I could return to it, even though by then Justin Hirsch had taken over his father's studio. I knew he'd be looking for whoever took those coins. Did he know the truth that I was still alive? I imagine he did."

The scene cross-fades to daytime exterior shots of early 1970s Las Vegas, the downtown Golden Nugget casino, the iconic cowboy sign, and other landmarks.

"My daughter Jane grew up. Ray kept tabs on her and sent updates that I received through José. By 1972, she had become a young woman and had married a nice Negro man—excuse me—by then the use of that word had gone out of fashion. 'African American' was now the proper term. He was really of mixed-race heritage, too, like Jane, but there seemed to be a notion in America called the 'one-drop rule'—if there was one drop of African blood in a person, then that person was not considered white. But there had been some improvements in the United States. The civil rights actions of the sixties changed the landscape for African Americans, although, like Hank had told me—there would always be racism in my native country. Anyway, Jane and her husband Maxwell moved to Las Vegas, where he worked as a waiter in one of the big casino restaurants and she had a job as a cashier."

Cut to the interior of a modest ranch house. We see a young mixed-race woman, Jane, setting up house with the help of her husband. She is pregnant.

"When Ray told me that Jane was going to have a baby, I had to come out of hiding and find a way to come back home."

An interior nighttime shot of a casino floor pulls in to reveal Jane behind the barred window, counting out bills to customers as they turn in their chips. The camera pans to the bar, where Blair sits with a drink and a cigarette. She still wears sunglasses.

"Like before, I watched my daughter from afar, keeping my distance. I knew that Franco's people were watching her, too, just in case I showed up. It was like walking a tightrope. However, I knew where Franco and his henchmen liked to hang out."

Cut to the exterior of a small diner in North Las Vegas, an area populated by working class minorities and those on skid row. The Sunshine Diner is an old-fashioned joint with just a few booths by the window, a counter with round "soda fountain"–style stools, short-order cooks, and chain-smoking waitresses.

The camera focuses on sixty-year-old Buddy Franco, his face now creased from aging and stress. Still bald, the facial hair graying. Seen through the window, he sits in one of the booths. Across from him is a younger, tough-looking man. They are eating breakfast, having coffee, and smoking. We pull away from the diner to a Ford Tempo parked across the street. Blair, in her "Penny Miller" disguise with sunglasses and scarf, watches Franco. She, too, is smoking. With a disgusted look on her face, she flicks a near-finished butt out the window, starts the car, and drives away.

"Yep, he was still watching Jane, hoping I would turn up. I had to be extra cautious. But I wasn't going to miss the blessed day, which, in 1973, finally arrived. I became a grandmother."

Blair, wearing a scarf and sunglasses, entered Southern Nevada Memorial Hospital and walked with purpose past the reception desk and to a stairwell that she knew would take her to the basement level. Earlier in the day, she had phoned the hospital to inquire what room Jane was in—but before she could visit, she needed a disguise. Taking a quick look in both directions to make sure she wasn't being followed, she opened the door and scurried down the steps. Now in her mid-forties, Blair maintained her physique by what she called the "anxiety diet." It wasn't the healthiest way to stay slim, but it did curb her appetite. The constant concern over whether Justin Hirsch's spies or his Las Vegas crime partners would find her or catch her in the act of keeping tabs on her daughter often took its toll. She did tend to drink more than she should, and these days there was more pressure for people to give up smoking. Blair couldn't do it. She'd tried for one year while living in Costa Rica, but everyone there smoked around her, so it was impossible. She resigned herself to the fact that she would either die of lung cancer, be murdered by Hollywood fixers or Vegas mobsters, caught by the police, or live to be a hundred as a fugitive from society.

Blair reached the basement and snuck out of the stairwell as if she were a common criminal—which, she often told herself, she was. *Blair Kendrick—Femme Fatale.* By the sixties, that French term had started being used to describe the "bad girl" characters in the old Hollywood crime movies of the forties and fifties. Critics in France had also coined the expression film noir to describe the pictures of that genre. Back when she was working and making the movies, no one called them that.

Femme fatale. A badge of honor? Perhaps.

She quickly found the room she was looking for—LAUNDRY. She stepped inside and addressed a woman wearing all white who was pressing nurse and orderly clothing.

"Hi, I'm looking for my uniform, I left it here the other day and then forgot to pick it up."

The woman nodded her head at the stacks of folded whites on a table. "Just take one in your size."

Blair quickly looked through the garments and found one. "Thanks," she said, and left the room.

"Nurse Penny" stepped out of the elevator of the maternity ward and headed down the hall before anyone could see that she wasn't wearing a photo ID clipped to her dress. The uniform alone would have to do to disguise her, but she didn't plan on staying long. She just wanted to *see* her granddaughter.

Halfway down the hall was a large common area, the waiting room for nervous fathers and families who expected to hear good news at any moment. She almost smiled at a couple of men who sat there with newspapers—when she felt a slice of terror rip through her spine. Blair immediately made an about-face and bolted for the nearest ladies' room.

Oh my God . . . oh my God!

She'd seen Buddy Franco and his cohort.

Blair caught her breath at the sink. Now that she thought about it, he didn't look so imposing anymore.

She opened the bathroom door slightly just to peer out across the hall at the men. The other fellow besides Buddy was the younger man she'd seen at the diner, probably now the muscle behind the team. Blair watched the two men for a minute, debating whether she should simply dart out, run to the elevator, and leave the hospital. She could see her granddaughter another day. Yes, that was the best plan. She took a deep breath, ready to slip out the door, when the other man put down his newspaper and stood. Then Franco put down his own paper, grabbed his cane, and started to stand with some effort. His pal offered to help him, but Franco practically slapped the hand away. Once they were both on their feet, the men left the waiting area and headed for the elevators. For a man with a cane, Franco could walk fast. He didn't appear to be having too much trouble.

She stepped into the hall and watched their backs as they turned into the elevator bay. After hearing the "ding" of the car arriving, Blair went the other way to the room where Jane was recuperating.

The door was open. Blair simply stood there, mouth agape, as the sight took her breath away.

Jane was in bed, nursing her baby.

Blair had never even spoken to her daughter.

She walked into the room. Jane looked up and smiled at her. "Hi," Jane said.

Blair couldn't find her voice. She just stared with wonder at the two living beings in front of her. Daughter and granddaughter. Tears came to her eyes.

"Isn't she beautiful?" Jane asked.

Blair cleared her throat. "She sure is. How . . . how are you feeling?"

"Just fine. A little tired. I was in labor for seven hours."

Blair didn't respond to that. She simply stepped closer and felt her heart melt.

The baby had fallen asleep. Jane gently moved her from her breast. "Can you . . . can you hold her a second while I fix myself?" she asked.

Blair nearly gasped. *Can I hold my granddaughter? Really?*

"Sure." She came around to the other side of the bed and carefully took the girl in her arms. Blair had a vivid, lovely flashback of when she had first held Suzanne—now Jane—as a newborn.

Jane fastened her hospital gown and then reached for her child. "Okay, thanks."

Blair laughed. "Nuh-uh. I get to hold her for at least another minute!"

Jane also giggled. "I know, you can't help it, can you? She's so sweet. What time is it? My husband is supposed to be here as soon as he gets off work."

"It's about three o'clock."

"Oh, good. He should be here in a half hour."

Blair couldn't take her eyes off the baby's sleeping face. Her skin was paler than her mother's.

"What's her name?" Blair asked.

A man's loud voice interrupted the conversation from outside the room. "Yeah, get me a Coke if you would," he called to someone down the hall.

Blair looked up and saw Franco's partner standing in profile in the corridor.

She immediately handed the baby back to Jane. "Here you go. I know you will enjoy her." Blair ducked her head, moved around the bed quickly, and scooted out the door. The man didn't look twice at her. She was just another nurse.

Franco stood at the end of the hall, looking toward the elevators. Apparently, the men hadn't gotten on one earlier. Blair entered the next patient's room to wait for an all-clear. The mother there was asleep, but a father sat next to the bed with his new baby in his arms. He looked up at Blair with a deer-in-the-headlights expression of utter fright.

If she hadn't been so rattled by Franco and the other man, Blair would have laughed aloud. "Don't worry," she said to the new father. "It will be great. You'll see."

The man nodded and grinned.

She turned and stuck her head into the corridor. Franco was gone. The other man was possibly in Jane's room. What would he say to her? *Have you seen a woman that looks like the old movie actress, Blair Kendrick?*

Blair scuttled down the hallway and into a stairwell, avoiding the elevator altogether and leaving the hospital without being discovered. She resolved that she had to find a way to see her daughter and granddaughter more often.

40

KARISSA

On the way to Wasco, California, Karissa had the nagging feeling that she was being followed again. The same dark car appeared behind her along state highway 126 as she traveled east from the 101 to connect to I-5. However, she lost track of it once she got on the interstate heading north to Bakersfield.

The landscape in this part of the state was flat and arid. The desert. Hardly any trees in sight. The sky was 180 degrees of blue that met the scorched earth in all directions.

Who would want to live here? she wondered.

The trip took nearly three hours. The town of Wasco was as she had expected—tiny, sparse, and quiet. She used her GPS to find the post office on E Street and pulled in to the parking lot at the side of the small building. Marcello's Corvette was already there, but he wasn't in the car. Karissa pulled out her phone and dialed his number.

"Hey," he answered. "You here?"

"I'm at the post office. Where are you?"

"I walked down to the Pueblo Market to get something to drink. Man, it's *hot* here."

"Well, come on back. I'm in the parking lot."

"Be there in a jiff."

He returned after five minutes, bringing her a cold bottle of water. "Where's yours?" she asked.

"Done drunk."

She took a swig. "Thanks, I was dumb not to bring any water with me. Come on, let's go." They headed inside the post office.

"How do you want to do this?" she whispered to him. "I talked to a Mr. Stevens on the phone, and he wasn't too forthcoming."

There were two tellers working—a Hispanic woman and an African American man, both in their late forties or early fifties. No one was in line. Marcello said, "Let me handle this." They approached the man, who looked up, nodded, and smiled.

"Help you, sir?" he asked.

"Yeah, I'm trying to locate Gregory Webster, who has this P.O. box here." Marcello showed him the envelope Karissa had received. "Do you know Gregory?"

At first, the teller's eyes revealed subtle alarm. He lowered his voice, but remained friendly enough. "May I ask why you need to find him?"

"Well, I was doing some business with Gregory in Los Angeles, but his phone number got disconnected. I need to speak to him about some money matters. I understand he has something to do with growing nuts?"

"Are you a bill collector?"

"No, sir. He stands to receive some cash, and I need to talk to him in person." Marcello then looked intently into the teller's eyes and nodded.

The teller seemed to get the message and, after a beat, grinned. "Gregory does change his number a lot. I have no idea why he does that."

"Can you help us out?" Marcello asked quietly.

The man looked at Karissa, who gave him her best smile. He seemed to like that. Finally, the man sensed that he could trust them. "Sure, he's at the Bass Player Farm on Paso Robles Highway, heading toward the state prison. Just take E Street up to Paso Robles, hang a left, and go about five miles. You can't miss it."

"Bass Player Farm?"

The teller shrugged. "I don't know why he named his farm that. He grows almonds and pistachios."

Karissa and Marcello gave each other a fist bump in the parking lot, and then her cell phone rang. The caller ID indicated a Santa Barbara area code.

"Marcello, it's the nun. Wait a second." They leaned against her Murano as she answered the call and put it on speaker so Marcello could listen. "Hello?"

"Ms. Glover? This is Mother Superior Phyllis Anne at Our Lady of Hope Children's Home."

"Hello! Thanks for getting back to me."

"I was able to locate a record regarding your inquiry. I'm afraid there isn't much I can tell you, but I can give you what I have."

"I would greatly appreciate it, Reverend Mother."

"It goes against our ethics here, but the donation you provided will be very helpful. Our Lord Jesus appreciates charitable efforts, and I believe he would forgive me for telling you these things, especially since they occurred so long ago."

"Oh, I agree with you," Karissa said with enthusiasm. She heard the nun chuckle under her breath, as if they were sharing something conspiratorial.

"Little baby Jane Doe was adopted by an African American family not long after the orphanage took her in. Their names

291

were Lewis and Mabel Channing, and they lived in Phoenix, Arizona."

"Phoenix."

"That's right. As far as I know, they continued to call the girl Jane."

"Jane Channing. Lewis and Mabel Channing."

"Yes. Now, I went ahead and attempted to see if the Channings are still at the address listed in our records. They are not. I'm not sure if you'll be able to trace the family beyond this, but I'm no private detective. That's all I have—good luck!"

"Thank you, Reverend Mother."

Karissa hung up and said, "I don't know if any of that information is helpful. But at least we know that Blair Kendrick's daughter found a family. What became of her? Can we find out?"

Marcello indicated his own phone. "The Internet is our friend." He opened a browser and searched for "Jane Channing Phoenix AZ." Karissa looked on as he scrolled through various hits. "Well, there're a few Jane Channings in Phoenix. How old would she be?"

"She was born in '49, so, what, she'd be *seventy* today. If she's still alive."

He backed up and typed "Jane Channing Phoenix Obituary." Again, he started scrolling, but there weren't many hits. Then Karissa caught something.

"Wait. Stop. Look, that name." She pointed to the text excerpt of the article that appeared beneath the hyperlink headline. "It mentions Mrs. Mabel Channing. Open that one."

"Good eyes, Karissa." The link went to a piece in *The Arizona Republic*. Marcello read the brief entry. "Jane Eliza Channing Bradford, age Twenty-Five, formerly of Phoenix, died in Las Vegas, Nevada, on May Third, Nineteen-Seventy-Five. Survivors include her mother, Mrs. Mabel Channing of Phoenix."

"Oh, no. Damn. What a disappointment. It doesn't say what she died of."

"Nope." He Googled "Mabel Channing Phoenix Obituary." It came up with a date of 1991 and indicated that the woman had left no survivors, but that she was "joining her husband, Lewis, and daughter, Jane, in heaven."

"Well, I guess that's a dead end," Karissa said.

"Wait a second." Marcello then Googled "Jane Channing Bradford Las Vegas Obituary." Several hits appeared, but none of them were obituaries. There were, however, several stories about a double murder.

"What the hell?" he murmured as he opened one. He read the entry from the *Las Vegas Review-Journal*, dated May 4, 1975. "Police are investigating what appears to be a double homicide at a residence on Reynolds Avenue. Maxwell and Jane Bradford were found shot to death in their home, apparently victims of a break-in. Sergeant Sean Wallis indicates the crime could be drug-related. Particularly troubling is that the couple's infant daughter is missing and believed to be dead. The Bradfords were both employees of the Golden Nugget Casino." He looked at Karissa, whose eyes exhibited horror. "Hoooly shit," he said.

"What a tragedy. Look for some follow-up stories," Karissa prodded.

He did so and found something dated May 5, 1975. "This is hardly a mention. Says police have no leads in the double homicide of Mr. and Mrs. Maxwell Bradford or the disappearance of their daughter. Again, they say it's drug-related." He kept searching and scanning the hits. "Wait. Here's something from the sixth." He showed it to her.

"Oh my God." Karissa put a hand to her mouth. She reads aloud, "'Police found evidence that the Bradfords' baby daughter was possibly killed. The little girl's clothing was found in a trash dumpster a block away from the scene of the crime. Blood on the pajamas matched the toddler's type, but no corpse has been recovered.' This is horrible."

Together they scanned the other entries on the page, but ultimately determined that the case had never been solved.

"Wow. That's so sad." She sighed heavily. "Blair not only had a daughter, but she had a *granddaughter*, Marcello. Too bad she never knew about it." Then Karissa remembered something. "Wait, when was Buddy Franco shot in that diner? That was in Las Vegas, wasn't it?"

"Yeah, 1975!" He punched in some terms into his phone and got the date. "May 9. That's damn close to May 5."

They looked at each other. "Coincidence?" she asked.

"Maybe."

"And maybe not." She looked at her wristwatch. "It's nearly five o'clock. Come on, let's get going. I want to get to that nut farm before they close."

They went to their separate vehicles and Karissa followed Marcello out of town on Paso Robles Highway. As the postman had said, they didn't have far to go. A short road led from the highway to Bass Player Farm, which consisted of a warehouse, a front office administration building, another structure that appeared to be where the products were processed, and a house behind everything else. The buildings were surrounded by a sizable orchard of almond trees.

They parked and approached the building. Marcello added, "I did a quick look-see on their website. Says the owner and operator is someone named Harold Green. Is that an online alias for Gregory Webster? I think he'd be making sure to cover his tracks. They grow and process their own almonds here, and then sell them to a different distributor. They're organic, too."

"Interesting," Karissa murmured, but she was more concerned about what she was going to find inside.

They entered the front office, but found no one there. "I didn't see anyone outside, either. Don't they have employees?" Marcello asked. He hit a desk bell button on the counter. When they were just about to give up, they heard someone approaching from the back room. A black woman in her late sixties appeared—they immediately recognized her as Carol Webster, Gregory's wife, whom they had seen at Ray Webster's funeral.

"Hello, how can I help—?" Her eyes grew wide when she saw Karissa. "Oh, my."

"Hello, Mrs. Webster," Karissa said. "Is your husband here?"

"Just a minute. I'll get him." She went through the door and they heard her pick up a phone. Her voice was low.

"He's not going to come out shooting, is he?" Marcello whispered to Karissa.

They waited a few minutes, and then Gregory, his wife, and a woman who looked vaguely familiar came into the space. The woman was also black, in her thirties, and dressed in jeans and a T-shirt. In a swift movement, she stepped forward and lifted her hands to embrace Karissa.

"Karissa!" the woman said, as if they were old friends. "You made it. You found us!"

Karissa paused, tilting her head. "Do I know you?"

The woman laughed. "I was dressed in a nice pantsuit when we met in the lobby of the Executive Suites. I'm Serena. Serena Brantley. I'm the one who told you about the house in West Adams Heights."

"Oh! Right!" Karissa put a hand to her mouth. "But . . . wait a second . . . I don't . . ."

"It was the only way we could drop a big ol' bread crumb so that you'd go to the house. We figured you'd rent it—it was a good deal, wasn't it? We made you an offer you couldn't have refused. After that, it was just a matter of time for you to explore the history of that house and then eventually come here to us." Serena laughed again. "You should see your face right now. Girl, you been punk'd! I ain't no real estate agent."

"Serena's my niece," Gregory said. "I was wondering when you'd finally find us." He moved around from behind the counter and held out a hand first to Karissa and then to Marcello. "I'm Gregory Webster, and that's my wife, Carol."

They all shook hands. "I'm a little freaked out," Karissa said. She addressed Serena, "You mean . . . you told me about the house for a reason?"

"Just like Serena said. It was to get you to follow your nose and find us," Gregory answered. "Sorry we had to be so indirect about it. And I'm sorry we couldn't speak at my father's funeral. We were being watched. Luckily, I've managed to remain hard to find outside of Los Angeles."

"Are you . . . Howard Green?" Marcello asked.

Gregory grinned again. "There are people in town—you know, brothers—who know me by my real name, but to the public this place is run by Howard Green. We're not very big, compared to other almond farms in California. We stay under the radar by just growing almonds, processing them, and whole-saling them to distributors that package them and take care of the retail end. That's why the men looking for me have been unable to do so, and it's also why I don't stay in Los Angeles but for a few hours at a time when I visit!"

"Wait," Karissa said. "I'm really trying to get my head around this. It was your *intention* to get me here?"

"That's right," Serena said. "We thought you'd be the perfect producer to tell Blair's story."

"I'm not sure what the story *is*!" She said, still dumbfounded. Then she addressed Gregory. "I mean, I mentioned to you at the funeral—and sorry again for your loss—"

"Thank you."

"—anyway, I mentioned that we are trying to make a movie about Blair Kendrick and Hank Marley, and we'd spoken to your father at Vernon Healthcare before he passed. He said we needed to talk to you. Is that why we're here? Do you have something you can tell us?"

Gregory just smiled. "Let's go back to our house." He looked at his wife. "Carol, lock up the office, we'll close early today. No one's coming in, anyway." She nodded and did so while he and Serena led Karissa and Marcello out the back of the administration office. They crossed a paved area that served as a connector to the various buildings. A separate driveway from the parking lot also went to the two-story home that stood behind the warehouse. It appeared to be several decades old, but recent models of a Ford pickup and a Chevy SUV sat in an open garage connected to the building.

"Carol and I got a windfall and bought this property in 1990," he said as they walked. "It was already an almond farm, and the family who had run it had been here since the Great Depression. That's how old our house is. The garage was built in the eighties. Serena lives in town and works at the Walmart Supercenter."

"Carol's my aunt," Serena explained.

Gregory continued, "As you can see, right now there's no work being done. Harvesting isn't until the fall. Employees are hired seasonally. We just take care of orders for the nuts from last year, and Carol and I can handle that ourselves." He then gave Karissa a lovely smile. "I'm really quite pleased to finally talk to you, Ms. Glover. We've been expecting you."

"Call me Karissa."

They entered through a side door that opened to the kitchen. "Can I get you some coffee or something?"

Karissa looked at Marcello, who shook his head. "No, thanks, it's too hot for coffee," she answered. "We're fine."

"Okay, let me or Carol know if we can get you anything." By then his wife had caught up with them and came into the kitchen. "Oh, come with us upstairs, will you? There's someone I want you to meet." They followed him to the wooden stairs, and then climbed to the second floor. He pointed to a bedroom. "In there."

Karissa and Marcello walked into a small room furnished with a hospital bed, an IV drip pole and bag, and a tray table. There were also a couple of empty chairs where visitors could sit. The tube from the drip was connected to the arm of a very old woman who lay in the bed. She had white hair and wrinkled pale skin, and she was smoking a cigarette. It appeared that her knees were propped up with pillows underneath the sheets that went up to her neck.

Karissa gasped aloud, for she recognized the brown eyes that were gazing at her with interest.

Gregory entered the room behind her and said, "I'm pleased to introduce to you . . . Blair Kendrick."

"Oh . . . my . . . God," Marcello muttered, his jaw dropping.

41

THE MOVIE

An aerial shot of Las Vegas zooms down to a quiet neighborhood on the west side, and then the camera settles on the exterior of the modest Bradford ranch house. A 1970 Chevrolet Impala pulls up into the driveway. Maxwell and Jane Bradford get out of the car. Jane opens the back door, reaches in, and pulls out her daughter, now almost two years old. As the family goes in through the front door of the house, we pan across the street to a 1971 Ford Tempo parked at the curb. Blair, in her guise as "Penny Miller," with sunglasses and a scarf, watches.

Her voice-over tells us, "Time crawled by, but I remained in Las Vegas and lived off the proceeds of selling Eldon's old coins, one by one. By the year 1975, things had settled down a little. I hadn't seen Buddy Franco in months, nor had I received any indication that the mob was keeping tabs on my daughter's family. Franco stopped showing up at the Sunshine Diner, where I'd always spotted him. Had he and Justin Hirsch given up? Or was I just blind? Maybe I'd gotten careless. Whatever—I began to wonder if I could take the risk of getting to know Jane and her family in person. I really wanted to hold my granddaughter again!"

*

Blair, carrying a wrapped present under one arm, rang the doorbell and waited. The house was not in the best of neighborhoods. A good portion of the African American population lived in North Las Vegas, and, as it was in most cities in the United States, minorities had a more difficult time making things work. Crime was an issue, along with low income, systemic racism, and the whole nine yards.

Jane answered the door. "Yes?" she asked, somewhat surprised to see a white woman standing on her porch.

Blair had known she was off work that day. Maxwell was at the casino on his shift. "Hi," she said with a smile, "I was wondering if you might need a nanny? Someone to look after your child and fix your meals or whatever?"

Jane looked at her as if she were mad. "We can't afford a nanny, but thanks." She started to close the door, but Blair stopped her.

"Wait! I . . . I'm not looking for any pay. In fact," she handed over the wrapped package. "I know your daughter's birthday is around the corner, and I brought her something to play with."

Jane tried to give it back. "I can't accept this. Who are you? Don't I know you from somewhere?"

"I'm Penny. I, uhm, I used to go to your church sometimes. Maybe you've seen me there."

"Well, I can't take the present. Thank you anyway."

"Please. It's a gift. I want her to have it."

Jane looked at her sideways. "Who are you? Why are you doing this?"

Blair shrugged. "No reason. You seem like a very nice family. You have such a cute daughter." She pushed the present back into Jane's arms. The woman attempted to shove it away.

"No, lady, I don't want it!"

"It's for your girl!" Blair practically broke into tears. "It . . . it

300

was for my own granddaughter, but she died . . . in a . . . in a car accident. Please take it. It's her birthday present. Please?" She abruptly turned and walked away, not giving her daughter the chance to protest.

"Hey! Wait!"

"Too late, dear!" Blair got in her Ford, started it, and backed out into the street. A bewildered Jane just stood on her doorstep, the present in her arms, watching the crazy woman drive away.

Tears welled in Blair's eyes as she pulled out onto Pecos Road and gained speed.

Damn you, Blair! she told herself. That had been a mistake. What had she been thinking? Be a *nanny?* No wonder Jane had thought she was a mad, old white woman. Perhaps she was.

The man wearing a Los Angeles Dodgers cap noted what had just occurred at the small house on Reynolds Avenue. He sat in an unmarked white van, sweating profusely in the Nevada heat; at least he was being paid handsomely for watching the home.

Old man Tonino would reward him even more for the information he had just obtained. It was the third time he'd seen the Ford Tempo on the block, and in each instance a white woman had been the driver. That was more than coincidence.

He started the van and drove away, turned on Pecos, and stopped at the closest gas station. He got out of the vehicle and went to the pay phone that was on the side of the building. He dialed the number he knew by heart. When the line was answered, he said, "It's Delbert. Tell Tonino I saw the woman again, third time. Fits the age and description. No, I wasn't close enough to get the license plate. But she'll be back."

Delbert hung up and returned to the van, ready to continue the surveillance. Tonino would get the word back to Franco.

They wanted that woman dead.

42

KARISSA

"Welcome," Blair said slowly, with a hoarse, gravelly voice. "Come in, have a seat."

"Blair Kendrick?" was all Karissa could say. "We thought . . ."

"That I was dead? That I'm buried in Westwood?" She just grinned and shook her head. "That's some other bitch."

"Blair, you know smoking isn't good for you!" Serena said. She went over to the bed and plucked the cigarette out of the woman's fingers. "The doctor said you have to stop."

The woman merely winced a little. She seemed to be too weak to object, but she mumbled something under her breath when Serena stubbed the cigarette out in a plate on the tray table. Blair then looked at Karissa and said softly and with considerable effort, "I'm ninety-one goddamned years old. I've had . . . two strokes and I can barely walk. I could die tomorrow. Why does the doctor give a . . . damn about me smoking?" She coughed.

Karissa thought the woman had chutzpah. "Sorry, I don't know what to say. It's a bit of a shock to find out you're alive!"

Gregory said, "Now you know why I don't want to be found.

302

Carol and I have been watching over Blair since she came back to the States from Costa Rica. She's always been like family to us. I've known her since I was a little boy." He looked at Karissa. "She lived in Costa Rica during the fifties and sixties, and then again from the late seventies to the nineties. My father, bless his heart, was in love with her. But he was Hank Marley's best friend, so he never did anything about it. But my dad and Blair remained good friends, though, isn't that right, Blair?"

She nodded.

"My dad helped to keep her out of harm's way, which was what Hank wanted, and then I guess you could say Carol and I took over after Dad got too old to do it. He refused to leave LA. We figured the best place she could hide was here on the farm."

"A *nut* farm," Blair said with sarcasm, but with humor in her eyes. "Please, sit down."

Karissa and Marcello took the two empty chairs. Carol left the room, while Gregory and Serena remained standing by the door.

"Ms. Kendrick," Karissa started, "we haven't told you who *we* are. My name is—"

"I . . . know."

Gregory continued, "She knows you are Karissa and Marcello. And that you want to make a movie about her."

"Well, yes," Karissa said. "That's right."

"And you call me Blair. None of this . . . 'Ms. Kendrick' stuff." The woman raised her arm and pointed toward a bookcase beside the closet. A short stack of notebooks—the kind used as journals—sat on a shelf. "Take those. They tell . . . my story. And why it's not my body in that grave in Hollywood."

Gregory added, "Over the last twenty years, she wrote it all down."

"It's all the truth," Blair said. "From my . . . viewpoint, anyway."

"Oh, my." Karissa reached over and grabbed them. After a quick glance at the handwritten entries, she said, "Thank you. I can't wait to read them, and thank you for trusting me with them."

Blair weakly lifted a hand and waved it at her. "They tell a sordid little soap opera."

"Did you—did you send me those rare coins?"

The woman smiled. "Did they come in handy?"

"Yes, indeed!"

"I'm sorry it had to be so . . . mysterious." Her breathing was becoming labored. "They came in handy . . . for me, too."

"For all of us," Gregory said. "The money helped us buy this farm. Got our son William into Howard University in Washington, DC."

Blair coughed and gasped.

"Are you all right, Blair?" Serena asked.

The woman shut her eyes, swallowed, and nodded. Karissa could see, however, that something was wrong. "Is there anything I can do?"

When Blair opened her eyes, they were full of tears. She sniffed, and then her face became distressed. "My story . . . you will see . . . I'm really . . . a terrible person . . ."

"What do you mean?"

"A . . . murderer." She coughed again, and it was more of an effort for her to catch her breath. Finally, she continued. "Your movie . . . my life isn't important. I want . . . I want you to do it . . . for Hank Marley. He's the real . . . victim here." A tear ran down her cheek, but she tried to keep smiling at her visitors. Then, the next cough was worse, and she winced in pain.

Marcello approached the other side of the bed and took Blair's other hand. "You don't have to talk about it now." He looked at Gregory. "I think she needs to go to the hospital."

"No!" Blair whispered forcefully and then struggled to say, "I want . . . to tell you . . . I do have regrets . . . so many regrets . . . but not for what I did . . . to those two men."

Karissa urged, "Hush, Blair, save your strength."

"No . . . *listen* . . ."

43

THE MOVIE

The movie picks up with a daytime interior shot of Blair's apartment kitchen. She sits at the table, reading the newspaper. The music evokes an ominous mood and begins to build as Blair turns the pages and then stops to read a small article.

She speaks in voice-over. "Then, one morning, I opened the Las Vegas Review-Journal *and saw it."*

Her face registers shock and horror. She gasps, puts a hand to her mouth.

Cut to a close-up of the newspaper article:

N LAS VEGAS HOMICIDES

Police are investigating what appears to be a double homicide at a residence on Reynolds Avenue. Maxwell and Jane Bradford were found shot to death in their home, apparently victims of a break-in. Sergeant Sean Wallis indicates the crime could be drug-related. Particularly troubling is that the couple's two-year-old daughter is missing and believed to be dead. The Bradfords were both employees of the Golden Nugget Casino.

Cut back to Blair, in shock, tears streaming down her face.

"My world came crashing down. Everything I had ever loved had been taken from me. First Hank, and then my daughter, and finally my granddaughter."

Blair runs to the bedroom, throws herself on the bed, and beats the covers with her fist. She screams, thrashes, and sobs in extreme distress. A lifetime of loss, as well as murder and guilt, comes crashing down.

"I knew what had happened, of course. It was Buddy Franco and his goon who had done it. They had probably gone to Jane and Maxwell, thinking the couple knew where I was hiding. At first the fate of my granddaughter was unknown, but I later learned that her bloodstained pajamas were uncovered in a trash dumpster near the house. And it was most likely all my fault. If I hadn't been so stupid in going to the house to give my granddaughter a birthday present . . . !"

Blair sits up and wipes the tears from her cheeks.

"It had been done to draw me out . . . they figured I couldn't help going to my daughter's funeral."

She opens a nightstand drawer. The camera cuts to a close-up of its contents—a handgun.

"There was only one thing left for me to do. Fortunately, I knew where Buddy Franco liked to have breakfast."

At nine in the morning on the day prior to the Bradfords' funeral, Blair parked the Ford down the street from the Sunshine Diner, facing away from it, and waited. She wore a red wig, sunglasses and a scarf, blue jeans, a plaid blouse, and tennis shoes. Her appearance was altered enough that any witnesses wouldn't be able to identify her as Blair Kendrick. She did, however, ironically resemble an older Malena Mengarelli.

She sat backward in the seat and watched the building with

her binoculars, but Franco was not inside. It was still early, though. When she had seen him there, it was usually around eleven. He liked his breakfast for lunch.

She had purchased the Smith & Wesson in Las Vegas at a gun show. It was identical to the one she had used on Eldon Hirsch and Buddy Franco in Hollywood.

The past few days had been dark as she drowned in the depths of despair. There were moments when Blair didn't think she could go on living. However, when the idea of revenge had taken shape in her mind—once again—then she had a purpose. History was repeating itself. She was all too aware of this dark parallel of inescapable fate she had inherited, a common trait of a femme fatale in a film noir. The irony was not lost on her. Blair was convinced she was insane—a madwoman, a killer—but she also believed she would be ridding the world of an evil.

Her escape route was all set. If she was able and the timing was right, she would drive directly to the Las Vegas airport. She had a bag packed, a change of clothes, and her "Penny Miller" passport. Blair had already studied the various departures and the cities to which they flew. She would make her way back to Costa Rica and remain there indefinitely. If the timing didn't work out, she knew of a lot near the airport where she could park and wait, hidden from view, until it was nearer a suitable departure time.

Buddy Franco arrived at the diner at 11:20, parked his car in the back of the diner, and walked around the building with a cane. He was alone, which made Blair's job easier. She had no idea where his cohort was, but she didn't care. He was probably off running an errand for his masters. The diner wasn't crowded— only one other booth was occupied by three people, and there were two others sitting at the counter.

She started the Ford, pulled it out into traffic, made a U-turn, and drove back toward the diner. Double-parking parallel to the front door, Blair left the car running and got out. The pistol was in her hand.

Franco was sipping coffee. He smoked a cigarette while reading the newspaper in a booth by the window. He hadn't noticed her. The man was slipping in his older age.

Blair entered the diner and walked determinedly to the booth. She raised the gun when she stopped in front of him.

"You killed my lover, my daughter, and my *granddaughter*," she said softly. "My *granddaughter* was only two."

Franco's eyes widened and his mouth dropped. "Wait—!" he snapped.

She squeezed the trigger. The round struck his chest. The man spasmed in his seat and grunted loudly. A waitress screamed.

Franco clutched the wound. He struggled to breathe as he gasped, "No . . . she's alive . . ."

Blair's heart was pounding, but his words caused another surge of adrenaline. "Where is she? *Where?*"

But the man couldn't answer. His eyes bulged as he tried to speak.

"*Tell me!*" she barked.

It was no use. Franco slumped over toward the window, his eyes staring blankly at the coffee cup on the table.

She lowered the gun. The waitress was still screaming. Most everyone else in the diner was cowering under the tables.

One man frozen at the counter said, "I think you killed him, lady."

Blair took a deep breath, turned, and walked out of the diner, her head held high and not looking at any of the witnesses. Once outside, she got in the driver's seat of her car and drove away before anyone in the joint could call the police.

44

KARISSA AND THE MOVIE

The film reaches the final scenes as Blair Kendrick's story moves into the present day. The setting is a quiet almond farm in Wasco, California, where the former actress has come to live in her twilight years. In a montage of short vignettes, we see the Webster family conspiring with Blair to attract the attention of a film producer in Hollywood—a woman named Karissa Glover.

In a voice-over, the Blair character declares, "After doing a lot of research about producers in Hollywood, I knew Karissa was the one who could tell the truth about what had happened. If we could get her into my house on South Harvard Boulevard, I believed that she would become interested in it. Our hints could not be overt, but I knew she was smart enough to eventually figure out the path she needed to take. Then, when we were finally face-to-face, I could give her my journals and tell her the whole thing. The absolutely wonderful truth about this story."

Actors portraying Karissa Glover and Marcello Storm are stand-

ing next to Blair's bed in her room at the farm, holding her hands.

"But, unfortunately, she had to learn all the nasty parts first."

Blair had not shifted her position under the sheet that covered her raised knees and chest, although relating the tale of how she had killed Buddy Franco had taken a lot out of her. The woman continued to wheeze as she spoke to Karissa. "I've been waiting . . . for you. I've wanted to meet you . . . for so long. There is so much . . . I have to say to you."

"And I look forward to it. But maybe you should rest now, Blair."

Blair shook her head. "Franco . . . he . . . wasn't the only one . . ."

"You don't have to talk," Karissa insisted. "I'll read the journals. You need to—"

"I also killed . . . Eldon Hirsch . . ." She squeezed both of their hands tightly.

Karissa had figured that was so, but the revelation was still startling. "Hush now. Save your strength."

But the floodgates were open. "And there . . . were . . . others . . . I—"

A muffled scream and scuffling in the stairwell interrupted her. Gregory started. "What the—?"

Karissa and Marcello turned to see Barry Doon burst into the room holding Carol Webster, one hand over her mouth, and the other holding a semiautomatic pistol that was pointing at her head.

"Hey, mister," Gregory began, "Please don't—"

"*Shut up!*" Doon shoved Carol into the room and into her husband's arms. "Get in there with them." He remained in the doorway, his bald head soaked in sweat, his gun trained on everyone and no one. Karissa and Marcello remained frozen by the bed. Gregory held Carol, and with Serena they moved so that their backs were against the wall. Blair kept silent, her eyes boring holes through the intruder.

"You!" Karissa snapped with venom.

"So, this is where she's been hiding all this time," Doon said. "Tonino and I knew that if we kept tabs on missy there"—he indicated Karissa—"that she'd lead us to her eventually." He addressed Karissa. "You sure don't know how to lose a tail." Then, to both her and Marcello, he barked, "Let me see your hands."

Together they raised their arms.

"Stand over there with them, your backs against the wall."

The couple joined Gregory, Carol, and Serena.

"This all ends here." He laughed and addressed Karissa. "You just don't take a hint as easily as we thought you would, even when I shot at you on your front porch and missed on purpose."

He shook his head, and then his free hand dipped into a pocket. He pulled out a colorful, wrinkled business card and threw it on the floor, where it landed faceup. Karissa was horrified to see that it was from the gold and rare coin collector shop, with Seymour's cartoon caricature.

"Once we knew you had some of the coins, my orders changed from scaring you away from making your stupid movie to keeping tabs on you to maybe lead us to this woman. Your talk with the Trundys clinched it," the man snarled. "I'd sure hate to be the police detective whose job it is to figure *this* one out! Six bodies in an upstairs bedroom, nothing stolen. Two Hollywood film producers, a couple of nut farmers, some dame, and an old bag who everyone thought was dead for decades."

"Mr. Doon—" Karissa started.

"*Shut up!*" He glared at her. "There's nothing you can say

that's going to change anything. When I'm done with you, I'll go back and take care of the Trundys."

"Wait."

Blair had spoken in a quiet, tentative voice.

Doon was surprised to hear her speak. "Did you say something?"

"Wait," she repeated. "Come . . . here . . ."

"What?"

"I want . . . to . . . tell you . . . a secret . . ."

"I don't care to know one."

"About . . . coins?"

Doon's eyes narrowed. "You still have them? Where are they?"

"Come . . . closer . . ."

He kept the gun trained on the other five people standing against the wall. "You people don't move. Keep your hands up. If any one of you so much as flinches, I'll shoot. I can't guarantee which one of you I'll hit, but someone will go down. Do you understand?"

No one said a word.

"Do you understand?"

They all nodded and spoke together. "Yes." "Yes, sir." "Uh huh."

Doon walked further into the room, still aiming the pistol at them. Slowly, he moved sideways toward the bed. When he reached it, he kept his eyes on the quintet as he spoke to Blair. "Okay, talk, lady. I'm here."

"Please . . . come . . . closer," Blair whispered, barely able to speak.

Doon awkwardly leaned over so that his ear was nearer her face. "Okay, tell me."

Blair's arm, which had been hidden beneath the sheet, moved and emerged into view. Her shaking hand held a Smith & Wesson revolver—but her age and weak condition slowed her timing, spoiling the surprise.

Doon snapped his left hand around Blair's wrist and thrust her arm away from him. "What the—?"

Her finger squeezed the trigger and the deafening retort elicited cries of fright from the captives standing against the wall. The round perforated the ceiling, causing bits of plaster to sprinkle over Doon and Blair. She attempted to force her arm toward him, but his strength was too much for her. The gun fell away from her hand, slid over the bed, and dropped to the floor.

"You bitch!" Reflexively, he brought his own gun-wielding right hand over and struck her, prompting Marcello to instinctively leap forward, grab Doon's gun arm, and force it upward so that his pistol also pointed at the ceiling. Marcello then quickly wrapped his sinewy left arm around Doon's neck and applied intense pressure. Doon writhed and struggled, attempting to backkick Marcello's leg and knee.

The others stood frozen, unable to fathom what was unfolding before them. Karissa, however, looked down and saw that Blair's weapon was inches away from her feet. Without hesitation, she stooped, picked it up, and pointed it at Doon. She then moved closer and rammed the barrel against the studio fixer's temple.

"Drop your goddamned gun, Doon!" she growled.

Marcello's arm tightened around the man's throat. "Do it or I'll break your fucking neck!"

"Or I'll blow your brains out," added Karissa.

The struggle didn't last long. Doon let go of his semiautomatic, allowing it to fall to the floor. Gregory came to life and rushed to pick it up. Marcello jerked Doon away from Blair's bed, knocking over the guest chairs, and pulled him toward the door.

"You have a place where we can keep this bastard on ice?" Marcello asked.

"I have just the spot," Gregory answered. "The cold storage freezer. Come on, let's get him downstairs." He turned back to

Blair and Karissa. "You were right, Blair." To Karissa: "She wanted to be armed in case you guys were followed here. She's one smart lady." He nodded at his family. "Carol, Serena, are you all right?"

"I think so," Carol answered.

"Yeah," Serena replied with a swallow.

"Better go call the police, and they should bring an ambulance, too. Tell them we've had a home intruder who tried to kill us."

Carol gathered her wits and left the room. Serena followed, saying, "I'll go, too—I think I need to throw up."

Marcello eyed Karissa, who was still holding the Smith & Wesson. "Are *you* all right?"

"God. I don't know." She was trembling. "I can't believe this. I'm so sorry. I *knew* he was following me. I thought I'd lost him. I was stupid."

"No, no," her partner said. "Your quick thinking just now saved us. Come on, Gregory."

The men strong-armed Doon out to the stairs, leaving Karissa alone with Blair. She righted a chair, set the gun on it, and moved closer to the bed to take the woman's still-quivering hand.

"What about *you*? God, Blair, are you okay?"

Blair's breathing was terribly strained, but she managed to emit a quiet little laugh. "Now *you're* . . . the femme fatale."

Karissa smiled but shook her head. "No, I'm not. Try to take it easy. Help is on the way."

"No use. I'm . . . dying," she whispered.

"The ambulance will be here soon."

Blair gently squeezed Karissa's hand. "Don't worry . . . about me. My time . . . is up. Finally."

"Don't say that."

They were quiet for a moment, save for the pronounced

wheezing. Then, Blair said, "I . . . must tell you . . . about my granddaughter. Don't stop me or I may not . . . finish."

Karissa nodded. "All right. I was going to ask if you ever found out what happened to her."

The woman closed her eyes. After a beat, she spoke slowly and softly, barely getting the words out. "After Franco . . . I went back . . . to Costa Rica. I hired a private detective in LA . . . to help Ray find her. She was placed in an orphanage . . . in Las Vegas. We learned she was . . . adopted. To a loving home."

"Did you ever see her? How long have you been back in the States?"

Blair started to gasp for air.

"Oh, Jesus," Karissa muttered. She heard faint sirens approaching the farm.

"I came back . . . in '91 . . . when Ray became ill. Carol and Gregory . . . were already here, so I . . . came to stay and work with them. It was a quiet . . . anonymous life. But I knew all about my . . . granddaughter and kept tabs on her. The girl's family lived . . . in a town upstate. She grew up and . . . made a life of her own."

Karissa smiled. "Oh, that's good. What's her *name*?"

The woman managed to answer, "Her name was . . . Julia."

Karissa blinked. She felt as if she'd been punched in the chest. "Julia?"

"Does that name . . . mean anything to you?" Blair prompted gently.

Karissa swallowed, unable to find her voice.

Blair added, "Her adoptive parents . . . renamed the little girl. They thought it might be . . . better for her, so she wouldn't have any . . . traumatic psychological attachments to the name . . . Julia." Then the woman spoke ever so faintly, "I once gave her . . . a birthday present . . . a doll . . ."

Karissa closed her eyes as they welled. ". . . with the name

'Julia' sewn into her dress. Oh my God . . . her parents renamed the little girl—"

Blair squeezed her hand again. "—Karissa."

Looking at her grandmother through tears, Karissa bent down, embraced the woman, and held her tightly until Blair Kendrick died in her arms—just as the police and paramedic vehicles pulled up to the house.

45

KARISSA AND THE MOVIE

The Present

Karissa and Marcello made their movie during the many passing months after the incidents that occurred in Wasco, California. Following the advance press screening of *Femme Fatale—the Blair Kendrick Story*, early reviews hit the Internet and created a tremendous buzz in Hollywood. Karissa and Marcello took a little more time and directed their production team to make some changes to the film. This was predicated by the aftermath of Barry Doon's trial and conviction for conspiracy to commit murder, as well Justin Hirsch's own prosecution.

Finally, the night of the world premiere had arrived.

Karissa, along with Marcello and his wife, Angelina, Serena Brantley, and the Websters arrived at the theater in a limousine, dressed to the nines, excited and nervous at the same time. Even Willy Puma was on the guest list. The event was sold out and throngs of people stood outside the building awaiting the opening of the doors. A red carpet, naturally, had been placed on the pavement that went from the curb, through the front doors, and into the lobby.

Karissa and Marcello joined the stars, director, writer Miranda Jenkins, and other essential crew members in front of the "step and repeat backdrop" for press photographs. The producing couple also posed for pictures by themselves and with each other. Afterward, a woman approached the pair.

"Ms. Glover, Mr. Storm, I'm Randi Ellen from *Entertainment Weekly*," she said. "Could I get a minute of your time before the film begins?"

"Sure," Marcello answered for them.

"Great." She held up a microphone as her cameraman hovered to shoot the interview. "Please tell us about this journey. I understand you had some, well, *interesting* obstacles."

Karissa laughed. "That's putting it lightly. Let's just say that Marcello and I believed in the picture from the beginning, and we're happy to be reinstated into the indie-producers film festival."

"I understand the ending of the movie went through some changes?"

Marcello fielded that one. "It did. After Karissa learned about her true connection with Blair Kendrick, we bundled all that history into the movie. Blair wanted her story told, so she crafted Karissa's entire journey, as you call it. Threw clues her way, sent her some, uhm, start-up funds, and guided her toward the truth."

"How do you feel about Justin Hirsch's passing?" Randi Ellen asked next. "As you know, his heart attack occurred as soon as the judge delivered the sentence for Hirsch's conviction of conspiracy to commit murder and racketeering. I understand that's why Barry Doon was stalking you, trying to scare you, and then ultimately attempting to kill you. Hirsch didn't want the history about what had happened to Hank Marley to come out."

Karissa hesitated, measuring her words, before answering. "Well, it's right out of a movie, isn't it?"

"Do you think the studio, Ultimate Pictures, can be salvaged?"

"Sure," Marcello answered that one. "There's a bidding war going on since it's up for sale. What really makes us happy is that all of Blair Kendrick's movies will be restored and rereleased."

Then the interviewer asked, "Speaking of Blair Kendrick, Karissa, how well did you get to know your grandmother?"

Karissa took a breath. "Hm, not well at all. She died in my arms about a minute after I realized who she was. I feel like I've gotten to know her, though, after reading the journals she left behind and piecing together her story from all the research Marcello and I did. She had kept tabs on me since I was a child, but she felt that she could never reach out for fear of the men—both in Las Vegas and in Hollywood—who wanted to kill her. Whether or not they knew about my existence is a mystery. Perhaps that knowledge died with Buddy Franco. I like to think it did."

"How do you feel about the fact that Blair was indeed a femme fatale? After all, she took the law into her own hands and killed several people. I noticed you changed the title of the film."

Karissa pursed her lips and said, "Yes, we got rid of that *Femme Fatale* thing in the title after our first screening. I don't condone what she did, but you need to look at it from her perspective. The man she loved was brutally murdered by evil, selfish, bigoted men. She avenged his death. And then, when her own daughter—her flesh and blood—was also brutally killed, she did it again. The woman in the beach house was provable self-defense. Sure, murder is wrong. But so were the cruel circumstances in which she had to navigate to survive and stay afloat. A higher power will judge her, but, frankly, in my opinion, I think my grandmother kicked some butt. She was caught in what became a cycle of destruction and sadness, but now, with our film telling her true story, perhaps that cycle is finally broken. She's a femme fatale no more."

The journalist then asked, "What does your movie have to say about racism—during Blair's time and today?"

Karissa took a breath. "Oh, boy. I think the film shines a light on many of the problems in Hollywood—and the rest of the country—regarding race, as well as sexism and harassment, too. Look, we totally accept that this is a story about a white woman and a black man who chose to be together in a racist society—and the outcome of that. This is my grandmother's and grandfather's tragic love story. Along the way, the film evolved into a highly personal project for me, too. Sure, I felt I had a duty to tell my grandmother's story; but ultimately it was also a way to tell *my* story—my own forgotten history, my heritage, and my ancestry, and how the prejudiced environment in which my grandparents found themselves created . . . me. Through all the odds, my grandparents persevered, and *I* am the result!"

"I understand you continue to live in your grandmother's old house?"

"I do, and I love it. What's also ironic is that my landlord, James Trundy, turned out to be my cousin, and his mother is my great-aunt! Neither of them knew this. My grandmother kept my true identity from them for their—and my—safety."

The reporter assumed a serious tone. "How much do you remember about the incident that's now become public—when you were separated from your birth parents as a child?"

"My birth parents were murdered on the orders of Justin Hirsch to draw my grandmother out of hiding," Karissa said. "It was a last-ditch pathetic attempt. All that stuff about the crime being drug- or gang-related was nonsense spread by Hirsch and Buddy Franco. I was eighteen months old when it happened. My connection with 'Julia' is rather surreal because that part of my life occurred so long ago. And don't get me wrong—my adoptive parents were the best parents I could ever ask for. I love them dearly; may they rest in peace in heaven. But I also wish I had known Jane and Maxwell Bradford a little better."

She took another deep breath, regained her composure, leaned into the microphone, and spoke with confidence. "That said, I'll always be Karissa, not Julia. I also want to add that this experience—the discovery of my birthright—has helped me identify with the two histories of which I am a part. I am biracial. That is who I am. I say that with pride."

"Thank you, Karissa Glover and Marcello Storm! Have a fabulous evening and enjoy your night!"

Along with Angelina and Serena, the couple followed the line of VIPs into the auditorium. They found their seats and sat with heady anticipation.

Karissa said a silent prayer, thanked her lucky stars, squeezed Marcello's hand, and settled back to enjoy the film.

The house lights dim to darkness and the movie begins with the obligatory studio and production company logos.

Orchestral music on the soundtrack blares with a sassy, seductive theme that cries out: film noir.

After the studio logo fades to black, the orchestral music swells and the title appears:

BLUES IN THE DARK—THE BLAIR KENDRICK STORY

The audience applauds.
Then a title card proclaims:

THIS IS A TRUE STORY.

The music crescendos and crashes to an abrupt silence.
The words fade and are replaced by another declaration:

DEDICATED TO THE MEMORY OF HANK MARLEY.

ABOUT THE AUTHOR

Raymond Benson is the author of nearly forty books. His most recent novels of suspense are *In the Hush of the Night* and *The Secrets on Chicory Lane*. He is primarily known for the five novels in his best-selling serial, The Black Stiletto, as well as for being the third—and first American—author of continuation James Bond novels between 1996 and 2002, penning six worldwide best-selling original 007 thrillers and three film novelizations. Raymond's other novels include *Dark Side of the Morgue* (Shamus Award nominee for Best Paperback Original), *Torment—A Love Story*, and *Sweetie's Diamonds*, as well as several media tie-in works.

The author has taught courses in film history in New York and Illinois and currently presents ongoing lectures about movies with film critic Dann Gire. Raymond is also a gigging musician. He is an active member of International Thriller Writers Inc., Mystery Writers of America, the International Association of Media Tie-In Writers, and ASCAP. He served on the Board of Directors of The Ian Fleming Foundation for sixteen years. He is based in the Chicago area.

www.raymondbenson.com
www.theblackstiletto.net